DESTROY
THE
PAPER TIGER

HOWARD HARRISON

ISBN: 1456478125
ISBN-13: 9781456478124
Library of Congress Control Number: 2010919319
Outback Press, Coolah NSW Australia (02) 63771950

CHAPTER ONE

No sound stirs human emotion more than the wail of a siren competing for air space in the deserted streets of a major city, especially in the early hours of the morning and especially in London.

The streets of London are never completely deserted. True Londoners, quite justifiably, fiercely defend their city's reputation of being a city that never sleeps.

But the streets are deserted enough to allow the clanging of fire engine bells and the *eee - aww* sirens of the police vehicles to echo at will through the old buildings, the narrow lanes, and major roads that play host to a unique group of people. People who are somehow joined to that indefinable emptiness, which breeds unabated, in those early hours. The homeless, the addict, and the prostitute; bar attendants treading their weary way home and the office cleaners treading their equally weary way to work; the adventuresome tourist, seeking out that one special experience to set their holiday apart; and, of course, the unsung heroes, the street cleaners, the taxi drivers, and the occasional police officer.

It was twelve minutes past three on the rainy morning of Tuesday, 2nd of May, 1989. The two fire engines from Stonegate Fire Station sped towards the old Goldberg building in Victoria Street on the outskirts of Hothamstone.

Not unreasonably, the average person would imagine fire-fighters were probably justified in expecting a quiet time on rainy nights. But fire is not a reasonable or predictable element, and those in the business know only too well it doesn't always work out that way. In fact, quite the opposite is often the case. The one thing every firefighter knows is that, if you are called out to a blaze on a wet night, and assuming it's not one of the numerous false alarms or hoax calls received by all emergency services, the odds are it will be a damn big one. A house fire caused by an act of human careless-ness; or in a factory, fuelled by some highly flammable substance, often stored illegally. And with the escalation of terrorism across the globe, there is always the constant threat of fire and other dam-age related to the detonation of some strategically placed explosive.

The red glow in the sky confirmed their worst fears. They could see the sparks and flames leaping high into the early morning sky, even though they were still half a mile away from Victoria Street.

Everyone has been told at one stage or another of their lives, and accepted as absolute, that the strongest human trait is self-survival, and that may very well be true. But what they probably don't know or haven't yet realised is that the second strongest human trait is an unbridled desire to state the obvious.

The Chief Station Officer Steve Watkins turned to the driver. "Looks like we're in for a long morning, Fred."

"Right."

The single-word reply was as short as the first comment was superfluous. Fred Gumble had always been a man of few words. It had been a long-held theory at the Stonegate Fire Station that the song, "Right said Fred," had been written about Fred Gumble.

As Fred Gumble manoeuvred the large vehicle around the tight corner into Victoria Street, it was obvious there was little that could be done to save the old three-story building. Built some time in the early nineteenth century, the wooden framework in the main structure and the surrounding brickwork had seen better days. Containment was to be the name of the game. It was essential that all efforts were directed at trying to prevent the fire from spreading to the surrounding buildings.

Before the first vehicle had come to a complete stop, the Chief Station Officer turned to his crew. "OK, men, you all know what to do."

"Right," said Fred.

To the wide-eyed spectator, and there are always plenty of them no matter the time of day or night, the human activity of the next few minutes appeared as a blur of random happenstance. Of course, nothing could have been further from the truth. Each and every firefighter is trained to the *nth* degree, fully aware and accepting of his or her own responsibility, competent in carrying out an individual task, each one knowing the lives of fellow firefighters depend on others' personal ability and expertise. Hoses ran out across the ground. Ladders were erected. Fire Hydrants were located and activated.

The fire crackled, as an eerie yellow glow lit the area. Puffs of black smoke, balls of flame, sparks and debris blasted through windows as burning goods inside the building exploded. *"Get back! Stand right back!"* Voices of authority shouted in vain. The growing band of spectators crammed as close as they dared, hampering the efforts of the fighters of the blaze. Flashes of white light pierced the air, as excited onlookers took pictures with their automatic, zoom-lens cameras, cameras previously used to snap the gates of Buckingham Palace and Trafalgar Square from the top of some roofless double-decker bus.

The Chief Fire Officer's car and two more fire engines arrived. More activity followed as extension ladders, each with a lone firefighter positioned precariously on the top, hovered over adjoining buildings. Thousands of gallons of water cascaded down walls, roofs, and into now broken windows. In life there is always a penalty. The adjoining buildings may well be saved from the ravages of the fire, but the occupiers of those buildings would soon learn that water damage can often be equally as devastating.

It was after midday before the blaze had been subdued and the building secured. As expected, the Goldberg building had been gutted and, with the exception of the outer walls, very little of the structure had been left standing. The firefighters had done a good job containing the blaze and, apart from the water damage, very little other damage had been done to any surrounding property.

Victoria Street remained closed as the fire crews rolled up hoses, and began the task of ensuring that what little remained of the blackened walls, posed no danger to passing pedestrians and traffic. The closure of Victoria Street during the early hours had thrown the morning peak traffic into chaos, and it was looking as if that might spill over into the afternoon peak, as well. It was another half an hour before the Chief Fire Officer, the Chief Station Officer and members of the Fire Investigation Unit could begin their preliminary investigation.

* * *

Detective Inspector Bill Harrigan sat in his office at the Stonegate Police Station. Patricia Hedrich had just brought in his afternoon mug of tea. He took a sip of the black liquid—no sugar with a dash of lemon juice.

"Ahh, perfect. Thanks, Trish." The image of the 1938 Vauxhall Tourer disappeared from view as he placed the mug on a coaster from his favourite vintage car set.

"Of course," she replied, in a tone of undeniable confidence and self-praise, which followed her as she left the room.

Bill Harrigan had almost finished reading Sergeant Bill Buckle's reports into the murder case completed thirty-six hours previously. He thought of how extremely difficult the case had proved to be, probably the most difficult of his career.

* * *

Bill Harrigan had lived in a Police family for his entire forty years. He was born in London as the only child of a Metropolitan London policeman. Bill Harrigan had not long celebrated his second birthday when his father, like many Englishmen, had grown discontented with his post-war homeland. Taken by the promise of a new life of milk and honey in a land where the "sun always shines", Bill Harrigan's father packed up his wife and son and immigrated to Australia. His father joined the police force in New South Wales, a state on the eastern side of Australia, and the family spent the next fourteen years living the almost nomadic life of an Australian Outback copper.

They were harsh years.

It didn't take his father long to realise that the Australian Outback was a fair, yet unforgiving, land. You worked hard, you played hard, and you learned fast.

Academic learning in many areas was difficult. Sometimes learning was done in a small country school, sometimes over the

School of the Air, via an antiquated two-way radio—school by remote control.

Learning life skills, however, was an entirely different matter. You must learn to be tough. You learned to survive on the very basics. You learned to be a self-motivator. You learned to make do with what you had. You learned that if it didn't fit, you must adapt it, modify it. You learned that God helped them that helped themselves. No one owed you a living. You learned to defend yourself and your family against any odds. You learned to be satisfied and happy with what you had. And, of course, you didn't complain. You couldn't if you wanted to; you were usually too busy or too tired from being too busy to complain anyway.

The people of the Australian outback were among the toughest in the world. With an air of resignation, they suffered drought and floods. They accepted the inevitability of the locust plagues and mice plagues. The years of hot winds and searing summer heat was etched deep into their faces.

So it was that Bill Harrigan spent his formative years, travelling in the outback with his parents from area to area, staying no longer than two years in any particular place.

Like many kids from the outback, having completed his third year education at the local high school, shortly after his sixteenth birthday, Bill Harrigan was forced to attend boarding school in Sydney to finish his education. He was eighteen when he gained his Leaving Certificate. He was an above-average student, quick to learn, with an ability to automatically separate the minutia from the relevant.

The curiosity of the young is indeed a powerful force and with Bill Harrigan, it was no different. Once his schooling was complete, it was time to spread his wings and so, instead of returning home straight away, he chose to drift from job to job, gaining experience in city life.

But despite his desire to travel and gain new experiences and see new places, Bill Harrigan was no drifter. He had just turned twenty-one years of age when he decided that like his father, he would become a police officer. His natural flair for police work soon became obvious, and his rise through the ranks could only be described as meteoric.

He could have done even better had he possessed the temperament to play the political game. Growing up in the bush had taught him plenty, but the one thing it hadn't taught him was how to gladly suffer bureaucrats and politicians. He detested the game of manipulation for self-gain. He was a straight up and down man with a firm belief in justice. He was paid to uphold the law, and he did that very well, but his belief in justice far outweighed his commitment to the law.

He remembered he'd been in the force about four years when his father retired. He also remembered being a little surprised at the time. His father wasn't a young man but he'd never thought of him as being old enough to retire; in fact, he never thought of his dad retiring. Dads were always at work. But retire he did, and his parents moved to Umina, a quiet little town on the Central Coast just north of Sydney. They bought a little cottage constructed of fibro asbestos sheeting with a tiled roof, typical of the area and prepared for a long and well-deserved life of rest and relaxation together.

Allowing his memories to fade slowly back into that part of the brain where they waited patiently to be summoned once more, he finished his mug of tea, closed the files, and buzzed his Girl Friday.

"Finished with the files, Inspector?" Patricia Hedrich asked as she strode across the highly waxed floor and stood across from his desk. She was a civilian employee at Stonegate Police Station and acted as Girl Friday, cum receptionist, cum secretary to the senior ranks. Patricia was married, had three children and was of a similar age to Harrigan.

Bill Harrigan liked Trish.

"Yep. Everything looks good." He replied and handed her the files. "You know what to do. The Barlow file goes back to the cold case files and the Leach and Willis files go to the archives. And good riddance to all of them," he added. Trish took the files and with a slight nod and a smile, she turned and retraced her steps towards the door. "Oh, and tell Sergeant Buckle they're OK too, will you?" He called after her.

Patricia answered with a simple wave over her shoulder

"Thanks, you're an angel."

Patricia Hedrich was one of the few women Bill Harrigan felt genuinely at ease with. What a shame she was already married. He opened his Teledex. To close off the Willis case, he needed to contact Margaret Willis, the widow of the victim, and tell her the final results of the investigation. Mrs Willis had been living estranged from her husband for some considerable time before his death, and during the investigation, Bill Harrigan and Margaret Willis had developed a genuine feeling of comfortableness around each other. Her mere presence, had stirred Harrigan's innermost feelings. As he reached for the telephone handpiece, the thought of speaking to Margaret Willis, or maybe even better still, being able to arrange a time to visit, sent a feeling of boyish excitement surging through his body.

He was startled as the telephone rang beneath his outstretched hand. *Damn,* he thought, as he realised that his call to

Margaret Willis would have to wait. He allowed himself time to regain some sense of equilibrium before lifting the handpiece to his ear.

"Bill Harrigan."

Despite his best efforts to sound even the slightest bit interested, the dullness in his voice betrayed his disappointment at the postponement.

"My my, don't you sound like a little ray of sunshine. 'afternoon, Bill…Grahame Bell."

"Grahame, please don't take this the wrong way," the pause was almost undetectable, "but right at this moment, I thought I would be talking to someone much more interesting and definitely more fun to be with than you are."

"Thanks very much." Mock indignation filled the voice of the Chief Fire Officer.

"How's the fire business?"

"Too good I'm afraid, Bill. It never stops."

"Keeps you in a job."

"It's going to keep you in a job for a while, too."

"Oh? Since when have I been attached to the Fire Investigation Unit?"

"You haven't. We've found a body. Looks like it's right up your alley."

"You sound serious."

"I am serious."

"The fire this morning in Hothamstone?"

"What a great detective you are."

"They do say that sarcasm is the lowest form of wit, but then you are only a fireman."

The fire chief chose to let the remark pass. "The Goldberg building, it's easy to find."

"Look for the big red fire truck?"

"Something like that…and if it's dark before you get here, I'll leave a light on."

"Thanks. Give me thirty-five minutes." He returned the handpiece to its cradle.

Harrigan mused over whether he should or should not telephone Margaret Willis before he went to meet Grahame Bell. He decided against it. He donned his jacket and laid his overcoat over his arm. He looked at the old wind-up wall clock with the yellowing face, Roman numerals, and octagonal wooden case. Many of his friends and workmates had suggested he should upgrade to a more modern clock, but Bill Harrigan preferred the nostalgia a clock such as this brought. The loud tick had a soothing way about it. Even the simple act of having to wind it every three days with the big brown key he kept in his desk drawer, somehow served to hold him within a slower era, a period when people had time for each other, when people had time to relax, to sit back and think things through. The good old days. He walked into the main office.

"Trish, I'm off to the site of this morning's fire in Hothamstone, in Victoria Street. I suppose you heard about it?"

"Heard about it!? I come that way to work! I got caught up in the bloody traffic for three quarters of an hour!"

"Sorry I asked."

"You be out long?"

"I'm not sure. It's two-forty-five now and by the time I get there, have a look around," he paused as he did the mental calculation, "I'll probably go straight home." He concluded.

"You be on your mobile?"

"If I must." Bill Harrigan was the first to admit that, although a mobile telephone could be extremely useful at times, he still harboured some reservations.

"See you t'morrow then."

"Right." He began to move away. "Oh. I'll be taking Sergeant Buckle with me."

"No you won't. He's just gone out."

"You know where?"

"Not exactly. He made some comment about the Dickens' jewellery robbery as he left, if that helps."

"Bugger! Oh well, I'll just have to go on my own." He had walked halfway to the front door before stopping and returning to the desk. "And would you also tell Superintendent Wilkinson I asked if he has given any more thought about a replacement for Sergeant McAdam?"

Sergeant Shirley McAdam's untimely death during the recent Willis, Barlow and Leach murder investigations had unnerved everyone at the Stonegate police station. It was a subject no one wanted to speak about, but life must go on, and it was only fitting that Bill Harrigan was the one to get the ball rolling.

"I realise it's only early days, but we're already desperately short without her." He added.

It was ten minutes after three when Harrigan stopped his ZX Mazda coupe near the scene of the fire. The eastern side of Victoria Street had now been opened to traffic. The eastern side was normally used by traffic coming into London, but to ease the congestion of the evening's peak hour traffic, it had been temporarily redirected for traffic leaving London.

Harrigan offered his hand. "G'day, Grahame." He still used a few of his favourite Australianisms. "What have you got for me?"

Grahame Bell took his hand in a firm grip. "Hello, Bill."

Their handshake and greetings completed, Grahame Bell reached for an orange safety helmet and threw it casually to the newcomer. "Here, you'll need this."

Harrigan placed the poorly fitting helmet onto his head and chased after the man disappearing into the building.

"Follow me…" he heard him call, "and mind your step."

"Who's here from the Fire Investigation Unit, Bert Simpson?"

"No he's on holidays…mind that wood there, it's still hot. There's a bloke from Leighton Hole filling in. He's not actually with the brigade anymore; he transferred to the police force several years ago. Damned shame really, he was a good investigator. Apparently, he's a newly made-up detective senior constable waiting for a posting to come through. We were short staffed so we got him on secondment while Bert's away."

"Do I know him?"

"Name's Colin McIver. If you've met him you'd remember him. Like I said, a good investigator but a little strange if you ask me."

They picked their way slowly through the smouldering debris. The inside of the building had been totally destroyed. The ceilings and floors of the second and third stories had collapsed, leaving only smouldering ash on the ground floor. Metal braces had been erected against the walls to keep them from falling in.

"Strange?" Harrigan asked.

"Pardon?"

"Strange. You said this McIver bloke was *strange*."

"Not quite one of the boys, if you know what I mean."

Harrigan took notice of the burned debris. A mixture of what looked to be washing machines, carpets, plenty of paper ash, gas cylinders, refrigerators, and mattresses.

"What the hell was this place used for?"

"Dunno. Storerooms of some description. The boys from the FIU are trying to locate the owner or owners now."

He stepped over a charred pile of blankets. "Here we are."

Harrigan followed Grahame Bell to the black pile.

He nodded to the uniformed policeman standing guard, hands clasped behind his back, and looked to the spot to which the Fire Chief was pointing. He shook his head sadly as he looked towards the remains of what was once a human being.

"No one deserves to die like that."

"You can say that again," the fire chief replied.

Harrigan kneeled next to the skeletal remains. The skin had been completely burned, along with most of the inner organs. Small lumps of charcoal lay where the liver and heart should have been. The mouth area in the skull was abnormally wide and showed no teeth. As his gaze wandered to the extremities of the body, he noticed there were no hands or feet. A belt buckle lay on what was left of the pelvic bone. To Harrigan's untrained eye, the shape of the pelvic bone suggested this person had most likely been a male.

"It's for sure someone doesn't want us to know who this poor bastard was."

Harrigan stood, looking around. "The medical examiner been yet?"

"Not yet. He's on the way."

"Where's this McIver fellow?"

"Ummm…" Grahame Bell uttered to himself as he looked about. "I don't see him, he may have…no, there he is, over there!"

He pointed to the far side of the building, or more accurately, what was left of the far side of the building.

"Senior Constable McIver! Over here!" Grahame called loudly.

McIver looked towards the booming voice. In reply to Grahame Bell's motion for him to join him and Harrigan on the far side of the warehouse, McIver began to make his way towards them very slowly, careful not to disturb or dislodge anything.

"McIver, I'd like you to meet Detective Inspector Harrigan, Stonegate Police." Harrigan shook his hand. The senior constable's handshake was almost strong enough, but the flamboyant mannerisms were unmistakable.

"Inspector."

"Senior Constable."

"It looks as though this poor chap had a few bad moments towards the end," McIver remarked, as his eyes angled toward the charred remains of the mutilated body.

Harrigan looked at Grahame Bell. "I'd say *a few bad moments* would definitely cover it, wouldn't you Chief?"

The Fire Chief nodded, a wry smile crossed his mouth.

"Any ideas yet, Senior?"

"Ideas, Sir?"

"How the fire started…where it started? All that arson stuff."

"A little early for anything definite, Inspector." McIver's voice was clear and crisp. He had a cheerful tone, edged with almost a touch of the melodic. Harrigan understood Grahame Bell's remark about not quite being one of the boys.

"How about an educated guess then? I won't hold you to it," Harrigan persisted.

"The difficult part with a building of this age is that everything burns so fiercely, it makes it more difficult to pinpoint where the fire actually started. But if I had to guess, I would say it started somewhere around this area, where we're standing now."

He bent and carefully picked up some of the blanket ash. "A pile of blankets is a very dense item. It's unusual for a fire of this nature to completely reduce such an item to ash."

He held the ash for his audience to see. "A pile of blankets is more likely to smoulder." With a touch of the theatrics, he allowed the ash to fall. "But be reduced to fine ash? I doubt it."

He tentatively clapped his hands together, ridding his fingers of the ash residue. "No, there was definitely *intense* heat around this area, and if there was any doubt about it, the condition of our friend here confirms it."

He raised his fingers to his nose and smelled carefully. "I would also venture that an accelerant of some description was used. By the smell, I'd say probably ethanol, but we'll confirm all that later."

As the three men stood talking, the medical examiner approached the scene unnoticed.

"You lot got nothing more to do than stand around talking?" Doug Roberts asked.

The trio looked up in surprise. Harrigan was the first to speak. "G'day, Doug. Do you know everyone here?"

"Hello Bill, Grahame."

Doug Roberts looked at the victim as he acknowledged his long time acquaintance. "Doesn't look like there's much for me to look at here."

He kneeled for closer inspection. Harrigan continued the introductions.

"This is Detective Senior Constable McIver from Leighton Hole, on secondment to the Fire Investigation Unit."

Having finished speaking to the back of the medical examiner's head, Harrigan turned and looked directly at McIver.

"Meet Doug Roberts, our local medical examiner."

"Pleased to meet you, Dr Roberts."

McIver's bright, enthusiastic and almost wispy lilt hung defiantly in discorded tone amid the trio of male bastion. The medical examiner slowly looked up at the smiling McIver, then to Harrigan, then back to the body.

"Nice to meet you, too, Detective Senior Constable." A distinct lack of enthusiasm filled his words.

For the next few minutes, small talk and meaningless comments passed between them as they surveyed the ruins of the building and the burned and twisted remains of the goods that had been stored inside.

Doug Roberts struggled as he got back to his feet. "Like I said before," he said, "there's not much I can do here. We'll get the body, or what's left of it, back to the morgue."

"Any idea what killed him? I assume it's a him?" Bill asked.

"Oh, it's a him alright! But cause of death? Hard to say. If he was alive when whoever it was chopped his hands and feet off and smashed his mouth area, he could have died from shock, or even loss of blood. Of course, he may have been dead before all that occurred."

"What are the odds he died in the fire?" Harrigan already had doubts that the fire was the cause of death.

"Unlikely, but not out of the question."

"That's how I figured it."

The medical examiner picked up his bag, nodded to McIver, said goodbye to the fire chief and as he walked away, called back over his shoulder, "I'll contact you when I know something more, Bill."

"Thanks, Doug." Harrigan replied as he turned to McIver. "Well Detective McIver, it's getting dark. I don't think there's much more to be accomplished here tonight."

McIver looked around. "I agree Sir."

"I'll get some men down here to watch over the place to-night, and tomorrow we'll start sifting through this bloody mess."

Two men in white coats, each carrying one end of a stretcher, hovered anxiously in the background. "Can we take the body now, Inspector?"

It was probably almost time for them to knock off and have a pint.

"Certainly Gentlemen, it's all yours."

Harrigan, McIver and Grahame Bell carefully picked their way outside.

Colin McIver was suitably impressed when Harrigan removed the large mobile telephone from his inside jacket pocket and dialled Stonegate Police Station. Mobile telephones were not a common sight and McIver wondered if there would ever be a time when they would become available to everyone.

Harrigan arranged for two policemen to be on duty throughout the night. With only the mopping up left to be done, Grahame Bell said his goodbyes and returned to the fire station.

McIver used Harrigan's telephone to organise a crew of specially trained Fire Investigation Unit inspectors to be at the site at first light to begin the arduous task of clearing the debris inside, piece by piece. It would have been much simpler had they been able to just get a few front-end loaders inside the building to scoop it all up and truck it away, but because of the body, it would now be a painstaking process.

Harrigan overheard the detective ask if the owner of the building had been notified.

McIver finished his conversation. Several silent moments passed as Harrigan watched McIver trying to figure out how to end the call on the mobile phone. Eventually, with an exasperated huff and quick shake of his head and shoulders, he thrust the mobile phone towards Harrigan.

Harrigan pressed the button with the red telephone motif.

"What'd you find out? The owner coming down?"

"No. The owner is a Muhammad Asif Mahmood. He lives on a Greek Island somewhere, but the occupier of the building is shown as Sidhu Trading, a shipping company. The directors have Pakistani or Indian sounding names, too long for me to remember."

"Is *someone* from the company on the way?"

"I'm afraid I have to say no to that as well, Inspector. Despite all our efforts, we have not been able to make contact with anyone from Sidhu Trading as yet."

"Alright, let's leave all that until tomorrow. What's at the rear of the building, anything interesting?"

"Not really. There's the usual pile of junk you'd expect to find behind a warehouse. There's also a small car park with two car-parking spaces on one side of the yard and a large shipping container on the opposite side. It looks like it could be used for a storeroom."

"Usual pile of junk?" Harrigan asked as he began to walk to the rear of the building.

McIver followed, talking as he went. "You know the stuff, a couple of broken pallets, empty boxes, a rusty washing machine, a fridge with no door, weeds growing around the fence line. Nothing to get overly excited about."

Harrigan stood surveying the area. McIver's description had been extremely accurate. It looked like the rear yard of a thousand other buildings in the area.

"What's in the shipping container?"

"I don't know, Sir. The doors are locked, and we really need to secure the walls of the warehouse a bit more before we start doing too much."

"Fair enough."

Harrigan gave the building a final look over. "Well, Colin, I think we'll call it a day. See you tomorrow."

"Very good, Sir."

Harrigan went to his car and looked at the clock in the dash. Three minutes after five. There was no real reason to go back to Stonegate, so he edged his Mazda into the traffic and prepared himself for a slow journey home.

He could have done without this murder right now. The last case had left him emotionally drained, and he still had to talk to Margaret Willis. He wasn't looking forward to that. Well, he *was* looking forward to talking to her, but not to confirm that her husband had been killed by what appeared to be his homosexual lover. Granted, she and her husband had been living apart, but no woman wants to hear that her husband fancied another man.

Damn it, he thought, *I might as well get it over with.* He'd programmed Margaret's telephone number into his mobile telephone a few days earlier and didn't take him long to recall it. He pressed the call button.

"Hello?"

"Mrs Willis?"

"Yes."

"Inspector Harrigan. Stonegate Police."

"Inspector. I was just thinking about you."

"Nice thoughts I hope."

Good God I sound like a bloody schoolboy.

"Of course, Inspector." She replied a little flirtatiously. A moment of silent apprehension crept its way through the speakers in Harrigan's car before she continued more cautiously. "Does this telephone call mean it's all over? The case is closed?"

"The report is being filed as we speak."

"What's in the report?" The tentativeness in her voice failed to mask the anxiety. Did she really want to know the truth?

"I'd rather speak to you in person; I'm not fond of telephones, especially mobile phones."

"You sound as if you're trying to spare me, Inspector. You needn't bother, just tell me."

"The report supports the prevailing theory, Mrs Willis. He was murdered by Leach."

"The homosexual?" Her voice echoed with hurt.

"Yes," he said, struggling with the answer.

There was a long and uncomfortable silence.

Harrigan could only imagine what might be going through Margaret Willis' mind at this moment. He allowed her silent moments to wrestle with the acceptance of the unthinkable. If her estranged husband had been murdered during a homosexual tryst, could he have been in a gay relationship when they were together?

But Harrigan also needed those silent moments to deal with his own sense of guilt. He knew the death was much more than a simple murder. He knew the *real* truth about her husband's death.

He'd had his own reasons for going along with the prevailing theory. The theory detailed in the final report. The theory seen as being in the best interest for all concerned by the Home Office. But in a case such as this, there was no *best for everyone* result. Someone always got hurt. And worse still was the fact that now he'd told Margaret of the report's findings, he would never be able to tell her the real truth.

"I'm sorry, Mrs Willis, I didn't want to—"

"I told you to tell me." Her reply was quiet and, Harrigan thought, measured.

"Are you alright, Mrs Willis? Would you like me to come around and sit with you a while?"

Another pause.

"That's very kind, Inspector, but no, not tonight. I think I want to be on my own."

Harrigan felt the disappointment pulsate through him.

"What about tomorrow night?" she continued. "Maybe we could go to Ali's?"

Harrigan's mood brightened immediately. "You're on!" he blurted amateurishly. "We could go out for dinner. How does seven o'clock sound?"

He hoped his enthusiasm sparked a fleeting moment of happiness within her.

"I'll be waiting…and Inspector."

"Yes?"

"Thank you."

Her words were soft, and trembled slightly as she spoke. Harrigan knew she was in for a bad night.

It was ten minutes to six when he eventually found a parking spot two doors up from his home. He grabbed his overcoat, put the mobile telephone into his coat pocket, checked the car for anything else he might have left, and eventually pushed the button on the remote. As he turned towards his home, he listened for the beeping sound of the Mazda's central locking system, to tell him it had secured his car. He heard no tell-tale beep, and was almost at his front gate, when he remembered that the battery in the little black remote control thing that operated the central locking device, needed to be replaced.

He returned to the car and, standing close by, he pressed hard on the remote control button. He didn't know why, but when batteries started to get weak in any remote control device, the temptation was always to press the button harder. He heard the single beep of the alarm.

Reminding himself to have the battery changed in the little black thingy, he retraced his steps.

"I'm home, Mum," he called from the hallway.

"Is it that time already?" came the standard reply.

He heard his mum clattering around in the kitchen.

"Do you want your tea now, or are you going to pop down to the Kings Arms for a bit?" She stood at the kitchen door wiping her hands on a frilly apron.

"Is tea ready?"

"Almost, but I can keep it warm."

He threw his coat casually towards the hallstand and walked to the frail little lady standing in the hall. He kissed her on the cheek.

"Have a hard day, William?"

"You could say that."

"Well, why don't you go down and have a pint or two before tea," she urged.

"To be honest Mum, I don't really know if I want to."

He stood thinking of Margaret. "I'm going to Ali's tomorrow night, so tonight I think I might just pour myself a Scotch and relax in the lounge room."

"Whatever you want, Dear."

The years of being married to a policeman, and now living with her policeman son, had given his mother a deep understanding of the pressures of the job. She understood the value of a few quiet moments.

He went to the liquor cabinet, poured himself a large Ballantines, and settled into the huge floral armchair. He took a long sip and laid his head back against the soft chair.

He called to his mother who had returned to the kitchen. "I'm taking Margaret Willis out for dinner tomorrow night, so you won't have to cook anything for me."

"Margaret Willis? She's that woman whose husband was murdered, isn't she?" His mother's tone of disapproval was evident in her voice. The description of Margaret Willis as *that woman* was just the icing on the cake.

He was in no mood to continue the conversation. He poured another whisky, pressed the television remote, and watched the last ten minutes of the news.

CHAPTER TWO

There are mornings when it's a pleasure to wake up. Mornings when Bill Harrigan was ready to tackle the world, when he just knew that everything was going to fall into place.

Then of course, there are mornings just like this one.

He had not slept well. Whether it was the surge of almost teenage enthusiasm caused by the anticipation of his dinner date this coming evening with Margaret Willis, or the many questions raised by the mutilated and burned remains in the fire at Victoria Street, he didn't know.

He dressed for work, went downstairs to the kitchen, and ate the two boiled eggs his mother had carefully prepared. Harrigan didn't like his eggs too runny or too hard. His idea of the perfect boiled egg is one that is just soft enough to allow him to dunk fingers of bread and butter into the deep yellow or orange yolk, and raise it into his mouth before some defiant yolk droplet leaps in some, death-defying egg-world base jump, and lands expertly on his tie. He drank his mug of tea.

It was three minutes to eight o'clock when he walked into the kitchen at Stonegate, made his second mug of tea for the day, and settled into his overly large, soft, leather chair.

He turned the page on his desk diary, Wednesday, 3 May. Harrigan had an intense dislike for the modern way of writing dates. What happened to the little *th* or *rd* after the number? No longer was it 19th or 3rd, it was just 19 or 3. And what about 1*st* and 2*nd*?

A reminder to wind the clock was written in bold letters across the middle of the page. He took the large brown key out of his desk drawer, walked to the old yellow-faced clock and opened the hinged glass face. A voice sounded from behind him.

"For goodness sake, why don't you buy a new one?" An exasperated voice asked from, the doorway.

"Why don't you mind your own business?" There was good humour in his voice.

Having finished his task, he returned the key to its resting place in the desk drawer and smiled at the old sergeant standing just inside the office, a mug of steaming tea clutched in his large fist.

"Good Morning, Bill."

"Good morning, Inspector."

Sergeant William Buckle had been stationed at Stonegate for the past twelve years. He was a good and honest policeman, who was proud that he was a person who could mind his own business. His most-often-used phrase was *I keep myself to myself*.

William Buckle liked his boss. He had never served under anyone like Detective Inspector Bill Harrigan. Harrigan was able to get more out of him than anyone he'd known. It was probably because he could see a lot of himself in the inspector, or maybe, more accurately, more of how he would *like* to be. One the other hand, maybe it was because he admired the inspector's stolidness, the *courage of his own convictions* as they used to say, or was it simply the inspector's unwavering belief that, while he was paid to uphold the law, justice should be the ultimate outcome. He took a sip of his tea.

"A message on my desk said you were looking for me yesterday afternoon. Sorry I wasn't here. I was out on that damn Dickens' jewellery robbery case. I'm beginning to believe that maybe there was no jewellery to be robbed in the first place."

"Insurance scam?"

"Could be, but anyway, that's where I was."

"That's O.K.; this morning'll do."

Bill gestured to the seat opposite his desk. "Sit down."

The old sergeant brought his mug of tea over to the desk and made himself as comfortable as possible on the visitor's chair. Bill Harrigan took a 1940 Standard Ten coaster from his coaster set and pushed it towards Buckle.

"What was on yesterday afternoon?"

"That fire in Victoria Street, Hothamstone."

"Why'd they want you? You're not in fire investigation."

"That's what I said." He paused before continuing. "They found a body, or more accurately, what was left of it."

Bill Buckle put his mug down, sat up, and leaned forward.

"All quite grisly if you must know," Harrigan said, as he opened his notebook and ran through the events of yesterday afternoon in minute detail.

Obeying the second strongest urge of human nature, Bill Buckle stated what he believed to be the obvious. "It's obvious then that someone doesn't want the body identified."

"Maybe," Harrigan eventually replied.

"Maybe?" Bill Buckle's eyebrows shot up. "What other reason could someone have to cut off a bloke's hands and feet and smash his mouth, if it's not that they don't want the body identified?"

"I don't know, Sergeant." Harrigan lay back and placed his hands behind his head. "What are the reasons someone doesn't want a body identified?"

Bill Buckle took another mouthful of tea as he thought about his answer. "You don't want it known that a certain person is dead?" His reply was tentative.

"Could be, what else?"

"You're trying to wipe out any trace of being connected to the victim."

"Yes, you could be right again. Alright then, let's suppose you're right." Harrigan leaned forward and rested both arms on the desk. He looked directly at Bill Buckle. "You don't want the identity of the victim to be known, and you don't want to be connected to the victim. Why then, Sergeant, would you leave the body in such a place that ensures the authorities will find it? Why not bury it in the country? Dump it at the bottom of the sea?"

"Well, it depends on whether the murder was premeditated or a spur-of-the-moment thing," Buckle replied. "Maybe the murderer didn't have time to get rid of the body. Maybe setting fire to the building was the easiest thing to do at the time."

"Hmmm…could be the way it happened, I suppose." The vagueness of his tone indicated very clearly to the old sergeant that his inspector was far from convinced.

They sat in silence.

Patricia Hedrich knocked politely before entering the room. "You two early birds want a fresh cuppa?"

With one quick gulp, Harrigan finished his tea and handed her his mug. "Thanks, Trish, I'd love another one."

Bill Buckle said nothing and simply held his mug up above his head.

"I knew you wouldn't say no, you old reprobate."

Bill Buckle smiled.

The interruption had put a spark back into the conversation.

"Bill, I want you to get Constable Watts to contact Detective Senior Constable McIver at Leighton Hole. He's on secondment to the Fire Investigation Unit and—"

"*Colin* McIver, Sir?" Bill Buckle interrupted, as he sat bolt upright.

"Yes. Why, do you know him, Sergeant?"

"You could say that, Sir." Then as an afterthought, he said, "but then, most of us do."

"Is there something I should know about McIver, Sergeant?"

"You've obviously spoken to him, Sir. Didn't you notice anything that, well...you know...strikes you as a little odd about McIver, Sir? You know, the way he speaks, his mannerisms."

"I must admit he does have a certain lilt in his voice."

"Lilt!?" The old man exploded.

"And as far as his mannerisms are concerned, maybe they're a little over done..."

"A little overdone!?" A large purple vein stood out on Buckle's broad forehead. "Sir, the bloke's a raging...you know..." He looked quickly to his left and right, then leaned forward and spoke in whispered confidence. "He's not one of *us*!"

"Not one of *us,* Sergeant?" Harrigan asked innocently.

"You know, Sir...he doesn't like...*girls*."

Harrigan smiled and watched the expressions cross the old sergeant's gnarled countenance. He had a look somewhere between anger and uncertainty. Bill Buckle had a definite feeling of uncomfortableness with Colin McIver's sexual preferences.

"So?" Harrigan half laughed the single-word question.

"So!? Let me tell you, Sir, there were none of his kind in the police force when I joined. Men were men in those days, Sir."

Harrigan let the remark go through to the keeper. He hadn't the heart to tell the truth to this soon-to-be retired policeman. Politically correct or not, Bill Buckle would never qualify as a police *person*.

"Well, let's just say that times change, Sergeant."

He rummaged through his pockets. "Now, I did have McIver's card here somewhere...yes, here it is."

He wrote a number on a yellow Post-It Note and passed it to his companion. Bill Buckle reluctantly took the note, handling it as if it carried some evil disease. Patricia Hedrich came in and placed the two mugs of tea on the vintage car coasters. She remained silent, simply smiling as she left.

"I want Constable Watts to assist detective McIver with the routine investigation. Interview witnesses, knock on doors, all the boring stuff."

"OK."

"I want *you* to follow up the Sidhu Trading Company, the names and addresses of the directors. Find out what it is they trade in. Get some telephone numbers. Talk to Colin McIver. His men have already started work on the directors. And, as soon as you have contacted anyone from Sidhu Trading, I want to talk to them."

He waited until the sergeant had finished writing.

"And I want to know about one Muhammad Asif Mahmood. He owns the building and reportedly lives on some Greek island."

"*The* Muhammad Mahmood, Sir?"

"That, Sergeant, is precisely what I want you to find out."

"You be here, Sir, in case I need to contact you?"

"Either here or on the mobile. I'm going back to the site of the fire."

As Bill Buckle began to stand, Harrigan waved for him to retake his seat. He reached for the telephone and picked up the handset.

"Before you go, I'll find out if Doug Roberts knows any more. Knowing how that poor bastard died might be a help."

They drank their tea as the telephone rang forlornly at the other end. Harrigan was about to hang up when it was answered.

"Doug Roberts."

"Doug, Bill Harrigan."

"I could have bet money it would be you. That's why I didn't hurry."

"It's nice to have friends."

"I suppose you want to know how Mr Lords died."

"Mr Lords?"

"You know, Lords…cricket…the Ashes and all that."

"Why do you people always have to be so bloody macabre? Where's your respect for heaven's sake?"

"As I've told you before, Bill, it's the only way to keep sane, and besides, the dead'ns don't care."

"Yes I know, but it still…argh, it doesn't matter."

He waited a few moments for Doug Roberts to tell him the results. Roberts said nothing.

"Well?" he prompted.

The medical examiner took a while to answer. "To be honest Bill, I'm not one hundred percent sure how he died. There is so little to work with. There are no indications that a gun or a knife was used. There's no heavy blow to the back of the head."

The medical examiner paused, sounding like he changed the handset to his other ear. "That's better," he continued as he opened the file with his right hand. "Now, the only real clue comes from preliminary tests on what was left of the lungs, and I can assure you there wasn't much left."

"What'd you find?"

"It's not a *find* as much as it's probably more like an educated guess at this stage, but there could be some indication of the presence of some sort of crude anaesthetic, could be ether based."

"Could that've killed him?"

"Not directly, no. Well, once again, I don't *think* so."

"What the hell does that mean?"

"It means that a positive cause of death may never be known. He may have even bled to death."

Harrigan remained silent as he ran the details he had just heard through his mind. With a tone of almost exasperation he asked his next question. "You're suggesting he could have been anaesthetised, had his hands and feet cut off, his mouth smashed, and then just left to bleed to death?"

"It's possible. Of course, even though the victim may have been unconscious at the time of mutilation, the body would have experienced some level of shock. Maybe that did the final deed. It could also have been the fire that finished off anything left alive, but yes, loss of blood could also have been the cause."

"Anything else?"

"Not yet. I'll get my final report to you as soon as I can…but don't hope for much more."

"Thanks, Doug."

He replaced the handset and looked up at the sergeant.

"You get most of that, Bill?"

"Enough, Inspector." Bill Buckle closed his notebook and once more rose from the chair. "I'll get Constable Watts started immediately and then get onto the names of the directors."

"Thanks."

Harrigan quickly flicked through his in-tray. There was nothing that couldn't wait. He looked out his window. He stood admiring London in the spring. The sky was grey, yet bright. Even though he missed the constant blue skies and sunshine of Australia, there was just something about England in the spring. He left his overcoat on the stand and walked towards the car park.

As Harrigan struggled to fit the key into the door lock of the Mazda, the voice of Superintendent John Wilkinson, his superior officer, sounded loudly behind him.

"How's the investigation into the fire coming along, Inspector?"

Harrigan had bent the key a couple of months ago, while leaning over a pool table with the keys in his pocket. Despite the key not being perfectly straight, it fitted into the ignition lock with ease, but the door lock was another matter. But up until now, he'd had the little black remote control and alarm sensor thingy, so it hadn't mattered that the key was a mongrel to get into the door lock. But now the little black thingy battery had gone flat, the once simple act of inserting the key into the door lock had become a major task and a matter of extreme annoyance and frustration.

He stood erect to face his inquisitor. Not wanting to go through the hassle of trying to fit the key in the door lock for a third time this morning, he left the key hanging.

"Slowly, Sir, but it's early days yet."

"Identify the body?"

Harrigan thought it unusual that the superintendent should have taken such a keen interest at this early stage. He was the sort of boss that usually didn't appreciate preliminary supposition. He was only interested in substantiated facts.

"No, not yet, Sir. But like I said, it's early days." He considered the wisdom of asking the next question, but asked it anyway. "Do you have some special interest in this case, Sir?"

"Not at all, Inspector," Wilkinson snapped, as he turned away sharply. "Just keep me informed, that's all." Then, in a complete reversal of attitude, he added understandingly, "If there is anything you need, Inspector, please don't hesitate to ask."

Wilkinson moved across the car park towards the old sandstone police station.

"Thank you, Sir!" Harrigan called, as he reached back toward the key still hanging patiently in the door lock.

He suddenly thought of McIver. He spun around and called after the retreating figure. "Oh, Sir! There is *one* thing!"

The superintendent stopped and waited as his inspector moved swiftly towards where he stood near the exit gate.

Twenty seconds passed.

"There's a Detective Senior Constable McIver from Leighton Hole on secondment to the Fire Investigation Unit, he's working on the fire in the Goldberg building. Well, his *team* is really doing the work; despite what Grahame Bell says, I'm not sure of his expertise in Fire Investigation. If the truth was known, he's really only making up the numbers until Sergeant Simpson gets back from annual leave. Anyway, I was—"

"*Colin* McIver?"

Harrigan noticed the eyebrows rise in unison with the upward inflection of the voice.

"Yes, Sir...*Colin* McIver."

A few silent moments passed. "Well, what about him?"

"Well, Sir, as we are a bit short staffed since Sergeant McAdam's...er, well since Sergeant McAdam is no longer with us, I was wondering if you would consider contacting whoever's in charge at the Leighton Hole Station and have him seconded to us. To speed up the investigation," he added quickly.

"I've heard this Colin McIver is—"

"Is what, Sir?"

"You know...not one of the boys, so to speak."

"Not...one of the boys, Sir?" Harrigan again played the innocent. "What do you mean, Sir?"

Wilkinson cleared his throat, shuffled one hundred and eighty degrees, and once again moved toward the Police Station building. "I'll see what I can do."

"Thank you, Sir."

Harrigan felt a hand touch his arm.

"Excuse me, Inspector." A beaming young constable, wearing the smile of self-satisfaction that comes from helping your fellow man, placed Harrigan's car keys into his open hand. "I noticed you had left your keys hanging in the door in your car."

* * *

The footpath area in the front of what was left of Goldberg house was still cordoned off. Barricades had been erected on the road, allowing pedestrian access around the site. Traffic flow was still only open one way. Harrigan drove into the rear lane, identified himself to the constable standing at the rear of the building, and parked in the yard next to the container. Much of the rubble around the container caused by the fire had been cleared away, and it was now obvious that the situation wasn't as he'd first assumed. This was not a disused container relegated to the status of spare storeroom; this container was still in use as a bona fide shipping container. He inspected the two large security padlocks. They were firmly locked. He noted the name and various numbers painted on the end of the Container. Indstani Shipping Line. Container LNF 1045. Gross 59040lb Tare 8160lb 2390 Cubic Feet. He thought it unusual that the name of the shipping company was only in letters about twelve inches high. If he owned a shipping line, he'd have the name plastered all over it.

As he copied the letters and numbers into his notebook, a voice with a distinctive lilt sounded from behind him. He turned quickly.

"Good morning, Inspector."

"Good morning, DSC." He finished writing. "How's it going inside?"

"Nothing very exciting I'm afraid. It's a painstaking business." He continued talking as they walked slowly toward the rear entrance of the building.

"First job at hand is to separate the burned remains of the building from the contents of the building. Once we have examined the *building* remains and are satisfied they can't help in our inquiries, we'll load them onto the tip truck."

"And the other stuff?"

"We'll load that onto another vehicle and take it to a more secure location for further investigation." McIver shook his head from side to side, gasped slightly, and gestured violently with both hands. "There is so much of it!"

Harrigan smiled as he imagined what Bill Buckle's reaction would've been to such gesticulation and exclamation. "Has the medical examiner been back to the site?"

"Not that I know of, Inspector, but a couple of men from forensic arrived a little while ago. I think the ME may have sent them back to carry out further investigation. They're taking more samples from where the body was found."

Remembering what Doug had said about the deceased maybe bleeding to death, Harrigan wasn't surprised he'd asked forensic to have another look. He looked over at the two men busily photographing articles, marking them, and carefully sealing them in little plastic bags. He stood quietly and surveyed the area. With the building debris slowly being cleared, he was now able to see in more detail the array of destroyed goods that had been stored in the building; washing machines, video recorders, refrigerators, the remains of couches, arm chairs, and gas bottles. He looked towards the far corner.

"Even the mandatory bathtub," he muttered, as he walked towards a bathtub lying upside down, half buried by timber that had once been part of the ceilings and floors of the two stories above.

He absently nudged the bathtub with his foot.

"I wonder if all this stuff is insured."

"We'll know once we talk to someone from Sidhu Trading."

Driven by a compelling desire to contribute more, Colin McIver waved an all-encompassing wave. "Looking at the amount of goods destroyed, it could be a motive in itself."

"Could be." Harrigan squatted next to the bathtub.

"Yes, you could be right, Sergeant. Burn the place down, collect the insurance."

The thought of a detective of such standing agreeing with him, made McIver stand just a little straighter.

"And then I suppose," Harrigan continued, "just to make it interesting, they murdered some poor bastard, lopped off his feet and hands, pulverised his face, and threw what was left into the fire for us to find."

McIver's ears reddened as he stood awkwardly, consumed with embarrassment. He knew he hadn't thought it through before he spoke, he should have kept his mouth shut. It had been a stupid thing to say, even though this was his first involvement in a murder case.

"DSC."

"Yes, Sir?" Eager to please, he answered a little too quickly.

"Get a couple of men over here, will you? I want to have a look underneath this bathtub."

"Yes, Sir."

As McIver hurried away, Harrigan looked at the glowing redness at the back of McIver's ears and smiled a compassionate smile. McIver couldn't know that the inspector admired someone who was willing to put forward his ideas. Someone who is *willing to chance their arm,* as they say. And maybe all the more importantly, Harrigan didn't always expect you to be right.

Harrigan felt disquiet, as he continued his survey of the building. Something just wasn't right! Something in this burned out shell and debris gave Bill Harrigan a sense that this was going to be one hell of a case. He couldn't put his finger on it right now, but given time, it would come.

McIver returned. "They're coming now, Sir."

"Thank you, Colin."

Harrigan felt it was time to tell McIver of his request to Wilkinson. "You should probably know, I've asked for you to be attached to my team."

Still smarting over his previous gaff, McIver was again taken by surprise by this very astute and unusual inspector. This was, of course, Harrigan's intention.

"You *asked* for me to be attached to your team, Inspector?"

"Yes, why? You sound surprised."

"Oh…no reason, Sir." McIver looked away sharply. This display of acceptance wasn't something he'd encountered since joining the force. He turned back to Harrigan.

"Thank you, Sir."

"Don't thank me yet; nothing's been confirmed. But to be honest, I doubt if there will be much opposition."

"I think you are probably right, Sir." He agreed knowingly.

The two constables moved between Harrigan and McIver.

"Excuse me, Sir," the larger of the two constables said, before he began the tiresome task of bending from a waistline more suited for less physical activity. "We'll just move all this debris away, before we lift the bathtub for you." While showing the correct amount of respect, there was no doubting the real feeling behind the constable's last few words.

Bill Harrigan moved to one side. It took them almost ten minutes before they were able to stand clearly on either side of the heavy iron object and prepare to move it to an upright position.

Curiosity is an almost uncontrollable failing of human nature, and as they bent to begin the lift, all eyes of those in close proximity were fixed to some point where the rim of the tub met the floor, watching expectantly.

Harrigan listened to a rather strained *one, two, three-ee…* and watched as the bathtub was raised.

Colin McIver gasped and hastily rummaged through his trouser pocket, searching for his ironed cotton white handkerchief. Once firmly in his grasp, he placed the material over his mouth and nose as the stench of rotting human remains invaded his nostrils.

The two heavily-laden, bathtub-carrying policemen turned their heads and screwed their faces. With as much dignity as the occasion allowed, they staggered four paces to the rear and quickly lowered the bathtub onto the floor. They then both followed McIver's lead and placed handkerchiefs over their faces.

Bill Harrigan looked for a thin metal rod, and finding one to his satisfaction, he squatted beside the body.

His many years growing up in the Outback of Australia had hardened his sense of smell against the stench of dead and rotting carcasses. Sheep, cows, kangaroos, and bodies of a myriad of other fly-blown and maggoty animals were commonplace, offending all nearby, except the ever-hungry crows that picked at the flesh. Granted the stench of human remains was probably the worst, but the foulness was just the same. At an early age, Bill Harrigan had learned to overcome such reactions as displayed by his colleagues.

Being careful not to disturb too much of the evidence, he used the rod to gently poke at the burned remains of what looked to have been some kind of rigid briefcase, similar to that which a pilot might use to carry his flight maps and weather charts. At the touch of the rod, the form of the briefcase disintegrated. A second gasp sounded from McIver. Harrigan released a soft whistle.

"A damned lot of good that'll do this poor buggar now," Harrigan said unnecessarily, as he gave a few more prods and then stood slowly.

"Before we touch anything else, we'd better get those two blokes from Forensic over here…and contact Doug Roberts."

"Yes. Yes, Sir, right away." A still shocked McIver hurried away.

Harrigan turned to the two constables. "You two had better stand guard over this lot."

He turned and began to walk away through the rubble. He smiled, as he called over his shoulder, "And don't get any fancy ideas. Gold bullion weighs too much to carry in your pockets, and it shows."

The two bobbies stood silently, their facial expressions distinct and humourless.

Harrigan re-entered the rear yard area and once again looked at the shipping container.

The ringing of his mobile telephone interrupted his thoughts. He removed the offending instrument from his pocket, and placed it to his ear.

"Harrigan?" The superintendent's voice echoed down the phone.

"Sir?"

"McIver's yours. Leighton Hole is sending someone to take charge of the Fire Investigation."

"Thank you, Sir." Harrigan needn't have bothered to offer his thanks; the superintendent had already hung up.

He looked once again at the markings on the container. Indstani Shipping Lines. The container number LNF 1045. Tare weight, Gross weight. "Two thousand six hundred and eighty four cubic feet." He read aloud slowly.

He walked the length of the container and thought, *that's a bloody big container.*

More because he wasn't sure what he should do next than to check the size, he went to one end of the container and began to count three feet at a time as he paced the length. "Three... Six... Nine... Twelve..."

"Everyone's on their way, Inspect—" McIver stopped in mid stride.

He looked up at the markings painted on the container and then back to Harrigan.

"You have some reason to doubt the size, Inspector? Believe me, it's forty feet long."

"Twenty one…twenty four…" Harrigan's voice trailed off as he realised how stupid he must have looked and stopped pacing.

In a bid to save face, he looked back to where he'd started pacing, then looked to the far end, thought a moment and, with a slight nod of his head, confirmed with as much authority as he could muster, "Yep, it'd be forty feet alright."

McIver admired Harrigan's recovery and fell in behind him as he moved to the rear of this metal monstrosity. Each door had its own locking device. A strong metal bar ran the vertical length of each door. On the top and bottom end of each bar was an interlocking claw, which married to a partner claw on the container. In the centre of each bar was a hinged metal handle, about eighteen inches long. With the doors closed and the handles pushed in against the container, the claws interlocked and sealed the container. Padlocks were then fitted to each handle. Both handles on this container had been fitted with Lockwood *Security* padlocks.

"I think it's about time we looked inside this thing, Colin. Find someone with a decent set of bolt cutters, will you?" He absently took one of the padlocks in his hand and gave it a tug.

"Back in a flash," McIver enthused, as he spun on his heels and hurried away.

As Harrigan watched McIver's individually characteristic departure, he couldn't help thinking that Bill Buckle was right. The sight of a flouncing policeman, *while thoroughly modern and there was nothing wrong with that*, was somewhat unnerving.

He winced as the mobile telephone rang in his pocket.

"Harrigan."

"Bill Buckle here, Inspector."

"Sergeant Buckle…I was just thinking about you. What have you got?"

"It's sort of a good news, bad news story, Sir. The good news is I have located the Sidhu Trading Office."

"And the bad news?"

"There's no one here of any authority. I've spoken to the staff, mainly shipping clerks organising containers for goods and ships for containers. Looks like a good business to be in."

"There must be a manager."

"There's an office manager, one…" he consulted his note book, "Muhammad Singh. He's kept fairly busy in this office but doesn't appear to have anything to do with running the overall business."

"What was his reaction when you told him of the fire?"

"No reaction, really. He said he'd read about it in the news-paper, and while he had sent many containers there, he hadn't known that Sidhu Trading actually leased the building. Well, that's what he told me, anyway."

"Do you believe him?"

"Hard to say. But why would he lie about a thing like that?"

"Was he surprised to find out Sidhu Trading leased the build-ing?"

"No. Sidhu Trading apparently has diverse interests through-out the world. Mr Singh sees his role in the company as looking after his office in Bichirst. Nothing more, nothing less. He did say he had a container there, waiting to be picked up."

"Yes, I'm standing beside it now. What about the directors of the company?"

"They spend much of their time overseas. Most of Singh's contact with the hierarchy is by telephone or fax."

"Anything else?"

"Not yet. How are your investigations getting along, Sir?"

"Nothing much. A bag full of gold bullion, another body, all the usual stuff," he said off-handedly.

"I'll keep on to it then."

The casualness of Bill Buckle's last remark suggested to Harrigan that not for one minute, did he think Harrigan was serious about the gold bullion or the body. Ambushing any opportunity the old sergeant had to ring off, Harrigan continued hurriedly. "There was a distinctive buckle, probably a belt buckle, we found lying in the remains of the body we discovered yesterday. I didn't pay much attention to it at the time, but go to forensic and see if there is anything about it that may help with the identification of the victim. It's a long shot, but it's about all we've got at the moment."

"Right you are, Sir."

The phone went dead.

"I hope these bolt cutters are big enough, I borrowed them from the demolition people." McIver opened the jaws of the bolt cutters, placed them around the shaft of the padlock on the left-hand side door, and slowly squeezed the handles together. A vein in the DSC's neck stood out as he channelled all his strength into the task at hand.

"I've heard from the superintendent. You're now officially assigned to my team for this investigation."

Harrigan heard a very strained *"thank you, Sir,"* squeeze from between two white lips. Except for the neck vein growing to breaking point, nothing happened for what seemed an eternity. Suddenly, there was a loud snap and the bolt cutter's handles crashed together.

McIver's shoulders sagged, as he folded his body forward from the waist. His chest heaving as he gulped for breath. "Ahhhhh, that was tough."

Harrigan moved around the gasping figure and took hold of the padlock. "Tougher than you think, Sergeant, the padlock is still in one piece."

McIver looked at the padlock then at the bolt cutters. It didn't take long to realise that it was the hinge pin in the cutters that had given way, not the padlock.

"Get a locksmith, that's one hell of a padlock."

McIver was still standing mute, looking down at the limp and shamefaced bolt cutters, when a black 800 series BMW drove into the yard.

A man of East Asian appearance climbed slowly from the car. He wore a grey suit, white shirt, and black tie. Gold rings and bracelets glistened.

"My, my, my goodness gracious me. What a mess. What a damned mess." While he spoke with the distinctive East Asian accent, his voice was deep and definitely educated.

Harrigan held out his hand. "Inspector Harrigan, Stonegate Police. I'm the officer in charge."

"How do you do, Inspector. I am Khalil Ramachandran. I am also a director of the company that leases this building." He shook the inspector's hand and bowed slightly.

"Sidhu Trading?" Harrigan asked by way of confirmation.

"I see you know already." He looked past Harrigan's shoulder at the burned remains. "Dear, oh dear, oh dear." His gaze returned to Harrigan. "Do you know what caused the fire, Inspector?"

"Not yet, Mr Ramacha...Rama—"

"Most people call me Ram; it's much easier," the Asian man interrupted.

Harrigan took this opportunity to introduce Colin McIver.

"This is DSC McIver. Colin, this is Mr Ramachandran, he's a director of Sidhu Trading."

The two men shook hands.

"Please, call me Ram," the director invited, as he glanced towards the sad tool dangling from McIver's left hand.

"Trying to open the container," McIver explained a little foolishly.

"Then it appears I have arrived just in time."

Ramachandran returned to the BMW and took a small bunch of keys from his briefcase. Two minutes later, the doors of the container swung open, revealing a wall of cardboard boxes. Harrigan counted nine boxes.

"What's in the boxes, Mr Ramachandran?"

"A variety of goods, Inspector. Mostly items one uses around the house. Washing machines, small refrigerators, blankets, clothing, material, that sort of thing. I can get you a bill of lading if you like. That's like an inventory," he explained unnecessarily.

"Thank you, we'll need to see that."

Harrigan stood a few feet away from the boxes and looked at the markings on each box. Some markings were stencilled, some hand written. The packing tape used to secure the top and bottom flaps of each box failed to cover the remains of tape that had been used to seal the cartons on previous occasions. It was obvious these boxes had been opened at least once before.

"These boxes appear to have been opened and resealed, Mr Ramachandran."

"Many times, Inspector. Like the majority of the goods we export, they are not new."

"Oh?"

"There are poor and underprivileged people in every corner of the globe, Inspector. There are millions of people who have never seen a new washing machine or a new anything for that matter."

He took a few silent paces and stood beside Harrigan. "And of course, many areas do not have the basics, such as electricity, so even second-hand electrical goods are of no value."

"Hence the blankets, clothing, etcetera." Harrigan observed.

"Correct. Always remember one thing, Inspector. As there are those who need, so are there those who have a surplus. We simply, shall I say, help with the re-distribution."

"It must take some organising, getting the right stuff to the right people."

"Not as difficult as you might imagine. Not in the age of the computer. We have traders all over the world that list surplus or damaged stock, or stock traded-in, so we know what is available. What is required is also listed. So, if there is a shortage of afford-able refrigerators in Harlem NewYork, and a surplus of affordable refrigerators in Birmingham, England, we correct the imbalance."

"The world's most diverse Op shop."

"You could put it like that, I suppose." Harrigan's disrespect was not lost on Khalil Ramachandran.

Harrigan looked across to the BMW. "It seems to be a profit-able business."

Ramachandran gave a resigned laugh. "Not really, Inspector. There is a small profit, but you wouldn't want it as your core business. Sidhu Trading is, among many other things, a successful shipping and trading agent. This is more a, how would you say, service to humanity?"

Harrigan turned to McIver. "Get a crew over here to unload this stuff and check it against the bill of lading. I'm sure

Mr Ramachandran has no objections?" His statement changed to a question as he faced the well-dressed man.

McIver moved away to prepare the search of the container.

"I do not see why you are interested in our cargo, Inspector, but if you must, you must." He shrugged and gestured openly with his hands. "I have no objections. Please, do what you want, but I would ask that you do whatever it is you have to do quickly. This container is due to be picked up this afternoon, and it is a costly business when a container misses the ship on which it is booked."

"We'll be as quick as we can, Mr Ramachandran. Oh, Colin!" he called across the yard.

"Yes, Sir?"

"Bring a sniffer dog, too."

A hint of hostility crept into the East Asian man's demeanour. "Sniffer dog, Inspector? You think we have drugs in that container?"

"I don't think anything, yet, Mr Ramachandran, but when I have two unexplained dead bodies, I investigate every possibility."

Harrigan studied Ramachandran closely. Ramachandran stiffened slightly and slowly turned his head to a position that allowed him to stare directly into Harrigan's eyes.

"I beg your pardon, Inspector?" His words were unhurried, yet definite.

"I said, I have to investigate every possibility," Harrigan replied, deliberately misinterpreting the reason for the question.

The two men held the stare.

"I meant about the two dead bodies."

Harrigan had known what he meant. He was trying to satisfy himself as to the real character of the man he was dealing with.

His cold, unblinking stare told Harrigan he was dealing with a man of considerable inner strength.

His answer was not immediate. "We found two dead bodies in your building, Ram."

Harrigan had purposefully not used the invited and more familiar name until now. Whether it was the fact that he used it now, or the fact that there had been two dead bodies found in the building that shook Ramachandran, he was not sure. But be it ever so slight, shaken he definitely was.

"One yesterday," Harrigan continued, "and one today. One body was under a bathtub, the other just lying on the floor in the open."

"Any identification, Inspector? Do you know who they were?"

"No, not yet. One body will be fairly easy to identify, very little damage. But the other one will be much more difficult."

"Difficult, Inspector?"

"Yes. Both hands and feet had been hacked off and the face smashed, totally unrecognisable. We haven't found the missing hands and feet yet, but we will." The truth of the matter was that he was more hopeful of winning the National Lottery than he was of finding the missing body parts, but that would remain his secret.

Ramachandran looked away and then back to the Inspector. "Are we allowed inside?"

"Yes, but we must be careful. There's a lot of activity and mess inside, and we haven't moved the second body yet."

Harrigan stood aside and motioned for Ramachandran to go ahead. Ramachandran took his mobile phone from his pocket. "I'll arrange for a copy of the bill of lading to be delivered."

Harrigan listened as Ramachandran spoke to the Bichirst office.

"And hurry, Muhammad," he concluded. "This container must be loaded on the ship this evening!"

He replaced his phone, nodded to Harrigan and, with an "it's on its way" the director walked towards the charred remains of what once was a doorway.

The constable on duty gave Harrigan and Ramachandran orange hard hats. "You must wear these inside the building, Sir."

"Thank you, Constable."

They stood inside the doorway and surveyed the ruins, as a swarm of workmen and police officers went about their tedious business. Harrigan picked his way toward the upturned bathtub. As they approached, Harrigan noticed a sheet had now been placed over the body. The two constables on duty closed ranks, as Ramachandran neared. He turned to Harrigan.

"Do you want me to try to identify the body, Inspector?"

"Not yet. It's better to wait until we clean him up a bit."

"And the other body?"

"We took that away yesterday."

They moved towards the area of the first discovery.

"We found it over here." Harrigan gestured to the broad area.

The man from East Asia surveyed the area for a few moments. "Well, I certainly hope we can soon identify these two," he said, almost offhandedly, maybe a little too offhandedly.

"As I said before, it's not going to be easy."

Ramachandran glanced around the ruins, looking up, sidewards, and behind. He shook his head.

"Dear, oh dear, oh dear. This is so very terrible. I think I'd like to go back outside."

By the time they returned to the rear yard, McIver's team was hard at work. The two heavy doors had been swung completely open and locked to the side of the container. Two police officers with jackets off were inside the container handing down the cartons to other jacketless officers on the ground. McIver was arranging the cartons in such a way to allow them to be checked and reloaded in the order they came off.

Ramachandran went to McIver. "It doesn't matter which way they are reloaded Senior Constable; they're all destined for the same location. All I would ask is that you would make sure the heavy cartons are on the bottom."

"Certainly, Mr Ramachandran."

A large forklift and driver, complete with a load of empty pallets, had been commandeered from a factory three doors up the ally. Following instructions from McIver, the driver placed the pile of pallets to the side of the container. The slower task of removing the heavier cartons on the bottom row had begun. The forklift driver raised one pallet at a time to the back doors, and the two officers in the container manoeuvred the cartons onto it.

Harrigan walked alongside the container and studied the concrete structure on which the container was sitting. Ramachandran followed.

"Unusual."

"Why so, Inspector?"

"I thought that when containers were left at a depot, the lorry driver simply wound down the front legs of the trailer and dropped the trailer, container and all. Much simpler than lifting the container off the truck and placing it on this concrete...what would you call it...platform?"

"Yes, Inspector, you're right, that is what usually happens. But we do have special circumstances, here. Our yard is small and a forty-foot container takes up so much room. If you look at the end of the platform, you will notice a wooden door. We use the space inside the platform for storage, mainly for the empty cartons. There is another door in the top of the platform that we use to pass the empty cartons through when there is no container here. It's easier to pass the cartons through that way. It's underneath the container at the moment so you can't see it, but if we can find the key to the other door," he pointed to the burned ruins, "in there, I'll show you if you like."

Harrigan shook his head. "That won't be necessary at the moment, Sir."

"The other important fact, Inspector," Ramachandran continued, "is that Sidhu Trading own the containers. Sometimes, they stay here for two, maybe three, weeks at a time. Trucking companies don't like their trailers held up for that period of time."

"That's understandable."

"So, it's easier for us to have the container delivered by a self-loading trailer, which simply lifts it off the back of the truck and places it on the platform. Being about the same height as the lorry, it's not difficult, and we get to use the extra storage."

Satisfied, Harrigan said no more.

They stood watching the activity in the yard. A neatly dressed man, also of East Asian appearance, arrived in an Opel Corsa van and, after being directed to McIver, he gave the DSC a large envelope. As soon as McIver opened the envelope, the man immediately began gesturing in a manner that made it obvious he was explaining the contents of the large sheets of paper.

"That your man from Bichirst?" Harrigan asked.

"Yes, Muhammad Singh. Good man. Very reliable."

Once he had finished explaining the document to McIver, Muhammad Singh returned quickly to the Corsa van and sped off, almost clipping the police van arriving in the opposite direction bringing the sniffer dog and handler.

"I hope his reliability is better than his driving," Harrigan said over his shoulder, as he went closer to the activity and asked Colin McIver for an estimate of how long the entire operation would take.

"It'll probably take another hour to unload. We then have to spot check the contents of cartons against the bill of lading, which should take another good hour. Providing all is as it should be, and of course if our four-legged friend finds nothing, we could then start to reload. The cartons are all the same dimension, so that makes it easier. I'd say with a bit of luck, it should take no more than a couple of hours to reload."

McIver looked at his watch. "It's ten-thirty now..." He paused, as he ran the sums through his mind. "My guess is it should be ready about half-past two."

"Thanks." Harrigan returned to Ramachandran. "If all is as it should be, Mr Ramachandran, we'll try to have your container ready to move sometime time around half-past two, maybe half-past three."

"Thank you, Inspector."

"I'm going to find a cafe and get a cup of tea. Do you want me to bring you something, Colin?"

"No thank you, Sir. I've already arranged something for the boys."

McIver was somewhat taken aback by the fact that a superior officer had offered to fetch him a cup of tea. A gesture certainly not common in the London police force.

"Mr Ramachandran. You up for a cup of tea?"

"That sounds like an excellent idea, Inspector," he replied, with a slight bow from the shoulders and a nod of the head.

Ramachandran moved towards the BMW. "There's a small cafe around the corner. Just give me a few moments, while I move my car out of the way."

The cafe was literally just around the corner and was typical of many cafes on the high streets in the industrial and poorer outskirts of London.

The linoleum was polished but worn. The tables were scratched and rickety. The shelves were empty, with the exception of a few jars of coffee and packets of tea bags. Cigarettes were available from behind the old glass-fronted counter. The checked curtains hanging at the semi-clean windows were faded, matching the equally faded advertising signs promoting goods, which had ceased to be available many years prior.

They found the cleanest table and sat opposite each other. The waiter, who was probably also the owner of the establishment, wore traditional Indian dress and stood ready, pad and pencil in hand. He had an almost annoying habit of bowing every time he spoke.

Harrigan ordered black tea with a dash of lemon. The waiter said he didn't have any lemon, so he changed his order to black coffee, two sugars, not too strong. Ramachandran ordered one of those little strong coffees that are served in a cup that looks like it comes from a child's tea set. Harrigan had tried that coffee once. It was bloody awful.

"Would you like something to eat, Sir?" the bowing proprietor asked.

Harrigan looked at the man opposite who gave a non-committal shrug.

"Do you have scones?"

"The very best scones in all of London, Sir."

"Two lots of scones. No jam, just butter."

The waiter bowed and shuffled off. As an afterthought, Harrigan half turned and called. "The scones hot?" His voice echoed loudly in the small room.

"But of course, Sir," he said, bowing, bowing.

The two men looked directly across the table. It was one of those situations where they didn't want to hold each other's stare, but to be first to look away would feel like a defeat.

"Well, what will you do now, find another warehouse?" Harrigan's question gave Ramachandran the excuse to look away.

"Life must go on, Inspector. We'll look around the area close by. There's bound to be something."

"We?"

"My fellow Director Manjit Singhabahu and myself."

"Have you contacted him? About the fire I mean."

"No. He's overseas at the moment."

"I would have thought it at least rated a telephone call."

"Inspector, I must make it very clear to you, our work takes us into some extremely remote areas. Communication is often very difficult, sometimes non-existent. Especially in some regions of remote Africa."

He leaned back to allow the waiter room to serve the drinks and scones. The scones had been cut in half, and steam rose from beneath the melting butter, soaking slowly into the soft, fluffy dough. The serving technique was, to say the least, basic but polite. Harrigan spoke over the waiter's outstretched arm.

"Maybe you could flog them some second-hand telephones."

Bowing, the waiter retreated.

Ramachandran ignored Harrigan's attempted humour.

The two men went through the ritual of repositioning their cups and scones to a more personal position, and absently, but very carefully, selected what each decided looked to be the best scone on his plate.

Harrigan had come to realise many years ago that the protocol of eating treats such as hot buttered scones was directly opposite that which applied to eating main meals. With main meals, you ate the Brussel sprouts first, saving the best until last. With scones, you always ate the best one first, just in case you fill up before you finish. Secondly and probably more importantly, and as never happens with main meals, someone else might come along and take it before you get to it. Worse still, of course, was when someone else came along and you had to offer him one, something you never had to do with a main meal. And, as Harrigan had often discovered, if you're saving the best until last, that's the one they will choose.

As Harrigan took a bite from the carefully selected scone half, the little bell on the door rang. He looked up and saw Bill Buckle trundle in.

"Well, well, well. Sergeant Buckle."

"Good morning, Sir. The boys unloading the container said you'd be here."

"Mr Ramachandran, Sergeant Buckle."

"Good morning, Sergeant…please, call me Ram," he insisted.

The sergeant offered a nod of recognition. "Mr Ramachandran."

The waiter appeared, pad and pencil in hand. Harrigan slid to the inside of the seat as Bill Buckle ordered a cup of tea. The waiter wrote, bowed, and left. Buckle sat next to his inspector who offered him his plate of scones.

"Scone, Sergeant?"

Harrigan watched Bill Buckle's hand move, as predicted, towards the other half of the best scone on the plate. He took a large bite and looked at the remaining quarter in his hand. "Hmmm. Not bad."

"And to what do we owe this pleasure?" Harrigan asked.

"Well, I spoke to Dave Wilson at forensic as you suggested, Sir. It appears that particular style of belt buckle is fairly rare and so we may be in with a good chance."

"Belt buckle, Sergeant?" Ramachandran sipped his coffee and failed miserably at trying to inject an element of casualness into the question.

"Just a lead we're following Mr Rama...Ramac..." As Bill Buckle struggled with the pronunciation of the inquisitor's name, he felt the downward pressure on the toes of his right foot. The sudden pain inflicted by Harrigan's left foot was more than enough to make him hold his silence.

Harrigan took up the conversation.

"Just boring Police work, Mr Ramachandran. I'm sure you have enough problems of your own at the moment without bothering yourself with what we're doing. We'll let you know if anything turns up."

"*If* Inspector? Do you not mean *when?*"

"Of course. Of course. When. I meant when."

The sergeant's tea was delivered.

"Do you wish anything else, Sir?" The waiter aimed the question at Harrigan.

Harrigan looked at Ramachandran who offered a slight shake of his head.

"No thanks. Just the bill."

The waiter moved the pencil up and down the pad, as he quickly tallied the account. He ripped the page from the pad, folded it, and handed it to Harrigan.

"Thank you, Sir." The bowing figure retreated.

Harrigan opened the paper. £7.50. He refolded the paper and placed one corner under his saucer. He took another scone and pushed the plate to Bill Buckle. Bill Buckle raised his hand indicating his refusal.

"Must think of the figure, Sir. Thank you, anyway."

"When do you expect Mr Singhabahu back, Ram, fairly soon?"

"In a couple of weeks, Inspector." Then, as an afterthought, Ramachandran added, " If he contacts me and learns about the fire he might return earlier. It's hard to say."

"We'd obviously like to speak to him, so if he does contact you…"

"I'll tell him, Inspector." Ramachandran assured him.

"Thanks." Harrigan finished the scone and, while deliberately not looking at Ramachandran, asked casually, "Do you have any idea who the bodies might be? Caretakers, employees?"

"No idea whatsoever." His reply was hurried. Deliberate.

"What about a security firm? Did you have some form of regular patrol check the premises?"

"No."

"Hmm." Harrigan had long ago perfected the art of injecting into his *hmm,* a tone of not so much disbelief, but more of being unconvinced, of having a problem with the answer. The unnerving tone prompted Ramachandran to offer more.

"To be honest, we didn't consider the goods in the warehouse had much appeal to thieves."

The answer was weak. A warehouse full of second-hand goods would be an extremely attractive proposition to those of the light-fingered temperament. Harrigan wondered at the real reason why Sidhu Trading didn't want security people coming and going. He looked into his cup, as he finished his coffee and thoughtfully placed the cup into its saucer. Ramachandran followed suit and, having placed his cup and saucer onto his empty scone plate, he moved them to the end of the table. Ramachandran realised this astute policeman was far from convinced by his previous reply and attempted to reinforce the message.

"The fact is, Inspector, we haven't had thieves. So I would have to say…we were right."

"Maybe no thieves, Mr Ramachandran, but we do have the bodies of two unidentified people, not to mention the fact that, now, you also have no warehouse."

At the mention of the two bodies, Bill Buckle realised that Harrigan hadn't been joking about a *second* body on the telephone earlier this morning. He wondered if there was really gold bullion as well. He resisted the urge to ask the obvious question and continued to sit in silence.

"Well, you're the policeman, Inspector. Maybe it's time you started trying to identify them." Ramachandran said and he took the folded paper from beneath Harrigan's saucer. "Please, let me get this." he continued, giving Harrigan no opportunity to object.

Ramachandran stood, turned sharply and walked to the counter, removed a ten-pound note from his wallet and gave it to the bowed figure standing behind the till. The man pressed the *No Sale* button and the old drawer opened. Harrigan heard the sound of coins dropping into the saucer sitting on the counter. The saucer had a hand written sign, which simply read *tips*.

Harrigan waited until Ramachandran was almost to the door.

"Oh, Mr Ramachandran, I'll need to talk to you, later. Do you have an address, telephone number?"

Ramachandran returned to the table and, reaching into his inside coat pocket, silently removed his wallet once again and handed Harrigan a business card.

The waiter cleared the table, as Harrigan sat back and read the details printed on the card.

Khalil Ramachandran. Director. Sidhu Trading. 145a Highview St Hawgate. 0171 - 774 9010. He turned the card over, placed it on the table, and took his pen from his inside pocket. "What's your home address and telephone number…just in case I need to contact you out of hours?"

"Twenty three, Elizabeth Grove, Kings Hill. 0175 - 8889166. Now, is that all, Inspector?" A slight hint of annoyance had crept into his tone.

"I think so…at the moment."

"Very well. Good morning, Inspector…Sergeant."

Ramachandran reached the door.

"Oh! Mr Ramachandran!" Harrigan called to him once more. "You will stay where I can reach you, won't you? Anywhere in London will do."

Ramachandran looked at the man behind the counter then back to Harrigan. "Of course."

The little bell rang, as Ramachandran opened the door with more force than was necessary.

"Tell me if I'm wrong, but you have some serious doubts about him, don't you, Inspector?" While the last three words were spoken as a question, they were more of a statement.

"Let's get out of here, Sergeant."

The man behind the counter watched closely as the two policemen left the cafe.

CHAPTER THREE

The tyres of the black BMW squealed softly as Ramachandran sped from the ally behind the burned factory and entered the main stream of traffic. He'd spoken to DSC McIver and, as nothing out of the ordinary had been discovered, the task of reloading had begun. He'd also telephoned the Sidhu Trading Office at Hawgate and left instructions for the container to be picked up at two-thirty that afternoon and taken to Tilbury Docks.

The Indstani Line's container flag ship, El Hal Monarch, was due to sail at first light tomorrow.

Amid the hustle and confusion of black cabs, red buses, and Ford Transit vans, Ramachandran allowed his mind to recall every piece of conversation that had taken place between himself and Bill Harrigan. Harrigan's attitude had made him feel uncomfortable. Uncomfortable, almost to a state of concerned nervousness. He could not rid himself of the feeling that Harrigan either knew something more than he was letting on or at least suspected something more. What that something might have been he had been unable tell. Harrigan had given no clue.

Of course, this had been a deliberate ploy by Harrigan. It was a natural ability, honed to perfection during his years as a policeman. The trick was that, irrespective of what you may or may not know, you must give the impression you are holding something back. Whether you actually do or you don't know more than you're saying is totally irrelevant. That you *appear* to know more is the important ingredient.

With the doubts planted by Harrigan playing heavily on his mind, Ramachandran realised that the time had come to call Muhammad Asif Mahmood, a call he wasn't looking forward to making, but he could put it off no longer. He pulled heavily on the indicator lever and swerved the steering wheel hard to the right, away from the direction of the Southwark Bridge, which led toward the Hawgate Office. He'd decided to drive to Manjit Singhabahu's home on the southern outskirts of London.

The black BMW seemed somewhat out of place, as it made its way down Brixton Road toward the A23. Out of place or not, this was the quickest route, and he needed to speak to Mahmood as soon as possible. He'd waited too long as it was. He had intended to contact Mahmood much earlier, but with the discovery of the two bodies, he really hadn't had the time, or enough information.

He couldn't use the mobile phone; mobile telephones were not secure. The police now knew both his office and home address so he was reluctant to use the telephones at either of those locations. Manjit's home was just under forty minutes away. With Manjit overseas and not aware of the fire, it would be unlikely, at this time of the investigation anyway, the police would want to tap his telephone. He would telephone Mahmood from there.

Once out of the traffic of inner London, he made reasonable time to the address in West Heathwich. Manjit was the homely type. His freestanding cottage was typical of the surrounding homes, each standing proud on a tree-studded half-acre property. Windows were multi-paned with double glazing and decorative wooden shutters fixed to the wall on either side. The two storeyed, high-pitched, thatched-roofed home, with heavy vines of Ivy creeping, like an old woman knitting a warm pullover, across the clinker brick walls. This was indeed an affluent community.

Apart from being able to see the large passenger aircraft a few miles to the northeast, flying low on their approach to Gatwick Airport there was little to remind him how close he was to London.

He stopped the BMW on the gravel driveway. He didn't use the knocker on the solid wooden door. Instead, he ran the zipper across the edges of his gold-stamped leather key pouch, tucked the BMW ignition key inside and withdrew a Lockwood door key. The door lock operated smoothly and the front door swung open.

"Aysha!? Are you home?"

As he called to his fellow director's wife, the deep Westminster carpet and maroon pile velvet wallpaper absorbed much of his voice. He walked to the bottom of the staircase and stood with one hand on the carved, stair rail post and one foot on the bottom stair.

"Aysha? Are you up there?" His voice hardened as he became impatient.

Manjit's wife appeared at the top of the stairs. Her raven hair shone as it cascaded across her shoulders. She wore a pale blue sari, emblazoned with a red Hibiscus flower pattern. Her perfect white teeth sparkled as a welcoming, yet somehow nervous, smile filled her dusky brown face.

"Khalil, what a surprise!"

A few seconds passed before she moved closer to the staircase.

"Well?" He demanded as he held his arms open to her.

The woman's beautiful figure seemed to glide, as she descended the stairs and placed herself close to him. He pulled her to him and with his right hand nesting in her long black hair, pressed his slightly opened mouth against her full red lips. Her embrace felt tense, her kiss almost dutiful. He felt the nipples of her rounded breasts soft against his chest. He opened his eyes and saw hers closed. Not closed with passion, just closed. He pulled away.

"Aysha? What's wrong?"

"Nothing...nothing, Darling." Her answer was stilted. "I'm...I'm just surprised to see you, that's all." She moved back from his embrace. "Would you like a cup of tea?" His silent stare of suspicion was brief but unmistakable. She felt a shiver of fear cross her body.

He turned toward the study. "I must make a telephone call. You will have to leave for while."

"Leave?" She asked, taken by surprise at being ordered from her own home. "Leave my own home? Why?"

She took a few brave paces towards him. "Who're you going to call?"

He continued to walk across the polished wood floor. "You know better than to question my actions, Aysha, now please leave."

The inclusion of the word "please," did little to detract from the ordered tone.

"If you're going to call Mr Mahmood…" He stopped in mid stride as she mentioned Mahmood. "I'll be quiet," she added timidly.

She could see the anger flood across his handsome face as he turned to face her.

He was so different from her husband. Where her husband was soft and gentle, this man was aggressive and assertive. It was this raw animal magnetism that excited her, attracted her to him. But there were times when he frightened her, when she feared for her well-being. This was one of those times.

"I…I'm sorry Khalil, it's none of my business. I'll go."

She clumsily grabbed her shawl from the coat rack, hastily picked up her leather bag, and hurried to the door.

"I have my mobile telephone with me. Please ring me when you wish me to return."

He walked silently to the window and watched as she reversed the dark green XJS V12 Jaguar from the garage and drove out the driveway through the opened iron gates. He continued his journey to the study.

As a rule, Ramachandran was not a drinking man. He'd been known to take the odd social Cabernet Sauvignon or maybe a small Cognac, but that was all. He was not a man to enjoy the frivolous side of life. He had material comforts beyond the imagination of most men, and in his own way, they brought him enjoyment. But like most men of wealth, he derived little enjoyment from the pleasure his material possessions offered; his enjoyment came more from the simple possession of them.

There is however, a basic and unnerving truth about possession. The more a man possesses, the more he has to lose. That is until he reaches the very top. Sadly, unlike Muhammad Asif Mahmood, Ramachandran had not yet reached the position of power needed to guarantee such possession, so by necessity, his life remained one of deliberate, controlled and calculated self-preservation.

Until his meeting with Harrigan this morning, there'd been only one man who'd had the ability to shake his confidence. Only one man who was able to loosen his grip on the control knob. But then, Muhammad Asif Mahmood was that kind of man. Mahmood was never ranked in the often-published lists of the most rich and powerful people. He simply would not allow it. He was beyond all that. He was much too influential to be caught up in all that childishness, and there was not a publisher alive who would dare intrude into his private life, let alone publish it.

There had been one publisher a few years ago that had ventured into these dangerous waters. Through the death of her father, she had inherited the controlling share in her not unsubstantial family company. Through manipulation and, if not corruption, at least dubious dealings at the level only money can buy, she had been able to gain control of a large slice of one of the major international satellite broadcast and newspaper corporations whose editorial content controlled public opinion around the world. Because of this, she had mistakenly dared to believe she had the right to investigate and report about Mahmood, his fortune, and his business interests.

Unfortunately, her blinded passion to prove that, as a woman, she could match it with the best, she had underestimated two vital elements. Mahmood's influence over the world's most powerful people and his absolute passion for privacy in these and other matters.

Mahmood had been furious, and it was merely seven months after her investigation had begun that she was forced to take steps to avoid personal bankruptcy. She was left no option but to split up the family company and sell it to other international media organisations.

To make matters even a little worse, rumour had it she was only able to sell it in parcel sizes approved by Mahmood, and only to organisations of his choice.

Four weeks after the last parcel had changed hands, during a trip from London to New York on her private yacht across the Atlantic, Lady Winsome Campbell Lloyd-Marshall mysteriously disappeared. Since that day, no one in any branch of the media had dared to repeat the folly of Lady Winsome Campbell Lloyd-Marshall.

Ramachandran respected Mahmood and his methods. He also feared him.

Man is indeed a strange and most complex animal. When he needed most to be in control, at a time when he should avoid anything that may slow down or hamper a quick mind and good judgement, is often the moment he will do the exact opposite.

Ramachandran approached the liquor cabinet and poured a large tumbler of Courvoisier XO Imperial Cognac.

He walked slowly to a high-backed Edwardian armchair near the window, carefully lowered himself into the softness, and took a large sip of the golden liquid and picked up the telephone handpiece. He looked blankly out of the window, as he held the instrument close to his chest.

The noisy burring sound of the dial tone echoed around him, as he rehearsed what he considered to be the best way to approach Mahmood.

Mahmood was going to be angry about the fire. Not because of the loss of the building, or even because Manjit was dead. Manjit had sealed his fate when he had gone running to Mahmood to tell what he'd discovered was really going on in the Goldberg building. No, Mahmood was going to be angry because Manjit's body had been discovered at the building and had brought the building to the attention of the authorities.

Mahmood did not like publicity. He'd made that very clear when he'd summoned Ramachandran to his yacht anchored in Shelter Bay at the Isle of Constopolu.

Constopolu was one of the lesser-known Greek Islands and had served as Mahmood's principle residential address for the past three years. Although privately owned by Mahmood through his International Phenomena Holiday Resort conglomerate, the world's largest such conglomerate, Mahmood had no current plans to build a resort on the Island. With the exception of his staff, he was the Island's only resident and, notwithstanding his private yacht, the *Dei Lucrii*, Constopolu was the one place in the world where his privacy was able to be enforced.

Mahmood held very little respect for Manjit. Manjit's innocence had been his only asset to the company. While ever Manjit continued in this innocence, demonstrating his genuine willingness to travel to the most remote areas of the world on his missions of mercy, transforming the unwanted goods of the affluent into desperately needed goods to the poor and disadvantaged, his worth to Mahmood's Empire was invaluable.

He gave the operation an air of respectability.

It's ironic really, Ramachandran reflected, *that it was Manjit's honesty that unwittingly brought about his demise.*

It was almost seven weeks ago now when Manjit had returned to the Hawgate Office unexpectedly, and as often happens with the unexpected, it changed the course of many lives.

Manjit's normal flight on Gulf Airlines had been delayed, so the airline transferred him onto a British Airways flight. Gulf Airlines always landed at Gatwick Airport, and being close to his home, his routine would have been that, on arrival at Gatwick, he would drive home that evening and go into the office at Hawgate the following day. As fate would have it, British Airways flights landed at Heathrow. His car being at Gatwick, Manjit had decided on this occasion to catch the Underground to Hawgate and finish his reports before travelling to Gatwick to pick up his car.

The suddenness of his arrival had caught Ramachandran completely off guard. He'd attempted to pass off his visitor as Mr Wei Yu Lee a Chinese businessman. But being caught off guard left him totally unprepared, and the attempted charade could not have been described as overly convincing by any stretch of the imagination. Manjit became suspicious and suspected that Ramachandran was trying to hide something.

He was even suspicious that he might even have been doing something under handed.

Manjit said nothing at the time, pretending to go along with the Ramachandran's explanations. However, the following day, he instigated a discreet and very private investigation into Sidhu Trading and Ramachandran.

It took comparatively little investigation to discover what business Ramachandran was really into, and against the wishes of his wife, Manjit left for Constopolu to lay out to Mahmood, a full and detailed report on the results of his investigation.

Mahmood had appeared shocked. He'd come to Manjit's side and placed his arm around the shorter man's shoulder.

"Manjit, you are a loyal and honest employee." He'd left Manjit's side and paced the Stateroom of his beloved *Dei Lucrii*.

"This is indeed sad news, Manjit. My heart is heavy." He'd paced in thoughtful silence.

"I...I'm sorry, Mr Mahmood," Manjit had faltered. "Maybe I was wrong to—"

Manjit was having second thoughts. Maybe he should not have spied on his friend. Maybe he should have said nothing.

"Allay your fear, my trusted friend. You have done no wrong."

Such praise from Mr Mahmood was rare and, suddenly, Manjit felt vindicated, his conscience cleared by this man's praise.

"But Ramachandran," Mahmood had given way to a thoughtful pause, "it is such a shock."

He'd slumped into a red velvet chair, rested his head on the blue antimacassar, brightly embroidered with a picture of two Bedouins riding camels and the pyramids of Giza in the background. He rested an elbow on each of the smaller but matching antimacassars, which protected both arms of the chair.

He'd rested his chin on his entwined fingers.

"We must keep this to ourselves, my friend. Our good name must be protected at all costs. Sidhu Trading's reputation must not suffer. Without respectability, your work with the less fortunate would not be allowed to continue, we must not allow that to happen."

"I understand, Mr Mahmood. Of course I will not mention what I know to anyone. Not even Aysha."

"*Especially* Aysha," Mahmood had enforced.

Manjit wondered at this last remark, but his thoughts were soon interrupted.

"....and when this is all over, Manjit, we must look at your future with Sidhu Trading. If what you say is correct, Ramachandran obviously cannot stay with us, and we will need the services of a new managing director."

Mahmood had left the softness of the velvet chair and was by now standing next to Manjit. Placing one arm around his back he began to usher him toward the gold-leafed wooden doors.

"Saheed!" Mahmood had summoned loudly.

"Yes, Mr Mahmood."

"Make sure Mr Singhabahu has a swift and comfortable journey back to London."

"Yes, Mr Mahmood."

"Thank you, Manjit, and remember, not a word…to anyone."

"Of course, Mr Mahmood. Thank you, Sir."

The rage within Mahmood grew violently. When Manjit had relayed the results of his investigation, Mahmood's reaction of shock was not feigned. He had been genuinely shocked. But not shocked at the results of the investigation, shocked that Ramachandran had allowed Singhabahu to get that close!

For Heaven's sake, Singhabahu was an honest man!!

To reach the position of power enjoyed by Mahmood, honesty wasn't always the first consideration. In fact, Mahmood's policy to *never trust an honest man* had held him in good stead over the years.

An honest man was the most difficult man to control. An honest man could not be bought. An honest man could not be blackmailed.

In the world of big business and politics, control comes relatively easy to those with the will and courage to exploit their fellow man. Most men can either be bought or have some indiscretion they wish to hide. But an honest man?

There was only one thing you could do with an honest man.

He'd summoned Ramachandran to Constopolu immediately.

It was three days after Manjit's visit that Ramachandran stood beside Mahmood. As the yacht sailed into the blue Mediterranean waters, Mahmood's tone was cold and matter of fact.

"You must kill him."

"Kill him!?"

Ramachandran had paced the outer deck. He'd looked over the rail at the disappearing shoreline then back to Mahmood.

"You want me to *kill* Manjit?!"

"You created the problem," Mahmood stated accusingly. "Do you have a better idea?"

"No…but…" He hesitated, trying to comprehend the reality of Mahmood's heartless instruction.

Mahmood looked knowingly at Ramachandran.

"I could do it another way, of course."

A cold chill had run down Ramachandran's spine, as he realised the implications of Mahmood's alternative.

The dial tone had ceased and the piecing beeping sound of the telephone brought Ramachandran back into the study. He looked through the window at the overcast skies, took another sip of the cognac, and dialled the number. He placed the hand piece to his ear.

He listened to the ringing, his heart thumped.

"Hello?" A strong Middle Eastern accent filled the voice.

"Mr Mahmood, please."

"Who is speaking?"

"Khalil Ramachandran."

"Yes, please. One moment, please."

Ramachandran's heart raced, as he desperately used these final seconds to come up with the right words, if there were any right words.

He heard someone pick up the phone.

"Well?" Mahmood was often a man of few words.

"The job is done, Mr Mahmood."

Ramachandran's tone of confidence belied his inner feelings. Along with honest men, Mahmood did not care for weak men either.

"Any problems?"

If Ramachandran thought he was going to be given a chance to skip around the facts for a while, soften the blow as it were, Mahmood's direct question put that to bed.

"Things could have gone better," he started unsurely, "but I've managed to overcome, well maybe not totally overcome, but I've—"

"I know about the fire."

Damn it!

But why should it have come as a surprise? Mahmood made it his business to know everything. Ramachandran did not have a chance to respond.

"I don't wish to discuss this matter over the telephone, Khalil, I'm on my way to The Badgers, meet me there at nine-thirty on Friday morning."

The phone went dead.

Ramachandran slowly replaced the handpiece. He sat thinking of the events of the early hours of Tuesday morning.

He'd been left no choice.

Maybe in the cold light of day and with the benefit of hindsight, he might have been able to do something different. But, at the time, he had made a calculated, albeit hasty, decision.

The longer he sat, the more able he was to convince himself that, at the time, he'd been right. He even persuaded himself that Mahmood would see it his way, once it had been explained at The Badgers.

He rang Aysha's mobile telephone. An afternoon of soft and seductive love making with the beautiful Aysha would make everything seem right again.

* * *

Harrigan and Bill Buckle stepped from the cafe, into the bright grey light of the English spring.

"Let's see how McIver's doing."

As they moved quickly across the narrow street, an early model Ford Corsair, painted in basic blue with patches of grey undercoat, went past and tooted its horn in reprimand, to what the driver perceived to be, errant pedestrians.

"I've had McIver attached to our team, Sergeant." Harrigan said casually.

Harrigan detected a slight faltering of his companion's steps.

"*Permanently,* Sir?"

"Well, only for this case."

"Oh. Right, Sir." The anxious reply spilled urgently from the relieved Sergeant's lips.

They walked a few moments in silence.

"For the time being," Harrigan added purposefully, smiling to himself.

The two policemen arrived back at the scene. The last of the heavier goods were being loaded onto the floor of the container. Harrigan walked over to the forklift and asked the driver to raise him up so he could see inside.

He stood on the tines and took a firm grip in the centre of the iron guard.

"Mind you don't catch your fingers on the mast as we go up, Sir, better if you hold on to the edges," the driver warned.

Harrigan did as was suggested.

"You know this is against the regulations, don't you, Sir?" The driver again tried to dissuade Harrigan from riding on the fork-lift.

"I'll take the responsibility, just lift me up." Harrigan gestured with his left hand.

Once at the desired height, Harrigan turned around and stared into the container. The boxes covered the floor neatly. Being of regular size, they made a level platform throughout the entire container for other lighter goods to be stacked on top. Harrigan thought if he'd been doing it, he would have done one row at a time, and slowly work towards the door, but then, he wasn't doing it.

He stared silently for a considerable length of time. He could see nothing amiss and eventually, disregarding his queasy gut feeling, turned on the tines and once again took hold of the edges of the guardrail.

"OK driver!" he called.

The driver needed no more instruction and lowered him to the ground.

"Thanks."

The driver nodded silent acknowledgment.

"Everything alright, Sir?" McIver desperately wanted to impress this police inspector.

"Looks fine, Colin." Harrigan took time to gather his thoughts. "Any news from the fire investigation team? How the fire started. Where it started?"

"Not yet, Sir. When I've finished here, I'll chase that up if you like."

"Yes, thanks." And then, changing the subject completely, he added. "As you're to be attached to us for a while, maybe you should gather your personal things from your desk at Leighton Hole and set yourself up at Stonegate Police Station. See Patricia Hedrich when you get there; she'll show you around."

"Right you are, Sir." Harrigan did have to admit that his enthusiasm was a little unnerving.

"I'll see you there around eight-thirty tomorrow morning." He motioned to Bill Buckle. "Let's go, Sergeant!"

The sound of Colin McIver tapping his pencil on his clipboard and calling *come on now, boys, we have a lot to do,* created the backdrop as Harrigan and Buckle went to Harrigan's car.

"You have a car here, Bill?"

Buckle nodded and pointed with his head as he spoke. "Young Constable Jones is waiting with it over there, Sir."

"Tell her to take the car back to the station. I want you to come with me."

Bill Buckle hurried away and, after speaking to the young Constable, he re-joined Harrigan, who was by this time, seated in the driver's seat dialling a number on the mobile phone, now nestled in its cradle. As he lowered himself quietly in the front passenger's seat, the old sergeant listened to the ringing of the telephone, clearly audible over the in-car speaker.

"Stonegate Police Station."

"Patricia, Inspector Harrigan."

"Hello, Inspector."

"A DSC McIver will be bringing some of his personal belongings over this afternoon—"

"*Colin* McIver, Sir?"

"Yes Patricia, *Colin* McIver. He'll be with us for a while. Help him settle into Sergeant McAdam's old desk and show him around the station, will you?"

"Yes, Sir."

"Sergeant Buckle and I won't be back until tomorrow."

"Very good, Sir."

Harrigan pressed the button with the little red telephone motif on it.

"O.K. Now, tell me about the belt buckle while we drive to forensic."

Bill Buckle described the belt buckle in minute detail. It was very distinctive, rectangular in shape, had a laurel wreath, which extended over the edges of the rectangle, inside of which was a triangle.

"And on top of the triangle is a dove," Harrigan said, completing the description.

Bill Buckle's head turned sharply toward Harrigan. "How did you know that?"

"It's the UCFAC symbol." Harrigan spoke the acronym and then spelled the letters individually. "U.C.F.A.C."

"UCFAC?"

"United Care For All Children. It's dedicated to the plight of children across the world and, from all reports, is a very highly respected organisation."

"Like UNICEF?"

"Similar. But the difference is UCFAC's membership is restricted to the world's elite."

Harrigan remained silent, as he attempted to negotiate the roundabout at Switham Cross. It was a difficult roundabout. Once half way around, you had to cross two lanes of traffic to get into Vicarage Road.

Twenty red buses, fifteen black cabs, ten minicabs, umpteen private vehicles, and one British Road Service's lorry later, he was sitting in traffic in Vicarage Road.

"What were we talking about?" Harrigan needed to get back on track.

"UCFAC—only the elite."

"That's right, thanks. It's a bit like an elite *club* if you like. A select few of the world's most rich and powerful do good things for the poorest of the world's children. Of course, a great number of these children and their families are poor, as a direct result of actions taken by these same rich and powerful people as they clawed their way to the top, but that's how life is, I guess. If the real truth were known, UCFAC is probably more like therapy to ease the conscious than an act of compassion."

"With respect, Inspector…you're a cynic."

"Thank you, Sergeant."

The traffic in Vicarage Road began to move.

"Is there anything else to know about the belt buckle?" The sergeant's curiosity had been aroused.

"It's an award," he paused, "not the same as, but also not totally unlike the more popular awards, such as the Nobel peace prize. The difference is that the popular awards are given out each year, not because someone has actually done something for world peace, but because another twelve months has gone by and some- one has to get it. The UCFAC award is only given when a genuine act of humanity, shall we say above and beyond the call of duty, has been fulfilled."

Bill Buckle sucked in his breath, as a cyclist swerved in front of the Mazda. Although it was only Harrigan's reflexes and driving skills that saved the cyclist from almost certain injury, the cyclist stuck his finger up and disappeared into the traffic.

"Since its inception twenty three years ago, there have been a total of twelve awards given. Seven to women and five to men. The original award was a Waterford crystal statue on which is etched the symbol of UCFAC."

"The same as the one on the belt buckle?"

"Give the man a cigar. Unfortunately, the rarity of these statues make them extremely valuable and make it extremely difficult for the recipients of the awards to display them; they were forced to store them in bank vaults and the like."

"I've often wondered why people steal things so identifiable, like a famous painting. They can't show them off." Bill Buckle commented.

"Who knows? When you have everything else you could possibly need, what else is there? Anyway, to enable the recipients of this most prestigious award to show it off, a couple of years ago, it was decided that, in addition to the statue, a broach for the ladies and a belt buckle for the gentlemen would also be presented."

"That makes sense."

"It certainly does, and despite that they still went ahead and did it."

Harrigan looked at his passenger. Bill Buckle had grown up in an era of strict discipline, where such open disrespect for the leaders of the community was unheard of. The slight shake of his head and the smile on his lips did, however, hint at a little envy for his Inspector's open and honest views.

"All we have to do," Harrigan continued, "is find out the names of the men who have been awarded the belt buckle, and we will be halfway to identifying the second fire victim."

"*Half*way?"

"There have only been two of these belt buckles awarded, Sergeant."

Despite the cynicism, Sergeant Bill Buckle was genuinely impressed with the Inspector's knowledge. He felt compelled to make comment. "How do you know all this stuff?"

"I'm a policeman."

The reply was instantaneous and matter of fact. Of course, had the old sergeant been watching BBC1 at eight-thirty, two nights previous, he would have seen the same documentary.

They drove into New Scotland Yard, and Harrigan nosed the Mazda into the visitor's car parking space nearest the arched doorway of the old stone building. Dozens of defiant and proud strutting pigeons were forced to vacate the space and reluctantly resorted to flight. As Harrigan wrestled with the damn door key again, he watched as a pigeon nestled in its new position on top of the head of a stone lion, which looked down dolefully, from the ledge one floor from the ground. The pigeon settled between two sandstone ears and almost with an air of superiority it went through a ritual of fluffing its feathers and preening itself.

Harrigan felt sorry for the stony-faced Lion, with its droopy half opened mouth and almost quizzical eyebrows. What a different story would have been told in the depths of darkest Africa. That bloody pigeon wouldn't be so cocky there.

The whirr of the central locking told Harrigan he was once more victorious in the challenge of the bent key.

"Remind me to get a battery for this bloody thing, Sergeant."

Having identified themselves to the desk Sergeant inside the lobby, the two policemen made their way towards the old rickety lift. They looked pensively at each other, as the lift creaked and groaned its way to the third floor.

In one motion, Harrigan knocked and opened the door of Dave Wilson's office.

"Hello, Bill! Come in."

Although carrying the rank of Sergeant, Dave Wilson looked at himself more as a scientist than a policeman. Rank was unimportant to him. He rarely recognised any superior officer's rank and, probably fortunately, was one of those people who could get away with it.

Harrigan entered, followed by Bill Buckle.

"Ah *two* Bills. It looks more like my letter box every moment."

"Don't give up your day job, Dave. How are you, anyway?"

"You know how it is, Bill, everyone wants everything yesterday." He raised his more than ample body from the old straight-backed chair. "I guess you're here about the bodies found in the fire?"

"You got it in one, Dave."

The forensic scientist reached for a blistering white dustcoat and, as he slid one arm into the sleeve opening, he headed for the door. "Follow me."

The sound of the three burly policemen walking the length of the well-worn but still highly polished brown lino floor in the high-ceilinged hallway, echoed in their ears.

If Harrigan had a weakness, it was his fondness of nostalgia. He found his visits to the many old buildings still used throughout the English legal system most enjoyable. And of all those old buildings, this building was his favourite. The smell of the wood panelling, floor wax, and a plethora of forensic chemicals used behind each of the frosted glass windowed doors filled the air with smells of yesteryear. This was more than nostalgia; they had actually stepped back into time.

He could visualise Sherlock Holmes opening one of these doors and, while adding the aroma of his pipe to the many other odours in the hallway, he turns impatiently to his faithful companion. *Come along now, Watson,* he could hear him say.

"In here, gentlemen."

Dave Wilson opened one of the frosted glass paned doors. With the exception of a computer and the odd piece of nineteen eighties' equipment, the room was as it would have been sixty years ago.

Glass cabinets lined one wall. Each cabinet was filled with brown bottles, proudly displaying labels on which were written unpronounceable names.

An old pair of assayer's scales, now unused, still conjured pictures of grey-haired and bent old men wearing pince-nez glasses carefully unlocking the clues of some dastardly murder.

"Is this what you've come to see?" Dave Wilson had removed a solid cardboard box, about the size of a hatbox, and placed it on the overly large wooden table in the centre of the room. The lid had been removed, and he held the very ornate belt buckle in his hand.

Harrigan went to him and took the buckle. "It's UCFAC alright."

He twisted it, inspecting the object from every angle.

"I'm no expert, Dave, but it doesn't appear to be as damaged as I would have thought."

"My sentiments exactly." Dave Wilson took back the buckle. He held it in one hand and pointed with the index finger of the other.

"See here." He held the buckle closer to Harrigan. "It has been burned alright, but not significantly. And here." He pointed again. "But once again, nothing serious."

He continued to speak to the object of attention, as he passed it to Bill Buckle.

"That thing may be extremely high quality, but even so, you would think that a fire of the intensity of the one at the Goldberg building would have done more...structural damage." His tone became dismissive. "What we have there looks like, well, surface damage. You can still read the serial number on it."

"Serial number? I didn't notice a serial number." Harrigan squinted, as he leaned closer.

"It's very small, on the inside edge."

Dave Wilson took back the buckle and pointed with his finger. "Just there."

He returned the Buckle to Harrigan who held it to the light. "I think you are right, Dave... Bill, write this number down."

Bill Buckle scribbled in his notebook as Harrigan called out the number.

"Let's hope that it *is* a serial number. Was there any belting attached?"

"Nothing."

"Did they find anything near to where they found the buckle that may have attached a belt to it? A press stud for instance?" Harrigan needed more information.

"No, nothing," Dave Wilson repeated more forcefully. "Everything appears to have been completely destroyed. Except the buckle, of course."

The man from forensic took the offered buckle and replaced it in the box.

"I'll contact UCFAC. Let's hope that is a serial number. If not, at least I can get the names of the two recipients," Bill Buckle said aloud, as he made notes in his pocket book.

"For a lowly sergeant, you're very well versed in the affairs of such an austere organisation as UCFAC, Bill."

"Not me, Dave. I can't take the credit; it's the Inspector. Told me all about it on the way over."

Dave Wilson had turned away from his visitors and was returning the box back to its position on the top shelf of the wooden cabinet. "You must have seen the documentary on BBC the other night too, Inspector."

It was a shame that, with his back turned, he missed the look given to Harrigan by the old sergeant. And Harrigan's wide grin and shrug of shoulders.

The ringing of Harrigan's mobile telephone interrupted.

"Excuse me." Harrigan walked to the far side of the room. "Harrigan."

"It's Patricia, Inspector, sorry to bother you."

Harrigan looked at Bill Buckle and smiled. "You couldn't have rung at a better time, Patricia."

"Oh good. Constable Watts is here. He has the information you wanted. He wants to know should he just leave it on your desk, or is there something you are waiting for?"

"Ask him what he found out about Singhabahu."

Harrigan heard faint voices, as Patricia Hedrich spoke to the policeman at Stonegate.

"Inspector?"

"Yes."

He said Mr Singhabahu was a very private man, but he does have his wife's name and his home address."

"Good, hang on a minute." Harrigan raised his shoulder and pressed the phone against his face. With two hands now free, he took out his notebook and pen.

"OK, shoot."

"His wife's name is Aysha. They live at number one, South Heath Lane, West Heathwich."

A few moments passed as he finished writing. "Thanks. Anything else?"

Again a few moments passed as the question was relayed.

"No, Inspector. Nothing that can't wait until tomorrow."

"OK. Ask Constable Watts to leave a report on my desk, and tell him thanks."

"Very good, Sir."

The phone gave an obedient beep as he cancelled the call and returned the instrument to his coat pocket.

"What about the other body, Dave? You got anything for us?"

"Now that is an entirely different story. You name it, we've got it."

He placed another hatbox on the table, removed the lid and began to lay out an array of plastic bags. Each with some object inside. Each carefully labelled.

The two investigating Policemen began to inspect the items, like bargain hunters at a Marks and Spencer's post-Christmas sale.

"What about the gold?"

"In the safe at the Yard."

"Don't trust you, eh? How much was there?"

"Around seventy ounces…my guess about five thousand pounds."

"Sounds just like my luck." He picked up a plastic bag containing a burned passport.

"Your luck, Inspector?" Dave Wilson asked curiously.

"Yes, Dave. Find myself with five thousand pounds in gold and then get burned to death in a bath. Sounds *exactly* like my luck. "This is in pretty good shape," he continued as he flicked through the pages of the Chinese passport. "Only the edges burned."

It wasn't a question, but his tone indicated that an answer was being sought.

"Most of the stuff is the same. He died lying face down. Anything underneath him is in fairly good shape. Even the money." Dave Wilson replied.

"Money?"

"Twenty-five thousand pounds. Some under the gold. Some in his coat pockets." Nothing gave Dave Wilson more pleasure than giving investigating police stunning news. It put a little excitement in his otherwise staid life.

Bill Buckle let out a soft whistle. "Twenty-five thousand pounds…*cash?*" He shook his head. "Now that sounds like *my* luck."

"Wei Yu Lee." Harrigan read from the Passport. "Place of birth, Wong Nee, China. Place of residence, United Kingdom." He continued to read every page aloud, as he turned them slowly. "It says here he arrived in the UK on…" he paused, as he turned the passport sideward, "the thirteenth May, nineteen eighty five."

He lowered the booklet. "What's that, about..four years ago?"

"About that." Bill Buckle confirmed as he rummaged through Wei Lee's final possessions.

Harrigan emitted a low but short whistle. "A resident visa for the USA. Issued almost three months ago. They're not easy to come by." He stood silently, deep in thought. "Dave, may I have a copy of this? Just the important pages."

"I knew you were going to ask that," he said triumphantly, producing several white pages from a nearby drawer, "so I had copies made." He handed them to the Inspector.

Harrigan threw his free hand into the air. "What can I say?"

He passed the papers to Bill Buckle, replaced the Passport into its little bag, laid it on the table, and scanned the other items. He spoke to the man from forensic. "This all there is?"

"It's not enough?" Dave Wilson replied disappointedly.

"You're sure this is all there is?"

"Yes, of course I'm sure." The tone of his reply reflected the fleeting resentment at the questioning of his professionalism.

"Hmm. Then that *is* strange." He absently moved the items around the table. "Very peculiar in fact."

"What are you looking for, Sir?" Bill Buckle leaned over the table and began to scan the items more closely.

"Keys. The man had no keys."

Bill Buckle casually joined the search for keys.

"Maybe he didn't need keys," Bill Buckle said, as he looked up at Harrigan.

"How did he get into his house, or flat, or whatever?"

"Maybe he lived in a hotel and left the keys at the desk."

"What about car keys?" Harrigan picked up each plastic bag in turn, searching for the missing keys.

"He doesn't drive. Goes by bus and train. Really, Inspector, not everyone carries a bunch of keys with them."

"Maybe you're right, Sergeant, but I think it unlikely he is going to carry a bag of gold and twenty-five thousand pounds on a train. Which brings us to the next question. Where was he going with all that money?

"Overseas somewhere is my bet," Dave Wilson chimed in.

"There's no ticket. No airline ticket."

Instinctively, Bill Buckle began to search the table for the missing ticket and his mind for a reasonable answer.

"Maybe he hadn't bought one, yet," the scientist suggested, now caught up in the intrigue. "Or maybe it's in a suitcase or bag with all his other stuff."

"So where's that bag now, Dave?"

"I don't know. A flat somewhere? A locker at the Airport? It could be anywhere."

"Which brings me back to the keys. Where is the locker key, or the flat key. There aren't any. Where are the damn keys?"

Bill Buckle increased the urgency of his search through the items on the table.

"You're wasting your time, Sergeant," Dave Wilson spoke up to save him the trouble of searching. "The Inspector's right. There are no keys."

The three men stood and looked at each other in silence.

"May I use your 'phone, Dave?"

"It's in the corner." He pointed briefly to the black instrument.

Harrigan withdrew his telephone book from his inside coat pocket and, as he crossed the floor to the telephone, he searched the pages for the medical examiner's number.

He dialled the number. The phone rang once.

"Roberts."

"Doug, it's Bill Harrigan."

"I was wondering how long it would be before I heard from you again."

"What's the latest?"

"Well, not much more than we knew at first, to be honest. There was so little left of the body, the actual cause of death is extremely difficult to determine. There are no signs of any instrument or weapon being used that would have directly caused death."

"What do you mean, directly?"

"Well, take the blow to the mouth. While it's not likely the blow itself killed him, it may have caused shock, which could ultimately have lead to the victim's death. Same as the severing of the hands and feet. But, unfortunately, there is no way we can establish beyond doubt one way or the other."

"What about your bleeding-to-death theory?"

"There is some evidence that the victim had been anaesthetised." A hint of optimism crept into Roberts' voice. "And, if the victim was alive at the time his hands and feet were cut off, yes it is quite possible."

"This whole thing just doesn't make sense, Doug."

"Inspector?"

"It doesn't matter, just thinking out loud. What about the other fella?"

"He was easy, asphyxiation. He simply ran out of oxygen."

"Being under the bathtub cause that?"

"Most likely. Fire needs oxygen and will seek it out and suck it up violently. The odds are the bathtub wasn't completely flat on the ground and, as the fire approached the bathtub with the victim hiding underneath, it just…" He made a sucking sound with his mouth.

"That would explain why there is only slight searing damage to the victim and his property. Except the bag he had his booty in."

"That was near the edge of the upturned bathtub. It probably caught alight before the fire actually sucked out the oxygen, and being leather, it would smoulder. Once the fire passed, the oxygen returned to the area, and the leather continued to smoulder, until it was simply a shell of ash. The way you found it."

Harrigan thought through the simplicity of the explanation. It was probably right, or that close to being right it didn't matter.

"Anything else?"

"I'm afraid not, Bill. That's the best we can do."

"Thanks, you've done well, Mate." He replaced the handpiece and returned to the large wooden table.

"Find anything else of interest, Sergeant?"

"Nothing much, Sir."

Harrigan picked up the passport and opened it from the back. He checked the section made available for names of people to contact in an emergency. Blank. He wasn't surprised.

"Make a note of all the details, Sergeant."

Bill Buckle held up the copies given to them by Dave Wilson.

"Oh yes, of course, I forgot. Thanks for everything, Dave. You've been a big help. Come on, Sergeant. I think we may pay a visit to Mrs Singhabahu."

He began to pick up some of the items to help tidy the table.

The forensic man quickly relieved Bill Harrigan of the few items in his hand. "It's alright, Bill, I'll do it."

"Thanks again, Dave."

"See you later, Dave," Bill Buckle called from beside the opened door.

"Yep. Bye, Bill."

It wasn't until they were halfway down the hall that Bill Buckle spoke. "What do you think?"

Harrigan had a thousand questions milling around in his head. A thousand questions and very few answers. "I think I wish that Sherlock Holmes *really* was here."

"I beg your pardon?"

"Forget it, Sergeant. Let's go see Aysha Singhabahu."

"Don't forget to get a battery for your door lock thing," Bill Buckle prompted.

As luck would have it, Harrigan saw a chemist across the road and just a few doors down. "Wait here, Sergeant. I'll duck across the road and see if I can get a battery over there."

Buckle watched his superior dart in and out of the traffic and into the chemist across the road. He was too far away to hear the little bell ring, as Harrigan opened the door.

"Good afternoon, Sir."

"Good afternoon." He held his keys out to the smiling gentleman in the white coat, who was rearranging his stock of ladies' shampoos on the centre counter. "Would you have a battery for one of these things?"

The chemist took the keys and inspected the remote car-lock sensor.

"I think so. Would you like me to fit it for you? There's no extra charge."

"That would be great."

"Very well, I won't keep you a minute."

Like most people who are waiting for the chemist to do whatever it is they do behind the high almost parapet like counter, Harrigan looked around the shop.

Cough medicines, headache cures, and cold and flu tablets were prominent. Hair brushes, a selection of various coloured pantihose, large and small nail clippers, and a range of nail polish in colours Harrigan had never known existed before were all displayed in a way to tempt the person now bored witless waiting for their name to be called. There was even a card of copper bangles for arthritis sufferers, similar to the one John Wayne wore.

In the far corner was a selection of crutches, wheelchairs, and walking frames, aids for those with temporary or permanent disabilities. He picked up a pamphlet advertising special shoes for those with troubled feet. Shoes handmade to specification. Chunky shoes, shoes with large heels or raised soles. *Must cost a fortune*, Harrigan thought. He replaced the pamphlet as the chemist returned.

"There you are, Sir. Good as new."

More by reflex than for checking, Harrigan took the keys, pressed the *doors* button and saw the little red light glow in its black socket.

"Fantastic...how much?"

"Six pound, fifty pence all together. Thank you, Sir."

Harrigan paid the bill and retraced his steps to the waiting sergeant.

"By the smile on your face, Inspector, I take it you were successful?"

Harrigan pushed the button and allowed the whirr of the central locking system to answer the question. "I certainly was, Sergeant. I certainly was," he repeated unnecessarily.

The two policemen settled into the comfortable bucket seats. Harrigan reversed carefully into the driveway, selected first gear and, before taking his foot from the clutch, gave a loud blast of the horn.

A startled pigeon flew from the head of the stony-faced lion. Harrigan smiled and eased the Mazda through the wrought-iron gateway and into the London traffic.

"What's the quickest way to West Heathwich?"

"Hawthorn Road and onto the A23."

"Hawthorn Road?"

"Turn right at the second roundabout."

Bill Buckle reached into the glove box and took out the A to Z. "What Street are we looking for in West Heathwich?" He asked.

"South Heath Lane."

Fifty minutes later, which included one wrong turn that took an extra ten minutes to go around the one-way system in the hamlet town of East Heathwich, Harrigan drove the Mazda into the gravel driveway and stopped behind the black series 800 BMW.

"Well! Well! Well! I seem to recognise that black beauty. I wonder what Mr Ramachandran is doing here?" Harrigan asked nobody.

The old sergeant's more than ample figure accentuated the crunching sound of gravel underfoot, as they walked passed the BMW and onto the front porch.

As he passed Ramachandran's vehicle, Harrigan stopped and peered first into the back seat area and then the front—not for any particular reason, just simply because he was a policeman. Many a piece of vital evidence has been found on the off chance: overhearing of a word spoken in innocence, a cursory glance that is taken by habit, not reason, even the reading of a pamphlet in a chemist shop.

The rich tone of the chimes filled the house.

The two visiting policemen followed the standard routine of most people who have just rung the doorbell of a new address. They turned away, leaving their backs to the door.

"Some house, Inspector. It's easy to spot where the police sergeants don't live."

The door opened. Both men turned back.

"May I help you, gentlemen?"Aysha Singhabahu stood in the partly opened doorway. Her dark beauty immediately struck Harrigan. Her perfectly shaped eyes, full lips, and high cheek-bones complimented her perfect white teeth that shone through her smile. Like many Middle Eastern ladies, a quality of innocent youthfulness masked her true age.

Making allowances, Harrigan guessed her to be early to mid forties.

"Mrs Singhabahu?"

"Yes."

He produced his ID. "Detective Inspector Harrigan, Stonegate Police...this is Sergeant Buckle."

"Very pleased to meet you, Inspector, Sergeant Buckle. Is this about the fire?" she asked a little too eagerly.

"In a way."

"Then I'm afraid you've wasted your time, Inspector. I know nothing about my husband's business. You must speak with him. When he returns from his trip overseas, of course."

"What about his fellow directors or business partners?"

"I... I don't quite know what you mean, Inspector."

"Do you have much to do with the people he works with?" He turned his head briefly towards the Black BMW.

"Mr Ramachandran for instance. That *is* his car in your driveway isn't it?"

"Oh," she gave a small laugh. Beautiful she was, an actress she wasn't. "Mr Ramachandran! I'm sorry, Inspector. Mr Ramachandran is a close friend of the family. I don't think of him as Manjit's *business* partner."

"Is that why Mr Ramachandran is here, Mrs Singhabahu, as a friend of the family?"

Ramachandran's voice sounded slightly muffled from an inside room and became clearer as he walked to the doorway.

"The purpose of my visit, Inspector, is to examine Manjit's papers in his study. Looking for more detailed information of his current trip. Where he might be at this very moment, that sort of thing. Something that may assist the police."

He opened the door wide and stood beside Aysha Singhabahu. Harrigan silently noted the comfortable togetherness, displayed within their closeness.

"If these policemen have more questions, Aysha, maybe we should invite the gentlemen in."

"I'm terribly sorry, Inspector, please, follow me."

She turned away and glided through the wide hallway, down one step and turned to the left. They followed her through the magnificent home and eventually into a drawing room. Harrigan stood at the double glass doorways overlooking a picturesque garden. The garden was typical of those so often displayed in magazines, such as *England's 10 Most Beautiful Gardens*, magazines whose glossy pictures remind the common gardener that, despite the hours of love and attention, their gardens will never rate among the best.

"May I get you gentlemen a cup of tea, or coffee?" Aysha offered.

Harrigan turned and shook his head. "No, we're fine, thank you."

He walked toward the ornately carved mantelpiece. Beneath the mantelpiece was a period iron fire-grate surround, complete with hand-painted tiles on either side. In the actual grate, an artificial log fire, apparently gas fuelled, lay dormant.

He carefully studied the photographs proudly displayed on the mantelpiece. After close scrutiny, from the position third from the left, he selected a photograph of a man sitting at a large wooden desk.

"Is this your husband, Mrs Singhabahu?"

She nodded, uttering an almost inaudible. "Yes."

"When was the last time you saw your husband, Mrs Singhabahu?"

"It was…what's today?"

"Wednesday," Bill Buckle offered.

"That's right, Wednesday, so it would have been…Saturday. He left around seven in the morning."

"He had an early flight?"

"Oh no, Inspector, Manjit drove his car."

"To Africa?"

"No." She gave a slight laugh. "Don't be silly, Inspector. I should have said, Manjit went to Scotland before he left for Africa. He had some business in Glasgow I think it was."

Harrigan turned back to the mantelpiece.

Bill Buckle watched silently as Ramachandran and Aysha Singhabahu exchanged glances. He thought he saw a coldness creep slowly across her.

Harrigan moved from one photograph to another. He needed time to gather his thoughts. Ramachandran had told him that his partner was in Africa and would by now be in some remote area where contact would be difficult to almost impossible. It would take Manjit eight to nine hours at least to drive to Glasgow. Manjit would get to Glasgow around four on Saturday afternoon. Even if he had done whatever business he went there to do that evening, he would have had to stay overnight. If he'd left Glasgow at seven the next morning, he wouldn't be back into London until four that afternoon. If what his wife had said was true, and she hadn't seen him since Saturday, he obviously didn't return home on Sunday and so he must have gone directly to the airport. He would probably fly first class, so he would not need to get to the airport until…say, one and a half hours before his flight. Therefore, he could have left London by five-thirty and if the flight took… Harrigan took a guess…eight hours? Manjit would get to his destination, allowing for time differences, around five-thirty to six Monday morning. Even if Harrigan's figures were not as accurate as he would have liked and he'd arrived three or four hours later, could Manjit have had time to do whatever it was he had to do after he'd landed and get to some remote area by Tuesday?

Yes, he had to concede to himself, it was possible.

Harrigan still felt uneasy. Why didn't Manjit *fly* to Glasgow? Why do all that driving just before his trip?

Like a lot of things developing in this case, it didn't make sense. He turned back to the waiting trio.

"Sergeant, why don't you go with Mr Ramachandran and see if you can find any information in Mr Singhabahu's papers? Especially travel arrangements. Maybe not for this flight, but previous flight details. They may give us a place to start."

"I must object, Inspector. There may be confidential material in my partner's documentation." Ramachandran paused before adding, "Don't you require some form of warrant to do that?"

"I thought you would welcome the assistance of a trained eye, Mr Ramachandran." A tone of surprise entered Harrigan's voice. "After all, Mr Singhabahu is your partner, and I'm told," he glanced briefly at Aysha, "he is also a close family friend."

"If Manjit was in some sort of danger, Inspector, I would have to agree with you, but Manjit is simply on a business trip and, as such, I feel I should protect the confidentiality of any of his documents."

"Mr Ramachandran, I am investigating the brutal murder of one man, and the very suspicious death of another." Only the venom in his voice matched Harrigan's icy stare. "Both men died in an equally suspicious fire, which guttered a building leased by a company with some very, shall we say, different trading habits of which both you and Manjit Singhabahu are directors. I must admit I have some grave doubts as to the whereabouts of Singhabahu." He walked to a position barely inches from Ramachandran's face. "And if you *dare*," he spat the word, "show any resistance or hinder me in any way, I will make your life more miserable than you could ever imagine a life could be."

Ramachandran backed away, the fear in his heart pumped adrenalin through his veins.

"Ram, please," Aysha pleaded, as she walked between the two men. "I'm sorry, Inspector, Mr Ramachandran has a very protective nature." She turned to Bill Buckle. "Come along, Sergeant Buckle, I'll show you the way to Manjit's Study."

Ramachandran seized the opportunity to depart with whatever dignity he was able. "It's alright, Aysha, you need not bother. I'll take the Sergeant…follow me, please."

"I feel I must sit, Inspector." Aysha said quietly. The silk sarong flowed freely as this woman, obviously of much stronger character than the first impression allowed, moved gracefully toward a round hand-carved table, which stood twenty inches in height, and nestled between two high-backed, heavily padded, antique chairs of almost Regal proportions.

While the chair fabric was of a heavy cotton type material, printed in a pastel like floral design, the chairs were of similar design and dimension to the two red velvet chairs, which occupied the spaces on either side of the log fire at The Kings Arms, Harrigan's *local* run by publican Roy Knight.

The light dusky colour of her shapely leg showed clearly as this woman of contrast made her ease in one of the chairs. She beckoned to the other chair and gave Harrigan a pleading nod.

"Inspector?"

Harrigan obliged his hostess.

"You appear to have some concern for my husband, Inspector."

"Concern may be a little strong, Mrs Singhabahu, and I do not wish to cause you any alarm, but yes, there is something that just doesn't feel quite right."

"May I be of any help to, how would you policemen put it, throw a little light on the subject?" There was a hint of light-hearted flippancy in her voice.

He sat thoughtfully, as he carefully considered his next question. "I don't wish to sound rude, Mrs Singhabahu, and please understand my good intent, but I find your attitude toward my..." he stumbled for the right word but was forced to revert to the closest possible, "*concern*, to be somewhat calmer, even a slight more disaffected than I would have imagined."

With unconscious movement, she re-crossed her legs, closed the exposure caused by the open sarong, and moved back and more upright into her enclosing chair.

"I don't know that I quite understand what you are asking, Inspector."

With the exception of some original embarrassment shown at the front door, caused, Harrigan guessed, by being interrupted during activities that would be described as beyond that of a family friend, Harrigan suspected, this was the first time he had felt an element of uneasiness in her demeanour.

Harrigan's experience had taught him that uneasiness is invariably the result of some level of guilt, feeling of guilt, or even the desire to hide something that may be perceived as being taken as guilt. It was an emotion to be explored, and to that end, Harrigan very deliberately reached into his inside pocket and withdrew his black covered notebook, on which was plainly printed, in gold and beneath an image of the British Coat of Arms, the words "Official Notebook."

Aysha watched silently as he made a notation in the book.

"Without wishing to sound overly argumentative, Mrs Singhabahu, I think you understand quite well," he replied bluntly. "You say your husband left here on Saturday morning to drive to Glasgow, or more correctly, you *thought* it was Glasgow." He paused as he made notes, "and you have not heard from him since?"

"Yes," she replied.

He looked up sharply and stared directly into her eyes. "Yes? Does that mean *yes* you *have* heard from him?" He deliberately misunderstood her reply.

"No! I meant *yes*, I haven't heard from him."

He continued to write. "Do you not find that a little strange?"

"Strange, Inspector?"

"Yes, strange. Your husband leaves for Glasgow on a Saturday morning, then on Wednesday, you learn he is in the Middle East somewhere and you haven't heard from him since he's been gone. I would think a wife could find that a little strange."

She smiled patronisingly. "Inspector, you must understand our culture. I am the woman in this house. My husband treats me well. But unless invited to do so, I am not involved in any way with his activities beyond this house, especially his business pursuits. I am not kept informed of his movements, and it is not our way to allow a woman to interrogate her husband. I am told what I am told and must be satisfied with that."

"And are you satisfied with that?"

"I know no other way, Inspector."

"May I ask how long you have been married?"

"Twenty-five years on the fourteenth of next month."

"You must have been married very young, Mrs Singhabahu."

"I'll take that as a compliment, Inspector. But yes, I was fifteen." Her body was again relaxed. "And to satisfy your curiosity, yes, it *was* an arranged marriage."

"Do you have any children?"

"No. Manjit is not able to sire a child, Inspector." Then, as an afterthought, she said, "it is the one sadness in our relationship."

"Is that why Manjit is so dedicated to the works of U.C.F.A.C.?" He spelled the letters.

The act of consciously giving a relaxed air had a tenseness of its own. Mrs Singhabahu was now obviously acting. Well, obvious to Harrigan. Probably not obvious to another person. But there are a few tell-tale signs: a slight twitch of a finger, a brief and unnecessary glance away, an all too innocent tone in an overly soft voice.

"U.C.F.A.C., Inspector?"

"United Care For All Children."

She regathered some of her composure. "Oh, yes. Now that you mention it, I do believe he has done some work or had some kind of connection with them."

"The culture thing again? You are only told what you are told?"

"Our culture is not meant as an object of derision, Inspector," she chided.

"I meant no offence, Mrs Singhabahu, but tell me, does your culture allow you to prepare your husband's clothes? You know, iron his shirts and lay out his socks, trousers, tie, that kind of thing."

"Yes, very definitely. This is my work as a wife."

He sat quietly, making notes. "What about his belt?"

"His belt, Inspector?" The quiet innocent voice made its return.

There are many people, Aysha Singhabahu being one of them, who, when given a leading question, will stall for time by repeating the question. The ploy is meant to create time to think of the answer, or at least *an* answer. Harrigan always thought that it made the person look guiltier. It was Harrigan's way if he needed time to answer a question, to just say nothing and think.

Is thinking before you answer a question a crime? Harrigan remembered getting into trouble at school for *not* thinking before he answered.

"Yes, his belt," he repeated, a slight agitation in his voice. "For holding up his trousers."

"Oh, I see, of course. How silly of me. Yes, Inspector. I prepare everything."

"Do you pack his suitcase when he goes away?"

Once again she needed time to think. As if being able to read his mind she did not repeat the question. She chose instead to sit silently thinking over the question. She knew where Harrigan was leading her, but she could see no way out.

"Yes, Inspector."

"Did you pack his bag when he went to Glasgow?"

"Yes."

"I would have thought that before you packed his things, he would have told you he'd be travelling on to Africa or the Middle East or wherever it was he was supposed to be travelling to."

"Well, he didn't." Her voice rose in volume and all traces of friendliness and cooperation had now disappeared.

* * *

In the study, Ramachandran looked toward the doorway as the sounds of the woman's raised voice reached the two men. "I think we should return to the others, Sergeant. We're not doing any good here."

"Oh, I don't think that's necessary, Sir. I'm sure the Inspector has everything well in hand."

"Well I don't—"

"What's this, Sir?" The sergeant handed a Mid Eastern Frequent Traveller statement to his decidedly anxious companion.

Harrigan and Aysha Singhabahu continued uninterrupted.

* * *

"So that means your husband either didn't know he'd be going to fly out of the country after his visit to Glasgow, or," he placed a pensive look of thoughtfulness on his face.

"Or what, Inspector?"

"Or he didn't fly out of the country, after all."

He made a grandstand display of noting this assumption in his Official Notebook.

With a violent rush, she raised herself from the chair and stood by the double glass window, staring at the garden. "That's rubbish, Inspector! Of course he did! Where else could he be?"

"That's what I'm trying to find out, Mrs Singhabahu."

He closed his notebook and returned it to his inside coat pocket. He too stood and walked toward the mantelpiece.

"May I take one of these pictures of your husband, Mrs Singhabahu? I promise to take great care of it and will return it as soon as this unpleasant business is all over."

She shrugged, as if to say she didn't care one way or the other. He selected a wedding photograph of Manjit standing next to his new bride. It was also the only photograph of Manjit not sitting behind a desk or table.

He walked to the door used previously by the Sergeant and Ramachandran.

"Are you ready, Sergeant?" His voice echoed through the large downstairs section of the house.

Thirty seconds later, the two men re-entered the room.

"You find anything?"

"Not really, Sir. Although, according to his Frequent Traveller statement, it appears he travels mainly with Gulf Air."

"Well that's something." He turned and spoke to the woman's back. "Thank you for your time, Mrs Singhabahu, we'll show ourselves out."

He nodded to the other man. "Mr Ramachandran."

The two occupants of the house remained silent as they listened to the sounds of retreating footprints, and the front door being closed tightly.

Eager to ensure the two policemen had left, Ramachandran hurried through the house and watched from behind the full length curtains hanging at the front window, as Harrigan's Mazda reversed down the driveway and into the tree-lined road. He returned to the drawing room. Aysha Singhabahu had not moved.

He grabbed her by the shoulders and spun her around. He continued to hold her tightly by the shoulders.

"What the hell was that all about!?"

"What was all what about?"

"Getting me out of the room with that damn Sergeant, while you stayed here with Harrigan!"

"Ram, please, you're hurting me."

His dark eyes blazed with fury. "I'll hurt you in a minute, if you don't tell me what Harrigan wanted to know!"

Quickly, the frightened woman told him everything that had passed between her and the inspector. She finished with the words, "and he thinks that Manjit may not even have gone to Africa."

The angry man threw her roughly against the far wall. He looked around the room and his gaze fell on the empty space on the mantelpiece. He moved quickly across the room and looked carefully at the remaining photographs. The wedding photograph was missing.

"Damn you!" he shouted. He stormed out of the room, out of the house, and into the BMW.

A single tear rolled down the woman's cheek.

* * *

Harrigan steered the Mazda towards the A23.

"Did you find what you were looking for, Inspector?"

"Now who said I was looking for something, Sergeant?"

"If you don't mind me saying so, Sir, I've never known you to do anything without a reason. And let's be honest, if you hadn't thought there would be something important there, you wouldn't have come down. You always send the likes of me to do the routine questioning."

"The likes of you, Sergeant?"

"The underlings, Sir. We usually get to ask all the dull, boring, and uninteresting questions of all the dull, boring, and uninteresting witnesses."

"Every piece of information is equally important, Sergeant. It's just that some information I want to get first hand. It's usually quicker."

"Oh, I'm not complaining, Sir. I've been in the 'force long enough to understand how and why the system works as it does. And I might add, it's proven to be a pretty good system over the years, too."

"You won't get any argument from me on that count, Sergeant."

Deciding that Harrigan would tell him the results of his talk with Aysha Singhabahu in his own time, Bill Buckle fell silent.

The two men sat in the silence, as Harrigan guided the Mazda onto the outside lane of the A23 and fell in behind the typical endless line of traffic,

"I want you to get onto U.C.F.A.C. as a matter of priority, Bill. I need to know the names of the two recipients of those two belt buckles. And don't be surprised if Manjit Singhabahu is one of them."

"You think that the body, or what was left of it, may have belonged to Manjit Singhabahu?" Bill Buckle was unsuccessful at keeping a tone of the incredulous from his voice.

Harrigan didn't answer the question directly. Instead, he removed the photograph from his pocket and, without taking his eyes from the road, handed it to the Sergeant.

Bill Buckle looked at the photograph. It was a typical wedding photograph of the bride and groom standing together on the steps of a church. Well, it looked like it could have been a church. They were standing on the top of eight wide stone steps, with giant wooden doors swung from an old sandstone doorway.

"It's a nice photograph, Inspector, but what am I looking for?"

"Take a look at the shoe on the groom's left foot."

Bill Buckle held the photograph closer to his eyes and pointed it more to the light coming through his side window. Not being able to see any better, he placed the photograph on his lap and took out his reading glasses. Having positioned them on his nose, he again studied the photograph.

"Well bugger me, however did you spot that?"

"I was looking for it. Had I not been looking for it, I would have probably missed it as well."

"What tipped you off?"

"When I was waiting inside the Chemist shop getting a new battery put in my door lock thing, I was looking around the place —"

"As you would."

"As we all do," Harrigan corrected, "and I came across a pamphlet advertising handmade shoes for those with foot complaints. It was then I realised why someone would not only get rid of any fingerprint or dental identification, but also hack off the bloke's feet. The victim must have had something wrong with his feet, or foot, that would help lead us to the identification of the body."

"By the looks of the left shoe in this photograph, Manjit Singhabahu had a club foot."

"Talipes. Yes, that's right."

Buckle again examined the photograph. "Well, you were still lucky to see it. It's damn easy to miss."

"The one thing that made me look as closely as I did was that, in every other photograph, Manjit was sitting behind a desk or a table. That was the only photograph where his feet were visible."

"It certainly appears that Manjit could well be the victim."

"And that the killer was someone who knew him."

"And the killer also knew he had a club fo.. Talipes."

"Exactly."

"Someone who knew him, eh?" the sergeant repeated.

"That'd be my guess, Sergeant. In fact, you could probably bet your pension on it."

Bill Buckle handed the photograph back to Harrigan. "You didn't press the point at the house?"

"No." His reply was thoughtful, as if still questioning his decision to say nothing at the time. "I did consider it, but I want to get a little more information before I show too much of my hand."

"You suspect his wife?"

"Of the murder? No, I don't think so. But she *is* definitely hiding something."

One of Bill Buckle's strengths was he knew when to say no more, and so apart from the odd remark like. *Bloody traffic doesn't get any better* or *turn left here*, the two men again sat quietly.

A lot had happened since Tuesday afternoon, and Harrigan was trying to piece it all together. One thing he was sure about was that the fire was deliberately set. He didn't need any expert to tell him that. He was also ninety-nine percent sure that Manjit Singhabahu's Talipes was the reason for the feet being hacked off the victim.

As for the rest of it...

They were two blocks from Stonegate Police Station when Bill Buckle interrupted his thoughts. "Just drop me outside if you want, Inspector, save you going inside and getting caught up."

The old Sergeant was right. The last person Harrigan wanted to see right now was the superintendent. "O.K., Bill, thanks."

He pulled the Mazda to the curb and, with a considerable amount of difficulty, Bill Buckle manoeuvred his overweight personage from the low-to-the-ground sports coupe.

With a twinkle in his eye, he put his head back inside. "Have a good night, Sir. See you tomorrow."

The door closed.

Cheeky bastard. But then why shouldn't he have a good night? He'd almost forgotten he was taking Margaret Willis to Ali's for dinner.

He looked at his watch. He had two hours.

CHAPTER FOUR

Harrigan forced his way through the traffic. If he was to pick up Margaret Willis at seven o'clock, he had to get a move on.

He ran the timetable through his mind. *It's five now. Twenty minutes to get home, one hour to have a shower, shave, get dressed, that'd make it around twenty minutes passed six.* If he allowed ten minutes to catch a taxi, and twenty minutes to half an hour to get to Margaret's place, he would be there pretty close to time.

It hadn't taken him long to decide that tonight he would catch a taxi, especially after the last time he visited Ali's.

It was the night he'd solved the Robert Willis murder case and needed somewhere to get away. Ali's was the perfect place. As the night had gone on, he'd had much too much to drink, and if it wasn't for Ali insisting one of his men drive him home, God only knows how he would have got home. Who knew? He had been in such a mood he might even have tried to drive home himself, not a clever thing to do.

No, tonight he would take a taxi.

The absence of cooking smells floating up the hall as he opened the front door confirmed his mother had remembered he was going out for dinner.

"I'm home!" he called, as he closed the door behind him.

His eyes automatically focused on the entrance of the kitchen, expecting to see the figure of his mother appear, saying something like *you're early William* or *how was your day, William?*

When she didn't appear, his pace quickened as he hastened to the kitchen.

"You there, Mum?" The concern edged in his voice echoed across the empty kitchen.

"I'm in here, William."

Following the direction of the voice, he went back up the hall and into the front room. His mother sat quietly in the lounge chair nearest the small bay window.

"You alright, Mum?"

"Yes, I'm fine, Dear. Just a little tired, that's all."

"You're not feeling crook?"

"No William, I'm not feeling… ill." His mother had never accepted the slang of the Australians. "Like I said, just a little tired."

William loved his mother dearly, but she did have a habit of suddenly *coming down with something* whenever he was to take a lady friend out to dinner of whom she didn't approve. And there was doubt that she did not approve of his planned evening with Margaret Willis.

Satisfied this was one of those occasions, he shrugged off his concern.

"Well, have a nice rest, Mum, I must hurry and get ready to go out. I'm running a bit late."

Not having to stop and talk as he prepared himself, Harrigan took less than forty-five minutes to get ready. He checked himself in the mirror, gave his clean-shaven face one more quick spray of his favourite *Georgio* aftershave and went back to the front room.

"O.K. then, Mum, I'm off. I'm taking a taxi and don't wait up." He bent and kissed his mum on the forehead. She felt slightly clammy.

"You sure you're alright, Mum? You feel a bit clammy."

"It's probably a slight cold William, don't worry, I'll be alright. I'll get into bed once you've gone."

"I'll take my mobile telephone with me. Ring me if you need me."

"I'll be alright…now, off you go!" she urged forcibly, "and have a nice night." She added with little or no conviction whatsoever.

She sat quietly as she heard the door close. The old lady watched through the window as her handsome son passed the front of the house and walked towards the High Street.

* * *

The black FX4S London Taxi took twenty minutes to manoeuvre its way from the High Street in Finchenham to Margaret Willis' address in Sprigham Wells.

The distinct rattle of the 2.5 litre Rover Diesel, echoed up the wide driveway as Harrigan directed the driver to stop behind the BMW Compact parked outside the front door on the eastern side of the large house.

For the six months, immediately prior to the untimely death of Margaret's husband, she and her husband had lived apart. The family mansion had been split into two distinct homes, with

Robert Willis living on the western side of the divided building, she on the eastern side.

From what Bill Harrigan could see, the western side of the house remained empty.

Harrigan looked at his watch. Ten minutes to seven. Harrigan liked to be on time. Neither early nor late. Concerned that his companion for the evening might feel obligated to rush those final touches, and not wanting the sound of the diesel motor of the waiting taxi to add to that obligation, he leaned forward and spoke loudly to the driver.

"You can cut your motor if you like, driver, we're ten minutes early."

"Thanks Guv, but it's better for th' motor t' leave it runnin'."

Of course it is, thought Harrigan fatalistically.

There was really no other choice but to get out and go to the front door, albeit ten minutes early. That's the trouble with not having your own car, you're always in the hands of somebody else. But his anxiety proved to be ill founded.

Before he had taken the last few steps, the front door swung open and Margaret Willis stood smiling in the doorway. Her long-sleeve, green woollen suit, with knee length skirt, had obviously not been bought off the rack. The cut of the suit, while highlighting the shapeliness of her body, did so with the grace and dignity that only money could buy.

"Good evening, Inspector." She turned her back as she closed the door. "I trust that was a look of approval I saw on your face."

"Very much so, m'lady. Very much so."

She placed her hand delicately through his outstretched arm.

"Your carriage awaits," he announced with grand gesture as they walked the few paces towards the taxi. With his head initially facing the driver, he continued as he opened the door. "It awaits very noisily, but nevertheless, it awaits."

"That *is* the sound of London, my dear Inspector."

"Take us on to Ali's Restaurant please, driver."

"Ali's, Sir? The one in Beckingham?"

"No, the one in Abby Towers. Off Millbank Road...near Albert Tower Gardens."

"Yes...I know where it is!" The tacit suggestion that he may not have known where it was, had had a distinctly negative affect on the driver's manner. London taxi drivers prided themselves on their competency in the London Transport *Knowledge* test. But competency in the *Knowledge* or not, and despite the training in the art of diplomacy his years as a London Cabbie had provided, the driver was noticeably taken aback. He gave Harrigan the once over and he returned to the job at hand.

Harrigan was not offended as he saw the driver's head give a little shake of amazement. The driver's amazement was really quite understandable. People of Harrigan's status are not usually the type of clientele allowed inside Ali's.

The Ali's that is, not the one in Beckingham.

In 1975, Ali, then a recent immigrant with limited funds, saw a notice for the auction of the entire sixth story area in a building at Abby Towers. The building had been built in 1623 as a warehouse, and while there had been some renovations and alterations over the years, as it was one of the few London buildings left untouched during the great blitzes of the Second World War, it was still in an extremely original condition. After the war, the bottom five floors were converted to residential suites. The sixth floor was divided into two areas. One third of the floor was a penthouse suite, with the rest of the space being set aside for a restaurant.

Whether it was because of the shortage of money after the war, or because of the resistance by the other tenants, the restaurant was never completed, and for many years only the penthouse suite was used.

When Ali saw the auction notice, he could see the potential immediately. He had a dream of completing the restaurant. But not *any* run-of-the-mill restaurant. He wanted a restaurant for the rich, for the top one or two percent of the population. He would supply a place to meet, do business, and dine in the midst of utmost discretion and privacy, far removed from the ever-prying eyes of the less affluent.

The occupancy and conditions-of-use restrictions that applied to the sixth floor area, coupled with the much-publicized protests of the other residents, had kept the price to a level that enabled Ali to purchase the start of his dream.

Of course, he would still have needed to raise more money, and he still had the fight with the other tenants to contend with.

But there is often an irony in life. Believing that Ali did not have the funds to mount a strong defence, the tenants took Ali to court, claiming that should he open a restaurant on the sixth floor in accordance with his building application, they would suffer large losses in their property values.

The case dragged on for more than three years, at the end of which time, Ali was left almost penniless. But the wait and the fight proved to be worthwhile, and on the sixteenth of October 1979, the court disagreed with the tenants and dismissed their claim. Now comes the irony part of it. The court also awarded damages to the penniless Ali, and it was the payment of those damages, which were a lot more than Ali had in the first place, that had given Ali the money to renovate and open his elite and private restaurant.

To call Ali's a *restaurant* was grossly understating the true nature of the place. It was, as Ali had originally envisaged, more of an elite club.

With the exception of a very select few, reservations were always required and even then, reservations were only available to those persons *known* to the staff at Ali's. To become *known*, a person must firstly be introduced and recommended by another *known* person at some previous dinner or attendance.

In *the normal course of events, the Bill Harrigans of* the world never see the inside of such a place, unless on police business of course. And even then it would be doubtful.

But fate often steps in and demonstrates that life is not always going to be the way we planned it. In Bill Harrigan's case, it was shortly after joining the London police force, and it was on his way home from his local pub, when fate decided to put a little of *the other side* into his life.

He had walked about one hundred yards towards his home when he saw three teenage louts kicking a middle-aged man who lay huddled on the ground. A position they had presumably beaten him to just a few moments earlier. Without fear for his own safety or even considering the odds, Bill had thrown himself into the melee and turned the attack onto the three louts.

It wasn't long before three very sore and sorry little hooligans were running off down the alley, proving once again how much heart it takes for three heroes to kick a man as he lies defenceless on the ground.

Fortunately, due mainly to Bill Harrigan's timely intervention, apart from a few fairly serious cuts and bruises, Ali Shamir, the well-dressed Pakistani man on the ground wasn't too badly injured and, despite Bill's protestations and offers to take Ali to the hospital, Ali just wanted to go home. Bill Harrigan escorted Ali to his home.

Ali was a man of honour. He saw Bill Harrigan as the man who put his own personal safety at risk and saved his life. He felt a debt he knew he would be unable to repay in full. But the debt was not a burden; it was a joy. Whenever he saw Bill Harrigan, he was reminded that cruelty of man to mankind was not as universal as some would have you believe. The night of the beating also served to remind him of the good that co-exists with evil. It was Ali's belief that to be reminded of this so rarely published fact, was indeed a bigger gift than the original act of rescue.

Bill Harrigan was a close friend and Ali's number one *known* visitor. Ali Shamir and Bill Harrigan were almost as kin.

The Taxi clattered to a noisy stop outside the old building on the bank of the Thames. A uniformed coloured man opened the door and Harrigan got out of the taxi. The handsome face of the uniformed man nodded gently as a white-gloved hand offered a salute of friendly greeting.

"Good Evening, Mr Harrigan."

"Good evening, Samir."

While Harrigan paid the driver, Samir assisted Margaret Willis from the Taxi.

"Thank you, Samir."

"It is my pleasure, Mrs Willis."

Margaret Willis was taken by surprise. She had been here only once before, and that seemed so long ago now. She remembered it was just after she had formerly identified the body of her husband. Her emotions had been an unexplainable mixture of relief and sadness, and Inspector Bill Harrigan had asked if she would like a quiet drink to settle her emotions. She had accepted his kind offer and he'd brought her here. If her memory served her correctly, she had not been introduced to Samir that late afternoon, which made his greeting this evening all the more special.

Margaret replied with a simple warm smile.

She again placed her arm through Bill's and they walked towards the old wooden doors. The sound of the electronic door lock being released reached their ears as the doors swung silently open on well-oiled hinges. The lift stood directly in front of them on the far side of the foyer.

"Good evening, George." Harrigan called without a hint of a glance to either left or right.

"Good evening Mr Harrigan," the deep-throated voice boomed from a direction behind the couple.

The lift to the sixth floor proudly displayed an old wrought-iron cage and door with a cabin of ornate and well-polished wood. A heavy brass plaque, screwed to the wall with large brass screws, announced the year 1923 and the name Otis.

As nostalgic as all this might be, the Old World charm of the lift was only a facade. The slow and laboured speed of the ascent and descent of the lift still reflected an age gone by, but fire and building regulations demanded the operation of the lift be of the most modern design.

But despite laws and regulations, the only hint of the modern design was one obvious, distinguishable feature. The exposed floor indicator buttons on the left side of the lift only went to the fifth floor. Harrigan explained that they were only there for show and weren't connected to anything. The residents of the first five floors had a separate entrance to the building a little further down the street. Above the fifth floor button was a small six-inch by four-inch metal door in which was a keyhole of an unusual shape. Only *known* persons had a key to the little metal door.

Behind the door was a numeric keypad.

Each key had its own coded number, and only those with a key and who knew the specific code for that key could take the lift to the sixth floor.

Once inside the lift, Harrigan placed his key in the lock of the little metal door. After what seemed an interminable time, the lift glided smoothly to a halt at the top floor and the doors opened.

Ali stood ready, with a broad white-teethed smile. "Welcome, William Harrigan."

The two men greeted each other warmly.

"Good evening Mrs Willis, it is a great pleasure to see you here again."

"Good evening, Ali, thank you."

He led the couple through this most lavish of restaurants.

The main area was the size of a small ballroom where the original warehouse beams remained exposed and featured. The oak panelling, cornices, and decor had been carved and erected by master tradesmen. Like all older-style buildings, massive wooden pylons created automatic barriers. But these barriers had been put to good use.

Innovative design allowed these barriers to create the formation of cubicles, each of small room size and each designed to be self-contained. Each had an antique table, and six equally antique chairs. The chairs were those high backed chairs with spindly legs that, while ornate, never gave the user a feeling of complete confidence in the chair's ability to cope with the weight.

A cocktail bar, four lush leather armchairs and fireplace, completed the basic comforts. Every area possessed an unobtrusively positioned fax machine, Teledex, and telephone.

A variety of bookshelves, fish tanks, and climbing vines guaranteed the privacy in each area. White-coated attendants waited discreetly in the shadows, available to attend to the needs of the privileged clientele.

Harrigan and Margaret Willis were led through to a smaller but more open room. This area was Harrigan's favourite place, and was the area they had occupied on Margaret's first visit. Being sensitive to the circumstances surrounding that visit, Harrigan suggested that maybe they should sit somewhere else. Margaret quickly squeezed his arm.

"No...no, Bill, this is fine."

Ali stopped near two leather lounge chairs positioned in such a way that, while allowing panoramic views of the Thames, the occupants were still able to face each other during conversation.

"Champagne, Mrs Willis?"

Margaret looked at Harrigan who shrugged a tacit *it's up to you* kind of answer. She nodded to Ali.

"Your usual, William?"

"Thanks, Ali."

They sat quietly for a few moments, as Margaret looked around her, re-familiarising herself with the luxurious and peaceful surroundings. As before, it reminded her of pictures of the Old World men's clubs. All that was missing was the cigar smoke and corpulent old men with waistcoats, double-breasted, blue pin-striped suits, and red bulbous noses, all with a glass of sherry clutched in puffy hands.

Bill Harrigan watched her as she reaccustomed herself to the atmosphere. He thought what a handsome woman she was. He felt proud to be seen with her, and yet he was finding conversation difficult. In the Taxi it was easy. There was always the initial small talk when you first met, and during the journey, there were always the standard remarks about landmarks and the traffic conditions.

But now they sat alone. Now he had to say something meaningful. He found himself searching for the right words.

"A penny for your thoughts, Inspector."

Margaret had a way of making the word *Inspector* sound like a term of endearment. It was almost as if it were a lover's pet name.

"You want the truth?"

"The whole truth and nothing but the truth," she affirmed.

"I was thinking how proud I was to be with you, and I was searching for some very clever words designed to set the mood for the evening."

His companion lay back in the comfort of the chair, crossed her right leg over her left, and arranged her skirt in the most modest of ways.

"Well, Inspector, as we're being honest, I must admit to have had reservations about this evening." She paused and looked briefly around her. "You know. Coming here. Wondering what memories it would bring. Seeing you. Knowing the part you had to play in the investigation into Roger's death, and maybe worst of all, you knowing all the sordid details. But I have decided that life must go on." She uncrossed her legs, leaned forward, and touched his hand.

"We are here to have a pleasant evening. There will be words said and actions taken that will remind us of the past. But the past remains the past, and talking about the past is in the present. And right now, the present is us, here, together." She lay back once more. And, my dear Inspector, you can stop thinking about searching for the right words…the words you said could not have been nicer." A smile crossed her lips and, for a brief moment, Harrigan saw the smile glint in her eyes.

The next few hours were filled with childhood reminiscing and details of their formative years, fond memories relayed between each other. Both were interested in each other's stories.

Both were searching for some element of sameness in the little things of each other's lives now passed.

Like servants of a bygone era, the waiters silently responded to their every need.

The meal was served at the table beneath the window. They ate in elegance and sipped their wine. The blackness of the Thames was broken only by the reflected light of a busy London City.

The evening slipped quietly into early morning.

"It's one-thirty Margaret. I'm afraid we must be making a move. The life of a working policeman and all that."

"You know, that's the first time tonight you have spoken about your work."

She is right, Bill thought. He was a dedicated policeman, and work was never far from his thoughts. But tonight…

They walked slowly towards the lift door. A white-coated man stood at the door holding Margaret's coat.

"I trust all was in order, William?"

"As always, my friend."

"Please, come again soon."

"You try and stop me."

They laughed as true friends do. As Harrigan laughed with Ali, the thought struck him that as Ali was from the same part of the world as Mahmood, maybe, just maybe, he could shed a little light on a few things. He turned to Margaret, asked her to excuse him for a moment and, placing an arm around Ali's shoulder, moved two or three paces away. He spoke quietly.

"What do you know about a Muhammad Asif Mahmood?"

He felt Ali's body stiffen slightly beneath his arm.

"Oh, my dear William, please do not ask me such a thing. Mr Mahmood is a powerful man. No one, and I mean *no one*, asks about Mr Mahmood."

"Ok, then, if you won't tell me about Mahmood, what do you know about a company called Sidhu Trading? It's a shipping Company mainly, but also deals in second hand goods."

"Goodness gracious me, William, I don't know what you are mixed up in, but listen to me, my friend. Whatever it is you are doing—"

"I'm investigating a murder, Ali. Two murders in fact." Harrigan interrupted.

"As I was saying, whatever it is you are doing, I would advise you to stop it."

"Stop it!? I'm a bloody policeman on a murder investigation! I can't just stop it!"

"Oh you English," Ali shook his head. "I will never understand you." He paused and looked up and into the face of his friend.

"Dear William, there is nothing I can tell you about Mr Mahmood, or Sidhu Trading, except," he moved from beneath Harrigan's arm, "to remind you to always remember one thing. In my country, seldom is anything as it may appear."

Harrigan frowned as Ali took him by the arm. "Come, your lady is waiting."

Harrigan felt suitably chastised.

The Taxi was waiting outside as the couple stepped out of the lift doors. Being one of London's better addresses, taxis frequented Ali's. Even so, while Harrigan and Margaret were preparing to leave, Ali had ensured that a taxi *was* waiting outside. Had there not been one, he would have telephoned the local cab company. There was no need for Harrigan to ask Ali to do this; it was all part of the service.

The Taxi was an almost new Gucci model, so-called because of the plush interior and polished driver. It was typical of the taxis that serviced Ali's. As Margaret laid her head against his chest, Harrigan placed his left arm comfortingly around her.

"What a beautiful evening." Margaret whispered, as she moved slightly to gain a more comfortable position "It will always remain one of those special times."

He felt a glow inside. There was nothing he could say that could add to her sentiment, so he replied simply with a slight squeezing of her shoulder. They sat quiet in a vacuum of silence, as the taxi manoeuvred the streets of an early morning London. It was a cosy kind of quiet. The noise of the taxi and the sounds of the city were all there, but they could not intrude. These outside noises were like a shell of an empty container.

But nothing lasts forever.

"*I've* heard Roger talk about a Muhammad Mahmood." Her head remained firmly fixed against his body, as she spoke in a soft, almost matter-of-fact tone. "And Sidhu Trading for that matter."

Harrigan turned his head to look at her. He spoke to the top of her head.

"What!?"

"Roger, my husband."

"Yes I know Roger," he replied quickly and a little too impatiently. "What did you just say about *Mahmood*?"

"Before all the trouble started between Roger and me, Roger often used to talk to me about his work. And as a senior Civil Servant, he often took telephone calls at home, mostly at night." She paused, "all hours of the damn night," she added bitterly.

Despite his policeman's instinct to will her on, she remained silent for the next few moments. Harrigan repelled the urge to hurry her.

"If I remember, it would have been about eighteen months ago, maybe two years." Harrigan moved his arm as she sat up straight and continued to recount from memory. "Roger was involved, indirectly of course, in the investigation into an alleged paedophile ring supposedly operating in the circles of some of London's, dare I say, select elite?"

"Yes, I remember that case. There were some Peers of the Realm and a high-flying Judge involved, too, as I recall."

"That's right. Lord Banbury was one I remember and that Supreme Court judge. What was his name...?" Her voice trailed into thoughtfulness.

"Archibald Lapsley-Midwinter." Harrigan declared.

"That's him!" She patted him on the leg. "Well done, Inspector."

"Not really. I was on the case of his disappearance; I never did get to the bottom of it. It's been stuck in my gizzard ever since," he confessed. "The whole business was very, very strange."

"Strange?"

"Well, maybe more baffling than strange, I suppose. When someone disappears, especially someone of his position and wealth, there is always some trail to follow. Always some small clue left behind. But Lapsley-Midwinter? He just disappeared off the face of the Earth! Vanished without trace."

Margaret became excited and almost bounced on the seat, as she turned to face him. "That's right, now I remember! It was in the context of Lapsley-Midwinter's disappearance that I heard Roger on the telephone, and it was then he spoke of Mr Mahmood."

"Do you remember what he said? Who was he talking to?"

"Not word for word. But I know he was angry," she added quickly.

"Go on."

"I remember it clearly. When he had finished his conversation, he slammed the receiver down so hard that I asked him what the matter was. He told me to forget what I had heard and never repeat it to anyone."

"Will you repeat it to me?"

"Of course, what I can remember that is. What difference could it make now, anyway?"

"Well, tell me, and then we can decide if it makes a difference or not," he replied in a friendly but slightly impatient manner.

"Let me think..."

"Do you remember what the conversation was about?" He urged.

"They were definitely talking about the paedophile crisis, Lord Banbury, and the judge."

"How do you know that? Are you sure?"

"Positive. I only heard snippets of Roger's half of the conversation, of course, but I clearly remember Roger saying, '*I realise we must quash this damn paedophile thing, but we must find that bloody Midwinter bastard first.*' I remember that quite clearly, because Roger had raised his voice at this stage and the word *bastard* was not a word Roger often used. I remember thinking that he must have been very angry."

"What else do you remember?"

"It was not long after that he said something like, '*I don't care how damn powerful Mahmood is,*' or maybe it was, '*I know Mahmood is a powerful man,*' I...I'm not sure exactly."

"It doesn't matter, that's close enough. You said your husband also mentioned Sidhu Trading?"

"Yes..." She paused, trying to get the story as accurate as possible. "Just after the Mahmood statement, he threatened '*to have men crawling all over Sidhu Trading first thing in the morning.*'"

Margaret sat back into her seat and returned her head to his shoulder. Harrigan put his arm around her and remained thoughtfully quiet.

"Do you have any idea who he could've been talking to?" he eventually asked, with little expectation of any positive response.

"Not really. Not a name anyway, but it must have been someone above Roger. One of Roger's superiors."

"What makes you say that?"

"At the end of the conversation, Roger slammed the phone down and said, '*fucking politics*,' or it may have been '*politicians*.' I'm not sure, but I knew he'd been overruled, and Roger hated being overruled."

Harrigan was taken by surprise at the casual way she'd used the "f" word. It was the last thing he'd expected.

She looked into his face and saw his surprised expression. "Well, I'm sorry, Bill…that's what he said."

Unable to resist her almost girlish charm any longer, he smiled and kissed her on the lips. She returned his affection.

They didn't notice the taxi driver watching in the mirror.

* * *

It was six minutes after three when Bill Harrigan opened the front door of his home and silently stepped out of the drizzling rain. As he climbed the stairs to his bedroom, he heard the sound of a rasping cough from his mother's room. He slowly opened her door a little way and whispered. "You alright, Mum?"

"Yes, I'm fine, Dear…Good night."

Being unmistakably dismissed, he closed the door and continued to his own room. As he prepared for a few hours sleep, his concern for his mother heightened. It wasn't so much the cough, it was the fact she hadn't passed some remark about the lateness of the hour, or his being out with *that woman* that was significant. He decided that if she were no better in the morning, he would have Doctor Mainsbridge call around.

With thoughts of Margaret filling every corner of his mind, Bill Harrigan fell into a peaceful sleep.

Unlike his mother, the weather was no better when he arose just a few hours later. He ate his soft-boiled eggs, dunked his buttered bread fingers into the yoke, of course, and having put on his overcoat, he kissed his mum on the cheek.

"Now, if you don't feel well, call Doctor Mainsbridge," he instructed.

"I'll be all right. Now, off you go, and for goodness sake stop fussing!"

The Mazda coupe idled smoothly in the heavy traffic. Like most drivers in London, he constantly complained about the traffic; but he had always enjoyed driving, it relaxed him. He rarely used the radio or cassette player in his car, preferring to let his thoughts ramble to wherever they wished to go. Of course, during the working week, his thoughts were invariably of work and whatever case he was working on at the time, but when on holidays, he was able to turn work off and indulge himself. Like last summer when he drove to Scotland.

With the exception of the two days he spent on the Isle of Iona, he'd spent much of his time behind the wheel. He even took his car on the ferry to the Orkney Islands. It was a damn expensive ferry trip but well worth it. He'd stayed at the Ferry Inn at the ferry wharf. For three days, he'd driven around the island, visiting fascinating sites like Neolithic cairn at Maes Howe and the village remains at Skara Brae, built around 3000 BC, older than Stonehenge or even the great pyramids. The history on the island fascinated him, and he vowed he would one day return. He thought he might like to take Margaret.

But Pleasant as it all was, the point was that, while driving up the west coast, around Orkney, down to Loch Ness, over to the east coast and then home, he'd been able to switch off, recharge his batteries, and be ready once more to face the challenges of a London policeman.

The *click clack* of the windscreen wipers brought him back from the brisk, sunny days of the Scottish Highlands.

Although the first body in the Goldberg building had only been discovered on Tuesday afternoon, just one and a half days ago, this case was growing more interesting by the moment. Like any mystery, while there were many clues and indicators, there was always one major key that had to be found: a motive, some vital element that tied it all together. And once that key had been found, the rest usually fell into place. Bill Harrigan knew he was a long way from finding the key in this case.

Despite the weather, the traffic was reasonably fast and, at five minutes to eight, Harrigan walked into the Stonegate Police Station.

Colin McIver was already at his newly acquired desk. Harrigan noted how disgustingly tidy it was. A black and gold onyx pen and pencil holder held pride of place, immediately above the large scribble free desk pad. The silver pen and pencil appeared to be of medium quality, probably a Parker. A large china cup and equally large saucer rested on a coaster to his left. The saucer hid from view, *that* picture of a San Francisco tram printed on the coaster. The "bunch of dates" calendar, which sat on the right of the desktop, had the appearance of having been moved from place to place until absolutely correct viewing angle had been achieved.

McIver was writing in his one-day-per-page diary. Harrigan stopped and looked across the desk. "I see you've settled in okay?"

"Yes, thank you, Sir."

He closed the diary and made to stand. Harrigan held up his hand. "Don't get up; I'm an informal sort of bloke."

"Thank you, Sir."

"Give me a couple of minutes to get settled, and then come into my office." He nodded to the cup and saucer. "And bring yourself in a cup of tea."

"Thank you, Sir."

Harrigan picked up the "bunch of dates" calendar and, after a few moments of examination, replaced it at a different angle.

"Handy things those," he called over his shoulder, as he resumed his journey. He could picture McIver once again trying to get the "bunch of dates" back to the right spot. *Harrigan, you're a bastard,* he chuckled to himself.

Having eventually re-settled the desk calendar, Colin McIver waited a few minutes before taking up his cup and saucer and heading for the kitchen. To his surprise, Harrigan was in the kitchen making his own mug of tea. McIver hadn't met many police officers of senior rank who didn't think they were above making their own tea. In fact, he couldn't remember any.

"Kettle's boiled; there should be milk in the refrigerator. It'll be yesterday's. Patricia brings the fresh milk in with her."

"Yesterday's milk will be fine, Sir."

McIver busied himself, washing his cup and saucer and filling the cup with the ingredients. The casual atmosphere of the kitchen seemed the right time and place for Colin McIver to get something personal off his chest.

"Sir, there is something I'd like to tell you, about me. Something personal."

"Very well, but before you do, let me tell you something first. And I want you to listen carefully and understand what I'm about to say. If what you're about to tell me doesn't affect your duties as a police officer, you owe me no explanations. If you want to tell me for some personal reason, that's different. I'll be pleased to listen. But don't think you owe me any explanations."

He finished stirring his tea and threw the spoon noisily into the sink. Carrying his mug of tea, he moved to McIver and placed his free hand on his shoulder.

"What I'm trying to say, Colin, is I'm not interested in what you think you *should* tell me, only what you *want* to tell me… okay?"

"Yes, Sir. Thank you, Sir."

"Now, what is it you want to tell me?"

McIver looked directly into Harrigan's eyes. He knew exactly what the inspector was telling him. "It's not important, Sir, thank you."

"OK. Now let's get to work."

As Colin McIver followed Harrigan into his office, Harrigan gestured casually to the visitor's chair opposite his desk.

"Take a seat."

"Thank you, Sir."

Captured by the loud ticking noise, McIver looked up at the old clock. Harrigan heard McIver issue a slight sucking sound. "What a *wonderful* old clock! I simply adore it!" he exclaimed in a tone best described as overly dramatic.

Harrigan looked at the clock, then at McIver, back to the clock, and then gave a slight shake of his head. "Well, that makes you and me, Colin. Everyone else in this place thinks I should buy a new one."

McIver straightened with indignation and with a slight upward tilt of his head. "A new one!? Replace that beautiful clock with one of those...those..." He struggled for the right words. "Those modern day monstrosities? That, Sir, would be an unforgivable sin." He could not keep the incredulous from the emphatic statement.

Harrigan smiled, as he thought of what Bill Buckle's reaction would've been had he been here.

As if by some physic phenomenon, there was a loud knock on the door, and Sergeant Bill Buckle entered, carrying his mug of tea.

"Come in, Bill."

"Good Mornin', Sir. I——" He stopped short when he saw McIver sitting in *his* usual chair.

"I don't think you have officially met Detective Senior Constable McIver yet, Bill. Colin McIver...Sergeant Bill Buckle. You'll be working together."

Harrigan leaned forward and continued in a whispered voice, "and you're sitting in his chair."

McIver stood in a manner reserved only for the guilty and held out a well-manicured hand. "I'm very pleased to meet you, Sergeant Buckle. I'm sorry about the chair. I, I didn't know."

Bill Buckle slowly changed his mug of tea to his left hand and warily extended his right. As their hands met, Bill Buckle squeezed firmer than was necessary, but the look of superiority in Bill Buckle's eyes soon changed to one of surprise as Colin McIver's vice-like grip took effect. They held each other's stare. The hint of pained understanding of the motive behind Bill Buckle's overly firm handshake was hidden deep within McIver's eyes.

McIver released his grip and moved his cup of tea. "I'll get another chair."

Bill Buckle settled into his usual chair. McIver took his new position at the opposite end of the desk.

Bill Buckle felt he should say something. "You're an early starter, DSC McIver."

"He likes my clock, too." Harrigan added casually.

It was time for all three policemen to take a sip of tea.

"Alright, let's get down to business." Harrigan opened his notebook. "Let's see what we've got."

They watched as he flicked through the pages.

"How'd you and Constable Watts go with the door knocking of the area around the Goldberg building, Colin?"

"Nothing worth reporting, Sir. We learned nothing of any consequence. It's mostly light Industrial around that area, very little residential. It's in the Constable's report, Sir." He gestured to the small pile of neatly typed papers.

"Yes, I saw it. What about derelicts, drunks, the homeless? There are usually plenty of them hanging around that sort of location."

"Nothing, Sir."

"Nothing." Harrigan repeated. "Well, if that gave us nothing, let's look at what we *do* have."

He continued to search the notebook.

"One burned out building. Two dead bodies. One with no hands, no feet and no dental records, burned beyond recognition, and only an UCFAC belt as means of identification. The other body, almost untouched with full identification, a resident visa for the USA, twenty-five thousand pounds sterling in cash and five thousand pounds worth of gold bullion."

He looked at the two policemen sitting opposite, who in turn looked at each other, and then back to the inspector. Not knowing what he expected them to say, both chose to sit quietly.

"In the early hours of last Tuesday, the Goldberg building was guttered by fire and the contents completely destroyed. The fire seems to have been deliberately set and the contents, mostly items for dispatch to the poorer regions of the world were not insured." Harrigan felt it was time he went through the whole situation to date.

"The building is owned by one of the world's richest men," he continued. "And was used by a company called Sidhu Trading, which is also owned by the same man. Sidhu Trading not only makes its living as a shipping company, but is also the world's largest second-hand store. Sidhu Trading has offices in various parts of London and is primarily run by two directors. One of these directors we are told, is currently wandering around unknown regions of the Middle East or Africa or wherever. We are also told that this is not unusual, because he spent most of his life travelling to the poorer parts of the globe, redistributing superseded, used, and no longer required goods. We, however, do not believe he is missing or wandering and is, in fact, our number one suspect as being the unidentified body. The other director stays home, runs the business from London, and has his dirty little way with the first director's wife."

Harrigan began to make notes on an A4 size notepad. McIver stood.

"I saw a whiteboard in the room next door, Sir. Would you like me to wheel it in?"

Harrigan was not a whiteboard man. He preferred to get things sorted out in his mind, but if it made McIver happy. "If you want to." He shrugged disinterestedly.

Undaunted by his new inspector's lack of enthusiasm, McIver dashed to the next room and, five minutes later, he wheeled in the whiteboard and set it up. He took up the special thick black pen and began drawing a series of horizontal and vertical lines. Each line had a heading followed by another series of horizontal and vertical lines.

Harrigan continued his summary. McIver followed him on the whiteboard.

"Manjit Singhabahu's wife Aysha told me her husband had left for Scotland last Saturday and has not been seen or heard from since. Khalil Ramachandran, on the other hand, had already told us that his fellow director was in Africa."

As the black pen suddenly screeched against the whiteboard, Harrigan and Bill Buckle looked sharply at McIver, their teeth still on edge.

"Sorry," McIver said softly.

"Anyway, as I was saying, what I have trouble coming to grips with is that, although Aysha only mentioned packing Manjit's bags with enough clothes for a trip to Scotland, she had not been in the least surprised to learn that her husband was now in Africa."

Harrigan deliberately omitted any reference to the photograph he had taken from Manjit Singhabahu's home or Margaret Willis and her dead husband's telephone conversation.

The slight knock on the door announced Patricia Hedrich. After the formal good mornings, Patricia collected the two empty mugs and McIver's cup and saucer. As she picked up the cup and saucer, Harrigan did not miss the look that passed between her and Bill Buckle, slight as it was.

"Patricia."

"Yes, sir?" A slight feeling of guilt rushed her words.

"When you see Constable Watts, ask him to come in here would you?"

"Yes, Sir."

Harrigan leaned back, hands behind his head. The loud tick of the clock filled the room. "Well, gentlemen, where do we go from here?"

Bill Buckle had known Harrigan long enough to understand that Harrigan already knew what the next steps were going to be, but the inspector's leadership style was to involve everyone, give everyone a chance to feel part of the team, as it were.

"We've listed what we do know. I think maybe we should list what we don't know." Bill Buckle felt a need to be the first between himself and McIver to offer a suggestion.

"Good idea, Bill, so do I. Colin, is it possible to make a copy of that stuff you've written on the board?"

"In a wink, Sir!" McIver pushed the first button on the right of the small control panel and, after a few whirring sounds and a couple of seconds, a sheet of paper emerged from the side of the whiteboard. He made three copies, and then with the gentle touch of a second button, the white board face slowly rolled out of sight leaving a second blank face, ready to use. McIver distributed the printed copies and stood ready once more with the thick black pen.

"O.K., let's start with the building. Question one, was the fire in the building deliberately lit?"

McIver drew one column down the left side of the whiteboard, headed the column *Building* and began writing the first question, in abbreviated form.

"I can answer that, Sir." McIver spoke as he wrote. "And the answer is a definite *yes*. I received the report on the fax this morning."

"Did the report say *how* it was started?"

"It was much as we'd thought, Sir. The primary ignition point was in the area occupied by the currently unidentified body. The body had been doused with some type of accelerant, probably Ethanol, but that needs to be finalised. Ribbons of the accelerant were also spread in various directions, except towards the rear door."

"The fire was intended to spread quickly, but had to allow time for the arsonist to escape." Bill Buckle ventured.

"I'd say that was a sure bet." Harrigan was interrupted as the three teas were brought in.

"Constable Watts is just getting a mug of tea and then he'll be right in." Patricia turned towards the noise behind her. "And here he is now."

When the four policemen were alone and, after another round of *good mornings*, while Harrigan quickly brought Malcolm Watts up to date, McIver returned the original white board face to the front and printed another copy.

"And as Sergeant Buckle has just stated, the fire was intended to spread quickly, but had to allow time for the arsonist or arsonists to escape," Harrigan concluded.

McIver stood poised, black pen at the ready.

"If we accept then that the fire was deliberately lit, that brings us to the second question. *Why* was the fire lit?" Harrigan's brief pause denied the others any opportunity to answer. "Well, we know it wasn't for the insurance. Ramachandran told us there was no insurance, and I find it hard to believe that a man as intelligent as Mr Ramachandran would tell a lie over a matter that we can easily check on, and we *will* do a thorough check."

Harrigan took a sip of tea. Bill Buckle recognised this gesture as the signal to participate and took the lead.

"With the information we have at the moment, I would guess that the fire was lit to further destroy any identity of the body, and also, maybe disguise *how* the victim was killed."

Harrigan sat in deep thought.

"If it *wasn't* started for those reasons, it certainly had that effect," Harrigan declared.

"Sergeant Buckle's suggestion does sound logical, Sir." Malcolm Watts offered in support.

"On the surface of it, Constable, I must agree. But if after killing somebody you go to all the trouble this killer did to hide the victim's identity, including setting fire to the building, why leave the UCFAC buckle? There's no logic in that."

"What if the killer didn't know the significance of the buckle?" McIver asked as he wrote.

"Maybe he thought the buckle would be destroyed in the fire," Bill Buckle offered optimistically. A few seconds later, he came up with a third option. "Maybe the buckle was hidden by the dead person's coat. Remember, we don't know how he was dressed; that's all been destroyed in the fire. Maybe the killer simply couldn't see the buckle. Didn't know it was there."

After a few moments of silence, Harrigan reluctantly agreed. "OK, I'll accept that for the moment." He turned to Bill Buckle.

"How're you getting along with the UCFAC buckle, Bill, you get an ID?"

"I left a message with a Mrs Thistlewaite at UCFAC yesterday afternoon. I hope to have an answer this morning."

"Okay." Harrigan glanced towards McIver. "You'd better draw another column on that thing, Sergeant, and we'll move on to Wei Yu Lee."

McIver obeyed and wrote "Q1" in bold figures.

"The first question is, where does Mr Lee fit into all this, and did he have anything to do with the murder?" Harrigan's questions were almost statements.

"That's two questions," McIver reprimanded light heartedly as he wrote.

Harrigan liked this man's sense of humour.

McIver finished writing and walked away from the whiteboard. "If I may, Sir, I don't believe Wei Lee had anything to do with the murder."

"And why is that?"

"Well, Sir, if he'd had anything to do with the actual murder, and if our theory is right about the murderer lighting the fire, why would he hide under the bath after he'd lit it? Surely he would have gone outside!"

"You're suggesting he was simply someone in the wrong place at the wrong time?" Harrigan asked.

"It could be something like that, Sir." McIver assumed his writing duties.

"If you are right, Colin, if he wasn't the arsonist, why *was* he there?" Harrigan mused as he leaned forward, placed his elbows on the desk, and intertwined his fingers. He rested his chin on his outstretched thumbs and stared silently into the immediate space in front of him; the two intertwined fingers closest to his face beat an irregular tattoo.

A quick shake of Bill Buckle's head caused McIver to close his mouth and remain silent.

Harrigan thought of the gold bullion, the twenty-five thousand pounds in cash, the passport and resident visa to the USA. More importantly he couldn't shake the thought of the missing airline ticket and absence of any keys that would suggest he had belongings elsewhere. Harrigan was convinced that Wei Lee was about to travel and that he'd had everything with him or at least, close by.

Maybe Wei Lee's belongings had been in the Warehouse.

Harrigan leaned back, placed his right hand on the arm of his chair, and hung his left arm down the side. He stared at the ceiling for a few moments and then slowly moved his line of sight to Malcolm Watts.

"Constable Watts."

"Yes, Sir." Came the eager reply.

"I want you to find out if the container that left the Goldberg building yesterday afternoon is now on the high seas or if it is still in the country. If it is in the country, I want it back! If it's not, I want to know exactly where it's going."

"You want me to do that right now, Sir?"

Harrigan copied the Container number and the name Indstani Lines on the bottom of the A4 pad and, using a ruler, tore it away from the rest of the page.

"Right now, Constable. Right now, if not sooner."

Constable Watts rose from the chair, took the paper, and left the room.

"All right, Colin, let's get back to your whiteboard."

Three sets of eyes quickly scanned the orderly and clearly marked notes on the board.

"Are we all satisfied that whoever killed the mutilated victim also started the fire?" Harrigan asked.

There was a general nodding in agreement.

"Is it also agreed that the death of Wei Lee was, for the moment anyway, unintentional?"

All heads nodded in unison once more.

"And would I be right in assuming that, unless the UCFAC belt buckle comes up with a different answer, you gentlemen agree that the unidentified body is that of Manjit Singhabahu?"

McIver nodded quickly in agreement. Bill Buckle, however, allowed a few moments to pass to give the question a little more thought before he, too, finally agreed.

"All right, now we're getting somewhere. The next question then, is—"

"Why did someone want Singhabahu dead?" McIver interrupted.

"That's quite right, Detective Senior Constable, and that is exactly what Sergeant Buckle and I are going to find out. And once we get the answer to that question, we'll be one step closer to finding the identity of the killer."

"What would you like me to do, Sir?"

"I want you to try and locate Manjit's car, Colin. He supposedly drove to Scotland. He is also supposedly in Africa somewhere. But it seems that he actually ended up in Hothamstone. It would be interesting to know where his *vehicle* ended up."

"Right, Sir."

"I also want you to check the validity of Lee's USA resident's visa. Make sure it's kosher if you know what I mean."

"I know exactly what you mean, Sir."

McIver placed the thick black pen on the ledge in front of the whiteboard and began writing in his notebook. Harrigan waited until he'd finished writing and had returned the notebook and pen to his pocket.

"I also want you to find out if Muhammad Asif Mahmood has a residence in the United Kingdom."

McIver withdrew his notebook and pen once again.

"And take Constable Watts with you."

As if on cue, Malcolm Watts entered the room.

"How'd you go, Constable?"

"I'm afraid the ship sailed early this morning, Sir."

"Pity, where's it heading?"

"Houston. Due to arrive in the second week of June, Sir."

"Well that gives us some time, anyway."

The others had no idea what he was talking about, and all three were wise enough not to ask.

"Unless you chaps can think of anything else, I think that's about it for now. We all know what we've got to do." He nodded to McIver and Watts. "Let me know as soon as you learn something."

"Yes, Sir. Come along, Constable, you and I have work to do," McIver said.

Once the two men were alone, the atmosphere in the office became less formal, more familiar.

"Where the hell do we begin, Bill?"

"If it was up to me, Sir, I'd start at Singhabahu's office at Sidhu Trading's Hawgate address. There were very little records in his home office, so most of his stuff must be there."

"Good idea. And then I think we'll pay a visit to Bichirst and have a talk with Mr Muhammad Singh. Something just doesn't gel with that bloke."

Before leaving the Stonegate Police Station, Bill Buckle asked Patricia that, if Mrs Thistlewaite rang, to give her the inspector's mobile telephone number.

It was almost eleven o'clock when Harrigan offered his identification to the receptionist at Sidhu Trading's Hawgate office.

"Good Morning." He paused, as he leaned forward and read the embroidered name on the neatly pressed uniform blouse. "Marilyn. Is Mr Ramachandran available?"

She looked a little startled.

"Marilyn?" Her reply took Harrigan by surprise; it definitely wasn't the response he'd expected.

She glanced down at her blouse and gave a slight, if not uneasy laugh. "Oh, I'm not Marilyn, she left last week. I'm Nora, I started yesterday. I'm wearing this blouse to save my own clothes, until I order new uniform clothes for myself. If I like it here, of course," she added quickly.

At the risk of stating the obvious, Harrigan asked. "Doesn't that get confusing for the visitors?"

Nora glanced from side to side and, as if divulging some secret information, answered in lowered tones. "To be honest with you, Sir, we don't seem to have many visitors. Apparently, most stuff around here is done via the mail box or fax, and the telephone, of course."

"Mr Ramachandran?" Harrigan brought the conversation back to his original question.

"I'm afraid Mr Ramachandran is not here, Inspector, and I have no idea what time he will be back."

"Can you contact him on his mobile telephone?"

She rummaged through the papers on her desk, looking for his number. She looked up at a small yellow Post-it Note stuck on the wall.

"There it is!" she announced triumphantly.

"If you are able to contact him, tell him Sergeant Buckle and myself are here to look through Mr Singhabahu's office."

Nora dialled the number and held the telephone piece to her ear. She waited in silence for fifteen to twenty seconds.

"Mr Ramachandran? It's Nora." She remained silent while Ramachandran spoke at the other end of the line. "Nora," she repeated, "from the office." Another pause. "Yes, Sir, it must be hard to get used to. I have an Inspector Hartigan here—"

"*Harrigan.*"

Nora stopped talking and looked at Bill Harrigan.

"It's Harrigan, Inspector *Harrigan*." He placed strong emphasis on the last Harrigan.

She nodded in understanding and mouthed a silent apology to the inspector. "I'm sorry Mr Ramachandran, that's Harrigan, not Hartigan." She waited a few moments for Ramachandran to make the mental adjustment. She continued. "He has a Sergeant Buckley with him. They want to search Mr Singhabahu's office."

A few seconds followed as she listened to Ramachandran's reply.

"He wants to know if you have a warrant, Inspector."

"Just tell him there's two ways we can do this; he'll understand."

She sat wondering if she should repeat such a statement to her new employer.

"Go on," Harrigan encouraged urgently, "tell him!"

Reluctantly the message was repeated. She sat quietly listening intently to her instructions.

"Yes, Mr Ramachandran, right away." She replaced the handpiece onto the telephone. "I don't know if I like working in this place," she said, as she wiped her brow with the back of her hand.

"What did he say?" Harrigan asked a little impatiently.

"Oh, I'm sorry, Inspector. I'm not used to all this police business. Mr Ramachandran told me to show you to Mr Singhabahu's office and to assist you in any way possible. I don't know how much help I can be, I haven't been here long enough to know much. But if I can, just ask." Nora escorted Harrigan and Bill Buckle to an office on the left of the main foyer. "In here Inspector." She said as she opened the door and stood to one side, allowing the visitors to enter the room.

"Thank you, Nora." Harrigan said as he entered the modest, but tastefully furnished room. It was immediately obvious, that while Singhabahu spared no expense on the things he needed and enjoyed, he was by no stretch of the imagination, wasteful or extravagant. With the exception of Awards and Commendations, the walls were bare of any decoration.

Nora closed the door and returned to her chair behind the reception counter.

"I'll start here at the desk, you may as well attack the filing cabinet," Harrigan paused and then added with a smile, "Sergeant *Buckley*."

"Right you are, Inspector *Hartigan*."

The good humour subsided as the two men got down to some serious police work.

Real police work wasn't like the programmes on the television. Much of the real life work was boring and tedious. The fast cars, glamorous nightlife, and beautiful people of the small screen gave way to invoices for second hand, superseded, and other unwanted goods; pick up slips and delivery dockets; customs paperwork and shipping itineraries. There were many letters of request from far and wide from third-world countries, the unrecognised and unfashionable nations and, of course, the ever-increasing, mostly ignored and unaccepted poorer areas of the richer countries. These requests in the main part had been matched with offers of goods from the overly affluent, the generous, and the wasteful.

The countless flight schedules and used airline tickets showed that Manjit Singhabahu spent much of his life travelling, mostly to parts of the world, the majority of people spent their lives trying to avoid.

Hundreds of letters of gratitude also filled the files. Two hours of intensive searching failed to reveal one solitary clue as to why Manjit Singhabahu should be murdered. Not one bad word. Not one bad comment. In fact, if the files were a true account of the man, he should have been canonised, not murdered.

They thanked Nora and made their way to the outside of the building.

Harrigan suddenly baulked. "Hang on a second, Sergeant, I've one more question for Nora."

"Nora!" he called, as he returned to the reception area. "Do you have any idea why Marilyn left?"

The quizzical expression on her face told Harrigan he'd have to explain further.

"Her departure was obviously sudden. Was she sacked? Did she resign? Did she just fail to turn up?"

"I've…I've no idea, Sir. Although with the haste in which I was employed, I think I agree that her leaving was unexpected."

"You don't know if she was fired?"

"No, Inspector, sorry."

"Thanks anyway, Nora, cheers." He rejoined Bill Buckle. "Let's pay a visit to Muhammad Singh."

The drive to Bichirst was as uneventful as a drive across London can be. In complete contrast to Hawgate, the Bichirst office was a hive of activity. Seated behind old wooden desks were seven employees, five males and two females. Each desk was filled with copious amounts of paperwork and each with the latest model computer terminal. Harrigan saw the irony of the scene. It was his understanding that computers were supposed to minimise paperwork, not create more.

"May I help you, Sirs?"

Muhammad Singh approached the counter. His voice was educated but unmistakably East Asian.

Harrigan showed his Identification. "Mr Singh?"

Muhammad Singh bowed his head. "At your service, Inspector."

"I believe you've met Sergeant Buckle."

Singh returned the Sergeant's official *"Sir"* with a silent and very slight nod of his head. "How may I help you, Inspector?"

"Do you have an office where we can talk?"

"Most certainly, Sir. Please be following me."

He led them towards a dark-brown, solid wooden door, broken only by a large pane of frosted glass that had been inlaid in the top section. They passed through into a dark corridor, which eventually led to a small, poorly-lit office filled with paper records piled on every flat service available. One wall was completely hidden by a stack of brown archive boxes.

Muhammad Singh removed piles of paperwork from two old and frail looking wooden chairs and placed them at the desk. He sat in a cracked and well-worn green leather chair across the desk, leaned back into his chair, and gestured for his visitors to sit. He quickly sat forward and moved the fluorescent desk lamp to one side before leaning back once more.

"Now, Gentlemen, how may I be of assistance?"

"Do you know Mr Manjit Singhabahu?" Harrigan began.

"The Director, Sir? I know of him, Sir."

"Do you have much contact with him?" Harrigan continued. Bill Buckle knew this was not a time for him to be interrupting. He was quite content to sit back and let his inspector take the running on this one.

"Only through his good works, Sir. We arrange the shipping of his goods."

"Would you explain how those arrangements work?"

"Well, Sir, when Mr Singhabahu had a container ready, he would contact this office and supply to us all the details. You know, where to pick it up, delivery address, container size—"

"Contents inventory, bill of lading." Harrigan offered.

"Oh yes, Sir, that is very important, Sir, for Customs you know, Sir."

The *humble servant* malarkey was starting to grate on Harrigan's nerves.

"Sergeant Buckle got the impression from your previous discussion with him that you had never been to the Goldberg building, and that you were unaware Sidhu Trading actually leased the building from Mr Mahmood who, by the way, also owns Sidhu Trading. Is that true? You had never been to the Goldberg building? "

"Ohh, Sir, we pick up many, many containers every day... from all over London. I don't get involved with who owns what. My job is in shipping, Sir, not property."

"How many ships does Sidhu Trading operate?"

"Sidhu Trading owns fourteen vessels that I know of, Sir. But we use the services of many others."

"You have your own containers?"

"Of course, Sir."

"How many?"

"I do not know exactly, Sir, but many hundreds."

"Are Mr Mahmood's companies charged at a different rate than your other customers?"

"I don't know that I can tell you that, Sir. Such information is classified as commercially sensitive."

"I'm in the police business, Mr Singh, not the shipping business, and I don't give a damn about commercial sensitivity. What is important is that I am investigating a murder, maybe two murders, and I don't like being messed about, not even a little bit. Now, if I am forced to get a warrant, and I will if I have to, I will have no option but to put that into the being-messed-about category, and once that happens, things might not be as easy for you or Sidhu Trading. Do I make myself perfectly clear, Mr Singh?"

Harrigan's unblinking eyes could see Muhammad Singh's mind racing.

"If I remember correctly, you were asking about discount rates. Oh yes, now I remember, yes, Sir; a discounted rate is offered."

Harrigan nodded in a *that's a more like it* attitude.

"Looking at your computer system outside, I assume the accounts for Mahmood's companies could be easily identified." It was more a statement than a question.

"Yes, Sir. It would take some time, but we could do it."

"Good. Then I want it done."

"It will take some time, Sir," he reasserted.

"That's fine. The next couple of days will do. Except for the records of the Goldberg building pick-up address. I'd like those now."

"How far back would you like to go? We only went to the computer system around five years ago."

"Five years will do fine."

"I won't be a moment, Inspector."

The East Asian man excused himself and left the room.

The two policemen sat in silence. Four minutes passed before Muhammad Singh returned.

"It'll take about five to ten minutes."

He resettled in the old green leather chair.

"There is just one more thing, while we're waiting. What connection does this office have with the Hawgate office?"

"Only for shipping, Sir. As I said before, Sidhu Trading has many branches. Many different operations. We may work *for* the one company, Inspector, but we don't work *as* one company."

Harrigan was getting weary of having to extract the answers from Singh in such a painstaking way. It was like pulling teeth. He decided it was probably time to get a little more aggressive.

"Who's your boss, Mr Singh?"

"Sir?"

"Who is your boss? Who's the gaffer? It's a fairly simple question."

Singh was obviously reluctant to answer this simplest of questions. "I answer directly to Mr Ramachandran."

"I see." Harrigan took a deliberate pause. "What about Mr Mahmood?"

"Mr Mahmood?" Muhammad Singh gave a little laugh. "Mr Mahmood is a rich and powerful man, Inspector. He is not interested in the likes of me." He hung his head submissively.

"How do I contact him?"

Once again Singh uttered that small and damned-annoying nervous laugh. "No one *contacts* Mr Mahmood, Inspector. Mr Mahmood only speaks to those he wishes to speak to. It is *he* who contacts *them*."

"Does Mr Mahmood have a residence in the UK?"

"I would not be knowing anything such thing as this, Sir. I am but a humble servant."

Harrigan could take the humble servant routine no longer. He stood impatiently and indicated to Bill Buckle that it was time to leave. Having taken two paces towards the door, Harrigan stopped suddenly, turned sharply, and slowly and meaningfully retraced the two steps. He raised a clenched fist and brought it down hard on the table. The green shade on the fluorescent light slipped awkwardly to one side. A startled Muhammad Singh jumped in surprise at the sudden change in Harrigan's attitude. As Singh's knees gave the desk one final jolt, the green lampshade succumbed to the pull of gravity and crashed to the floor.

"Humble servant my arse! I've told you before. The sergeant and I are investigating at least one murder, maybe two…and I promise you, anyone who holds back any evidence or refuses to supply information will eventually be rounded up and charged as being an accessory to those murders, plus anything else I can think of!"

He leaned on the desk and placed his face a few inches from Singh's nervous stare. His voice became quietly menacing. "I don't make idle threats, Mr Singh, so listen very carefully. The Sergeant and I are going to wait outside in the reception and I suggest that while we are outside, you give some serious thought as to an address in the UK where we may be able to contact Mahmood."

He stopped at the door and spoke again to Singh.

"You had better believe it, Mr Singh, when I tell you that compared to me, Mahmood is a fucking pussy." He closed the door behind him.

"Do you think he knows if Mahmood has a U.K. residence?" Bill Buckle whispered.

"I have no bloody idea, Sergeant, but we'll soon find out."

Several minutes passed. Singh eventually appeared and handed a manila folder to Harrigan. "The account you wanted is all in there, Inspector. I'll have the others tomorrow, about two in the afternoon."

"I'll have someone pick them up." Harrigan stood staring expectantly.

"On that other matter, you might try an estate in Kent called The Badgers. I don't know where it is but I have heard it mentioned."

"Thank you, Mr Singh."

"And Inspector."

"Yes, Mr Singh?"

"Don't mention where you heard that, will you?"

"I'll try not to, Mr Singh...I'll try not to."

It wasn't until they were both settled in the car that Harrigan opened the manila folder. He plugged the mobile telephone into its holder and switched the car ignition to *accessories*.

"While I'm looking through this, Sergeant, contact UCFAC and see if they have identified the belt buckle yet."

He also suggested that he should ask Patricia Hedrich to start looking for an address for The Badgers.

Harrigan looked through the Sidhu Trading (Hothamstone) account. In the background, he heard conversations between Bill Buckle and Mrs Thistlewaite and then Bill Buckle and Patricia Hedrich. As the Sergeant finished the second conversation, Harrigan closed the folder and passed it to him.

"Just as I suspected, Sergeant."

Bill Buckle took the folder and began to inspect the contents.

"Did I hear Mrs Thistlewaite confirm that the buckle belonged to Singhabahu?"

"Yes, Sir."

Harrigan started the motor and drove toward Hothamstone.

"So the body is that of Manjit Singhabahu, Sir?"

"That's how it looks, Sergeant. That's what the buckle tells us."

"Is the buckle enough for a formal identification?"

"I think the better question, Sergeant, is what else do we have? Besides, I'll bet bodies have been officially identified on less in the past. And we do have some other evidence. For example, the body is the right height." He looked thoughtful for a moment, "or should that be *length*?"

"You sound more like a medical examiner every day."

"God forbid."

Bill Buckle pressed his feet hard to the floor as the Mazda raced towards the rear of a lorry loaded with barrels of Bass beer. Mere inches before impact, Harrigan indicated to the left and darted in front of a red-faced van driver and exited the round-about.

"And let's not forget the body was also found in the building leased by the Company of which he was a director," Harrigan continued. "It's all too coincidental. But maybe most importantly, the body had no feet. The killer would smash the mouth to hide identification through dental records; that makes sense. As does the removal of the hands to get rid of fingerprints and burning the rest of it. Macabre it may be, but still understandable. But the feet, Sergeant, why the cut off the feet?"

Bill Buckle released the pressure from the floor and desperately tried to keep the tremble from his voice, as the Mazda sped along its controlled yet seemingly reckless journey.

"Because the club foot would give it away. Even after the fire, bone structure would still be there. It looks like you were right, Sir. "

"Damn right it does, Sergeant. Thank God for family photos."

Bill Buckle did not know where they were heading, but the general direction gave him an inkling that it was probably the Goldberg building. He was right. They turned into Victoria Street and then into the rear lane. Police were still in attendance.

"Good afternoon, Constable."

"Good afternoon, Sir. I must advise you that the area is still declared unsafe and, if you wish to go inside, you must wear one of those hard hats, over there."

He pointed to an array of red and yellow builders' hard hats, laid out on a charred desk near what used to be the rear entrance of the building.

"Thanks, Constable, but we won't be going inside."

He walked to the now empty container platform.

"What are we looking for, Sir?"

"I'm not sure, yet, Sergeant."

He walked slowly around the platform, eventually stopping at a padlocked wooden door at the end farthest from the lane.

"Constable, do you have anything we can use to jemmy open this door?"

"I'll see if I can find something, Sir."

The constable went to the charred desk, exchanged his helmet for a builder's hard hat and disappeared into the ruins.

Bill Buckle stood beside Harrigan.

"Ramachandran told me they stored cardboard boxes under this platform. I would like to see for myself."

Any further conversation was cut short by the ringing of the mobile telephone.

"Harrigan."

"Inspector, it's Colin McIver."

Harrigan looked at Bill Buckle and silently mouthed, *"McIver."*

"Yes, Colin, what have you got?"

"Well, Inspector, we've managed to contact two people in Scotland who can confirm that Singhabahu visited them."

"That didn't take you long."

"Easier than we expected, too, Sir. We simply rang the Office at Hawgate and the receptionist gave us the telephone numbers and contact names."

"The receptionist's name was Nora?"

"Er, yes. Nora."

"She only started there Monday. Tell me, did she take much time finding the information?"

"No, Sir, not really. Now that you mention it, she had the information at her fingertips. Why do you ask, Sir, is that important?"

"Ring her and ask if there was any particular reason why she had that information so readily available. There's probably a simple explanation, but I'd like to hear it."

"Yes, Sir."

"Good work. Let's hope finding the car will be that easy."

"We've found it, Sir." He was unable to contain the gloating tone in his voice.

"You've found it? Where?"

The constable arrived back at the scene triumphantly carrying a jemmy. Harrigan nodded his approval, as Bill Buckle took the jemmy and began working on the locked door.

"I'm sorry, Colin, I was interrupted, what was that you just said?"

"At Gatwick, Sir," he repeated. "Parked in the eastern end, adjacent to the security guard's box. The parking ticket is stamped 2030 Sunday, 15 April."

"He left the parking ticket in the car?"

"Yes, Sir. On the dash."

"Well done." Harrigan's tone was vague. Maybe cautious would better describe it.

"Thank you, Sir."

"Have the vehicle taken to Stonegate and get the lads from the lab to go over it."

"Already arranged, Sir."

"Well done again, Detective."

Harrigan absently took the instrument from his ear and pressed the button with the little red telephone motif. Buckle meanwhile had managed to remove the hasp and clasp from the door and stood beside the dark opening. He looked at Harrigan.

"Everything OK, Sir?"

"Yes Sergeant, very much so. McIver has confirmed Singhabahu's Scotland visit and his car is parked at Gatwick."

"Blimey, that was quick."

Harrigan nodded in silence and, placing the telephone into his pocket, he stooped and stared into the darkness. The constable tapped him on the shoulder.

"You may need this, Sir."

"Thanks."

Harrigan took the torch and shone it inside. The beam of light showed the space underneath the platform to be empty. The space ran the length and width of the platform, which made it somewhere around forty feet long and ten feet wide. It had a concrete floor and, apart from the height, it was an ideal storage area. Harrigan noticed an electric light half way down, and it took very little investigation to locate the light switch. He turned on the light and returned the torch to the constable.

"Thank you, Constable."

Harrigan studied the trapdoor in the ceiling of this unusual storage room, and reaching up, slid back the two large bolts, which locked it in place. The door swung down, away from Harrigan.

Harrigan looked up at the sky through the newly created opening, then back to the tunnel. Harrigan's eyes refocussed, as he sat thoughtfully, staring at the door now hanging from the far side of the opening and obscuring the view into the tunnel.

He backed out slowly and stood beside the sergeant.

"Everything to do with this case gets *curiouser* and *curiouser,* Sergeant." He indicated the vacated space. "Take a look."

Being of more advanced years than Harrigan and of fuller figure, Bill Buckle noisily moaned and groaned as he bent down and peered into the waiting space. Harrigan meanwhile inspected the top surface of the platform.

"I can't see much with that door hanging down, Inspector." The strained voice floated up through the open door hole. "It blocks everything off."

"Precisely, Sergeant. As I said, curiouser and curiouser."

"You want me to close it up, now that I'm down here?"

"You may as well, I've seen enough."

The moaning and groaning sounds were eventually followed by the sound of the bolts being slid back into the locked position. Bill Buckle closed the outside door as best as possible and, as the locking device was now lying pitifully twisted on the ground, he placed an empty five-gallon drum against it to hold it closed.

Harrigan sat in the Mazda, dialling a number on the mobile telephone. Bill Buckle brushed the dirt from the knees of his trousers and waved in a gesture of appreciation to the constable who was once more preparing himself for the boring task of the solitary guardsman.

"Good, I've got that. Thanks Patricia. See you tomorrow." Harrigan ended the call and turned to Bill Buckle now seated beside him.

"We've got the address of The Badgers; it's at Upper Binstead. Trish says the local police station knows all about the place.

Apparently, it's empty most of the time, so they look in every now and then, for security reasons."

Harrigan drove to the end of the lane and nosed into the peak-hour traffic.

"Let's head back to Stonegate."

Bill Buckle nodded.

"You'd think someone like Mahmood would have security people looking after the place when he was away."

"Apparently he has."

"Then why do our people have to waste their time?" Harrigan took that to be a rhetorical question and remained silent as he steered his way over the Thames, and on to Stonegate.

It was well after five when Harrigan nodded at the desk sergeant and walked into the main office. Having sent Malcolm Watts home, Colin McIver sat alone.

"Come in and have a drink, Colin," Harrigan invited as he, and Bill Buckle passed his desk.

Before Patricia had left for the day, she'd handwritten a note and put it on his desk. He picked it up and read it to himself. *The Super wants to see you.* In an almost unconscious attitude, he looked through the window and across to the superintendent's office. It was deserted.

"I'll worry about that tomorrow."

The screwed up Post-it Note barely made a sound as it bounced off the side of the dark green metal wastepaper bin.

Bill Buckle accepted Harrigan's offer of a Ballantines. McIver declined.

"You've had a successful day, Colin," he said, as he took the aluminium tray of ice from the executive bar fridge. In an attempt to loosen the ice cubes, he twisted the tray, first to the left, then the right.

"Yes, Sir, easier than I thought it would be. The people in Scotland were very obliging."

"Did you get back to Nora?"

Being unsuccessful with the twisting, he hit the tray on the edge of the cabinet. The ice cubes jumped. One landed on the floor. "Bugger it!" he muttered loudly to himself.

"I'll get it, Sir." Bill Buckle offered.

"It's okay, stay there, Bill."

Harrigan picked up the ice cube, rubbed it on his shirt and dropped it into the glass on his left. McIver continued as Harrigan completed the ice cube task and poured two liberal servings of his favourite whisky.

"She said that Mr Ramachandran had rung her Monday afternoon and told her it was very important she take note of Mr Singhabahu's itinerary."

"She was sure it was Ramachandran?" He carried the two glasses to where Bill Buckle now sat. The old sergeant reached out and carefully selected the right-side glass. Harrigan either didn't notice or didn't care he'd been left the drink with the ice cube that had fallen on the floor. He changed the glass to his right hand and took a more than ample sip.

"She said she was fairly sure, but she'd only been there one day. Is it important?"

"Who knows? Maybe, somewhere down the track." He shrugged.

"Singhabahu's car isn't here yet, Sir, but I have the lab boys ready to go to work on it first thing tomorrow."

"And the visa?"

"It's very difficult to get information about that sort of thing without going through all the proper channels—especially from the Americans. Privacy and all that."

Harrigan sensed he had more to say on the matter. He played the game.

"But?" he invited.

"Well, Sir." He glanced at the silent Bill Buckle, and with an over-elaborate gesture of his left hand, continued. "I have a very good friend at the Embassy, and he has promised to look into it for me. As a favour if you know what I mean."

Bill Buckle's clenched knuckles whitened on the glass as he took a long draft of the whisky. Harrigan was sure he noticed a small gleam in McIver's eye.

Harrigan made no comment as he picked up Malcolm Watt's report of the previous day. "You did say there was nothing learned from the local door knock?"

"Nothing much, Sir. As I told you, there are very few residents in the area. It's all in the report." McIver didn't like to be doubted or re-questioned, and a sense of annoyance crept across his reply.

The tone in his voice wasn't lost on Harrigan.

"Mmmm. It's a pity, though."

"Pity, Sir?"

"That we couldn't have found *something*," he needled.

Harrigan watched McIver's expression tighten. He knew what this young police sergeant was going through; he'd been through it himself. In today's police force, promotion is everything, and irrespective of ability, in the end, it is your political skills that will get results in the promotion stakes. The first and most important skill to learn is to keep your mouth shut when some politician, top bureaucrat, or high-ranking officer starts talking nonsense. Or even worse, repeatedly questions your methods or results. The trick is, of course, to listen intently, agree wisely, and then carry on the way you intended to in the first place. If you are right, they'll stand beside you and take the credit, if you are wrong, well that's another talent to be developed.

Harrigan had *all* the skills, and if he'd ever found the desire to apply them, he could have gone far. But he was rebellious by nature and had scant regard for rank and authority. He just wanted to get the job done. It was only because of his extreme natural police ability that he'd reached the rank of Inspector. This young DSC, however, had his future in front of him. Harrigan was keen to test his mettle.

He purposefully discarded the report. "Alright then," he sighed disappointedly, "let's think about that tomorrow."

As if on cue, the old black telephone on the desk rang sharply. The style of ring indicated it was an internal call, and at this time of the afternoon, it had to come from the front desk.

"Yes, Sergeant."

"Inspector, the Station Sergeant at Upper Binstead has just called."

"Go on."

"He asked me to pass a message on to you. He said, that as you were inquiring earlier today about The Badgers, you might be interested to know that Mr Mahmood arrived there this afternoon."

"Did he say if he knew how long Mahmood would be there?"

"No, he didn't say, Sir."

"Okay." He thought for a few moments. "Sergeant, ring him back and ask him to keep an eye on the place. I want to know who goes in and out, and if Mahmood leaves."

"Righto, Sir."

"And ask them to be discreet. I don't want Mahmood to know we're watching."

"Gotcha."

Harrigan sat thoughtfully before enlightening his two inquisitive but patient companions. "Mahmood's in the country, at The Badgers."

"You going visiting, Sir?" Bill Buckle asked.

He shook his head. "Not tonight, Bill. I think I'd better speak to the Super first."

"My, my, aren't we getting cautious in our old age?" The slightest hint of a smile crossed Bill Buckle's lips, as he innocently finished his drink.

"No, you old reprobate, I'm not getting cautious. I just don't want to fuck it up."

McIver warmed to his new inspector. There was no doubt that Harrigan was the senior officer and was firmly in charge, but somehow he was still one of the boys. He hadn't become aloof and separated from those of lesser rank.

"You want another drink?" Harrigan asked.

Bill Buckle shook his head. The time by the old clock was ten minutes to six.

"Well let's call it a day then. Colin, I want you and Constable Watts to carry on as you are going. You have plenty to keep you busy?"

It wasn't really a question but McIver answered it any way. "Yes, Sir. Manjit's car, the visa, make sure there is no insurance on the Goldberg building or its contents, and I thought we might start checking all airlines to see if we can find what flight Manjit took."

"Great. Bill, I'll see Wilkinson first thing in the morning and then you and I will take a drive to Upper Binstead."

"Do you think the superintendent will agree to a visit? Mahmood's a powerful man. What I mean, Sir, is that maybe he might think someone from the home office would be...more suitable?" Bill Buckle uttered the last two words with as much tact as he could muster.

"I think you might just be right there, Sergeant, but with a touch of poetic licence and the words of Clarke Gable, *frankly old mate, I don't give a toss*. But while we're on the subject, where exactly is Upper Binstead?"

"Near the Kent Flats, Sir. We can take the M20 to Ashford or go via the A20 and turn off near Green Valley Hills. It'll take a couple of hours."

"Can we go via West Heathwich?"

"Manjit Singhabahu's house?"

"Correct."

"We could. It's not too far out of the way."

"Good. The boss gets in about eight-thirty, so I guess we'll leave somewhere around nine-fifteen to nine-forty-five."

"I'll be ready." The old sergeant lifted his heavy frame and stretched his legs. "Want me to wash your glass, Sir?"

Harrigan looked at his empty glass. "No thanks, Bill. I think I'll have another one before I leave."

"Good night then, Sir."

"Good Night, Bill." Harrigan nodded to McIver who had taken the lead from Bill Buckle. "Good night, Colin."

"Good night, Sir."

McIver pulled the door closed and Harrigan lay back in his oversized leather chair and let the silence overtake him. In a strange and comforting way, the ticking of the old clock was part of that silence. A few moments passed. He absently drained the few melted drops of barely discernible whisky-flavoured iced water from the glass.

CHAPTER FIVE

As Bill Harrigan had left for work earlier that day, after telling his mother to call the doctor, Margaret Willis had begun to stir. She had woken late. The turmoil in her life over the last ten to twelve months had denied her any meaningful rest. Her life had reached its lowest ebb.

But last night? Last night was different. If only it could've lasted forever. As she slipped her favourite satin housecoat over her naked body, she thought of the gentle and loving way in which her police inspector had treated her. He made her feel young and alive again.

She sat at the kitchen table, idly fondling her housecoat. She remembered it was the same housecoat she'd been wearing the afternoon Bill Harrigan had come to tell her of her estranged husband's death.

With her memory now awakened, she distantly stirred her cup of English Breakfast tea as she thought of her marriage before the pregnancy. At the beginning, Roger had been a wonderful husband. They had tried for so many years to have a child. A child. That son or daughter they'd yearned for to make their life complete.

The spoon suddenly stopped turning as she pushed it hard onto the bottom of the cup. Her body tensed at the memory of the beatings that had begun soon after the news of her pregnancy. The beatings had grown in intensity with the swelling of her child-bearing womb. The horror of the final beating and kicking she suffered at the mercy of her once loving husband stabbed mercilessly within her.

The beating that killed their unborn child. Their unborn daughter.

Her beautiful facial features were pale and drawn as she sipped her tea. There were no more tears left; she had cried a lifetime of tears. There is a special sadness reserved for those who can no longer cry.

Thoughts of the separation that followed forced a short, derisive laugh from within her. "Some separation," she said aloud. The mansion in which they lived had been divided into two large semi-detached residences. Builders had erected a wall separating either side of the house. Each had its own entrance and driveway.

The estranged couple did not speak and rarely saw each other and, in accordance with the separation agreement, Robert Willis continued to pay all the bills.

In an involuntary motion, she wrapped her housecoat closer to her body, as the thoughts of her "on the rebound" affair with Brian Winslow-Cammeron flashed before her. *Whatever did I see in that man?* she wondered.

As she stood motionless, staring through the patio doors into the well-kept garden, the warmth of her freshly made, second cup of tea, flowed into her hands. The sun was trying to brighten the remaining few moments of this late Spring morning. She loved England in the Spring, the new flowers, the young birds, and the fresh green leaves all evidence that life goes on. Despite the darkness, there was always light. Her body softened against the now free-flowing housecoat as the mental picture of Bill Harrigan passed before her.

Her family would not have approved. He would have been described as being *below her station*. But he made her happy. When she was with him, she felt relaxed, cared for, and dare she imagine, almost loved? Could such a thing happen? Could this police inspector who told her of her husband's murder, who discovered the devastating motive and sordid details of that murder, be as attracted to her as she to him? Was he to be her future?

The china cup almost fell as she was startled by the shrill ring of the telephone.

She went to the telephone and placed the cup and saucer on a table, as she hurried past.

"Hello?" The hope it might be *her* police inspector filled her greeting.

"Mrs Willis. You are to listen very carefully." The cold accented voice sent a bolt of fear through her.

"Who is this?" she demanded.

"I have a message to give you. Just listen, don't ask questions."

"I demand to know who you are. I'll give you just three seconds to—"

"Shut up! I told you to just listen!" The threatening tone in his voice forced her into silence.

"You will forget everything your late husband said about Archibald Lapsley-Midwinter. You will forget everything about the entire matter. You will not say another word to anyone, especially to your newly found policeman friend, do you understand?"

"What?"

"Do you understand!"

"Y…yes, but—"

"There are no buts! It is up to you, Mrs Willis. If you value your life and the life of your friend, you will no longer have any memory of this matter!" A quiet yet sinister tone tinted the threatening voice. "Do I make myself clear?"

"Yes."

"And this telephone call, it didn't happen."

"I understand."

A click at the other end of the line ended the conversation.

Margaret replaced the handset and sank slowly into the large floral armchair. She shook her head in disbelief.

At first she shrugged it off as a crank call, someone with a warped sense of humour who had picked her number at random. *But no! He knew my name and knew about Bill. God, it's like something out of a cheap detective story,* she thought.

Questions raced through her brain. Who would issue such a threat? What was it she *knew* that is so important? How did they know that she knew? How did they know about Bill? And apart from *who the hell are they,* Margaret mouthed the hardest question of all. "What the *hell* am I going to do?"

Margaret's almost aristocratic upbringing had trained her to be a woman of strong personal resolve. Anyone who had any contact with her soon learned she was not a person to be faint of heart. She did not take kindly to being threatened, and she had already decided she was *not* going to do *nothing*.

If there was only her own safety to consider, she would have called the police immediately. But they had also threatened Bill.

She needed time to think this through and, if the caller was to be believed, as long as she did nothing, there was no danger.

If the caller was to be believed.

* * *

It was twenty minutes past seven when Bill Harrigan fitted the key into the front door lock of his home and turned it with more haste than usual.

He'd finished his second Ballantines in his office at around fifteen minutes past six. Before leaving the office, he'd rung his mother to let her know what time he'd be home. The telephone had rung longer than normal, and when his mother did eventually answer, her voice was chesty and difficult to understand.

"Mum, are you all right? You sound terrible."

"I'm fine son. Just a touch of the flu'. Where are you?"

"I'm at work. I was ringing to say I was just leaving." After a short pause, he added, "do you want me to pick up some fish and chips for tea?"

"Just get a portion for yourself, William, I'm not hungry."

He listened in silence as the sounds of coughing filled the earpiece.

"Did you call the doctor?"

"No. I'm all right, William. Please don't fuss! You sound just like your father when you fuss."

He'd left Stonegate and driven almost three blocks before dialling 192.

He waited only a few seconds before the speakers in his Mazda delivered the voice of a female tele-worker who had obviously topped the class in the *bored and uninterested tone* school.

"Directory enquires, what name?"

"Dr J R Mainsbridge." "

What town?"

"Wrenleigh."

"Postcode?"

"I'm not sure."

He felt the distain come through the telephone.

Harrigan took the next few silent moments to wonder how many people who don't know a telephone number, would know the postcode of the address of the telephone number.

"Caller, here is your number." The tele-worker said in an, *even though you didn't know the postcode I have still found the number,* tone.

He'd been grateful the computer had repeated the number. London traffic was difficult enough without trying to write a telephone number on the back of your hand. He narrowly missed an open-top, double-decker bus half filled with tourists as he dialled.

"Dr Mainsbridge's surgery."

"Eileen, it's Bill Harrigan."

"Mr Harrigan, how are you?"

"I'm fine, thanks. I'm calling about Mum. I think Dr Mainsbridge should come 'round and see her."

"What's the problem?"

"She has this awful chesty cough." It hadn't sounded so drastic when he'd said it out loud.

"Has she had it long?"

"A couple of days."

"Has it got worse?"

"Much."

"Are you ringing from home now?"

"No, I'm on the mobile; I'll be home in about three quarters of an hour."

"One moment, Mr Harrigan."

He'd listened as he heard the receptionist rustle through the appointment book.

"Dr Mainsbridge has two more patients to see, and then he'll come straight over. It will be about eight o'clock…ok?"

"Thanks, Eileen."

"Knowing your mother, I'm surprised she has agreed to see doctor."

"She hasn't."

"Oh."

The clock on the dash had said 6.35. Good, that gave him time to pick up some fish and chips and be home in plenty of time to tell his mother he had called the doctor and to subsequently calm her down.

He removed the key from the lock and pushed the door open. The contents of the plain paper-wrapped package under his arm filled the hallway with the smell of freshly cooked fish and chips.

"Mum? Are you in bed?" He called up the stairs.

A rasping, chesty cough came from the front room. He placed the fish and chips on the hallstand and moved towards the sound. He walked into the lounge room and looked at his mother's sagging figure, sitting in her favourite chair, wrapped in a large woollen blanket. He bent toward her and needlessly rearranged the edges of the blanket.

"Now I don't want you to get mad, but I've called Dr Mainsbridge…he'll be here around eight."

He immediately felt vindicated, as she slowly lifted her pale and tired face, and with an air of capitulated approval gave him a weary smile. She blinked two teary eyes. Her body shuddered with a racking chesty cough.

It was almost fifteen minutes past eight when a knocking at the door announced the arrival of the doctor.

The usual repartee took place as Harrigan opened the door.

"Thank you for coming Doctor."

"Where is she?"

"In the front room."

The Doctor hurried past him and entered the room. With the mechanical actions of repetition, accompanied by those familiar words, *"Not feeling too well today? Let's have a look at you,"* the doctor placed his small black bag near the patient, opened it, and began the examination. The stethoscope was moved to various positions as the doctor listened to the rasping and gurgling sounds of the fluid-filled lungs. The thermometer, placed under the tongue, slowly pushed the thin line of mercury farther up the narrow tube. Ignoring the involuntary bout of coughing, the examiner unhurriedly prepared the apparatus to take the old lady's blood pressure. Finally, after placing everything back into the little black bag, he carefully withdrew the thermometer and held it askew to the light.

He shook the thermometer about six to eight times, carefully inserted it into a protective tube and packed it alongside the other equipment. As the clasp of the bag clicked shut, he took the son's left arm at the elbow and ushered him into the hallway.

"I'm going to have to send your mother to the hospital. She has severe pneumonia and, without immediate hospitalisation, she may not even make it through the night."

"What?"

"Bill, your mother's not a young woman. This is not uncommon. Let me use your telephone. I'll get an ambulance on the way."

The powerfully-built, case-hardened police inspector leaned gently against the wall. In no way could he be described as a mother's boy, but they had shared a long and full life together.

They had shared much happiness and sadness, the good times and the bad. They shared the same house but lived their own lives. They were good mates and, as he had at the death of his father, he again had to accept that no one is immortal, and if not this time maybe the next, he could lose this lifelong friend. The thought hit him harder than any physical blow he had endured.

* * *

As Dr Mainsbridge telephoned for an ambulance, Margaret Willis sat in her favourite chair watching *the Bushtucker Man* on the BBC. Her association with Bill Harrigan had kindled an interest in Australia. She was somewhat surprised at her lack of knowledge of a nation that had such close ties with the United Kingdom. Whether her desire to increase her understanding of this far away land was driven by the self-satisfaction that can only be experienced with the gain of knowledge, or simply to impress Bill Harrigan when the topic came up, she wasn't sure. Maybe it was a little of each. But, through books she had purchased and by watching selected programmes on the television, she had definitely increased her knowledge. Not that she really had any real interest in the man in the strange hat eating some form of tree root right at this moment. She had other things on her mind.

The man at the other end of the telephone had made it quite clear what would happen if she didn't do exactly as he'd instructed. She had no idea how long it was, before she eventually made the decision that she would tell Bill about the telephone call. Despite the obvious danger, she refused to let anyone stan-dover her. She was not going to allow some anonymous coward, bully her into submission. She was tougher than that!

She had hoped he'd have rung her this evening so she could have arranged to meet him. It wasn't something she wanted to talk about over the telephone. She looked at the clock, twenty minutes past ten. The chances of him ringing tonight were now about as great as persuading her to eat whatever it was that the aboriginal man on the BBC was about to slide down his throat. She flicked off the TV.

For the second time today she was startled as the telephone rang.

"Margaret Willis," she answered tentatively.

"Margaret? It's Bill. Are you alright?"

"Oh, Bill." Not wanting to give anything away at this time, and although desperately trying to keep her voice steady, she was unable to keep a hinted air of relief from her voice. "All right? Yes I'm fine. Just surprised you rang so late. That's all."

"I'm sorry. I almost didn't call you because you're right, it's late."

"I'm glad you did," she answered hurriedly.

"I was going to call you earlier but Mum's been taken ill with pneumonia."

"Pneumonia? Is she all right? Well I know if she has pneumonia she's not all right but how is she?"

"She's in St Luke's hospital. I'm there now." He spoke uninterrupted for the next four and a half minutes. He recounted the events leading up to the doctor's visit, the arrival of the ambulance, the packing of his mother's bag, and the eventual settling in at the hospital. "God only knows if I've packed the right stuff. Still, that can be worked out tomorrow."

"Do you want me to come over?"

"No, I'm leaving now. I have a big day tomorrow, but thanks anyway."

"Will I see you tomorrow?" She felt a little forward asking such a direct question, but considering what she had to tell him, she really had no choice.

"I'd love to see you tomorrow, but it would have to be late. This Sidhu Trading case is beginning to take some shape. I'm off to visit our Muhammad Asif Mahmood first thing in the morning. He's in residence at his estate in Kent at the moment, and I want to talk to him before he takes off again. I must also call in to West Heathwich on the way and, before I leave, I'll have to report to the superintendent so, like I said, it will have to be late."

"You'll have to see your mother too." There was silence as she thought for a few moments. "Why don't you ring me from the hospital?"

"I was hoping you'd say that. Goodnight, Margaret, and thanks for understanding."

She obviously couldn't tell him about the telephone call, now; it would just have to wait. "Good night, Bill…and Bill?"

"Yes?"

"Please be careful."

* * *

It was a little after midnight before Bill Harrigan finally climbed into bed. Despite the long and tiresome day, he found difficulty in sleeping and, at twenty-four minutes past five, he abandoned his fitful night's sleep and began to prepare for the day ahead.

He showered and shaved and, as he stood in boxer underpants and singlet, he ironed his shirt, tie, and handkerchief.

In the kitchen, he brought the water to the boil, selected the biggest eggs in the carton, and carefully lowered them into the bubbling water. He checked his watch. Three minutes later, with the buttered bread for dipping into the soft yellow yolks and a cup of tea, he returned to the saucepan. One of the eggs had cracked and the egg white stringed from the shell. With the gourmet expertise possessed by most men, he allowed the eggs a few more seconds to make sure they would be just right and then relocated them into the two large eggcups.

Disappointment crossed his face as he knocked the top off the cracked egg and saw the hard-boiled yolk. Deciding the egg was overcooked because of the cracked shell he moved to the second egg. Expectantly, he repeated the action of decapitation. With a sigh of disappointment he shook his head.

"Why does this always bloody happen when I cook these damn things!"

Giving away all thoughts of dunking bread fingers, he set about the task of making warm boiled-egg sandwiches. He awkwardly raised the hard-to-hold sandwich to his mouth, taking extra care to avoid the melting butter, now escaping from all sides, from dripping onto his tie.

He telephoned the night sister at the hospital who told him his mother was resting comfortably and she would tell her he'd rung.

The last job to do before walking out the door was to pick up the plain-wrapped parcel of fish and chips he'd placed on the hall-stand last night and throw it in the bin in the kitchen.

Harrigan was of the opinion that Superintendent John Wilkinson was generally a good man. Considering the restraints of being a career policeman and having to play the political game, his efforts to still be a good policeman and administer equal justice were commendable. They were not always achievable of course, but still quite commendable. Harrigan of course, put equal justice first. But not in some altruistic way. He didn't see himself as a knight riding a white charger through the halls of Westminster, righting the wrongs of the system. There were plenty of people to do that, mostly from the left side of politics and often with one of the more modern academic qualifications. It did also appear to Harrigan that a Bachelor of Arts in Social Rights and Understanding was invariably accompanied by the desire to wear an unkempt beard, climb trees for the good of mankind and the manufacture of raffia hats. But that was ok too, if that was what they were good at.

He, on the other hand, had long realised and accepted that law and justice were two entirely different commodities. As demanded by his oath, he upheld the law as was his sworn duty, but he always tempered his actions with a sense of justice.

"I missed you yesterday, Inspector." The superintendent entered Harrigan's office and settled himself in the visitor's chair across the desk.

"I'm sorry, Sir. By the time I received the message, you had left for the evening."

"That's alright, nothing urgent. I was wondering how the Goldberg building fire case was progressing."

Harrigan outlined everything that had been discovered to date and the status of the investigation. What he did omit, however, were his own assumptions and suspicions.

"And do you think the dead man is Manjit Singhabahu?"

"All evidence points that way, Sir. I think it's a pretty safe assumption."

"Ramachandran murder him?"

"It looks that way. But we need more evidence before we can take any more action in that direction."

"Agreed. What about the other dead man?"

"I don't think he was murdered. I think his death was an accident. I'm more interested in who he was and why he was there in the first place."

"You have doubts as to his identity? Didn't you say he had a passport?"

"Yes, Sir. But personal papers are not always what they first seem to be. DSC McIver is checking on that."

"How's McIver fitting in?"

"No complaints. In fact, I think he is a good policeman. He could go a long way, if he's allowed."

"Allowed, Inspector?"

"Yes, allowed. You know, prejudices. No poofs in power, that sort of thing."

Wilkinson gave a slight cough and shuffled in his chair.

"What about Muhammad Mahmood, do you think he may be involved in any of this?"

Despite the casual manner of the question, Harrigan knew this was the main reason for Wilkinson's visit. A man as rich as Mahmood had influence in every corridor of power throughout the world. Wilkinson had been sent to find out what Harrigan had planned as far as Mahmood was concerned and to be steered away from any action that might affect the positions of those who enjoyed the privileges of high authority and influence.

"I have no idea, Sir. That's why I will be visiting Mr Mahmood this morning."

With his tongue firmly planted in his cheek, Harrigan added. "It's only a courtesy call, Sir. Tell everyone not to panic."

"That attitude is going to get you into trouble one day, Inspector." Despite his desperate efforts, the hint of a smile crept into the corners of Wilkinson's lips. "But I'm pleased to see you understand the sensitivities."

"Yes, Sir. And in all seriousness, there is no reason for concern. If I do uncover or suspect something, I won't want Mahmood hiding behind his position. Everything will be done according to the book."

"Thanks, Bill. You know it was suggested that the matter may better be handled by the Home Office."

"I didn't know, but we had suspected something like that might happen."

"We?"

"Sergeant Buckle."

Wilkinson gave a knowing nod, and placing his left hand on the desktop, stood slowly. "I'll support you as far as I can, Bill, but you must keep me informed."

"I will, Sir."

Harrigan lay back in his chair. He looked through the glass partition and watched Bill Buckle and the superintendent exchange greetings as they passed in the aisle.

"Come in, Bill," Harrigan called before the old sergeant had time to knock.

"Good morning, Sir. How'd you go with the super?"

Harrigan gave a non-committal shrug. "All the usual stuff. Mahmood is a powerful man, be careful, don't rock the boat." He finished the last of his morning mug of tea. "Ready?"

"As I'll ever be, Sir. I assume we're taking your car?"

Harrigan's reply was to simply jangle his keys in front of him. He checked he had his notebook, pen and wallet. "Let's go."

It was nine-thirty when the Mazda stopped in the driveway, adjacent to the front door of number one, South Heath Lane in West Heathwich.

"The place looks deserted. I can't see her car anywhere."

"Let's hope the car's in the garage and the lady of the house is still in bed." Harrigan crunched around the car as he walked on the gravel driveway to the front door. He pushed the doorbell. He heard the chimes resound throughout the house. Bill Buckle walked to his side.

"Any luck?"

"Not yet. Take a look around the back."

Harrigan rang the bell again and looked as best as he could through one of the panes of the patterned glass that surrounded the entrance. He could see no movement. He hammered his fist on the door, as Bill Buckle returned.

"I can't get around the back, Sir, the side gate's locked. But what I could see didn't show any sign of life. I don't think she's here, Sir."

"I think I am going to have to agree with you, Bill." Harrigan was annoyed. He had particularly wanted to speak to Aysha Singhabahu face to face. He could have asked her if she'd heard from her husband over the telephone, but he wanted to watch her reaction as she answered. He could gather much more from watching a person's bodily actions and facial expressions than he could from listening to the words over a telephone.

"We may as well head for The Badgers." He could not resist the urge to look back twice as he returned to the car.

As there was no suitable motorway, the journey from West Heathwich to Upper Binstead took longer than Harrigan had imagined. Not that Harrigan minded all that much. A drive through the English countryside was a very pleasant and relaxing experience. It gave him time to gather his thoughts before he met with Mahmood.

The south-eastern region of England was a welcome change from the streets of Stonegate. Fast trains to London had seen an upsurge of London workers settling in these areas, and he wondered how long it would be before these newcomers eventually destroyed that small village atmosphere, the very atmosphere that had attracted them in the first place.

Harrigan allowed his mind to wander into the future of one of these little villages. He saw how the new settlers eventually realized what they had done to their little area and someone would form a *Save the Small Village Atmosphere* committee. The committee would organise fundraisers and invite hundreds of friends from outside the area to come and experience the small village atmosphere they were trying to save and to purchase their unique arts and crafts.

In their frantic pursuit to purchase wonky pottery mugs and poorly-welded candlestick holders, these supporters of nature and Ye Olde England would come in their Range Rovers, ploughing up lush fields and knocking down hedgerows. Badgers and finches would flee in terror before the committee raised enough money to build a *Save the Small Village Atmosphere* meeting hall, which two years later would become the *Small Village Memorial Museum*. Unfortunately, the committee would never understand that it was the museum, complete with its sprawling car and coach parking area, increased traffic access, and three extra sets of traffic lights that sounded the final death knell of what they were trying to preserve.

They drove through Royal Tunbridge Wells, turned onto the Hastings Road, and then turned left onto the A262. Harrigan found it impossible to think of Hastings or read a sign or a mention of it in the paper without thinking of 1066, the year of the Battle of Hastings. He has no idea why that date stuck in his mind. It's the only date of the many dates learned at school that he remembered. Ask him when the Battle of Waterloo was or what year Australia changed to decimal currency and he hadn't a clue. Speaking of Australia, one date did come to mind, 1932. The year they opened the Sydney Harbour bridge, or was it 1933? He actually had to admit to not fully understanding what the battle in 1066 was all about, but 1066 it was.

Having stopped at Ashford for tea and scones at a small café called *The Teapot and Cosy*, Bill Buckle directed Harrigan through the back lanes of the Kent Downs and into the main street of Upper Binstead.

Well that was not strictly correct. The Main Street of Upper Binstead, as Harrigan was about to find out, was now closed to traffic.

They parked the Mazda in the car park on the outskirts of the village and walked towards the huge stone archway which heralded the village entrance. Beside the archway were several orderly piles of stones that indicated the remains of the early village wall. Harrigan stood and read the hand-painted history of the village.

The original village of *Binstead in the Valley* was built sometime during early 600 A.D. It was the site where James Binstead, mead maker to Aethelberht, the King of Kent, first plied his trade. It is said that it was at the request of Justus, the then Archbishop of Canterbury, the land was granted to James Binstead. The village of Binstead thrived until 1011, *fifty-five years before the Battle of Hastings*, thought Harrigan, when the village, being in a valley and unaware of the danger, was razed to the ground by marauding Danes whose prime target was actually Canterbury. The mead factory was destroyed and the Binstead family, with the exception of the village gravedigger John Binstead who, having overindulged at the mead factory the previous night and was asleep in the graveyard, were all killed.

Not wishing to be put in the same position again, the surviving villagers rebuilt Binstead, but this time they moved to higher ground.

Upper Binstead was not a village to be described; it was a village to be experienced. Harrigan walked alongside his companion, the cobblestones difficult to negotiate without twisting an ankle. Neither man spoke as they meandered toward the blue police sign at the bottom of the old street. Many of the buildings had come long after the relocation. The latest building Harrigan saw was a book shoppe dated 1537. The Men of Mead hotel boasted 1013 across the door, and like many thousands before him, Harrigan stopped and touched the stones marked with small plaques announcing that these stones were from the original village of Binstead.

The doorbell at the whitewashed Police Station jingled as they opened the door. It was not quite three paces to the front counter; yet, before they had reached the counter, the local police sergeant had come from another room and was waiting for them behind the wooden barrier.

"Good morning, Gentlemen." The local bobby was something straight out of an Agatha Christie novel. His manner was friendly but official. His uniform, complete with starched collar, was immaculate. Harrigan subconsciously straightened his tie and checked to make sure the bottom of his coat was hanging correctly. He produced his ID.

"Bill Harrigan, Stonegate Police."

The sergeant stood smartly to attention.

"Good morning, Inspector. Sergeant Alan Mudford at your service."

"Good morning, Sergeant and this is Sergeant Buckle." Formal introductions seemed in order.

"Sergeant."

"Sergeant."

"You're here about the Badgers I presume, Sir?"

"That's right, Sergeant. Anything happen overnight?"

"Not that we know of, Sir. Of course, as there are only three of us here. We don't have the manpower to keep a twenty-four-hour observance of the Badgers, but as far as we know——"

"Thank you, Sergeant, I'm sure you are doing your best."

"Thank you, Sir."

"I suppose we'd better make a move. Can you direct us to South Heath Lane?"

The Sergeant lifted the trap door in the counter and came into the front reception area. He opened the front door. The bell rang. Harrigan knew it wouldn't take long before that bloody bell got on his nerves.

"When you leave the car park, I presume you're in the car park at the other end of town?"

Harrigan nodded.

"Well," the Sergeant pointed to a small hill in the distance some two miles from the village, "when you drive out, you will be on the road that leads you up to there."

The road itself wasn't visible, but the two hedgerows, which presumably lined the road, were quite distinct.

"When you reach the top, you will see a road signposted to Acacia Downs. Turn right and," he moved farther into the street, "if you come out here…" he beckoned.

Harrigan and Buckle followed.

"You can see a large Oak tree up the top there. Not the smaller one directly above the bakery, farther around, over there."

"Yes, I see the one."

He lowered his arm. "Well, when you get to that Oak tree, Hedgerow Lane is straight opposite. You can't miss it. The Badgers is a couple of miles down, on the right-hand side."

"Thank you, Sergeant."

"My pleasure, Sir, and if you need any further assistance, just call."

"Very kind, see you later."

Fifteen minutes later, Harrigan stopped at the two enormous iron gates that barred the entrance. A small section of the guard-house was visible through the pedestrian entry, also barred by an iron gate. He watched through the side window of the small stone building as the security guard stood slowly, presumably from behind a desk, and walked toward the door. The guard disappeared from view and thirty seconds later re-appeared at the smaller gate. He wore the typical uniform of most private security firms, sported the almost obligatory short-cropped hair-cut, and walked with the unmistakable gait of the well-rehearsed security guard.

The clipboard carried in his right hand negated the entire effect. Storemen carry clipboards; a guard carries a thick leather strap to which is attached a foaming-mouthed Alsatian with a studded collar.

He leaned towards the open car window. "May I help you, Sir?"

Harrigan showed his ID. "I'm here to see Mr Mahmood."

"Do you have an appointment, Sir?"

"It's an official visit."

He made some notes on his clipboard and handed back the ID. He walked to the front of the car and recorded the registration number.

"One moment please, Sir!"

Harrigan glanced at Bill Buckle, and then they watched as the guard retreated through the small gate, disappeared, and then reappeared in the guardhouse. He lifted the receiver of the telephone and, glancing at the Mazda a few times, spoke into the mouthpiece. The conversation was taking longer than Harrigan appreciated and, just as Harrigan was about to leave the vehicle, the guard replaced the telephone handpiece and disappeared from view. Ten seconds later, the gates began their slow pivotal journey.

The security man stood at the open gate directing Harrigan to drive to him. *If he says 'have a nice day,' I'll run the bastard over,* Harrigan thought.

As directed, Harrigan stopped the Mazda in the gateway.

"Please proceed to the main home, Inspector, and please watch out for the deer."

"Thank you." A relieved Harrigan engaged first gear.

"Have a nice day."

The Mazda lurched forward.

* * *

"There's a police Inspector coming up to see me. I want you two to take your cars down to the stable buildings, and stay out of sight until I call for you."

"Is his name Harrigan?"

"I believe so."

"He's the one investigating the fire, and the death of Manjit."

"I know! Now get out both of you."

Mahmood looked at the Grandfather clock in the corner. Ten minutes past midday. He wasn't surprised at Harrigan's visit. It had been obvious since he'd been at the Badgers that the local constabulary had been involved in more than a simple cursory watching brief. And the death of Manjit Singhabahu at the Goldberg building was always going to lead some kind of trail to him. He did admit, however, to being impressed at the speed in which this Harrigan fellow had caught up with him.

Mahmood poured a glass of iced water, sat in the soft leather chair near the unlit fire, and carefully went over everything Ramachandran had told him a few moments previous.

To anyone other than Mahmood, Ramachandran's story would have sounded a trifle pathetic.

"Once I had come to terms with the fact that Singhabahu had to be eliminated," he'd said, "I had no compunction in carrying out the duty. After all, it would not have been the first time I had to—"

"Those were different times," Mahmood had felt compelled to interrupt.

"Maybe they were, Mr Mahmood, but killing is killing, no matter what the circumstances."

Mahmood recalled looking toward his second guest. "Aysha, maybe you would prefer to walk in the grounds?"

"I'm fine, thank you, Muhammad."

Muhammad!? Ramachandran felt the anger rise inside him. She'd called him Muhammad! Was there something between these two he'd wondered? Jealousy consumed his thoughts.

"Please carry on, Ram." Mahmood had invited.

Ramachandran related everything that had happened. From the time Mahmood had said that Manjit must die until his and Aysha's arrival at The Badgers that morning. Once the narration had begun and the jealousy had been pushed aside, Ramachandran spoke with the eagerness of a man relieving his conscience.

* * *

Bill Buckle let out a soft whistle as the Mazda followed the smooth asphalt road that led a winding path to the top of the hill. "How'd you like to mow that lawn every Saturday morning?"

The two policemen cast their eyes around the carefully tendered grounds. Harrigan could see no deer and began to wonder if that security bloke was having a lend of him. But the grounds themselves, now they were something else. The stone wall surrounding the property was still visible in the distance. Pruned and well-shaped trees and shrubs clustered in strategic areas. As they approached the crest, the main building of the estate slowly, and almost majestically, rose into view.

Once in full view, the aptness of the term, *majestically*, took an air of absolute authenticity. The turreted roofline almost promoted the building to castle status. Almost, but not quite. The large main building and east and west wings gave it somewhat of a palace look. The mind's eye could picture the queen of a time long past, walking the pristine rose garden, handmaidens tendering her every whim. Water glistened in what looked to be a Romulus and Remus fountain.

The indistinct line between the mythical and the real, blurred between the iron railings firmly fixed in a stone wall that surrounded the ten-acre area and the aura of fantasy that hovered eerily over the magnificent building.

"Don't forget to wipe your feet," Harrigan said, as they drove toward the slowly opening iron gates.

The security camera on the stone pillar told them that someone was watching.

Despite the ever-watchful eye of the security camera, it still took three minutes and two operations of the enormous bell button before the solid wooden door began the seemingly laborious task of creating an opening in this fort-like structure.

"May I help you, Sir?"

"Detective Inspector Harrigan and Sergeant Buckle of the Stonegate Police to see Mr Mahmood."

The faithful Fadhel closely inspected Harrigan's credentials.

"Please, come in." The East Asian man stood aside and motioned for the two men to enter. "Please wait in the main vestibule," he said from behind them, as he refastened the wooden door. It was not until he had passed the two stationary visitors that he continued.

"Mr Mahmood will not be a moment."

Although exquisite and definitely grande in design, the vestibule was fairly typical of this style of building. A massive stone staircase in the centre of the room, reached from the marble floor, to the heavens. Huge pillars bore the weight of the floors above. Ceilings were almost too distant to see, and the numerous doorways leading to rooms off the vestibule all looked to be at least ten feet high. Why anyone would want a ten-foot-high doorway, Harrigan could not imagine. Maybe it was a ploy to trick intruders into believing that the inhabitants were giants.

Mahmood was certainly no giant. Harrigan guessed him to be around five feet nine inches tall and weigh ten stone.

The man of wealth chose not to approach his visitors, but instead walked briskly across the vestibule to an open door on the right.

"This way, Gentlemen," he called in an almost offhand manner.

Once again, with the obligatory antique furniture, red velvet drapes, and heavily framed pictures, this room also lacked imagination.

"Make yourselves comfortable," he offered, as he walked directly to the unlit fireplace. With an obviously rehearsed move, he half turned, placed his right elbow on the mantelpiece and, with his right arm across his body, placed his left hand over his right. He clasped the right hand, raised his right foot, and placed it on the brass fire rail.

"I assume your visit is connected to the Goldberg building fire, Inspector?"

"And the two dead bodies."

"Of course. The two dead bodies."

In a deliberate attempt to minimise any advantage ownership of this mansion offered, Harrigan chose not to sit. He selected a space in the centre of the room and adopted the typical police-man's stance and, holding his "Official" notebook with pencil poised, he stared down towards the shorter man. Bill Buckle walked the walls of the room admiring the paintings, seemingly oblivious to the conversation.

"And how is your investigation coming along, Inspector?" Mahmood asked.

"We know the fire was deliberately lit."

Mahmood was singularly unimpressed and allowed boredom to fill his countenance.

"We have no positive motive for the fire, as yet. The contents were not of great value, but we are checking with the insurance companies, there may be something there, you never know."

Mahmood gave a dismissive shrug. "The bodies. Do have you any idea who they might be?"

"The man under the bath carried identity papers of one Wei Yu Lee, a Chinese National with USA resident status." Harrigan's tone was very matter of fact.

"You say he carried the papers. Does that mean you don't believe the dead man to be this Wei Yu Lee person?"

"Not at all. What it means is that we have not checked the authenticity of his papers, and until such time as we are able to do so, his identity cannot be officially confirmed or denied."

"I see. Very proper indeed."

"Indeed. He also had significant amounts of gold and cash with him."

"He sounds like a well-prepared fellow, Inspector."

"Maybe, but I must admit to doubting the preparedness of someone who dies in the manner this person did. Would you have any idea why he would be at the Goldberg building, at three in the morning?"

"While I am never too far removed from the day-to-day operation of my businesses, Inspector, please do not expect me to know every minute detail." He stood thoughtfully. "However," he continued, "if I had to guess, I would suggest that maybe he was hiding from someone?"

"Hiding from someone in a warehouse full of second-hand goods? Who would he be hiding from?" Harrigan could not keep the tone of disbelief from his question.

Mahmood shook his head and moved toward the French doors, overlooking the gardens. "And what of the other man?"

Harrigan was annoyed that he could not see the man's face as he spoke. "We have evidence that it was one of your employees. A Mr Singhabahu"

"Manjit?" He spun around and looked directly into Harrigan's steel cold eyes "Are you telling me that Manjit Singhabahu is dead?"

"Yes."

"Good heavens above." Mahmood moved a few paces towards the main table beside the red velvet drapes. With one hand on the table top, he slowly lowered himself into the chair at the head of the table.

"Goodness gracious. Dear, oh dear, oh dear, oh dear."

"I had no idea that a person in your position would have such, shall we say, affinity with his employees, Mr Mahmood."

"Oh yes, Inspector. I owe much of my success to my closeness with the senior managers of my operations." He paused and then spoke quietly. "Manjit dead, I find it difficult to comprehend." He waited a few more moments before regaining his composure. "Are you sure it is Manjit. I mean, could you be mistaken?"

"We can always be mistaken, Mr Mahmood, but I doubt it this time. There's just too much evidence."

"Does his wife know?"

"Not yet, she still believes he is in Africa, or maybe even in the Middle East somewhere."

"Then who identified the body. Ramachandran?"

"The body was burned beyond standard identification procedure."

"Then how, fingerprints?" Harrigan had difficulty believing that Mahmood didn't already know the answers to these questions.

"No, not fingerprints either." Harrigan replied patiently.

Mahmood stood defiantly and returned to his position near the French windows.

"Well, I am damned if I can believe you have a positive identification."

"There are several factors that support our theory. Manjit's UCFAC belt buckle for instance, we found that with the body."

Mahmood's shoulders jumped slightly as he issued a short grunting laugh and waved his right hand in dismissive derision.

"That trinket?"

"It may be a trinket to you, but trinkets like the UCFAC awards are very rare and all carry a serial number. The one found on the body is the one awarded to Manjit and, if you are as close to your senior managers as you would have me believe, you would know that Manjit would not lend that buckle to anyone. He was the only person who wore it."

"Of course, I apologise; one should not trivialise such things." Then as another thought came to him, he said, "Maybe someone put it there?"

"Who? Manjit was murdered by someone who did all he could to hide Manjit's identity. Even to the point of burning the building, so it's not likely the killer put it there. So who else could've put it there? The next person or persons to see Manjit, or what was left of him, were the Stonegate firefighters. Are you suggesting that one of them put it there?"

He shook his head resignedly. "No I suppose you are right."

Although Mahmood's attitude had been defensive and sometimes argumentative, Harrigan could not help notice how amenable he was, for a person of his influence, that is. Harrigan thought he would have been much harder to approach and even more difficult to converse with. He was almost a normal person.

"I'm sorry, Gentlemen, I have been very rude, may I offer you some refreshment? Tea, coffee, something stronger?"

"No thank you, Sir, we appreciate how busy you must be, so we won't take up much more of your time. Just a couple more questions and we'll be out of your hair."

"Very well."

"This always sounds like a stupid question, but it has to be asked. Do you know anyone who would want Manjit dead or who would benefit from his death?"

"No," he replied immediately. "Someone who wanted to take Manjit's life? That is almost unthinkable, Inspector. He got along with everyone."

"Well he didn't get along with *everyone*, Sir. Somebody killed him. What about his work? Is there anyone connected with his work?"

"No...no one." His reply was definite.

"What about his private life?"

"Manjit had very little private life, Inspector. His work was his life." He became thoughtful, giving the appearance of suddenly having thought of something. He continued hesitatingly. "Well, now that you mention it, there may be..." He answered his own query. "No! No it's nothing. Forget I said anything."

"If it could help our inquiries, Mr Mahmood, I do need to know."

"Well, his wife, Aysha."

"What about her?"

"She's, well, she's not as faithful as a wife should be."

"Are you referring to her affair with Ramachandran?"

Mahmood was genuinely taken aback. "You *know* about their affair?" Mahmood was unable to hide the element of anger that crept into his voice.

Harrigan deliberately ignored the question. "If I need to contact you again, Mr Mahmood, what is the best way to do that?"

"Just talk to Ramachandran. He knows how to contact me."

"Maybe I won't want Ramachandran to know I will be speaking to you."

A look of suspicion crossed Mahmood's face. "Ramachandran may have been having an affair with Manjit's wife, Inspector, but are you seriously implying that he may also be connected with his demise?"

"I'm not implying anything at this time, Mr Mahmood. I just want to know the simplest way to contact you should it become necessary."

"I will speak to the Home Secretary, talk to him if you need to contact me. Unless you have suspicions about him too?"

"No, Sir, I have no doubts about our Home Secretary, but he doesn't often answer the telephone when I ring, if you know what I mean."

"I'm sure you will find a way, Inspector."

Harrigan did not force the issue any further.

Mahmood called to Fadhel, who materialised immediately. "My guests are leaving, Fadhel, please show them to the door."

"One last thing, Sir."

"What is it Inspector?"

"We found Mr Singhabahu's car at Gatwick Airport…would you have any idea if Mr Singhabahu was planning a trip?"

"Gatwick?" Mahmood seized the opportunity. "Doesn't that suggest that Manjit has left the country? That the body in the warehouse *isn't* that of Manjit's?"

"Maybe. But on the other hand, maybe that is just what someone wants us to think. But examination of the vehicle will hopefully tell us more. The trip, Mr Mahmood, do you know if Manjit was preparing to take a trip?"

"My dear, Inspector, Manjit was always preparing to take a trip, as you so delightfully put it. That was Manjit's role in the organisation."

"Uh huh." Harrigan made a note and pocketed his pen and notebook.

Fadhel took this as a cue to silently lead the way toward the vestibule.

"Oh, Inspector!" Mahmood called, "the other chap...Wei Lee. I trust that matter will be cleared up quickly?"

Harrigan stopped by the door and half turned to his host "That depends where our investigation leads, Sir."

"I wouldn't like to think that any investigation would, how I can put it, lead to some false accusations toward my good reputation, considering my connection with the Goldberg building, if you understand me, Inspector. I would take a *very* dim view of that."

"The investigation will lead where it will lead, Mr Mahmood."

"Come now, Inspector, who is this Wei Lee anyway? Some illegal Chinaman?" His words were purposefully derisive. "Honestly, Inspector, how much attention should be paid to such a no account? How important could it be?"

Harrigan turned back into the room and withdrew his notebook from the inside pocket of his coat into which he had just replaced it.

"I get the distinct feeling you are advising me not to continue with the Wei Lee part of the investigation."

"I'm not suggesting Wei Lee's death not be investigated. But there are degrees of investigation, are there not?"

"Why is this so important to you, Mr Mahmood?"

"Oh really, Inspector, don't be so naïve. Try and see it from my perspective. A man in my position has many enemies. Any hint of scandal can have a disastrous affect on my businesses across the world. It could cost me millions of dollars and threaten the livelihoods of thousands of people, and for what? The life of some worthless Chinese illegal?" The venom in his words spat across the room.

"Your concern for the livelihoods of your workers is most admirable, Mr Mahmood, but let's get one thing very clear right now. The Wei Lee investigation will be treated like any other investigation. It will be followed through to the end, irrespective of where it may lead. And you need not worry, if Lee had no connection to any of your operations; you will not become involved and your reputation will be protected."

"I am already involved, Inspector! But you are right about one thing; my reputation will be protected."

Harrigan nodded to his host. "Good day, Sir." He turned purposefully to his companion. "Come along, Sergeant. Let's get out of this place. We have two deaths to investigate."

"Well, Inspector, don't say I didn't warn you."

Harrigan stiffened. "Warn me? What do you mean, *warn me?*"

Bill Buckle moved swiftly and stood closer to his superior officer.

"I don't bow to threats, Mahmood, so you can do your damnedest!!"

"Inspector..." Harrigan felt Bill Buckle's steadying hand resting on his arm. "Maybe it's better we continue this at a later time?"

"Yes, Inspector, your sergeant is right, and anyway, how could I *threaten* you? With the loss of your job? I think not! I know enough about you to know you would resign before bowing to a threat, and oh," he caught his breath, "please don't tell me your over-active imagination believes all that television rubbish about threatening the good guy's family!"

Mahmood turned his back and walked toward the French windows. He stood facing the garden, his hands clasped behind his back. "You are not married, you have no children, and your poor mother is in hospital, so really, Inspector, how could *I* threaten *you?*"

Harrigan didn't know what the threat was, but he knew the threat was there. His brain raced, as he tried to come up with the answer. Damn the man! Mahmood turned and held Harrigan's stare. It was as though he could read the angry thoughts running through Harrigan's brain.

Although Harrigan was furious that Mahmood knew so much about him, he was angrier with himself for underestimating this powerful man. *Of course,* Mahmood would have expected a visit from the Officer in Charge of an investigation to which he was inextricably linked. And, *of course,* he would have found out the identity of that officer, and all about him. You don't get to Mahmood's position by underestimating a potential adversary. You must always have the edge. Harrigan had to admit that Mahmood did have the edge, for now.

"I must confess to being disappointed in your overreaction, Inspector. I had a higher opinion of your capabilities."

Bill Buckle felt the hackles on the back of Harrigan's neck rise to the bait. With an old head and a firm hand grasping his Inspector's elbow, he gently guided Harrigan towards the door. The two policemen silently left the room.

Their silence continued as Harrigan sped down the smooth asphalt toward the front gates. Bill Buckle kept a sharp watch for any deer that might suddenly block their path, but even he was beginning to doubt the validity of the security man's earlier warning.

Harrigan seethed with the frustration of his first meeting with Mahmood. It had not turned out the way he'd planned. He'd hoped to unsettle Mahmood, to somehow get an angle on the current investigation. He was becoming more frustrated with this case by the moment. Nothing about the Goldberg building fire seemed to fit together. He had a whole bunch of ends, but no rope in the middle. He had hoped today's meeting was going to lead to some clue to finding the missing rope, but the exact opposite had happened. Mahmood had the upper hand and had won the first round by a TKO, and now he had to face that damn security drongo again. It was just all too much.

The big iron security gates were open when Harrigan arrived at the front entrance. The Security man, with the clipboard firmly secured under one arm waved the Mazda through with the other. Harrigan clenched his teeth, gave a nod of appreciation, and drove through the gateway with his eyes fixed firmly ahead. He brought the vehicle to a halt at the intersection of Hedgerow Lane. He fixed his seatbelt and slowly entered the road to Upper Binstead.

Harrigan plugged in the mobile phone. A loud beep announced he had a message on the message bank. He dialled the number and listened as the voice told him he had one new message. He pressed the replay button.

He recognised the voice straight away.

"Bill, this is Margaret. I must speak to you right away. There is something I think you should know before you see Mahmood. I'll wait by the telephone."

Harrigan looked at his companion.

"I wonder what that's all about." He said, as he dialled Margaret's number.

* * *

Ramachandran and Aysha drove their vehicles into the stable's garage. The garage doors closed behind them automatically, denying any view from the outside. With Ramachandran leading the way, they made their way silently up the stairway to the living quarters.

This was no ordinary stable building. These stables were built at a time when horses were treated vastly more superior than the servants. The horses were watered and fed and bedded like royalty. Of course, with Mahmood so rarely in attendance at the Badgers, there were no horses, but the stables and living quarters were maintained.

"Close those curtains like Mahmood asked," Ramachandran ordered, pointing to the windows facing the main building. Aysha, like the obedient servant, obeyed the command.

"Can I get you a drink, Ram?" She asked.

Ramachandran ignored her question. "What in the hell is going on between you and Mahmood?" Anger and menace filled his voice, his face contorted in jealous rage.

"What? What do you mean?" Aysha's tone was quiet, innocent.

"You called him Muhammad! You called the richest and most powerful man by his given name!! As casually as you would talk to a pet pussycat! Nobody does that. Nobody is allowed to be that close to Mr Mahmood, unless..." He left the sentence unfinished.

"Unless what? What *are* you talking about?" The line of innocence continued.

"Unless that person was *more* than an acquaintance or a friend!"

Aysha was frightened of the man now inches away from her. His chest was pounding, his eyes, fiery red. This man was almost beyond self-control.

"Oh, really, Ram, surely you're not suggesting that Mr Mahmood and I are lovers?"

Ramachandran held a clenched fist high above her side temple. "Yes, you bloody tramp," he raged, "that is exactly what I am saying!" The downward swing of the raised fist halted as a quiet voice sounded from the doorway.

"Are you alright, Miss Aysha?"

Like so many before him, Ramachandran had forgotten the hidden bodyguards of Mahmood. Mahmood demanded a feeling of solitude. Fadhel was the only manservant-cum-protector allowed to be seen. Fadhel was Mahmood's confidante. Fadhel spoke very few words. His was more of a watching and listening role. He displayed no emotion and was more than willing to sacrifice himself for his master if the need ever arose. Mahmood felt comfortable with Fadhel, and Fadhel worked tirelessly to maintain such comfortableness. Despite his loyalty and devotion, Fadhel knew and accepted without question that, should he fail his master's wishes, his life would be forfeited.

But a man of wealth and power makes many enemies, and one protector was unable to offer the levels of security required. It should really come as no surprise that a troop of twenty-seven highly trained and specialised bodyguards accompanied Mahmood's every move. They were paid well to be vigilant. They were paid better to be invisible. The quality of unobtrusiveness came as a natural ability to people of the East Asian regions. It was a talent peoples from other lands could well nurture.

"Yes, thank you. And I'm sure Mr Ramachandran feels as comforted by your presence as I."

Just as Ramachandran had not seen the man appear noiselessly at the entrance of the room, he did not see him leave. He did realise that for Mahmood to allow one of his protectors leave to follow Aysha, his suspicions of their affair were well founded.

As Aysha spoke, she left him in no doubt. Her voice was low. Spittle sprayed softly onto his face as she hissed. "Do you think you have the right to be the only one apart from Manjit with whom I can share some physical pleasure? Alright then, if you must know, yes! Muhammad and I *are* lovers. Not in any possessive way. We make pure basic animal-instinct love. Sex for the sake of sex. That *anything goes* kind of sex, experienced only by two people who are free of the shackles of jealous possession. You were always second, Ram. You were never the best, just convenient."

Aysha spun away from the man with whom she had spent many hours of love making in her marital bed. Her chest heaved violently. She turned and stared cruelly into his deep brown eyes, eyes that now breathed hatred. "And now, my dear Ram, with Manjit out of the way, convenience is no longer an issue!"

The shrill ringing of the telephone interrupted the surge of jealous rage, growing deep inside Ramachandran's body. He snatched at the handpiece and raised it to his ear. He wasn't given a chance to speak.

"Both of you get back up here." The phone went dead.

"Mahmood wants to see us."

Aysha pushed passed Ramachandran as he replaced the hand-piece. She hurried down the stairway and her Jaguar was speeding down the long driveway before Ramachandran had even reversed the BMW out of the garage.

Ramachandran hurried into the room. Aysha was sitting in the large armchair nearest Mahmood. A look of superiority nestled smugly on her face. Ramachandran thought it made her look ugly. Mahmood stood stony faced, his back to the French doors. Ramachandran did not know what to expect. What had she told Mahmood? His knowledge of the full extent of Mahmood's viciousness sent a twinge of fear through him.

"The inspector tells me that they have identified the muti-lated body in the warehouse as that of Manjit's, so your precautions were a waste of time, and a good building. Not to mention bringing the police to my front door."

"That's all very well with hindsight, Mr Mahmood, but I did what I thought best at the time. I told you, I made arrangements for Manjit to meet me at the Warehouse at three a.m. I told him I had discovered something untoward happening with the business and I needed to see him urgently. I told him it had to be during the early hours of the morning because nobody must know what I had uncovered."

"Yes, yes, Ram, you told us before!" Mahmood impatiently repeated a brief summary of Ramachandran's explanation up to the point when Harrigan and Bill Buckle arrived.

"You planned to have him accompany you in your car, drive to the Black Friar Woods, where you intended to, to *shoot* him, I think you said?"

Ramachandran nodded his bowed head.

"You were then going to put the body in a plastic bag, take him to our depot at Queens Docks, where the bag would be placed in an ice-packed container and later dumped in the Atlantic Ocean. I am not interested in the finer details Ram, but I am sure it was all very possible, maybe a little elaborate, but at least you were trying to be thorough. So what went wrong?"

Earlier in the day, Ramachandran had been surprised at Aysha's lack of concern when she'd learned of the death of her husband. Both men had spoken freely of the death, and Aysha had remained calm and almost uninterested. Her attitude had confused Ramachandran at the time, but since the episode in the stables, the reason was now all too clear. Any feeling Aysha might have had for Manjit had long waned, and the marriage had become a simple a union of convenience. *Much like our affair,* he thought. It was now abundantly clear to Ramachandran that Aysha was after the big prize, Mahmood.

"Ram, I said, what happened!" Mahmood did not like having to repeat himself.

"Oh, I'm sorry. As I was saying before the police interrupted us, I arrived at the warehouse at two-thirty in the morning. Not wanting anyone to know I was at the building, I left my car a block away and walked down the back lane. I had told Manjit to do the same. I used the rear entrance, and once inside, I thought it wisest to leave the lights off. The windows in the warehouse were fairly small, but there were a lot of them, and the streetlights gave enough light to be able to move around. I stood quietly near the rear door to let my eyes get accustomed to the light. As I did so, I heard a noise from the front of the building. I thought Manjit was already there, so I called out softly, 'Manjit, is that you?' But there was no answer. I made my way slowly into the building, and that's when I almost tripped over the body. Manjit was there all right, but he was already dead.

"So why did you set fire to the building? Why didn't you just get your car, load him in it, and carry out the rest of your plan? It would have saved me, both of us, a lot of bother."

"As I said before, Mr Mahmood, hindsight is easy. I bent down to have a closer look at the body. When I saw the hands and feet had been cut off, and his face, smashed beyond recognition, I almost threw up. Ugh it was horrible."

He paused for a few seconds as he relived the horror.

"God only knows why, but I started to go through the pockets of Manjit's clothing. I guess I did this through the result of some subconscious plan that was already developing in my mind, I don't know, but as I was going through his pockets, I heard another sound, this time at the rear door. It sounded like someone had just left the warehouse. Probably the murderer, I thought. I, I didn't know what to do. I couldn't carry the body outside because someone might see. Obviously someone else knew Manjit was dead, and a photograph of me carrying my partner's body out of the building could quite easily finger me as the killer. I had to think quickly. I knew the workers would start arriving in a couple of hours, and although I couldn't see it, I knew there would have been blood all over the floor. I decided the only thing to do was to destroy the body beyond all recognition and also destroy all evidence of what actually happened. I figured that if I lit a big enough fire, the police would have little to go on and, after the initial investigation, the matter would be just be another case to gather dust in the files. Of course, I didn't count on Wei Lee being in the building or that damn Harrigan."

"It is indeed unfortunate that a policeman like Harrigan is the investigating officer, but Wei Lee? Surely you must have known he was around there somewhere?"

"Not in the warehouse. I thought he would be—" He stopped and looked at Aysha. "Let's just say I didn't expect him to be in the warehouse. The noises I heard must have been Wei Lee moving towards the back door."

Ramachandran walked thoughtfully around the room as he began to form a mental picture of Wei Lee's final movements.

"For some reason, he obviously wasn't able to get to the rear door, and decided to hide under the bathtub until I had gone." He suddenly had an idea. "I wonder if it was Wei Lee who killed Manjit."

"Where are the hands and feet?"

"The police may find them somewhere in the rubble."

"Maybe. So go on, finish your story."

"There's not much left. I knew we had ethanol in the building, so I doused the body, piled as much flammable material I could find over and around the body, and ran trails of ethanol to various points of the ground floor and, well you know the rest." Ramachandran relaxed. The story had been told and Mahmood seemed to take it better than expected. Mahmood's perceived benevolence was short lived.

"What about Manjit's car?" he asked accusingly.

"Wha...? Er, I don't know. I didn't see it." He thought for a moment. "Which is odd when you think about it, because we had agreed where we were going to park our vehicles." A frown creased his brow as he asked a barrage of short, stammering questions. "If he was there before me, where was his car? Why didn't I see it? Maybe he just simply decided to park it somewhere else? Maybe he was killed somewhere else and dumped in the building? I don't know." Ramachandran again felt unnerved. He had completely forgotten about Manjit's car.

"*I* know where it is," Mahmood announced calmly.

"You do? How? Where is it?"

"Yes I do, the *inspector* told me." Mahmood's emphasis on the word *inspector*, clearly demonstrated his displeasure. "The car has been found at Gatwick airport."

"Gatwick airport? How the hell did it get there?" Ramachandran sounded genuinely surprised.

"I don't know, Ram, but I have no doubt our astute inspector will find out soon enough."

"Did Harrigan say they had any suspects?" Ramachandran tried to get away from the subject of Manjit's car.

"No, he didn't say," he lied. "Harrigan is no fool, and if I am any judge of the man, my connections won't be of much help in keeping me up to date with the investigation, either. I'm sure they'll do what they can, but Harrigan isn't the type who confides in people, *especially* his superiors. He may appear a little rough around the edges, but don't underestimate him. The worst of it is he is an honest cop, the most dangerous of all." Mahmood crossed his arms and raised his right hand to his face. He very slowly rubbed the thin forefinger back and forth across his chin. "No, we will have to watch Inspector Harrigan very carefully." Despite the unmistakable chill that filled Mahmood's words about Harrigan, the tension between the room's three occupants appeared to relax.

Ramachandran's anxiety began to wane. Being now able to see the beautiful Aysha for what she really was, his growing jealousy had changed to quiet disgust. With Mahmood's calm and calculating venom now directed at the police inspector and away from himself, he began to feel confident he had weathered the storm.

Unfortunately, his regained confidence was soon shaken.

"Of course, the inspector did mention your affair with Aysha. That gives him at least one motive." Mahmood paused and looked, first at Ramachandran and then at Aysha. "And two suspects."

"That's nonsense!" Ramachandran almost shouted the words as he took two paces toward the tycoon. A rustle of hasty movement from the doorway caused Ramachandran's motion to cease. "Aysha and I were very careful not to——"

Mahmood's body tensed. Anger flooded into his voice. Despite his own earlier intention of leading Harrigan toward Aysha's infidelity, he was angered at Ramachandran's lack of security. "You damn fool! How could you be so careless as to allow the inspector in charge of a murder investigation to find out you were having an affair with the dead man's wife? And you, you damn whore, can't you at least keep your legs together until your husband is buried?"

"Muhammad, please——" She sat forward quickly, desperately trying to retain his favour.

"Get out of my sight…both of you!"

Aysha had no option but to rise as Fadhel took her arm. "Muhammad…" she pleaded.

"Get out! And Ram, you had better fix this mess. And fix it now! I don't want any more visits from the police!"

Muhammad turned his back. He heard snippets of vitriol being passed between Ramachandran and Aysha, as, assisted by Fadhel, they scurried through the outer vestibule and towards the front door.

A smile crossed his face.

* * *

The telephone barely had time to ring twice before Margaret Willis snatched the receiver. "Hello?"

"Margaret? I got your message. Whatever is the matter?"

"Bill. Oh Bill, I'm glad you rang. I just had to talk to you." A nervous relief sounded in her voice.

"What is it, Margaret, what's happened!"

"I had a, a peculiar telephone call yesterday morning. I wasn't going to say anything, but—"

"What do you mean…peculiar?"

"Well, I guess threatening would be more accurate. It only lasted a few moments. A man with a thick accent told me to forget anything I'd heard about Lapsley-Midwinter. He warned me not to say anything. Particularly to you."

"Or else?"

"'*If you value your life or the life of your friend,*' I think he said. Bill, he meant you when he spoke of my friend."

"Why didn't you ring me straight away?"

"I was going to. But then I wanted to think. It all sounded a little unreal if you know what I mean. Some kind of sick practical joke. And besides, your mother had been taken ill and I didn't want to give you something else to worry about."

"Margaret, listen to me very carefully. I'm in Kent at the moment, so it will take me a little time to get to your address.

I'm going to send a couple of police officers to your house. Until they arrive, don't answer the door and don't go outside."

"Is, is that really necessary, Bill? I am concerned, even a little frightened, but don't you think that all sounds just a little bit melodramatic."

"Just do it!" he shouted.

"You're serious, aren't you?" She was silent as she thought for a few moments. "Do you know who made the phone call?"

"I don't know who made the call, but I'm damn sure I know who was behind it! Now I want you to listen to me very carefully and don't argue. I want you to hang up, lock the doors, and don't go anywhere until I get there. Is that clear?"

"Yes, but —"

"There are no buts!" He pressed the *end call* button on the telephone, dropped the Mazda into second gear and spun the wheels as he accelerated toward London.

Bill Buckle sat silently as they sped through the narrow Hedgerow Lane. He rapidly gained meaningful understanding of the mental strength of that band of people who spend their waking moments as navigators in off-road Rally cars. He prayed some local farmer with a tweed cap and a tractor load of hay wasn't around the next bend.

Mercifully, the lane was deserted, and it wasn't long before they were on the M20. Harrigan dialled Stonegate police station.

As luck would have it, DSC McIver had just returned to the station. He gave McIver, Margaret Willis' address and told him to take Constable Watts and get out to the house and allow no one near the place until he arrived.

"And I mean *no one!*" he concluded.

"Yes, Sir!" McIver answered without question.

The telephone clicked dead.

"That Bastard!"

"McIver, Sir?" Bill Buckle asked.

"No, not bloody McIver Sergeant, Mahmood. Muhammad bloody Asif fucking Mahmood."

Harrigan took a blue police warning light from the floor behind Bill Buckle's seat and handed it to the old sergeant. "Here, make yourself useful."

Bill Buckle placed the light on a small patch of Velcro, glued to the dash, adjacent to the windscreen. He plugged the cord into the cigarette lighter and switched on the flashing light. Immediately, the light flashed through the glass, directing motorists in front to move aside. Most drivers obeyed such direction, but there were always the exceptions. The young, up-and-coming executive male on the mobile telephone or the Ms who believes she has a right to drive wherever she likes and no male is going to tell her what to do. The teenager with the radio so loud the mudguards of the car vibrate with every beat and the twelve-seater mini-bus taking the residents of the local nursing home, back home after midday Bingo.

Despite the odd difficulty, they made good time; even the traffic on the M25 wasn't as bad as it could have been. They turned off the M25 and onto Sprigham Wells Road.

During the Motorway journey, and seeing Bill Buckle's obvious thoughts that he was overreacting, he had decided to confide in his passenger.

He gave Bill Buckle a brief outline of his association with Margaret and concluded, "and so on Wednesday night, Margaret and I had a night out at Ali's." Harrigan felt the stare of the old policeman.

"It was all terribly innocent, Sergeant. The truth of it is that, the previous day, I had told Margaret the results of our investigation into her husband's murder —"

"The *official* findings, Sir?"

"Yes Bill, the *official* findings."

Bill Buckle had been with Harrigan during that investigation and knew the whole truth. In fact, it was during that investigation when he'd realised the stuff his inspector was really made of. That realisation had helped create a special bond between the two men, a type of bond that few people experienced.

"How'd she take it?"

"Pretty well, considering. That's why I took her out the following night. She needed to get out, and I, well I—"

"Needed some female company," Bill Buckle ended the sentence.

"Something like that."

"You could do a lot worse."

"Thank you. Anyway, at the end of the evening, we caught a taxi home from Ali's. On the way, we started to talk about the current case, nothing in particular, just talk for talk's sake really. That is, until Margaret picked up on something I'd said, something about Mahmood." Harrigan related the detail of what Margaret had said in the taxi regarding her husband's telephone conversation and their conversation that followed. About the paedophile case, the disappearance of Lapsley-Midwinter, and her husband's reference to Mahmood and Sidhu Trading.

Harrigan could tell by the look on Bill Buckle's face that he still hadn't grasped the significance of what he'd just been told.

"Bill, that was the *only* time we have spoken of it." Harrigan reinforced.

"So, considering the caller's reference to Lapsley-Midwinter, you're suggesting that whoever telephoned Mrs Willis must have been privy to that conversation, or at least had the conversation reported to them?"

"That's right. And who was the only other person in that taxi?"

"The taxi driver."

"Right again."

"Blimey."

Blimey was right. Nothing more needed to be said between these two experienced policemen. They each knew the full meaning of the recent events. Mahmood had people in all walks of life across the world, reporting to him. That's how he kept control. The taxi driver was Mahmood's man. The question now was, was it simply a coincidence that it was that driver who took Harrigan and Margaret Willis home from Ali's, or had it been orchestrated?

"Do you think Ali is involved, Sir?"

Given Harrigan's affection for Ali, that question was one many people would not dare ask. But these two men's almost telepathic thoughts were demonstrated by Harrigan's preparedness for the question.

"I don't know. I would like to think not, but it does prove one thing."

"If it was orchestrated, for Mahmood to place a tail on you, he must have something to hide about the Goldberg building fire and the two dead bodies?"

"Exactly, my dear Watson."

It was at this time of the conversation they'd turned off the Motorway.

It wasn't until they were four miles from Sprigham Wells that the traffic congestion made it impossible to take any further advantage of the blue warning signal. Bill Buckle turned off the light, unplugged the cord, and placed it behind his seat. They sat in traffic, staring at the back of a shipping container carried by the lorry directly in front. As there was little else to see, Harrigan read the markings on the container. Nyugen Shipping Company. Max Tare 112 tonne. 2682 Cu ft.

"Of course, Bill," Harrigan continued the conversation of fifteen minutes ago. "The other big question is what has Lapsley-Midwinter got to do with the Goldberg fire? If I was being tailed because of the Goldberg fire, why was Margaret warned not to speak of Lapsley-Midwinter? Are the two connected, or is Lapsley-Midwinter just a coincidence?"

"Maybe it wasn't *you* being watched, maybe it was Mrs Willis."

"And *I* was the coincidence?"

"It's possible, Inspector. If you consider Roger Willis was a senior civil servant with top-drawer connections, it should at least be a consideration."

Harrigan took a few moments to digest the feasibility of Bill Buckle's proposition. "Yes Sergeant, you're right, it is very possible."

It wasn't until they had reached the driveway at Sprigham Wells that Bill Buckle broke the silence. "Do you think you'll ever tell her the truth? Tell her what really happened to her husband?

"I don't know, Bill. I honestly don't know."

Harrigan could see McIver as they turned into the driveway. He assumed that Constable Watts was keeping watch around the back of the house.

"Everything quiet, Sergeant?" Harrigan asked, as he approached the front door.

"Yes, Sir. Constable Watts is watching the rear of the house."

"Good work." He rang the front door chimes.

There was no immediate response. Harrigan looked at Bill Buckle, now standing beside him.

"She's probably upstairs. Relax Sir, it could take a few moments."

Harrigan unconsciously took three paces backward and looked up at the second storey windows. He heard the door being opened.

"Looking for me?" Margaret asked, familiarity filling her voice.

Harrigan smiled. "You alright?"

"Fine, thanks." She stood to one side. "Come in. Come in."

"Do you remember Sergeant Buckle?"

"I, I think so, vaguely. I'm sorry, Sergeant, so much has happened in my life lately, I —"

"It's nice to see you, Mrs Willis." Bill Buckle nodded politely then turned to Harrigan. "I'll wait outside, Sir," he offered discretely.

"No need, Sergeant. This is police business and two heads are better than one."

Margaret Willis gestured to the older man. "Please, come in Sergeant."

"Thank you, Ma'am." Margaret Willis disliked being called Ma'am. She closed the door and walked ahead of them.

"I assume you would both like a cup of tea?"

"I wouldn't say no."

"Black with lemon?"

Harrigan was pleased she'd remembered. "Thanks."

"Sergeant?"

"White with two."

They followed her into the kitchen.

"Tell me about this damn telephone call...do you feel OK now?" Harrigan added, almost as an afterthought.

"How could I feel otherwise with all these policemen to protect me?" she said light heartedly as she filled the kettle. "At first I was angry," she said into the sink, "but the more I thought about it, the more uneasy I became. Let alone that I have no idea who they may be, they knew my unlisted telephone number!" She rattled the cups, saucers, and spoons, as she prepared the basic utensils, ready for the boiling water. "Earl Grey?"

Both men nodded approval.

"They knew I had been with you Bill, and they knew that I knew something, albeit a *little* something, about Lapsley-Midwinter. How would they know all that? Have they been following me? And if they have been, why and for how long?"

"I can answer some of your questions and have a guess at the rest. The sergeant and I——"

"Have you rung the hospital about your mother?" she interrupted.

"Not since this morning."

"Well, before we get onto this other business, first things first. You know where to find the telephone. Go and check how your mother is while I finish making the tea. There's plenty of time for the other."

Harrigan looked at his sergeant's smiling face. It was obvious that Bill Buckle approved of the lady's suggestion and thoughtfulness.

"Thanks, Margaret."

"The sergeant and I will bring in the tea."

Six minutes later, the trio sat in the front drawing room. The ward sister had described his mother's condition as *comfortable but still has a long way to go.* There was nothing he could do at the moment, and she promised to tell her he'd rung when she woke up. Harrigan sat in a soft leather armchair, legs crossed and holding his cup of tea in front of him. He took a long, comforting sip.

"As I was saying, the sergeant and I discussed the matter on the way up here, and we agree that the only person who knew of our conversation, other than us, of course, was the taxi driver."

"Surely you don't think tha—"

"Let me finish. I have a strong feeling that Mahmood is more than an innocent bystander in whatever this is all about. How deeply he is mixed up I don't know."

"Mixed up in what?"

"Well, let's start with the fire at the Goldberg building. I'm not suggesting for one minute that he set fire to his own building, but I am willing to bet that, either directly or indirectly, he had something to do with the *motive* behind the burning."

The spoon rattled as he returned his cup to its saucer.

"The telephone caller warned you not to say anything about Lapsley-Midwinter. He also made special reference to me. As the taxi driver was the only other person who could possibly have heard that conversation, the driver was either following me because of the investigation of the Goldberg fire, or you because—"

"Of what Roger knew and might have told me." Margaret was quick to grasp the situation.

"Correct."

"The driver may not have been actually following either you or I," she continued. "Maybe he is paid to simply keep his ears open and report anything he might overhear."

"Possible. But what are the odds that the one driver out of the thousands of London taxi drivers who is on the Mahmood payroll, would pick us up and overhear our conversation by sheer coincidence?"

"Maybe we shouldn't assume that Mahmood only has one taxi driver on the lookout. He may have hundreds," Bill Buckle suggested.

"That's a good point, Bill." Harrigan thought that was a very strong possibility.

"He may also have none," Margaret reminded the two naturally suspicious police minds.

"No. There I must disagree," Harrigan replied definitely.

"Why? With respect, Bill, your reasoning is all based on the assumption that Mahmood is involved. Nothing you have said so far connects him to the telephone call."

Harrigan placed the empty cup and saucer on the coffee table next to his chair. He unfolded his legs and leaned forward in the chair, placed his elbows on his knees, and clasped his hands together. He looked at the floor.

"I should probably tell you a little more of what took place this morning." He related the details of Mahmood's veiled threat at the Badgers earlier in the day and then continued. "So you see, Margaret, he purposely itemised each reason why he couldn't threaten me, leaving out one…you. And if he knew my mother was in hospital, he would know about our relationship."

She sat silently. Her face grim.

"I was angry when I left The Badgers. Angry that he knew so much about me. Angry I had underestimated him. But I also had a nagging frustration that there was something else. Something he hadn't told me or something I had missed. As soon as I listened to your message on my mobile telephone, I knew what it was. The one thing he hadn't mentioned was the one thing he could use."

"Are you telling me that Mahmood thinks he can use *me* to threaten *you*?"

"Yes. That is exactly what I'm telling you."

She gave an uncertain laugh. "That's preposterous! We are just two people thrown together through the circumstances of life." Her language was too melodramatic. She stood deliberately and walked toward the empty cup and saucer sitting next to Harrigan. "For Mahmood to believe you can be threatened through me means he thinks you have…we have…we are…" Her voice trailed into silence as she looked into Bill Harrigan's eyes.

There were no words to be spoken at such a time. As she reached slowly toward the coffee table, her face came closer to his. Their eyes locked. Bill Harrigan felt a pounding in his head, as the blood rushed through his body. A feeling of wanting flowed from his unblinking eyes. She understood. She felt it too. The excitement of realisation mixed with uncertainty and fear made coherence a difficult task.

"I must…I'll get another, er, I'll…I'll be back in a moment." Harrigan watched as she left the room. He sat staring at the empty doorway.

"She makes a grand cup of tea," the sergeant's voice sounded from across the room.

Harrigan turned his stare to the old sergeant, sitting comfortably in the oversize lounge chair.

"Well she does!" he reaffirmed.

Harrigan sat thoughtfully. He was fairly certain that as Margaret had disobeyed the telephone warning, and had told him of the threat, she was probably now in danger. For her to stay in the house alone until this matter was cleared up, was not an option. But he didn't have enough evidence to get approval for twenty-four hour surveillance. With his mother in hospital, there was no need for him to go home, so *he* could stay with her. But that only solved the night-time problem. What the hell was he going to do with her during the day? And, of course, no matter what ideas he came up with, Margaret had to approve, and that wasn't going to be easy, either.

He heard Margaret open the front door and call to McIver.

"Would you like a cup of tea or something, Officer?"

"No thank you Ma'am, I'm fine."

Harrigan jumped up from his chair and hurried to the front door and called over Margaret's shoulder.

"Would you come in here for a few moments, Colin? I'm sure there's enough of us here at present to keep an eye on the place."

McIver followed Harrigan into the front room.

"Are you sure you won't have a cup of something?" Margaret again questioned McIver.

"Well, now I'm inside, a cup of tea would be absolutely lovely." McIver's hand movements and general mannerisms made Margaret look questioningly at Bill Harrigan. Harrigan gave a knowing *well it is the eighties* nod. Margaret Willis was not amused.

"Margaret, please let me introduce the newest member of the team, Detective Senior Constable Colin McIver. Detective, Mrs Willis."

Colin McIver crossed the floor and outstretched his hand. "Very pleased to meet you, Mrs Willis."

Margaret Willis took his hand and shook it more firmly than was ladylike.

"How do you like your tea, Detective?"

"Milk, no sugar, thank you."

Margaret Willis turned sharply and left the room. Harrigan looked toward Bill Buckle and saw him shaking his head with an air of disbelief. Harrigan opened his hands and silently mouthed the word *"What?"*

Bill Buckle held his head still, and with movement in his eyes only, looked toward McIver and back to Harrigan. Harrigan frowned and then, as the penny dropped, lowered his head into his hands. He sat for five seconds, then slowly stood and walked toward the door. He patted the old sergeant's shoulder as he passed.

Unaware of the circumstances surrounding the death of Roger Willis, McIver had no idea what he had done to so obviously upset Margaret Willis. "What did I say?"

"Nothing, Colin." Considering Bill Buckle's personal opinion on such things, the old sergeant was surprisingly understanding and sympathetic toward McIver. "It's not you, personally, I'll explain one day."

Harrigan entered the kitchen and saw Margaret standing at the sink. She felt Harrigan's presence at the door and her body stiffened as she straightened suddenly, dabbing her eyes with her handkerchief. She pushed the small piece of lace into the pocket of her dress.

"I'm sorry Margaret. I didn't think." He spun away from her. "God! How could I be so stupid!"

"It's alright, Bill. It's not your fault. It's me. With the results of the investigation into Robert's death still fresh in my mind, Roger being with that Leach person before he was killed, what they might've been doing together, my husband and that…that homosexual, I, I just…" Her voice trailed into silence.

Harrigan held her to him. They stood silently for several minutes, as Margaret gathered her thoughts and personal strength. "I'm alright now," she murmured, as he held her tightly into his shoulder.

"Bill…? I'm OK now," she repeated.

He released her gently and looked into her eyes, a little red from crying. "You go into the front room. I'll freshen up my face and bring your teas in. Well, go on," she ordered her reluctant companion.

"I'll ask Sergeant McIver to wait outside."

"No Bill! You mustn't do that." She saw the doubts in his eyes. "Please, Bill, let me deal with this my way, please?"

He smiled and gave her a wink. "You're the boss."

Harrigan took a deep breath and marched back into the front room. "Alright, Colin, let's hear what happened today. I hope you have some results?"

"Everything alright, Sir?" He nodded toward the open door.

"Everything's alright. Now give me your report!"

"Well, first on the list is the insurance. There was definitely no insurance on the contents of the building. The Building itself has a little insurance, but well below market value."

"I thought Ramachandran said there was no insurance on the building," Bill Buckle commented.

"The policy was taken out by the overarching company in the conglomerate of which Sidhu Trading is a part. Maybe he didn't know about it."

"It's not important," Harrigan said impatiently. "What else?"

"Manjit was booked on Africa Air but didn't take the flight."

"Are you sure about that?"

"Positive, Inspector. His seat was given to a Mr Joost Van Graan on stand-by. I have a picture of Van Graan being sent to the office."

"Ok. What about the car, any 'prints?"

"Plenty, but all Manjit's."

"So if the last person to drive the car wasn't Manjit, why weren't those fingerprints in the car? Or at least why wasn't the car wiped clean?" Bill Buckle queried.

"Gloves?" Harrigan asked.

"There is some evidence of glove marks, Sir."

"There has been some forensic success analysing glove prints in recent times, do we know what kind of gloves Manjit wore?" Harrigan continued.

"We could find out Sir, but the forensic suggest the gloves prints they found were from surgical gloves, Sir, not driving gloves."

"Surgical gloves," Harrigan said, as he shook his head. "Nothing in this investigation comes easy!"

"If it *was* Manjit who drove to the airport, why did he leave his car there when, for whatever the reason, he didn't take the flight? Why didn't he drive it away?" It was again Bill Buckle's turn to ask the obvious.

"Maybe he was kidnapped at the airport," McIver felt a little stupid as he listened to the drama of his own question.

"I doubt it. Too much security there. You'd think a kidnapping would take place before he arrived at the airport," Bill Buckle said.

"Exactly, Bill, it wouldn't make sense to do it at the airport," Harrigan agreed. "And if someone wanted us to believe that Manjit flew to Africa as planned, surely they would have had someone take his place on the aircraft. It's too easy to check on something like that."

"And why leave the car in the *daily* car park?" McIver queried. "Wouldn't it make more sense to use the *long-term* car-park, where it might not be noticed for weeks?"

"Well, maybe not, Colin. If someone wanted to make it look like Manjit drove his car to the airport, because Manjit flew regularly, the people in the long-term car park would probably know him by sight. They'd know it wasn't him driving. And why use surgical gloves? Whoever drove the car to Gatwick would have known that, eventually, we would establish they were surgical gloves. They would know we would realise that no one drives to the airport wearing surgical gloves, so it must be a set up. It defeats the purpose of trying to make it look like Manjit drove to the airport himself. Why not use regular driving gloves?"

Harrigan fell silent. McIver opened his mouth to speak. For the second time since McIver had joined the team, Bill Buckle shook his head at McIver, warning him to say nothing. Bill Buckle knew Harrigan well enough to know that, when he placed his chin between his right thumb and forefinger, and while covering his mouth with his hand, absently stroking his left cheek with the right forefinger you didn't interrupt, you just sat quietly.

A few minutes passed. The silence pounded inside their heads. Bill Buckle found himself searching for the slightest noise. For the first time that he could remember, he missed the tick tock of the old clock in Harrigan's office.

Harrigan moved his hand away from his mouth and said with an air of almost distant revelation. "You know, Sergeant Buckle." He rarely used Bill Buckle's full official title. "It is as if someone has set up a false trail with the intention of it looking like a false trail."

"Say that again?"

"I said, it is as if someone has set up a false trail with the intention of it looking like a false trail."

"Why would someone do that?" McIver blurted out.

Harrigan continued in his vague way, ignoring McIver's comment completely. "I wonder why someone would do that?"

"Do what?" Margaret Willis broke the spell as she carried in a wooden tray, complete with four cups of tea and a plate of biscuits, all resting on a bleached white doily. She carefully placed the tray on the centre table.

"I'm sorry I took so long. I made a cup for the constable in the back garden."

The three men stood and took the cups as they were handed to them.

"Inspector, Sergeant Buckle." The two men offered a quiet thank you and each took two biscuits.

"Detective, I hope it's to your liking."

"I'm sure it will be Mrs Willis."

Margaret Willis took a seat beside the inspector.

"Do what?" she repeated.

"Oh, nothing. It's not important," Harrigan said as he looked at McIver. "What about Wei Lee's US visa?"

"It seems genuine enough. All records indicate that Mr Lee has been granted permanent resident status of the United States of America through the normal channels."

"Nothing suspicious?" Harrigan continued to push the point.

"No, Sir, not really. The visa was issued with more haste than is usual, which does raise some questions but, apart from that, everything appears perfectly normal."

"From what I hear, visas for the USA are hard to get," Margaret commented.

"That's very true, Mrs Willis, and security surrounding the issue of visas into the USA is one of the toughest in the world. But any system can be broken, no matter how sophisticated it might be. All you need are the right people in the right places and lots of spare cash.

"But, as far as you are aware, the visa is genuine?" Harrigan reaffirmed.

"As far as we can tell Sir, yes."

They sat in silence for more than a few minutes but could find no other avenue for further conversation. They had more questions than answers, and nothing seemed to fit. It was time to shut it all out for a while.

"It's a quarter to five, Colin, so you and Constable Watts should be heading back to the station. I'll stay with Mrs Willis for a while."

"It's no trouble, Sir, I don't mind staying," McIver offered.

"I know that, Colin, but you go. Thanks anyway." Harrigan turned to Bill Buckle. "Your car's at the station, Bill. You might as well go with Colin. I'll see you all bright and early on Monday."

"What are you going to do, Inspector?"

"I think I will pay a visit to Ali's."

"Is it wise to go alone, Sir? I think that maybe I should go with you, considering."

"Nothing will happen at Ali's, Bill, but I appreciate your concern. See you on Monday."

They bade their farewells, and Margaret closed the front door after them. She came back and sat next to Harrigan.

"I'd like to come to Ali's with you, Bill."

"I had a feeling you were going to say that." He turned and looked into her shining hazel-green eyes. "And I'd love you to come with me Margaret, but I think it'd be much safer if you didn't."

"Safer? Safer than what, staying here?"

Harrigan knew she had a point. At least he could watch out for her until he could figure out how she could best be protected.

"Ok. But you must promise to do exactly as you're told. I have no idea what we might be walking into, if anything. If we have to take some immediate action we might not have much time to debate the issue."

"I can't believe that Ali has anything to do with this trouble, Bill."

"Neither can I, Margaret, but I don't trust Mahmood. Ali himself might even be in danger. I just don't know. That's why you must be ready to do whatever I say."

"Don't worry, I promise I'll be a good girl and do exactly what I'm told," she said playfully. "Grab yourself another cuppa, and I'll run upstairs and get ready."

CHAPTER SIX

It was almost 7:30 p.m. when Bill Harrigan escorted Margaret into Ali's.

Margaret had taken just over thirty minutes to be ready. Having commented on her efficiency and remarking how beautiful she looked, Harrigan had then driven them to Finchenham, where he too took a little over thirty minutes. He rang the hospital and was told his mother was resting comfortably and they would tell her he'd called. He reaffirmed that the hospital had his mobile telephone number, and finally they were on their way.

"You want to drive or take a taxi?" He asked.

"If you are going to have a few drinks, a taxi would probably be a good idea."

"Well there is that, but given the events of the last couple of days, I'm a little reluctant to travel by taxi at the moment. He gave himself a few moments to think about it. "But you're right. We mustn't change our lives because of these bastards; I'll leave the car at home." He turned left at Raven Crescent and headed back home. He re-parked the Mazda and they hailed a Taxi in the High Street.

Despite Harrigan's newly found suspicion of all London taxi drivers, the drive was uneventful. Once outside the Abby Towers building, the taxi door swung open, and the white glove rose in salute.

"Good evening, Inspector." Samir's words lacked that certain warmth Harrigan had grown accustomed to. Samir also avoided direct eye contact. An uneasy, strained quality was plainly obvious in the greetings ritual performed by the doorman.

"Good evening, Samir." Harrigan replied carefully.

"Good evening, Mrs. Willis."

"Good evening, Samir, thank you."

"Something's not right," Harrigan whispered. He placed his arm around her waist. "Stay close."

That's the most unnecessary piece of advice I've had all day, Margaret thought, as they entered the foyer and walked towards the wrought-iron cage doors of the lift.

"Good evening, George," Harrigan called over his shoulder.

"Good evening, Sir," George replied. Harrigan had been alerted. George never called him *Sir*. He squeezed Margaret's hand. It was too late to go back.

As they reached the lift, two coloured men, probably from the West Indies, slipped from the shadows, barring their way. Margaret had never been as close to anyone as large and powerful.

"I am sorry, Sir, the restaurant is closed for a private party." The voice had a deep richness.

"Really? Well my name is Detective Inspector Harrigan of the Stonegate Police, and I would like you to step aside, private party or no private party." Harrigan reached for his ID.

A huge hand grasped Harrigan's right arm.

"I must ask you not to reach inside your coat, Sir. I'm sure you understand."

Harrigan had to admit to himself that these were the most polite goons he had ever encountered. But he was a London policeman, in *London for heaven's sake,* and he didn't take kindly to being told what to do in his own city, especially by two bloody strangers. Harrigan's years of growing up in the harsh Australian outback had taught him that, on most occasions, you only had one chance. Whether it was looking for water in the Simpson Desert or facing a gang of drunken louts, you had to grasp the nettle and give it your best shot. Sometimes you won, sometimes you lost, but if you didn't have a go, you'd never know.

He was fully accepting of the fact that the towering mountains looking down at him were quite capable of crushing him without raising a sweat. But in true Harrigan style, he also knew that mountains could be moved relatively simply, you just had to put the dynamite in the right place. Not having the baggage of feeling bound by *gentlemen's rules,* with the speed of an angry rattlesnake, Harrigan's right knee struck the groin area of the man holding his arm. The grip on his arm released immediately, as Harrigan felt the considerable lumps in the man's trousers flatten against his knee.

The unexpectedness of this lone policeman's attack against such odds gave Harrigan enough time to aim a well placed right cross into the sensitive region of the second man. With the two men doubled at the waist clutching their groin areas, Harrigan took one pace to the rear, pushing Margaret back at the same time. Not wanting to face the consequences once the pain had subsided, Harrigan took one shaved head in each hand and with every ounce of strength he could muster, brought the skulls together. The sickening sound of cracking bone echoed through the marble vestibule. It made Margaret almost retch.

Harrigan allowed the two bodies to crumple to either side. He reached forward and pressed the button. The lift doors opened.

"Come on. Let's eat."

Margaret recovered quickly from her revulsion. She stared ahead, unable to look directly at the man standing beside her. She did not know what had frightened her the most, his savage display of violence or the casual way in which he'd said *let's eat*. Amid her indecision, a confused feeling of excitement began to fill her body. While the violence had repulsed her at first, she was now unable to repel a sense of attraction. This man, *dare she think her man?* was a true warrior, a protector. He was able to move from the gentle man she knew he could be to a man of cold, conscious-free action, willing to tackle any situation no matter the odds. She felt a certain pride and exhilaration.

Harrigan looked at her warmly as he felt her arm slide into his.

Ali was startled as the lift-warning chime sounded. He rushed, wide-eyed toward the opening doors.

"William! Wha...?" Ali was looking past the two occupants, searching for a glimpse of any others who might be there.

"There is only Margaret and myself, Ali. You seem nervous, my friend."

"Oh dear, oh dear, oh dear, what have you done, William?"

"Done, Ali? What have *I* done?" He pushed past his concerned friend. "What is going on here, Ali? You act like we're not welcome."

"Dear William." It was almost as a matter of secondary importance, that he nodded to Margaret as he rushed past his new visitors and stood in front of the policeman. He grasped Harrigan's hands in his. "You know you are always welcome. You saved my life. Maybe I'm trying in some small way to return the favour."

"Did you put those two goons downstairs?"

Ali pulled his hands away in offence. "Please, William. Give me some credit! Do you really believe I would employ people like that?"

"Then who did?"

The door of the Grande Lounge at the far end of the room opened and, for the second time today, the familiar manservant issued an invitation to Bill Harrigan.

"Please come in, Inspector. Mr Mahmood is waiting to greet you."

Harrigan gently removed Margaret's arm and said, "Wait here." He began to walk alone towards the open door. Margaret hurriedly reclaimed her position on his arm, matching him stride for stride. Recognising the determined look of a woman who was not about to be left behind, he restrained any words of argument and placed his hand over hers. With an air of the debonair that even the famous James Bond would have envied, he strolled through the doorway. "Thank you, Fadhel."

The Grande Lounge was, without question, the most elegant commercial dining room in Europe. There were many much larger, but in true Ali tradition, this room provided unparalleled elegance, privacy, and the most magnificent view of the heart of London. There were, of course, all the facilities needed to conduct business, from a simple facsimile machine to a computer connected to the fledgling CERN Internet. An automatic listening-device detector alarm was also featured in this sound proof room. Even the Secretary's office, positioned in the far left side corner, was designed so no one in that office could hear or see what was happening in the Grande Lounge, unless of course the occupants of the Grande Lounge so desired. Not that any secretary would mind sitting there from time to time with nothing to do. The office was as plush as the main dining area.

There were seven people seated at the table. A wine waiter poured a deep golden-coloured liquid from a finely shaped wine bottle. Muhammad Mahmood sat at the head of the table. His six guests were seated three on either side. Harrigan recognised some of the faces from the high society pages of the papers.

Muhammad Mahmood wiped the corners of his mouth with a white linen serviette, and placing it beside an empty entrée dish, rose and walked towards his new visitors.

"Inspector, we meet again." Despite his next comments being addressed to his seated guests, his fixed, icy stare remained steadily towards Harrigan's equally determined eyes. "Gentlemen, let me introduce Inspector Harrigan of the Stonegate police."

Harrigan acknowledged the men at the table. He noted two of the guests' slight overreaction to the introduction.

"And of course, the charming Mrs Willis."

"Please remain seated, Gentlemen." Margaret offered generously.

"How pleasant it is to meet you, Mrs Willis." Mahmood took her free hand and, with a half bow, combined the two accepted greetings, a handshake and a kiss to the hand, without actually completing either.

"I do not believe we have been introduced, Sir." Margaret's tone of cold aloofness momentarily shook Mahmood's air of flamboyance.

Harrigan allowed Mahmood a few moments of embarrassment before correcting the powerful man's lapse in social etiquette.

"Mrs Willis, please allow me to introduce Mr Muhammad Mahmood. Mr Mahmood, Mrs Margaret Willis."

Returning Margaret's polite nod, Mahmood quickly regained his composure. Maybe a mite too quickly, thought Harrigan.

"Have you come to see me, Inspector, or are you here for some quiet repast?"

"Quiet repast, Mr Mahmood. I try to avoid interrupting people when they are dining. But now that—"

"They must pay police inspectors very well?" Mahmood interrupted, as he gestured boldly to the splendour of Ali's.

"I get by. But, as I was saying, since you have introduced the subject of our reason for being here, surely you are a long way from Upper Binstead?"

"Business, my dear Inspector, business. And business knows no boundaries."

"I trust you refer only to the boundaries of distance."

"But of course."

Compared to the last time he'd spoken to Mahmood at the Badgers, Harrigan felt much happier with his performance. He judged himself to actually be a few points ahead.

"It has been a pleasure seeing you again, Mr Mahmood, but please, we must let you return to your guests."

"Thank you, Inspector. Good evening, Mrs Willis."

"Good evening, Mr Mahmood."

As Harrigan reached the door, he stopped and turned. "Oh, Mr Mahmood, about your two men at the lift..." he paused to allow Mahmood to make comment if he desired.

Although now at his seat, Mahmood remained standing. "I am dreadfully sorry about that, Inspector, security is very important in this day and age; you know how it is. I trust they didn't inconvenience you too much?"

"Not at all." Harrigan turned and walked past Fadhel. As the doors closed slowly behind them, Mahmood heard Harrigan's voice as he called over his shoulder. "I'm sure one of your men will be able to tell you which hospital they have been taken to."

The white-coated attendant led them to Harrigan's favourite area, and both he and Margaret settled into the high-backed leather chairs. They re-familiarised themselves with the happenings on the Thames and surrounds. The attendant dismissed himself and went to prepare the drinks that had been ordered simply as, "The usual for me please Omair, and a Gin and Tonic for Mrs Willis."

"What was all that about?" Margaret eventually asked.

"What was all what about?"

"Mahmood calling us in just to say hello."

"You thought there was something unusual about it?"

"Out of the ordinary to say the least. You know my background, Bill, my privileged childhood as you would call it. Even during my marriage, I was forced to live according to my station, and you can believe me, people such as Muhammad Mahmood do not simply invite outsiders into a private dining party just to say hello! Good Heavens, my parents would never contemplate such a thing; it's just not done."

The reference to her parents took Harrigan a little by surprise. He knew she came from a well to do family, but it had never been mentioned between them, not in any serious kind of way. Was this deliberate? He had to admit that the casual manner that Margaret always displayed when she was with him had easily breached the forbidden and often treacherous ground that lay between the classes.

He put those thoughts out of his mind.

"I must agree," he replied, "even *I* know it's not the done thing."

Realising her comment might have been offensive, she leaned forward and momentarily touched his arm. She was yet to learn that Harrigan didn't take offence at such things.

"That is why," He continued, "as you so correctly hinted at, we must assume he did it for a reason."

"Reason? What reason could there be?" After a few moments thought she continued. "Maybe when he saw you walk in he felt that, if you knew that he knew, that you knew that he was here and didn't acknowledge you, you might take that as some admission of guilt? You know, a trying-to-avoid-you kind of thing?"

Harrigan lifted his drink carefully from the tray and took a thoughtful sip. He shook his head. "I doubt it." The attendant retired discreetly into the background. "The likes of Mahmood are not intimidated by those types of thoughts. I doubt if such line of thought would even enter his head. No, I think the reason was far more sinister than that."

Sinister? she thought. She took a long draught of the Gin and Tonic as she considered Bill's use of the word *sinister*.

"I think it was probably more to do with you than with me."

"Me!?"

"He made a point of addressing you by name *before* being introduced."

"That's right, he did. And I've never met the man before, socially or through business." She began to realise the motive for the use of the word sinister. "So how would a man in his position know who I was?"

"And a man of Mahmood's obvious intelligence just doesn't make a mistake in the social graces like that. There is no doubt in my mind, Margaret, that it was a deliberate and calculated act."

"For what reason?"

"I think it was Mahmood's way of telling me he knew who you were."

"Why is that important?"

"Letting me know that he has seen us on a night out together, especially at Ali's, was his way of telling me, he knew you meant something to me. That you are the way he can get to me and force me to take the threat to you very seriously."

Margaret looked at Bill and, realising he was deadly serious, stifled a laugh of disbelief. "Well," Margaret replied with humorous, yet nervous, pride. "I thought I handled it excellently,"

"And so you did, congratulations." He held his drink in mocking salute and both took time out for a sip of refreshment. Feeling his light-hearted quip was more dutiful than from the heart, she chose to let him sit in silence and reason through whatever it was that was on his mind.

It was some considerable time before his next comment.

"But his little charade might just have backfired. His remarks at The Badgers this afternoon and the threatening telephone call had already told me he knew who you are and what you mean to me." This was the second time today that his feelings for her had been brought into their conversation, and Margaret fought hard to hold back *the* burning question.

"Did you recognise anyone at the table in there?" He asked.

"No…I don't think so…but then I wasn't really looking. You obviously did."

"Yes I did, three of them. Well, two positively. Sir Stanley Beckenham, Chief High Justice of the Supreme Court of Appeal and Lord Abel Twickenhurst, Chairman of many large companies and institutions."

"Twickenhurst International Merchant Bank would have to be one of them."

"Correct, and it is one of the most respected merchant banks in the world. Then there's the Cougar Motor Coach and Body Builders, manufacturer's of luxury vehicles for the richest of the rich, and of course, Alfred and Franks, Europe's largest chain of supermarket and variety stores."

"Who was the third person you recognised?"

"He is either an Archbishop or Cardinal, I'm not sure, but I know he's a top dog in one of the religions."

Margaret took her cigarette case from her purse and slowly took a cigarette and placed it in her mouth. Bill noticed this was her first cigarette today and wondered if she was trying to give it up. He was too polite to ask. He took his lighter from his pocket and moved the flame toward her. She inhaled deeply, blew the majority of the smoke high into the air and absently looked at the glowing tip of the long, expensive cigarette.

"I am trying to cut down on these things." She spoke these words of revelation to no one, and then, looking directly at Harrigan, she added, "who knows, I might give them up altogether."

There was no answer to that. If he agreed, it would indicate that he thought she should give them up and that he did not approve of her smoking. If, on the other hand, he said not to give them up, it would suggest he didn't care. He opted for a manly non-committal nod of the head and slight shrug of the shoulders. Margaret returned to the conversation concerning Mahmood's guests.

"One of the richest and most influential people in the world invites a few other rich and influential people to dinner. I fail to see the significance of that, my dear Inspector. Who would you expect someone like Mahmood to invite?" She leaned closer to him, placed her hand on his knee and whispered, "What's your point? What dastardly conclusion has your overly excitable imagination conjured from this major event?"

It was his turn to lean forward and whisper. "The point is, my dear Watsona, it is not that he has high flyers to dinner that matters, it's *which* high flyers that interest me."

Margaret leaned back into her chair and inhaled a second time. She returned her right hand, complete with the burning cigarette, to its position of resting on the arm of the chair. Harrigan watched the smoke of the burning cigarette wisp gently toward the ceiling.

"Mahmood said he was in London on business. Twickenhurst is a banker . I'd probably be surprised if he or even someone like him *wasn't* present, but the other two? What legitimate business could someone like Mahmood possibly have with the Chief High Justice or, for that matter, an Archbishop?"

Margaret went to reply but caught her words. Her immediate reaction had been to offer a simple reply to the question, but second thoughts made her realise that maybe she didn't have a simple answer. Maybe it was a worthy question.

Her curiosity was now aroused.

"You said Mahmood's charade may have backfired. That would indicate a serious blunder on his part. I must concede that his choice of dinner guests might be somewhat unusual, but a serious blunder?"

Harrigan crossed his legs and finished his Ballantines. The attendant appeared.

"The same again, Mr Harrigan?"

"Yes, please Omair." He did not give Margaret the option to decline. "And better still, make mine a double."

"Certainly, Sir."

Harrigan intertwined his fingers in front of him as he lay back contentedly in the Chesterfield armchair. Margaret could not help but compare this laid back man of almost blissful karma before her, with the man who not an hour ago had dealt so brutally with the two men at the lift.

"Margaret. Ever since this case began with the first body found in the fire at the Goldberg building, the investigation has led nowhere. It hasn't made one iota of sense." He took the offered drink. Margaret quickly finished her first, placed the empty glass on the silver tray and took her second.

"Do you wish to order your meal, Mr Harrigan?"

"Not yet, thanks."

"Maybe a little olive oil and bread baked fresh in the kitchen?"

He looked across at Margaret who nodded approval. "Yes, thanks Omair, that would be lovely."

Again they were alone.

"As I was saying, I could find nothing to bind this case together." He raised his finger to emphasise his next words. "Until *now* that is. Yes, Margaret, Mr Mahmood has unwittingly given me the key. All I need to do now is find the right doors to unlock."

Margaret had never found smugness attractive before. She watched him as he gazed out the window at the lights of London, the flashing cameras from boats on the Thames, the lights on the top floor of the red double-deck buses as they crossed Westminster Bridge.

"I love London," he said softly.

"Why?" Her interest was genuine. This man had travelled the world. He related stories and experiences of a life that many would envy, but when he talked of London he talked from the heart. He talked like someone seeing the beauty of London for the first time. It was a blinkered view of only seeing the good.

"I can't say exactly." He sipped his Ballantines thoughtfully. After a shrug of his shoulders he concluded, "I guess it just fits me, like an old pair of slippers. You know there are better slippers in the shop, but this pair's comfortable."

Margaret's life of the privileged childhood and young adult-hood followed by ten years of high-society marriage allowed her no understanding of such a relaxed and simplistic outlook. She understood what he meant, but was not able to feel the content-ment. It was like a politician declaring an understanding of the plight of the poor but not having the gut feeling of feeling hungry. That only came through experience.

Omair placed the fine china bowl of extra virgin olive oil next to the plate of delicately cut bread. Margaret leaned forward and dipped a piece of the bread into the oil. Harrigan followed the ritual, which until recent years, was seen as almost a totally Mediterranean thing to do.

"Mr Mahmood seems to think that you feel comfortable with me," Margaret said, trying desperately for an air of nonchalance.

"Mr Mahmood is a very astute man." Harrigan took a small bite of the oil-saturated bread.

"Do I take it from that remark he is right?"

"Margaret, I've felt an attraction toward you from the first day I saw you."

"Yes, I remember. It was cold the day you first came to my door and my nipples pressed hard against my silk housecoat. You had difficulty not sneaking a glimpse."

Harrigan shifted embarrassingly in his chair.

Margaret smiled. "I shock you, don't I?"

"Yes, I guess you do," Harrigan replied and gave a resigned laugh.

"Don't be shocked, my dear Inspector. Be assured it is only because of the way your manner relaxes me that I am freed from convention."

"I'm glad about that. We have had some nice times, haven't we?" He took another bite of the bread. "Remember that trip to the Cotswolds, to the Ferryman's Ghost Inn?"

"I will never forget it. It was my happiest day for years."

He leaned forward and gently took her hand in his. He looked down at her hand, silent at first. "Margaret," he looked directly into her eyes, "would you think me forward if I said I would like to share many more days like that with you?"

She held his gaze. An almost light-hearted seriousness came into her voice. "I thought you would never ask."

They smiled together.

"Come on, let's order."

The rest of the night at Ali's was fairly uneventful. Ali was openly edgy with Mahmood being on the premises, so Harrigan acted casually towards him. The last thing he wanted was to make trouble for his friend. He'd probably done too much already. They finished their meal a little after ten-thirty and, at eleven, prepared to leave. Harrigan knew Ali would be arranging a taxi to be outside, and deliberately said nothing to Ali about the last Taxi Driver. While he didn't suspect Ali, he just wanted to be sure.

The foyer was deathly quiet. There were no signs of the earlier altercation and two new minders stood in the shadows near the lift.

"Good evening, Gentlemen." Harrigan called. "Good evening, George."

"Good evening, Inspector."

"You know the number if you have any trouble, George?"

"Oh, I don't think there'll be any more trouble." Despite being closely covered by Mahmood's men, George still managed a knowing smile.

"Goodnight then."

"Goodnight, Inspector."

A taxi waited at the front door. "Where to, Guv?"

"Sprigham Wells, thanks, Driver. I'll let you know exactly where, when we get there."

He felt Margaret's body tense.

"What's the matter?" His concern was deep and genuine.

"Nothing really. I'm seeing bad-guys behind every bush at the moment."

"Don't worry, I'm not going to leave you. I'll be closer than your shadow until this mess is over, so you'd better get used to it."

"And when it is all over?"

"By then I hope to be just like an old pair of slippers." She smiled, gave his thigh a soft squeeze of approval, and snuggled into his shoulder. He placed his arm around her and they completed the journey in silence.

He paid the driver through the driver's window. "Thanks, Driver. Have a good night."

"Good night, Guvn'r." The rattle of the motor faded, as the black taxi reversed back down the driveway.

"Come on, you have a case to pack."

"A case? Where are we going?"

"I don't want you staying here, not until I can get some police protection arranged, anyway. There's a motel just around the corner. I think we'd be better staying there tonight."

"Taking me to a motel? My you *are* a fast worker," she said, as she unlocked the door.

"Shut up and get packing."

It took ten minutes for Margaret to throw in the things she needed. She also packed a spare toothbrush for Harrigan.

"I'm ready," she announced, as she descended the last few stairs.

"Alright. Now, just in case there are a few bad-guys behind some of those bushes watching this place, I want you to go through the house turning off lights like you would when going to bed."

She stood looking at him.

"Go on! I'll come with you."

They started in the kitchen, then the hall. The light at the top of the stairs came next, followed eventually by the bedroom light.

They sat quietly on the bed. Five minutes passed.

"Come on, it's time to go," he whispered.

He took her case, and she followed him down the stairs and to the back door. He quietly opened the back door and looked into the blackness of the night. They slid into the garden and stood against the wall of the house. Their ears strained, listening for any sound that should not have been there. Their eyes stared into the darkest areas, trying to see something shining or a movement that did not belong.

Eventually, he took her hand, and they moved through the garden to the back gate. Once again, careful scrutiny indicated there was nothing out of place in the street behind and, after entering the street and locking the gate, they made their way stealthily to the Royal Edward hotel/motel.

* * *

It was almost eight the next morning before Margaret and Harrigan stood at the buffet bar in the Heritage room at the Royal Edward. Harrigan glanced around the room at the diners already seated. The room could almost be described as being segregated into three sections. Two coach loads of tourists had each taken over an area deemed by the leader of the pack as being the best spot. In Harrigan's experience, no matter what coach you may travel on or what group you may travel with, there was inevitably always one in the group who knew better than any other, what to see, where to go, what was a bargain and what wasn't and, of course, where to sit in the restaurant. What qualifications this self appointed leader needed was unclear, except for the fact they were usually head of the body corporate in their block of home units somewhere or at least in charge of the local neighbour-hood watch. And of course, a hide thicker than a Rhinoceros was mandatory.

In the darker area of the room were seven tables set for break-fast. Two couples and one foursome occupied three of the tables; the other four were unoccupied. Being a Saturday morning, the breakfast crowd was probably down in numbers and of a different mix than a normal weekday.

Had today been a weekday, the people breakfasting would have unwittingly created a scene reminiscent of the thousands of similar rooms set specifically for breakfast in hotels and motels across the country. Across the world, in fact. Harrigan could imagine the majority of the tables would be set for ones and twos. As a general rule, the majority of the tables would be taken by a lone breakfast person. There would also be one or two couples and probably one table at which three or four sat. Despite the mixture of genders and genuine desire towards individual-ism, there would be a marked similarity. All would be on busi-ness. Their dress, mannerisms, breakfast selection, and choice of reading material merely served to offer classification. The two ladies in their early twenties, dressed smartly in tailored suits of a style once reserved for men, sat deliberately apart. While their similar bearing, general appearance, the choice of healthy breakfast, complete with a bottle of mineral water would have denied them their independence, it was their reading material that bound their individual sameness. The obviously placed folder of computer-generated graphs, columns, and general notes, would've also somewhat detracted from the image of the individual they attempted to create. Harrigan could almost hear the ring of the mobile telephones...in unison, of course.

Their young male counterparts suffered in much the same way, except that the mobile telephone, would've been displayed unashamedly on the table top for all to see. Another difference between the sexes was that, although both genders displayed a studious and thoughtful look as they concentrated on such important reading matter, the young up-and-coming males would occasionally and with great flair, remove a Mont Blanc pen from their top pocket and make notes and sometimes *even correct* the computer notes. This was very impressive.

Unfortunately, despite the efforts of those so eager to impress, the rest of Harrigan's imaginary breakfast people didn't notice any of this carry on. They were predominately male and dressed in various stages of well-travelled business clothes. They read the daily tabloid and ate either scrambled egg on toast, bacon with egg and tomato, or sausages with scrambled egg and tomato. Both choices came with fried bread and tea or coffee. The main similarity was the bored, "wish I was at home," expression etched into each face. The table of four always offered some light relief. It was usually four young lads in town for a seminar or some training and motivational course that their boss had seen advertised in a glossy brochure he'd received in the mail, titled *"Your business has been selected, etc etc."*

Three of the lads would laugh heartily and draw the odd glance of disapproval from the computer pages of the young and terribly important. The fourth lad looked like death. He'd played the mandatory role of the one who drank too much and will, much to the amusement of the other three of course, be useless and limp for the next few days. If one of these four had been female, she would also be trying to be one of the boys, but usually would fail miserably.

"You going to eat something, Bill?" Margaret's voice forced its entry into his reverie.

"Pardon?"

"Breakfast! Are you having any? You seem to be miles away."

Harrigan smiled.

"Well? Were you?" she persisted.

"Yes," he replied as he looked around the breakfast room. "And no."

Margaret looked at him quizzically.

"Yes and no, I was miles away," he explained hurriedly. "But yes, I am definitely going to have breakfast."

As Margaret prepared a plate of fresh fruit, a bowl of muesli and skim milk, and one piece of whole-meal toast, she watched horrified, as Harrigan piled a plate with bacon, sausages, tomato, and some doubtful looking scrambled egg.

"Want some juice?"

Margaret nodded. "Yes, please."

"Orange, tomato, or," he lifted a jug of juice closer to his eyes, "I think it's grapefruit."

"Orange juice, thanks."

"Where'd you like to sit?"

"You choose."

Harrigan selected a table in the corner and away from the window.

"Did you have anything planned for this weekend?" Harrigan asked.

"Not really." An almost wistful expression crossed her face. "I'm afraid that every day seems much the same as the other, lately. Weekdays or weekends, they have lost their meaning."

"Good." Again Harrigan felt the need to qualify his remark. "Good you have nothing planned, I mean."

They continued to eat in silence. Margaret tried hard not to stare as Harrigan struggled with the little sachet of tomato sauce. He could not eat sausages without sauce.

"Bill, do we really need to be taking that telephone threat so seriously? I mean, all this cloak and dagger stuff, police protection. Don't you think it's a trifle over the top?"

Harrigan placed his knife and fork on either side of his plate, wiped his mouth with the serviette, and sipped his tomato juice.

"To be honest Margaret, I'm not sure. At the best of times these things are always a bit of a guess, but really, what choice have you got? You can only look at what facts you have and make a judgment. The truth of it is that, unless there *is* some attempt on the life of the person under protection, you rarely know if your judgment was right or not."

He took another mouthful of sausage and scrambled egg. "This scrambled egg is pretty average."

"So don't eat it," Margaret offered helpfully.

"I've got it on the plate, now," he replied defensively. He looked thoughtful for a few moments and, then, as if making a major decision declared, "I think it needs a little more sauce."

As he wrestled with a second sachet of sauce, he returned to the previous conversation. "Let's look at what we have."

"I am." A hint of the aghast edged her remark as she stared at his plate watching the sauce tumble onto the yellow pile.

He chose to ignore the comment. "Only a moron kills or does serious bodily harm to another person for no reason, and we know that Mahmood is not a moron."

"I agree, but, " she argued, "you still have no absolute evidence that Mahmood is behind the threat."

"I know we have no absolute evidence, but absolute evidence is hard to come by. Most times evidence is circumstantial, especially at the start of an investigation. As far as I'm concerned, the important question at this time isn't *if* Mahmood was behind that telephone threat, the question is how *serious* is the threat?"

"How do we establish that? Besides the obvious, of course."

"The seriousness of his threat to you is directly linked to how big a threat he thinks *you* are to *him*. If he sees you at an annoyance-only level, someone who doesn't really *know* anything but might know enough to start somebody else investigating, the threat is probably just that, a threat and we are over-reacting. But, if he sees you as something else, like someone who knows too much, or knows enough to put Mahmood out of business or behind bars, who knows what could happen? And don't forget, Roger was in a position to be full bottle on this business, and Mahmood has no idea what he may have told you. So, until I know something more definite, I'm afraid you'll have to put up with me and my paranoia."

"I think I can handle that."

"Coffee?"

"Tea, thanks."

Harrigan noted that Margaret showed no reaction at the mention of Roger's murder. He brought a small pot of tea for Margaret and a pot of coffee for himself.

"I didn't think you drank coffee. I thought you preferred tea?"

"I didn't sleep too well last night, one eye open; you know how it is."

"I told you to sleep in the same room; there were two single beds."

"I know. But we managed to get two rooms with a dividing door, and with the dividing door open, I could keep and eye on you, metaphorically, of course, without intruding."

Margaret threw her head back and spoke to the ceiling.

"My God! I trust the man with my life! Surely I trust him with my bloody honour!"

Harrigan ignored the eyes of the other diners now looking in their direction. "Well, I'm sorry, but that's the way I am. Take it or leave it."

She smiled a broad, soft smile and placed her hand on his. "I'll take it." She took a sip of her tea. "So, what's next?"

"Well, being a weekend, investigation is more difficult. I have to go to the station and finish off a few things, and I must pop down to the hospital and see how Mum is. If we get a chance, I would also like to take a drive around the dock area."

"That last bit sounds like fun."

"I also want to visit Aysha Singh. There's something about that woman I just can't put my finger on."

Margaret was tempted to pass some comment about not letting him put his finger on anything of Aysha's, but she thought better of it.

"Where does she live?" she asked, unable to ignore the dullness of the alternate question.

"West Heathwich. Maybe we'll see her tomorrow morning and then go to lunch somewhere, what do you think?"

"Fine by me."

Having allowed the coffee to wash away the taste of the scrambled egg, Harrigan paused at the reception desk and paid the bill for both he and Margaret. He refused her offer to pay her share, explaining he was sure that the superintendent would approve the expense.

They checked both rooms and confident nothing had been left behind, dropped the keys at the reception and went outside into the spring air and hailed a taxi.

"Stonegate Police Station, thanks." Harrigan stored a mental picture of the driver and noted the driver's details.

With the exception of satisfying Margaret's curiosity by explaining he intended to have two police officers escort her home to repack her case, they rode in silence.

Margaret's first impression of the Stonegate Police Station was that it was old and tired and needed a great deal of renovation. Once inside, she was introduced to the desk sergeant with much the same description and needs as the Police Station itself, and was made comfortable in Harrigan's office. She sat and watched as he hung his coat on the ornate stand, took the big brown key from his desk, and wound the old clock on the wall.

"How many more times have I got to tell you to buy a new clock?"

Margaret looked towards the sound of Bill Buckle's voice, while Harrigan concentrated on the job at hand.

"What the hell are you doing here this morning?"

"Hello, Mrs Willis."

"Good morning, Sergeant."

"I don't know, Sir, it's this damn…" he turned to Margaret Willis, "excuse me."

"That's quite all right, Sergeant, I'm a big girl."

"It's this Mahmood business, nothing seems to…" he paused, as he struggled for words, "tie together, if you know what I mean. It's all ends and no middle."

Harrigan closed the glass door of his old clock and returned the key to the top drawer. "I'm pleased you're here this morning, Bill, I think I may be able to fill in some of that middle."

"Oh?"

"I'll just get Margaret off for a change of clothes." He picked up the telephone hand piece and rang the desk sergeant.

"Yes, Inspector?"

"Sergeant Harris, would you have a car and a couple of Police Officers I can use for an hour or so? I have an escort duty for them."

He watched the old desk sergeant through the glass partition. Harrigan figured that Sergeant Ernie Harris had been in the force for at least a hundred years of which at least eighty had been spent as a desk sergeant. He knew every trick in the book and, despite his gruff and intimidating manner, was liked by everyone. Harris moved the hand piece from his face as he motioned to two police officers about to leave the building. Harrigan saw Harris' right arm point towards his office. He replaced the hand piece to the speaking position. "Constable Finnegan and White are coming in to see you, Inspector."

"Thanks, Sergeant, I owe you one."

"Margaret, I want you to go with the two police officers, and pack enough stuff for two or three days, just in case." He saw the question coming. "Just casual gear, nothing too posh."

There was a knock on the door.

"Come in!"

"The sergeant said you wanted to see us, Inspector."

"Yes come in Constable Finnegan." He stood and shook hands. He didn't believe rank to be an excuse for bad manners. He looked at the policewoman accompanying the young constable.

"This is Constable Fiona White, Inspector. She joined us a couple of weeks ago." Harrigan offered his hand.

"G'day, welcome aboard."

"Thank you, Sir."

Harrigan was pleased there was a female constable. He introduced Margaret and they both knew Bill Buckle.

"I would like you to escort Mrs Willis to her home while she gathers some personal things and then return here. This may sound a routine task, and it may well turn out that way. However, I want you to stay with Mrs Willis at all times, be alert, and do not, I repeat, do not allow anyone into Mrs Willis' house while you are there."

"Do you want us to call in once we get there and when we leave?"

"That would be a good idea. Tell Sergeant Harris on the way out, will you? And take note if you think you are being followed. Take no chances and call for backup if you have any suspicions at all, is that clear? Any doubts at all!"

"Yes, Sir. Please come with us, Mrs Willis."

"Are you *sure* this is necessary?" Margaret was a little over-awed by all the fuss.

"I'll see you when you get back." Harrigan returned to his desk and looked at his old sergeant.

"Sit down, Bill."

Taking a few minutes to gather his thoughts, Harrigan relayed in minute detail the events of the previous evening and aired in confidence his suspicions. Bill Buckle's mouth hung open as Harrigan completed outlining his thoughts.

"Blimey! You really *do* believe Mahmood is involved."

"Why shouldn't I? He's not involved directly, of course. Men of his position are never directly involved; there is always someone else positioned to take the fall. But he's involved alright."

"I have to agree it does answer most of the questions." Bill Buckle sat and thought over everything his inspector had been saying. Realisation of the full impact of the situation, even if Harrigan was only partly correct, brought a solitary exclamation.

"Bloody hell."

"I think you have summed up the situation adequately, Sergeant. *Bloody hell* covers it nicely."

"What are you going to do?"

"I don't know yet."

"You'll have to tell the super."

"Well, yes." He hesitated. "I agree I'll have to tell him something."

"Something, Sir?"

"Really, Sergeant, you must know by now that you can't tell a superintendent *everything*. Sometimes there are some things a boss just does not need to know. If I told him everything, he would feel some urgent desire to actually do something about it. And you know how dangerous that can be!"

Bill Buckle smiled once more at the inspector's cynicism towards authority and those wielding the authority.

"No," Harrigan continued, "I'll tell him enough to make him worry, but not enough to act." He stood and walked towards the liquor cabinet.

"Whisky Sergeant?"

"No thank you, Sir, a little early for me."

Harrigan looked at the clock. 10:47. "It's a little early for me, too, but I'm going to have one anyway." He poured a substantial quantity of neat Ballantines into a tumbler.

"I'm going to talk to the super first thing Monday morning. I'll work out how much he needs to know and, hopefully, if I get it right, he'll agree to give me some level of police protection for Mrs Willis."

"Don't get too optimistic. To offer police protection is to give some credence to your theory, and he is not going to want to do that in a hurry."

Harrigan nodded reluctant agreement. "I think you could well be right on target there, Bill." He took a sip and swilled the liquid around his mouth in an action usually reserved for mouthwash and allowed the whisky to trickle down his throat. It was warm and comforting.

"You know, Bill, we have directed most of our attention on the death of Manjit Singhabahu. I think it's time we paid a little more interest on our other deceased member of the group, Mr Wei Yu Lee. First thing on Monday, I want you to get a decent photograph of Wei Lee, one that doesn't make him look too dead, if you know what I mean. See if you can find out more about him. Go to Chinatown. Show the photograph to everyone, ask questions, you know the routine."

"His passport says he has been in the country over four years. If we're lucky he should have made some friends, or enemies, in that time." Bill Buckle observed.

"I must admit I have never put much faith in personal documentation; it is too easily forged. Personal documentation is basically for keeping decent people honest. Ironically, it gives the illegal immigrant with the money to afford quality documents, the appearance of legitimacy." He took another sip of whisky. "And forged documents are easily available, in all parts of the world, especially the Middle East and Asian countries. They're very talented that way."

"You'll get no argument from me on that one, Sir. I've seen some dodgy documents in my time."

"Like I said before, Sergeant, quality is governed by price."

"So you believe Mr Lee hasn't been here for four years as his passport suggests?"

"That's what I want you to find out. Take Constable Watts with you. And Bill, keep a watchful eye out. If my theory is right, or even only partly right, it's quite possible there may be others who could be looking for Lee. If they know you're asking about him, they may have you followed. If so, you know what to do."

"Call for backup."

"And bring him or them in for questioning." Harrigan took another drink. "Anyway, I'll probably see you Monday morning and we'll talk about it then, but if I don't, you know what to do."

"I'll get Watts and get started."

"Thanks, Bill."

"What about McIver?"

"I want him to revisit his friend at the American Embassy. See if we can't find out more about Lee from that angle."

"I'd better be getting home," Bill Buckle said, as he stood slowly. "I have to cut the grass before I go down to the 'Hounds." Bill Buckle spent most of his spare time with cronies at the Hare and Hounds.

"If I don't see you Monday Bill, good luck."

"Thank you, Sir, you too. I think you'll need it talking to the super."

Harrigan gave a silent chuckle to himself. *You've never spoken a truer word, Sergeant,* Harrigan thought, as he drained the tumbler.

Harrigan busied himself for the next one and a half hours doing routine paperwork, checking time sheets, rosters, and expenses. He read through mail lying in the in-tray and disinterestedly threw it all in the out-tray. Patricia'd know what to do with it.

He switched on the PC on his desk. From Windows 2.0 he selected the Word program, opened a new document, went to *Save* and, with two fingers, typed "Goldberg Fire." Although Bill Harrigan was a two-finger typist, he didn't always use the same two fingers. While the index fingers were his favourite, some-times he got flash and used the first finger next to the index fin-ger. While unorthodox, his unique typing method allowed him to type at fifty words per minute with only a few mistakes here and there. Of course "few" is a relative term, but with the spell-ing and grammar check facility, he was generally satisfied, and it was easier than writing. He did have to admit to disliking with a passion the American dictionary, and its difficulty with words ending in *our*.

He opened his notebook and began transferring his notes into the computer. He persevered for several minutes and then sat back in the leather chair and stared at the keyboard. Harrigan loathed writing reports. After several minutes wrestling thoughts of self motivation and eventually admitting to himself that, no matter how long he procrastinated, the task still had to be done, he did what any right-thinking person would do on a Saturday morning and shut down the computer and moved the keyboard to one side.

He walked across the office to the filing cabinet and removed the Manila folder given to him by Muhammad Singh at the Bichirst Office of Sidhu Trading. He splashed a few drams of Ballantines into his glass and returned to his desk.

It took a full fifteen minutes to read through the accounts. As he studied the extremely comprehensive accounts, it became abun-dantly clear that up until now, he had seriously underestimated the enormity of the Sidhu Shipping and Trading Company. While these wére only the "Home Company" accounts, they gave a clear insight of the services offered. A Container Shipping Line, General Forwarding, Cargo, and Project services. Road Transport was also included, plus Warehouse and Customs Clearance. Multiple Receiving Depots, Cargo tracking and, of course, one of the largest Container Terminals and Stevedoring operations in the United Kingdom.

He read and reread the accounts. All seemed in perfect order. Containers were loaded at thirty-seven different locations: warehouses, vehicle manufacturers, white goods manufacturers, trading companies, and factories across the nation. It seemed that Mahmood had a finger in every pie. With such wealth and access to product, especially second-hand and reject product, Harrigan began to view with less suspicion Mahmood's altruistic operation run by Ramachandran and Manjit Singhabahu. In fact, he began to see it as an almost natural phenomenon. Especially when, if like Harrigan, you accept the fact that once people become excessively wealthy, they have an almost uncontrollable inner cleansing desire to be seen as benevolent. As cynical as this may sound, in reality it is of utmost importance to the needy that such inner cleansing be nurtured and encouraged, mainly through public recognition and especially by their peers, because let's face it, the average common man doesn't give a damn.

Margaret Willis poked her head around the door and saw Harrigan, head down and deep in concentration. With the almost childish intention of surprise, she walked quietly across the carpeted floor.

"You're back in good time," Harrigan said, looking up and not realising he had spoiled her surprise. "Everything go alright?"

"Perfectly."

He wondered at the coldness in her tone.

Constable Finnegan knocked and entered quietly at Harrigan's invitation.

"Any problems, Constable?"

"No, Sir, no trouble at all. Everything looked exactly as it should be."

"Thanks, Constable. Good work."

"Will that be all, Sir?"

Harrigan thought for a few moments. Would he have them drive Margaret and himself to pick up his car or would he catch a taxi?

"Yes, thank you, Constable, that will be all. Oh, and thank Constable White for me!" he called after the retreating figure.

He closed the folder in front of him and drained the tumbler.

"A little early for the hard stuff, Inspector?" she feigned rebuke.

"You're not my mother," he replied good humouredly.

"Speaking of your mother."

"Let's pick up my car. I'll pack a bag and then we'll pop around to see her at the hospital," Harrigan said decisively.

"We?"

"Well, I can't leave you alone, what do you suggest?"

"I think you are overreacting to the whole situation, that's what I suggest!"

"Maybe."

Having run a suspicious eye over the Cabbie, he asked to be taken to the Kings Arms. He didn't want to be dropped outside his house, just in case.

Harrigan kept the conversation at a level that could only be described as two notches below dull and uninteresting. The weather, the traffic, and the advantages of a Purpose Built Taxi vehicle were by far the highlights.

It was seventeen minutes before one, when Harrigan paid the cabbie and walked towards the Golden Labrador, lying on the front mat of the hotel. He bent and patted her on the head. Like all good pub dogs, Sally lay still and carefully rid her face of an, *"if someone pats my head once more today..."* expression.

"This is Sally, she's a good old girl. Likes to race me for the red chairs in front of the fire."

Margaret came to his side. "What a beautiful dog."

"Roy treats her like one of his kids. Give her a Pat. She loves a pat."

Margaret reached down and patted Sally gently. The large golden body heaved deeply, as Sally gave a big sigh.

They walked down Wickam Road to number thirty-three.

"Who's Roy?" she asked.

"The publican. We must go there one day if you'd like."

She threaded her arm through his. "I'd like."

It didn't take Harrigan long to pack a bag, give the house the once over, and lock the front door.

"I don't think I should come in with you to see your mother. You know how she feels about me and it won't help her get well."

"What do you mean *how she feels about you?*"

"Oh come on, Bill, please don't start pretending. Your straightforwardness is the one thing I love about you."

"Thanks very much," he pouted.

"You know what I mean."

He smiled. "Yes I do, and you are right." He paused. "OK, but you will have to stand in the hall where I can see you."

"If it will make you happy."

"It will."

And so, having parked the car, gone to the front desk, and caught the lift to the third floor, Margaret Willis stood in the hall opposite ward *three zero five* while Bill Harrigan visited his Mother. Even from the hallway, it was obvious that his mother was still very ill. She was awake and talking, but very quietly. Harrigan tried to hide the shock of seeing his mother looking so frail.

"Don't worry, William, I'll be alright." He never could hide anything from his mum.

He stayed for ten minutes and eventually, at his mother's insistence, prepared to leave. He bent over and kissed her on the forehead.

"See you again soon, Mum, I love you."

"Thanks for coming, William." She reached up and took his hand. "And William, your friend is very beautiful, why don't you bring her in next time? It gets cold in the hallway." She released his hand and closed her eyes. He thought he saw a hint of a smile flicker in the corners of her mouth.

The Mazda sped down Mile End Road, through East Ham and followed the A13 to Purfleet. Harrigan told Margaret about his mother's last remark.

"You can't keep things from mothers, Bill, you should know that."

"Tell me about it. But it does raise one question."

"Oh?"

He remained silent, concentrating on the road ahead.

"Well?" She pushed the issue.

He paused a few more moments, obviously having difficulty. "Where do we go from here?" His usual air of confidence and self-assuredness had deserted him.

Margaret looked a little puzzled.

"*Us* I mean. You and I. Where do *we* go from here?" He knew this wasn't coming out right, but he continued to ramble on like a tongue-twisted schoolboy. "I might be seeing things all wrong, but I would like to think that you, er…you have some…er…how do I say it?"

"Attraction to you?" Margaret assisted. "Is that what you are trying to say?"

Harrigan couldn't discern whether the tone in her voice indicated that she was incredulously happy that he felt that way or that he was incredulously stupid for broaching the subject. He moved uncomfortably in his seat. He wasn't very good at this type of conversation.

"Attraction?" His voice pitched a little too high. "Yes, I guess you could say that."

It was Margaret's turn to pause. "Why should I have to go first? What about you? How do you feel towards me?"

They had reached the M25 Purfleet junction.

"I think we have to turn off here and go through Gray's End,." he said unnecessarily.

"Of course you have to go through Grays End. Don't change the bloody subject," Margaret scolded playfully. "Get back to the question. Well, do you?"

"How I feel isn't the issue —"

"But how *I* feel *is*?" she interrupted. The playful tone was no longer apparent.

"Y…yes. But don't take that as it sounds."

"How else am I to take it?" Anger and disappointment tore through her.

"Margaret, I must be perfectly honest."

"At last," she interrupted. "My faith in your straightforwardness is taking quite a battering."

"Of course our feelings for each other are equally important. There's no question about that. And I've already told you I've been attracted to from the first day we met. Surely you must know my feelings for you by now. But that is not the issue, our past is the issue."

"Our past?"

"To be more accurate, the difference in our past."

"What are you talking about?" Margaret was having difficulty understanding.

"Well I mean, look at you. You're beautiful. You have money, a mansion on the outskirts of London, and a private-school upbringing. You've grown up and lived among the privileged few. Me? I'm a policeman who is the son of a policeman, from the other side of the tracks, as they say." He paused for a few moments, as he saw a look of disbelief cloud Margaret's face. He spoke hurriedly to correct any misunderstanding. "Please don't take my explanation to mean that I somehow feel inferior, I don't. I'm not apologising for my upbringing, far from it. I've had two wonderful parents, a good education, and an exciting life. I'm not suggesting that your lifestyle has somehow been superior to mine, because it hasn't been. But it has been *different*. We have lived and learned different ways. I just don't want you to walk with me down a path to a place you would ultimately not want to go."

Harrigan pulled the Mazda into the kerb in Slipway Road. He looked between the rows of containers at the fully-laden container ship in the distance. Not wanting to dwell on the thought that had probably just made a complete ass of him and killed off any chance he might have had with Margaret, he tried to concentrate on the reason he was there. It seemed to him that the majority of the containers on the ship were twenty foot in length.

A few forty-foot containers appeared to be loaded on the bottom with the outside row held in position with crossed metal braces. He assumed it was easier and more stable to load the larger containers first.

"Do you really think I'm beautiful?" Margaret asked.

Harrigan frowned. He spun his head and stared directly into her now almost green eyes.

"What?" It took Harrigan a few moments to grasp the true significance of the question. He threw his head back against the headrest of his seat, closed his eyes, and slowly moved his head from side to side.

"I spend five minutes of living hell trying to confront something that has plagued my mind since I first met you, I bare my soul, and you haven't heard a damn word!"

Margaret took his hand. He opened his eyes and turned slowly towards her. She smiled. "You chump. Of course I heard every word, but that stuff isn't important. Of course we have lived different lives and learned different ways, but so what? We are adults for heaven's sake, and if we are to walk down that path you so poetically referred to a little while ago, then our different pasts are not important."

"I did get a bit carried away, didn't I?" He interrupted.

"Let's just say you were led by the emotion of the moment. But let me finish. In my opinion, as long as we are aware of our differences and maintain a respect for them as we grow together, what's the problem?"

"I just wanted to get it all out into the open, that's all."

"And I'm glad you did. Now, back to the important stuff. Do you really think I'm beautiful?"

He smiled. "I think you are the most beautiful woman in the world."

They moved together violently, reaching to grasp each other in their arms. A mechanical grabbing sound resounded through the car as the retractable seatbelt locking devices snapped into action holding their eager bodies apart. The indecision of the moment faded as the small car filled with the sounds of uncontrollable laughter.

Ten minutes passed. Silence had replaced the laughter. Their hands remained clasped together as the lay back, silent, both coming to terms with the magnitude of the unspoken commitment they had just made to each other.

"What did we come here for?" Margaret was the first to break the silence and bring some normality back into the situation.

"I'm not sure, really. I have this crazy theory in my mind, and it is full of loose ends. I just wanted to look at the containers. See how they are loaded. Looking for inspiration, I guess."

He drove slowly along Slipway Road and pointed to a container holding-yard.

"Look at all those containers, there are hundreds of them."

Margaret looked at Bill then at the containers. She struggled to find enthusiasm. This must be one of those differences he had been talking about.

He stopped the car near the fence where three forty-foot containers were stacked. The doors of the bottom container had been left open.

Margaret felt she should say something. "It looks bigger on the inside. I suppose that's because it's empty."

Harrigan spun rapidly. "What did you say?" His voice was raised. Margaret wondered what she had said to get such a reaction; she was only trying to be sociable.

"I just said it looks bigger on the inside than it does on the outside. It's probably because it is empty, you know, like a room in a house. It looks huge, until you put the furniture in."

Harrigan undid his seatbelt, leaned across and kissed her long and hard. He eventually pulled his lips from hers. He stroked her soft cheek with the back of his fingers.

"Darling, you are wonderful!" His excitement was contagious. Margaret's heart pounded as she searched deeply for suitable words.

"Do you want to look at some more containers?" She asked suggestively.

He kissed her quickly.

"Not right now, I've seen all I want to see."

Margaret realised this *differences* thing was probably going to be harder to work out than she had first imagined.

He looked at his watch. Twenty minutes after three. "We have time to see Aysha Singhabahu this afternoon. What do you reckon? We shoot down to West Heathwich, see Aysha, and then we will have the rest of the weekend to ourselves?"

"Sounds fine to me."

The engine revved, as he did a sharp U-turn and headed back towards the M25.

Margaret sat in the car as Harrigan rang the doorbell at the West Heathwich home.

"Good afternoon, Inspector, what a surprise."

"Surprise, Mrs Singhabahu?"

"To see you so late on a Saturday afternoon. I would have thought you'd be at the football or some other such thing."

"Some of us have to keep working I'm afraid."

"I assume your visit has something to do with my husband?"

"Yes."

She stepped to one side. "Please, come in."

"Thank you all the same, but I do have a friend in the car, so I won't keep you long."

"As you wish. Have you located my husband, Inspector?"

"No, Mrs Singhabahu, I'm afraid not. I was hoping you might have heard from him by now."

"No. Nothing. I have heard nothing." She lowered her head. She stared silently at the ground for a few moments before raising it again and looking into his eyes.

"You think something has happened to my husband, don't you, Inspector? Something very bad."

"I'm afraid I do, Mrs Singhabahu." He looked towards Margaret. He didn't want to continue this conversation on the doorstep, but he couldn't take the chance of leaving Margaret alone. Aysha Singhabahu was very perceptive.

"Please ask your friend to come in. We shouldn't talk on the doorstep."

"I'm afraid she is not a member of the police force."

"Does that make such a difference, Inspector?"

"Well, if you don't mind."

She gestured toward the car. "Please, Inspector."

Harrigan moved swiftly to the Mazda and opened the front passenger side door.

"This is going to take a little longer than I first thought. She insists we go into the house."

"Both of us?"

"Both of us."

The formal introductions being completed, Aysha led the way into the room overlooking the garden.

"Please be seated, may I offer you a cup of tea?"

Both Harrigan and Margaret declined politely.

"Now, Inspector, you were saying, about my husband?" Harrigan sat silently, carefully selecting the right words. He needn't have bothered. His facial expression gave away his thoughts. Aysha answered her own question. "You think one of those bodies found in the fire at the Goldberg building belongs to my husband, don't you, Inspector?"

"To be honest with you, Mrs Singhabahu, yes I do. I do not believe your husband is in Africa arranging the delivery of a shipload of second-hand blankets. I believe he was lured to the warehouse in Victoria Road and murdered."

Margaret sat quietly looking through the glass doors at birds enjoying the beautiful garden. As the two conversationalists appeared to not notice her presence, she tried to remain as inconspicuous as possible. The harshness of Harrigan's last statement did however, force an involuntary, brief, but obvious, glance in his direction.

Harrigan continued quickly, not allowing Aysha time to respond.

"May I see your husband's UCFAC belt buckle?"

"UCFAC belt buckle, Inspector?" The innocent soft tone of her voice reminded Harrigan of their previous interview.

"Yes, his UCFAC belt buckle. Last time I was here, I asked if you packed your husband's clothes. I asked you especially about his belt. You told me you always pack all his clothes, including his belt, but you didn't mention the UCFAC belt buckle. Knowing how grand the buckle is and how much your husband would treasure such an award, as you didn't mention it at the time, I assumed you didn't pack it."

"I, well yes, you are right, of course. I didn't pack it." She stumbled over the words.

"Then may I see it?"

"Er, no. I mean, you could if it was here, but it's not, I gave it to someone."

"You gave it to someone?" Harrigan's voice echoed in disbelief.

"Well, not just anyone. A man came to the door. He said he was one of Manjit's work friends. He explained Manjit had realised at the last moment that one of the clients he was to visit had been responsible for Manjit winning the award. It would have been a great offence not to wear it."

"And what time did this man come to pick up the belt buckle?"

"It was five minutes past six, last Monday morning. I remember because his knocking woke me, and I looked at the bedside clock."

"Do you know the man's name?"

"No."

"Did you recognise him, by that I mean had you seen him before?"

"No I don't think so."

"Would you recognise him again?"

"I don't know. It was early, why is all this so important?"

"We found the buckle in the ashes of your husband's mutilated body." Harrigan's deliberate harshness had its affect.

Aysha gasped and fell back into the chair.

"Margaret, help Mrs Singhabahu, would you? I'll get a glass of water."

Margaret loosened Aysha's clothing and sat on the arm of the chair. She took the water from Harrigan and placed the glass next to her patient's lips. Aysha took a sip.

"Thank you, I'm sorry. I didn't mean to..." she said weakly.

"It's alright, Mrs Singhabahu." Margaret comforted as she glared at Harrigan, disappointed at the callous way in which he'd referred to the ashes of the woman's husband. "You've had a nasty shock."

Harrigan sat patiently.

With a slightly unsteady hand, Aysha eventually touched Margaret's arm. "I'll be alright now, thank you, Mrs Willis."

Harrigan felt the coldness of Margaret's icy stare as she returned to her seat.

"Would you like me to send someone around to be with you, Mrs Singhabahu?" Harrigan asked in a vain attempt to curry a little favour with Margaret.

"No. No thank you, Inspector. I'll be fine. But I would like to be alone for a while."

"Sure, I understand I'll come back another time." He rose from the chair. "We'll find our own way out."

"Thank you, Inspector."

Margaret refused his offer of assistance, said goodbye to Aysha Singhabahu, and led the way to the front door.

As Harrigan crossed the driveway, he heard the passenger door slam shut. He slid silently into the driver's seat and quietly closed his door.

Margaret sat looking stiffly ahead. "You callous bastard! How could you show such little feeling toward that poor woman?"

Harrigan started the motor and edged onto South Heath lane.

"Don't waste your pity, Margaret, she's lying through her teeth."

"And how do you know that, Sherlock? Policeman's intuition?"

"Maybe. But tell me, would you give one of your husband's—"

"Estranged husband," she corrected.

"One of your estranged-husband's most treasured possessions to a perfect stranger who knocks on your front door at six in the morning?"

"I might," she replied defiantly.

"Oh come off it! Tell me the truth, would you really?"

"Well, maybe, maybe not,

"Maybe not?"

"Alright! No, of course I wouldn't. But that was still no reason to be so hard on her."

"Really Margaret, do you really think I am that unfeeling? Give me some credit!" Their bodies jolted as he drove the car hard. "I have two dead bodies, one of which has been murdered, the other, who knows? Everyone I have interviewed so far is lying his or her arse off. Sidhu Trading is mixed up in who knows what illegal activity and, to top it off, one of the richest and most powerful men in the world is in the middle of it. I am a policeman and sometimes being a policeman means not always being the epitome of politeness!"

The Mazda lurched as he turned onto the A29.

"You're right. It's none of my business, and I shouldn't have made a comment. It's just that I, well…"

"Maybe it's all a mistake. Maybe we are too far apart."

"Hey! We knew it wouldn't be easy. Do you always give up so easily?"

"No. it's just that, well, I don't like to upset you."

Her mood mellowed. She placed her hand on his leg. "That's sweet. Let's say we forget all about it?" She rested her head on his shoulder "Where are we going?"

"Bognor Regis."

She sat up straight ."Bognor Regis? Why the hell are we going to Bognor Regis?"

"I don't know. I was angry when I decided. Maybe that's where angry people go."

"You're an idiot," she laughed.

"Thank you." He raised her hand and placed it against his lips. After a few moments, he returned her hand to its previous position and placed both hands on the wheel. "And Margaret, forget about Aysha Singhabahu. Believe me, she's not all she appears to be."

* * *

Aysha watched as the Mazda eased its way onto South Heath lane. She closed the curtains and turned back into the room, a smile on her face. It wasn't a pleasant smile, warm and inviting, it was an ugly smile, cold and calculating. She walked to the telephone and dialled. She didn't need to look in the telephone book; she knew the number. She'd dialled it often enough.

"Hello."

"Fadhel, it is Aysha. I must speak to Mr Mahmood."

There was a click at the other end of the telephone as Fadhel put the telephone on hold. The seconds ticked by slowly.

Aysha heard another click.

"Muhammad? It's Ays—"

"Mr Mahmood is in conference," Fadhel interrupted. "He wants you to give me the message."

"I want to speak to Mr Mahmood!" she demanded. "Tell him Inspector Harrigan has been here, asking about the belt buckle!"

Aysha was furious. She desperately wanted to regain favour with Mahmood, and this could only be achieved if she spoke directly to him.

She heard Mahmood's voice at the end of the line.

"What is all this about, Aysha?"

"Muhammad, it is so good to speak with you. When can I see you?"

"What is all this about that damn inspector asking about the belt buckle?"

Aysha relayed every detail of Harrigan and Margaret Willis' visit. She paid particular attention to the inspector's interest in the whereabouts of the buckle and her reply.

"I did well, Mahmood. I was very convincing."

Mahmood had not become rich and powerful by underestimating his opponent, and he viewed Harrigan as an opponent. A very worthy opponent.

"Why was the Willis woman there?"

"I don't know!" Aysha resented her lover's lack of appreciation. "He said she was a friend. What difference does it make anyway?"

"Aysha, I want you to listen to me and listen well. I don't want you to leave the house. I don't want you talking to anyone else, about anything. Is that clear?"

"Yes, Muhammad." The tone of the man's voice destroyed any sign of the woman's previously demonstrated defiance.

"It's not safe for you to be alone anymore. I want you to pack a suitcase—"

"Pack a suitcase?"

"I am going to send someone to collect you and bring you to me. Don't pack too much, just a few things to tide you over until we can buy you a whole new wardrobe."

The sudden warmth in his attitude filled Aysha with excitement. She could hardly believe her ears. Dare she think that, at last, she was going to be Muhammad Mahmood's woman?

"I will do exactly as you ask, Muhammad."

"Good." The phone went dead. Aysha leaned back in the chair. Her thoughts filled with optimistic reasoning. Why shouldn't she become Mahmood's mistress? With her husband dead, there was no obstacle. Mahmood's pride would not allow him to take her from Manjit, but now? She smiled with the realisation that no longer must she suffer Ramachandran's amateurish advances. She thought of Ramachandran's reaction when he learned that she was to become Mahmood's mistress. There was no question he would feel jealousy. He had even been jealous of Manjit! And frustration? Yes there would be frustration because there would be nothing he could do about it. No one dared question Mahmood, especially his subordinates. And finally fear. Ramachandran would fear the influence she may have over Mahmood. Ramachandran had said too much to her during times of heated passion. Told too many secrets, made too many promises, as he'd tried to woo her from Manjit. How much of what he'd told her would she pass on to Mahmood? Oh yes, she smiled, he would definitely feel fear.

She rose from her chair and laughed out loud.

* * *

Harrigan and Margaret sped passed the Arundel turnoff.

"We really are going to Bognor Regis, aren't we?" Margaret commented with a hint of disbelief peeking through.

"Yes, why not?"

"Wasn't it George the Fifth who said *Bugger Bognor?*"

"I think so. But it was also George the Fifth who gave the title Regis to the town Queen Victoria used to call *Dear Little Bognor.*"

Margaret looked at him with quizzical disbelief. "Why do you know such things? Apart from people who live there, who in their right mind knows, or even wants to know the ins and outs of Bognor Regis?"

"It's also the sunniest seaside resort in Britain."

Margaret slumped in her seat, crossed her hands on her lap, and stared at the dash, bored with the Bognor Regis history lesson..

"It was originally named after a woman," he tried to enthuse. Margaret shifted in her seat but her gaze remained stoically ahead.

"In AD680," he continued, "it was named Bucgan Ora, meaning Bucge's shore. Bucge was an early Saxon woman. Not many women had places named after them in those days."

"Shut up."

"Yes, Dear." Harrigan enjoyed their playful repartee.

Several miles from Bognor Regis, Margaret was talking of holidays she'd taken with her parents, mostly overseas. While she enjoyed the times in France, America, and Canada, she expressed regret at not getting to know her own country. Of course, she had learned about England. For heaven's sake, she'd grown up there. How could she not have learned? But her so-called "privileged" upbringing had denied her the chance to learn about it or experience the beauty of it the way the average child would. Not like the little white-bodied child on a cool and windy beach building sandcastles with a bucket and spade. She had never chased butterflies in a meadow or listened in wonderment to the chimes of a distant village church bell.

Harrigan slowed and turned off the A29.

"Where're we going now?"

"We mustn't forget that it was concern for your safety that brought us here in the first place! You are under police protection...well, my protection, anyway, and I'm a policeman, so that's close enough. After our experience with that London taxi driver, I doubted the wisdom of giving Mahmood's people another easy opportunity to report our whereabouts."

He drove carefully along a narrow wooded lane.

"There was a sign a few miles back advertising the *Yapton guesthouse — Where our doors are always open.* Since we are looking for a quiet weekend, I thought this place might fill the bill."

The Yapton Guesthouse was typical of an old stone farmhouse. It had probably seen better days, but it still had inviting warmth about it. It had been a long time since the acreage on which the Farmhouse stood had seen real farm activity. The Arun River flowing behind the property did much to enhance its transformation into a holiday retreat. Beautiful trees shaded swing seats, resting on the manicured lawns which ran between strategically placed flowerbeds of various shapes and sizes.

"What a beautiful place." Margaret was forced to remark, as she stood beside the Mazda.

"Let's see if there's a vacancy."

They were in luck. The guesthouse had been fully booked, but one couple who were due to arrive in an hour's time had just telephoned to say they were unable to get there and had cancelled their booking. The accommodation was not in the main house, but in the recently renovated farmyard outbuilding. *Why not just call it a barn,* thought Harrigan.

It was, however, far from being a barn. True, the old stone building may have started life as a barn, but the renovations had transformed it into one of the most inviting guest apartments either had ever seen. When coupled with the magic of a clear spring evening, the moss clinging to the old stonework and its setting on the edge of the woods, presented a fairytale aura.

"We'll take it."

* * *

It was eleven minutes after seven the following morning when Harrigan woke to the ringing of his mobile telephone. He gently moved his arm from beneath Margaret's head and rubbed some circulation back into it. He picked up the telephone and moved to the window.

"Hello?"

"Inspector Harrigan?"

"Yes."

"It's Sergeant Harris…Stonegate Police Station."

"Yes, Sergeant."

"I'm sorry to telephone you this time of the morning, Sir, but Superintendent Wilkinson told me to contact you."

"Yes, it's alright, Sergeant, what is it, what's happened?" Harrigan urged, wishing the sergeant would get on with it.

"It's Mrs Aysha Singhabahu Sir."

"What about her?"

"She's been found murdered, Sir." Harris replied bluntly.

"She's what?"

"She's been found murdered, Sir. In her house at South Heathwich."

"Do you know what time it happened?"

"What is it, Bill?" Margaret's sleepy voice asked from across the room. "Is it your mother?"

Harrigan shook his head and waved a dismissive hand.

"Sometime around three a.m. I think, Inspector," Harris continued. "The local boys are at the scene but, because of the connection with the Goldberg fire case, the superintendent arranged for you to take over the investigation."

Margaret came to his side and placed her arm around him. "What's happened?" she whispered more urgently.

"It's Aysha Singhabahu," He replied, after putting his hand over the mouthpiece.

"How long shall I tell them you'll be, Inspector?"

"Oh..." He hesitated as he formed a mental picture of what he had to do, and how long it would take to drive to West Heathwich. "A couple of hours. Don't let them touch anything. And Sergeant, get hold of Bill Buckle and have him bring Ramachandran to the address."

"Mr Ramachandran is already there, Sir. He found the body."

"Did he now." Harrigan paused again, "OK, thanks, Sergeant, I'm on my way."

"Do you still want me to contact Sergeant Buckle, Sir?"

"No. Let him sleep in. I'll contact him myself later if I need him."

"Very good, Sir."

The two men hung up simultaneously.

"What's going on? What's happened to Mrs Singhabahu?" Margaret's curiosity was getting the better of her.

"She's been murdered."

"Murdered!"

"Yes, murdered."

"Good heavens. We were only talking to her a few hours ago, and now she's dead. It doesn't seem real." She moved across the room and sat at the dressing table.

"It's real enough, believe me. *Now* do you think I've been overreacting about your safety?"

"No, I guess not," she conceded. Harrigan was proud of the way in which Margaret was taking the news of Aysha's death. Although obviously shocked, she had not fallen into a display of the melodramatic, as many people would've. Especially someone whose husband had also been murdered less than six months previous. *She is one tough lady*, he thought, as he moved towards her and placed his strong hands on either side of her neck. He looked at her in the mirror, gently massaging her slightly taut shoulder muscles.

"Mmmm, that feels lovely," she purred.

"I'm sorry I got you into this mess. If I hadn't taken you to Ali's that night, we wouldn't have caught that taxi home and you wouldn't be involved."

"And we wouldn't be here together, so let's not go down that path." She reached up and placed her hands on his. "OK, so what happens now?"

"What happens is that we must have some breakfast, pay the bill, and then head back to West Heathwich as fast as possible."

"Are you suggesting that I'm coming with you?" There was a touch of surprise in her voice.

"You'd better believe it! I am not going to leave you alone for a minute. And there'll be plenty of police at the house, so you'll be safe there." He bent down close to her. "Don't tell me you're squeamish," he teased.

"No, I'm not squeamish!" she replied defensively, "It's just that I have never been to a murder before."

CHAPTER SEVEN

It was a few minutes before 10.00 a.m., when Harrigan ushered Margaret past the uniformed constables at the front door of the West Heathwich address.

"Inspector Harrigan?" a fresh faced and enthusiastic young sergeant asked, as he strode towards the two newcomers.

"Yes."

"Sergeant Middleham, Heathwich Police. I was told you were on your way."

"Good." Harrigan was in no mood for cheerful young sergeants. He noticed Middleham staring at Margaret.

"Sergeant, I'd like you to meet Mrs Willis." The sergeant snapped to attention and bowed courteously with actions representing something from a second-rate German war movie.

"The lady is under my protection, and for the next hour or so, she will be under your protection." Margaret looked anxiously at Harrigan. "Don't worry, Mrs Willis, the sergeant won't let me down, will you, Sergeant?"

Sergeant Middleham again snapped into action. He designated two young uniformed constables to accompany Mrs Willis into another room and make her comfortable.

"And at no time will Mrs Willis be left unescorted, is that clear?" Harrigan snapped.

The two constables nodded in unison.

"Right! Get on with it then!" Middleton ordered.

"Inspector Harrigan!" an accented voice called from across the room. "Inspector Harrigan! I am so very, very pleased to see you. This is tragic. So very tragic."

"Good morning, Mr Ramachandran." Harrigan glanced to the covered body. "Yes, it is tragic."

The East Asian man crossed the room and now stood directly in front of him.

"Please, Inspector. I don't think these policemen understand the situation; they seem to think that I had something to do with the murder!"

"Mr Ramachandran, I suggest you return to your seat and let me have a look around. I'll talk to you in a little while." He turned to the sergeant. Khalil Ramachandran looked toward the sheeted body and walked sadly back to where he had been sitting previously.

"You know Mr Ramachandran, Sir?"

"You seem to forget, Sergeant, the only reason I was put in charge of this case is because it's connected to another investigation."

As the young sergeant smarted under the bluntness of the inspector's reply, Harrigan sensed he had been unnecessarily abrupt to this young police officer who was obviously trying hard to please. Harrigan's attitude had nothing to do with Middleham. He was angry because Aysha Singhabahu was dead. He'd had a lot of questions he wanted to ask, and now it was too bloody late! He glanced quickly around the room.

"You appear to have done a good job so far, sergeant, well done."

He knelt beside the body and removed the sheet covering Aysha Singhabahu's head. Apart from the gaping and bloodied wound to the temple area, she was still a beautiful woman.

"Just the one wound?"

"Yes, Sir."

Harrigan checked the dead woman's hands and fingernails and, returning the cover over the body, stood up slowly.

"Do we have a murder weapon?"

"According to forensic, it is probably that pedestal ashtray, standing over there near the body." He pointed to the tall, black marble object. "Forensic wanted to run tests on the blood stains, but I told them to leave it where it was until you arrived, Sir."

"Has it been dusted for fingerprints yet?"

"Yes, Sir. I thought that would be ok."

"What else do you have for me, Sergeant?"

The Sergeant flicked open his notebook. "Well, Sir, the station received a call at three-eighteen this morning from a neighbour across the road." He looked up at Harrigan momentarily. "That's Heathwich Police Station." He returned back to his notes. "Apparently the neighbour, a Mr Nicholas Rosenberg, owns a fast food shop near Gatwick Airport. He is up early every morning to cook food and prepare for the day." The Sergeant again looked up at Harrigan. "You see, Sir, even though his shop might not open until six a.m., there is a lot of cooking and—"

"Yes, Sergeant, I know how a fast food shop works."

"Very good, Sir." He returned to the notebook. "Anyway, as Mr Rosenberg was letting his cat out, as he does every morning, he heard a squealing of tyres and screeching of brakes. A car driving at very high speed suddenly approached and, without slowing down, turned into the driveway, almost knocking over the gatepost. That's the driveway out the front of this house, Sir," he explained unnecessarily.

Harrigan nodded. "That would've been the BMW outside."

"Yes, Sir, that's correct," he said with a surprised tone in his voice. He was about to return to his notes when he suddenly stopped, and looked back to Harrigan. "Can you tell me how you knew that, Sir?" he asked politely.

"Oh, just basic police work, Sergeant, nothing very brilliant, I'm afraid. As I came in with Mrs Willis, I noticed the gravel had been disturbed where the car had skidded to a halt."

The Sergeant suppressed his anger at not noticing that himself. "Mr Rosenberg then said he—"

"Is Rosenberg here, Sergeant? Can I speak to him directly?"

"Well, er no, Sir, Mr Rosenberg has left. You see, Sir, he had to open his shop. I thought that, as long as I had his statement, you could talk to him later."

"You're telling me that even though you knew I was coming here, you let a witness go without first consulting with me?"

"Yes, Sir. I...I..." Sergeant Middleham knew he had stepped well beyond the boundaries of normal protocol. He'd known at the time he wasn't following procedure and had prepared himself as best as possible for the consequences. But now he was beginning to wish he hadn't. He knew there was no point in trying to lie his way out of it, so he continued. "I know I shouldn't have, but Mr Rosenberg has a business to run and I thought, well, to be honest, Sir, we know where he'll be and I couldn't see any sense in him losing trade."

"Well done, Sergeant." Harrigan interrupted. "There's not enough people in the modern day police force with the balls to make their own decisions. Good work!"

"Th-thank you, Sir." Harrigan's attitude took him by surprise. "Thank you." This was no ordinary police inspector, he thought, not knowing how close to the truth he was.

"Carry on, Sergeant." Harrigan urged, nodding to the open notebook.

"Yes, Sir!" His newly found enthusiasm gave Harrigan satisfaction.

"Well, Sir, Mr Rosenberg said he heard the doorbell ring followed by a loud knocking on the door. He said he also heard the man shouting something. He couldn't hear exactly what the man was saying but it could have been, 'open the door, Aysha, open the door,' but he couldn't be sure."

"That's fine."

"When Mr Rosenberg heard the sound of a window smashing and the alarm going off, he decided it was time to call the police. He dialled 999 and as fate would have it, there was a police car in the area and the boys arrived within two minutes."

"The police who came, are they still here?"

"Oh yes, Sir, I wasn't that brave." He smiled, as he called to one of the two police standing near the doorway.

"Senior Constable, this is Detective Inspector Harrigan, from Stonegate. He is in charge of this case, and we are to give him all assistance. Inspector, Senior Constable Blake."

Harrigan offered his hand. "Blake."

"Inspector."

"The sergeant tells me you were first on the scene."

"Yes, Sir, me and Constable Wilson." He looked toward the constable in the doorway.

"What happened?"

"Well, Sir, we was patrollin' two streets over when we got a call that there was a disturbance at this address. We were here in a few seconds."

"Did you use your siren?"

"No, Sir, we were that close we didn't need to. And anyway, Sir, not in this neighbourhood, 'specially in the early hours of the mornin'…if you get my meanin'."

"Friends of the commissioner and all that?"

"Somethin' like that, sir."

"Well, that saves me asking why you were patrolling the area at that time of the morning."

"That's very understandin' of you, Sir. Anyway, when me and the constable arrives, we stops in the driveway. The lights were on, and the front door was open. Very strange for that time of the mornin' we thought. We entered quiet like and saw a gentleman kneeling beside the victim, Sir." He pointed across the room to Ramachandran, still sitting, head bowed. "That gentleman over there it was, Sir."

"Have you made your statement yet, Senior?"

"The sergeant has it all in writing, Sir."

"Good, I'll read it after I've spoken to Mr Ramachandran. Hang about will you? I might need you again."

"Very good, Sir."

As Harrigan moved towards Ramachandran, Sergeant Middleham spoke quietly from behind.

"Excuse me, Sir."

"Yes Sergeant."

"The ladies from the coroner's office want to know if you've finished with the body."

"Yes, Sergeant. They can take it away." He looked over to the two white clad figures standing patiently beside the stretcher. "Ladies, eh?"

"Yes Sir. But surely that doesn't *bother* you, does it, Sir?"

"I couldn't give a monkey's toss, Sergeant. It just beats me why ladies would want to do a job like that." As a second thought he added, "Oh, and Sergeant, you can tell forensic they can bag that pedestal ashtray. I don't need it anymore."

"Yes, Sir."

Harrigan took hold of a Jacobean high-backed chair and placed it in front of Ramachandran. He sat down, crossed his legs, and withdrew his notebook.

"Now, Mr Ramachandran, tell me your recollection of events."

"Well, Inspector ..." he began nervously. He spoke like a man wanting to get something off his chest. "Goodness gracious, where shall I start? It was eight minutes after two this morning, when I received a telephone call from Aysha. She was in a terrible state."

"Tea?" Harrigan asked.

"I beg your pardon, Inspector?"

"Cup of tea. Do you feel like a cup of tea?"

"Oh no, no, no, no, Inspector. Please, I want to tell you my story."

"Well I do."

"What?"

"Feel like a cup of tea!" He looked around the room. "Sergeant!"

"Yes, Sir?"

Harrigan waited until the Sergeant came close enough so he didn't have to shout. "Ask Mrs Willis if she would make me a cup of tea. She's a lady that likes something to do, and," he lowered his voice to a whisper, "she makes a *great* cup of tea."

"Shall I tell her that, Sir?"

"Why not? Now Mr Ramachandran, you were saying?"

Ramachandran was irritable and confused. The interruption had disarranged the thoughts he had so carefully organised in his mind. Harrigan was an expert interviewer.

"Aysha rang. She was terribly upset. She begged me to come over. She told me to hurry; she felt her life was in danger!"

"In danger from whom?"

"She didn't say. She just pleaded with me to come over immediately, and then the phone went dead."

"So you came over straight away?"

"Of course. I dressed quickly and drove as fast as I could."

"And what happened when you got here?"

"I ran to the door and knocked. No," he corrected, "I rang the bell first and then I knocked. Well banged on the door would probably be more accurate. I called to Aysha to let me in."

"Were the lights on in the house?"

"No. The whole place was in darkness."

"Here's your tea, Inspector."

"Thanks Constable. Carry on Mr Ramachandran."

"When Aysha didn't respond, I smashed a pane of glass in the door, put my hand through the opening and opened the door. Because I hadn't used a key, the alarm sounded immediately. I stumbled across the room and—"

"Why didn't you turn on the lights?"

"I don't know. I...I just wanted to turn off the alarm, I guess. As I came close to where the alarm pad is, I knocked my knee against that ashtray pedestal." He looked across and noticed it had now been removed. "It's not there now, Inspector."

"Don't worry about it. I know where it's gone. Please, carry on."

"Well, I picked it up and stood it out of the way, and then turned off the alarm."

"You know the code?"

"I was a regular visitor here, Inspector."

"Oh yes, I had forgotten," Harrigan lied.

"I went back to the doorway and turned on the lights." He paused for a few moments.

As Harrigan sipped his tea, he watched the man's face closely. "It was then that I saw…" He paused. "It was then that I saw Aysha, lying on the floor, her head bloody."

"It must have been a shock."

"Yes, it was. But to be honest with you, Inspector, at that time I didn't realise she was dead. Certainly the wound was clearly visible, but she still looked so beautiful. I rushed to her and kneeled beside her. I stroked her hair and whispered to her."

"Whispered to her?"

"Yes, I know it sounds stupid now, but I didn't think she was dead! I asked her if she could hear me, was she alright, that kind of thing."

"What happened next?"

"I eventually realised she was dead and looked around the room. I saw the pedestal ashtray standing next to her and thought that that must have been what I'd knocked over in the dark. It was after I'd picked it up and saw the blood on the end of it, that I realised it was probably the murder weapon."

"What did you do then?"

"I didn't have a chance to do anything. I heard a voice telling me to put the ashtray down and to remain where I was."

"Senior Constable Blake."

"That's correct." He pointed towards Blake. "That policeman over there. I did as I was told and didn't move. He came to me and handcuffed my hands behind my back. I protested my innocence but he led me to this chair and told me to sit there and not to move or touch anything. How could I touch anything? I was handcuffed."

Harrigan sipped more of the tea. He said nothing.

"Once the other police arrived," he continued, "Sergeant Middleham was kind enough to remove the handcuffs, but ordered me to stay seated. Apart from the time I came over to you, I have been seated here ever since."

As Harrigan stood and finished his tea, a young constable appeared at his side and took the empty cup and saucer.

"Thank you, Constable." He walked to where Sergeant Middleham was talking to Senior Constable Blake.

"What do you think, Sir?" Middleham asked.

"I'm not sure yet. He certainly had opportunity...but motive? It could be jealousy." He mused more to himself than anyone around him. "Maybe Aysha *didn't* tell him she was in fear of her life; maybe she told him she was leaving and he came over here to stop her." He reached for the telephone.

"Finger prints finished with this?"

"Yes, Sir."

He picked up the handpiece and pressed the redial button. The telephone rang five times. The deep accented voice on the answering machine began. "You have reached the residence of Khalil Ramachandran. I am unable to—" He replaced the handpiece.

"Well that part of the story checks out. Tell me, Senior, what was your first reaction when you came to the door?"

"I saw that gentleman, Sir." He again pointed to Ramachandran. "Standin' over the body 'e was, holdin' that tall ashtray." He broke off as he looked for the ashtray. "It was over there, Sir."

"Forensic have taken it, please carry on, Senior." He was beginning to wish he'd left the ashtray where it was. The senior continued.

"It looked like 'e had just killed 'er to be honest wiv you."

"How was he holding it?"

"Wiv his right hand claspin' down the bottom and the top, restin' in his uvver hand, Sir."

"Did he give you any trouble, Senior?"

"None, Sir. 'e did exactly like 'e was told, Sir. 'e did insist 'e didn't do nothin', Sir. Said 'e didn't kill the lady. It's all in me report, Sir."

"Thank you, Senior." Senior Constable Blake took his leave. "Sergeant, have the senior and his partner escort Mr Ramachandran to Stonegate Police Station."

"Shall I 'cuff him, Sir?"

"I don't want to frighten him anymore than necessary at the moment, Sergeant, but I don't want him getting away, either, if you get my drift."

"Very good, Sir, I understand."

Harrigan returned to Ramachandran. The nervous looking man stood as the inspector approached.

"Mr Ramachandran, I am going to have to ask you a few more questions."

"But why? I haven't done anything!"

"I didn't say you had, Sir, but Mrs Singhabahu has been murdered, and you were found at the scene holding the murder weapon."

"But I explained that."

"Exactly, but we must have your explanation in an official statement. Senior Constable Blake and his partner will escort you to Stonegate police station. I'll be along as soon as I can."

"What about my car? Why can't I just drive myself to the police station?"

"You go with Senior Blake. I'll arrange for your car to be brought to Stonegate."

Ramachandran's show of fear turned to an attitude of arrogant aloofness.

"Am I being arrested, Inspector?"

"Just a few more questions, that's all."

The conversation may have developed into an argument that Harrigan did not want at this time had it not been for the commotion at the front door. Voices were raised. The constable on duty was holding a man by the shoulders telling him he was not allowed in. The man demanded entry. Harrigan hurried over and placed a hand on the constable's shoulder.

"It's alright, Constable, I know this man. Please come in... Fadhel, isn't it?"

"Yes, Inspector, what's happened? Where is Mrs Singhabahu?"

Before Harrigan could answer, Ramachandran bounded from his chair and grabbed Fadhel.

"What the hell are you doing here?" he screamed. "You've come for her, haven't you?"

Harrigan grabbed the angry man's arm. "Take Mr Ramachandran away please, Senior."

With very little effort, Senior Constable Blake took a firm hold of Ramachandran and led him toward the door. Ramachandran looked at Harrigan and fell silent; he knew he hadn't done his cause any good.

"I apologise for Mr Ramachandran, Fadhel. He's a little over-wrought at the moment."

"Has some misfortune befallen Mrs Singhabahu, Inspector?"

"You could say that. She's been murdered."

"Oh dear."

Harrigan didn't know if it was the simplicity of the two words or the way Fadhel had spoken them, but the *oh dear* was far from the reaction he had expected.

"May I ask what you are doing here?"

"Mr Mahmood instructed me to come and pick up Mrs Singhabahu and take her to him."

"Do you know why he wanted to see Mrs Singhabahu?"

"Where Mr Mahmood is concerned, it is my position to simply obey, Inspector, not to question."

"I understand. But if you were asked to guess or maybe offer your personal opinion why Mr Mahmood wanted you to take Mrs Singhabahu to him, what would you say?"

"I would say I am Mr Mahmood's manservant. I do not have an opinion."

"Didn't you even wonder why?"

"Mrs Singhabahu often visited Mr Mahmood. It is none of my business, Inspector!"

"Where is Mr Mahmood?"

"On his yacht, off the southern coast of France."

"Does Mr Mahmood spend much of his time on his yacht?"

"Most of his time, Inspector. He feels safer on the high seas."

"It must be some yacht."

"It is no ordinary vessel, Inspector. Mr Mahmood lives very comfortably and he is more than able to run his worldwide operations from the vessel."

"I take it you were on the yacht when Mr Mahmood directed you to pick up Mrs Singhabahu?"

"That is correct."

"What time was that?"

"Around five o'clock yesterday afternoon."

"How did you get here?"

"By helicopter. The yacht has its own helipad. Makes commuting very simple. The helicopter is waiting for me at a small airport near Little Woping. About an hour's drive from here."

"Waiting for *you?*"

"Well, it was, and still is, I suppose, waiting for Mrs Singhabahu and myself, but Mrs Singhabahu won't be coming, will she, Inspector?"

"Why do you think Mr Ramachandran reacted so violently toward you when you came in?"

"I suggest Mr Ramachandran is best able to answer that, Inspector."

Harrigan called to the sergeant who had been standing discreetly in the background. "Sergeant, I want you take a statement from Mr ...?"

"Saheed." Fadhel offered.

"Saheed, I need to know how he can be contacted, and I may need to speak with his employer. I need those details."

"Will you need Mr Saheed once he has given me the statement, Inspector?"

"I don't want him leaving the country. We'll keep his passport."

As if that would stop him with that bloody helicopter waiting around the corner, Harrigan thought.

"I must object, Inspector!"

"I suggest you contact Mr Mahmood. Tell him what has happened and what I have said. I'm sure he'll have no objections. Take a week off, stay at The Badgers. It'd do you good, Fadhel, believe me. It's better than Bognor."

"I beg your pardon, Sir?"

"Nothing Fadhel. It's a private joke." Fadhel looked puzzled.

Harrigan walked away, picked up the suitcase Aysha had packed earlier and placed it on the table. He looked at the packed items. Two pair of shoes, one for casual wear, one for good. Two casual outfits and one good outfit. Three sets of underwear, one nightdress and a housecoat. Aysha had also packed all her jewellery. Harrigan could never understand why anyone needed that amount of jewellery in the first place. There were also a few personal trinkets and two photographs, both of Aysha in her youth. Harrigan left the items on the table and went into the room where Margaret still waited with her two protectors.

"Sorry I've been so long."

"That's alright. The two constables and I have been chatting away; well, it's been more like I've been chatting away and they've been listening patiently."

Harrigan spoke to the two policemen.

"Thanks for looking after Mrs Willis. I'll take over now."

"Very good, Sir." They turned to Margaret "Nice to meet Ma'am."

"Likewise, and thank you."

"Our pleasure Ma'am."

Once alone, Harrigan took her in his arms. "Thanks for that lovely cup of tea."

"I was glad to make it. It gave me something to do," she said knowingly.

He took her hand and led her back into the scene of the murder. "There's something I want you to look at."

"It's not too gory is it?"

"No, of course not. I need a woman's opinion." He showed her the contents of the suitcase. "This is what Aysha had packed in her suitcase. Does anything seem odd to you?"

Margaret looked at the shoes, clothing, and jewellery. "She certainly packs a lot of jewellery."

"That's right! If you have only packed three outfits, two of which are casual, why take all that jewellery?"

"Security maybe. She knew there'd be no one in the house once she'd gone to wherever it was she was going."

"Maybe. What about the two photographs and the other small items? There's *seven* bottles of perfume, and all these other bits and pieces."

"I must admit it seems a little odd."

"It most certainly does, Mrs Willis, it most certainly does."

As they approached the door, Harrigan interrupted Sergeant Middleham.

"Excuse me, Fadhel, you said before that Mrs Singhabahu often visited Mr Mahmood?"

"That is correct."

"Did she always take a suitcase?"

He took a few moments to answer. "Not that I can recall, Inspector. She usually brought an overnight bag."

"Thank you, Fadhel. Mrs Willis and I are going back to Stonegate, Sergeant. I'll leave you to clean up. Thanks for all your help and I'll be in contact soon."

"Right ho, Inspector."

* * *

Harrigan and Margaret were twenty minutes away from the Stonegate Police Station when the ringing of his mobile telephone interrupted their conversation. He pressed the green button.

"Harrigan."

"Inspector, it's Sergeant Davis, from Stonegate."

"Yes, Sergeant."

"Superintendent Wilkinson asked me to call you. He's waiting at the station to talk to you. Before you question Mr Ramachandran."

"Thanks, Sergeant, I'll be there in about twenty minutes. While I've got you on the telephone, would you try and contact Sergeant Buckle? I'd like him there when I talk to Mr Ramachandran."

"I already have, Inspector. He's on stand-by."

"Good work. Also, would you contact Sergeant Middleham at Heathwich Station and arrange to have Mr Ramachandran's BMW brought to Stonegate? I forgot to do it before I left."

"Certainly, Sir. Anything else?"

"No. See you soon."

The conversation ended.

"I don't know what the super wants me for, but I want to talk to him about your protection. Maybe now, he'll believe me."

"Don't tell me you're sick of me already."

"Don't be silly, of course I'm not." His tone was maybe a little too defensive. "I just think you'd be safer under proper police protection."

"I was only kidding, don't be so touchy."

"I'm not touchy. I'm just worried about you, that's all."

"I know. And that's nice."

It was thirty minutes later when they walked up to the Desk Sergeant at Stonegate.

"Good afternoon, Inspector, Mrs Willis," he greeted, noticing it was now ten minutes after noon. "Sergeant Buckle is on his way, and the superintendent is waiting in his office. Mr Ramachandran is in number one interrogation room."

"Thank you, and Sergeant, I need two more police officers to watch over Mrs Willis."

"I'll get Finnegan and White Sir."

"That'll be great. I can't impress upon you enough my fears about Mrs Willis' safety."

"You needn't worry, Sir. Mrs Willis is safe in my care."

Margaret and Harrigan said their good-byes, and Harrigan walked down the corridor to the superintendent's office.

Harrigan knocked on the wooden door. The word Superintendent was printed in gold lettering with a brown shadow on the frosted glass panel.

"Come In!" came the shouted reply.

"Good afternoon,. Sir."

"Come in, come in! Shut the door! Sit down!" Superintendent Wilkinson's obvious agitation made his speech rapid. Almost stuttered. "What the hell's going on Inspector? I've had the Commissioner ringing me and he's been ringing me because the home office has been ringing him! What the hell is going on Inspector?" he repeated.

Harrigan knew this was not the time to be flippant. He occupied the chair opposite his superior and, as calmly and briefly as possible, outlined all the events that had taken place since the first body had been found in the Goldberg building. He did omit some of the details of the previous evening, of course.

"And that, Sir, is where we're at," he concluded.

"You really believe that Mahmood is involved in all this?"

"To some degree, yes, definitely. But people like Mahmood are never close enough to get caught. They employ others to do their dirty work. Like getting the Home Office to annoy you through the Commissioner."

"I'll pretend I didn't hear that and ask you another way. Do you think Ramachandran is working under Mahmood's instructions?"

"I honestly don't know, Sir. I'm not sure how much of Ramachandran's behaviour is under instruction or how much is his own work. One thing I am certain of is that Sidhu Trading isn't the all-honest and above-board organisation Mahmood likes to make it out to be. And I am equally certain that Mahmood knows and condones whatever is going on there. But like I said, to what degree Ramachandran operates within Mahmood's knowledge and to what degree he operates on his own, for his own gain, I haven't been able to work out, yet, but I will."

"It's a brave man who would doublecross Mahmood."

Harrigan was taken by surprise by his boss's candid remark. He figured now was as good a time to ask the next question.

"I'd like to reopen the case involving Archibald Lapsley-Midwinter's disappearance. The paedophile case if you remember, Sir?"

"Of course, I bloody remember. Why the hell do you want to open that can of worms again?"

Harrigan had a theory. He was sure he now knew how Lapsley-Midwinter had disappeared and how he could trace him, but he didn't want to confide in Wilkinson just yet. It wasn't that he had any doubt that his superintendent was an honest and honourable cop, but it had been Harrigan's experience that the higher up the promotion ladder people climbed, the less likely they were to stick their necks out. It seemed that the lack of bottle needed to seek out the truth, no matter what the consequences, increased in direct proportion with promotion.

"The Margaret Willis connection, Sir," Harrigan said, choosing to offer a half-truth. "The threatening telephone call, Mahmood's veiled threat to me at The Badgers, and Mahmood's dinner guests at Ali's."

"Oh come on, Inspector, Mahmood's dinner guests?"

"I agree that on its own, it doesn't mean much. But coupled with the threats, especially the threat to Mrs Willis, I think it is significant. Businessmen and Bankers I can understand, but clergymen and judges? Give me a break!"

Harrigan watched as Wilkinson's inner conflict played its role across his worried face. He knew his leader was searching deep, looking for the bottle to give tacit approval to reopen what was obviously a very sensitive case.

"I'll see what I can do. If I can get it reopened, you must promise me you'll be discreet. You must be discreet, and of course, you must keep me informed."

"Yes, Sir!" It wasn't so much that Wilkinson had agreed to look into reopening the case that spurred Harrigan's enthusiasm, because Harrigan would have reopened it anyway. It was the fact that Wilkinson was able to grasp the nettle.

"Oh and one last thing, Sir, if I may?"

"Would it make any difference if I said no?"

"No, not really, Sir. It's about police protection for Mrs Willis. I believe she is in real danger. Mrs Singhabahu's death shows there is no compunction about killing a woman, and I will be poking around the Lapsley-Midwinter case again, so…"

Wilkinson waved his hand in defeat. "Alright, alright. See Sergeant Davis. I'm sure he'll be able to arrange it." He placed his arms on the desk. "Anything else?"

Sarcasm can tend to end a conversation, so Harrigan nodded appreciatively and left the room.

"Oh, Inspector!"

Harrigan reopened the door. "Yes, Sir?"

"How's McIver getting along?"

"Great, Sir. He is a good police officer."

"How's Sergeant Buckle taking it?"

"No problems, Sir. They're the best of mates, if you know what I mean."

"Yes, Inspector, I know what you mean."

* * *

Margaret and Harrigan argued about the level of police protection she was to receive. He wanted her taken to a safe house where protection could be assured. She was determined to move back into her own home.

"I'm tired of living like a damn gypsy, Bill. Please, let me take your two police officers and move back home. I'll be alright!"

Realising he was not going to win the argument, Harrigan relented, albeit reluctantly. He did however satisfy himself that Constables Finnegan and White were fully aware of their responsibilities, and a little more at ease, he watched as Margaret left the police station flanked by the two officers.

"Don't worry, Inspector, they're two good officers."

Harrigan turned to the man standing behind him.

"I know, Bill, but thanks anyway." He walked inside the building. "I'm sorry to get you in today, Sergeant."

Harrigan explained to Sergeant Buckle in brief summary, the events of the morning. How Aysha was killed and the instrument used. The testimony of Senior Constable Blake and Sergeant

Middleham's recount of the neighbour's statement. The items packed in the suitcase, Ramachandran's initial explanation, and his reaction when Mahmood's man arrived.

"I wanted you to listen to Ramachandran's version of events first hand."

"Do you think he did it, Sir?"

"Everything points in that direction, Sergeant."

As the two men walked down the poorly lit corridor, Harrigan counted three fluorescent tubes not working and one with that annoying flicker fluorescent tubes get.

"You'd think we could afford a few bloody fluorescent tubes in this place."

He opened the door to number one interrogation room. Ramachandran sat at the wooden table, an empty mug in front of him. Harrigan spoke to the constable sitting against the wall.

"Everything alright, Constable?"

"Yes, Sir."

"Hello again, Mr Ramachandran, you know Sergeant Buckle."

Ramachandran nodded quietly.

"Would you like another cup of tea?"

"It was coffee. But no, no thank you."

"Thank you, Constable. Wait outside. We'll call you if we need you."

"Very good Sir."

The room echoed slightly as the door closed. Harrigan and Bill Buckle sat across the table from the man who was now looking less confident than the man who had left the scene of Aysha Singhabahu's murder. He was the first to speak.

"I've been thinking, Inspector, about everything that's happened. It doesn't look good for me, does it?"

"Well, to be honest with you Mr Rama…Ram, it could look better. But let's not get ahead of ourselves. There're a few formalities we must get over and done with."

Harrigan pushed the switch that activated a tape recorder.

"First of all, I must explain that this interview is being recorded. The time is twelve forty-five p.m., Sunday twenty-third of April. This interview is being conducted by Inspector Harrigan, accompanied by Sergeant Buckle. The person being interviewed is Mr Khalil Ramachandran in the matter of the murder of Mrs Aysha Singhabahu." Although Ramachandran hadn't been arrested or charged with a crime, Harrigan performed the ritual of explaining his rights.

"I understand, Inspector."

"I must also explain to you, Mr Ramachandran, that you are entitled to have legal representation present and, in a matter such as this, it is my duty to advise you that legal representation is recommended. Do you wish legal representation at this time?"

"No. Not at this time. I will inform you."

"Very well."

"I have done nothing, Inspector!" Ramachandran could wait no longer. "I did not murder Aysha. My heavens, I loved her."

"No one is accusing you of anything, Mr Ramachandran. We are simply trying to formalise your statement of the events."

"I'm sorry. I understand."

"I want you to tell me everything that happened this morning. Just the way you told me at the murder scene. Take your time, and start when you received the telephone call from Aysha."

Ramachandran began his story. The details varied little from what he had said earlier. Harrigan noted the story was not told word for word, like it had been rehearsed, but more like an explanation of events as he remembered them for the second time.

The frantic telephone call from Aysha and his wild drive across London. His ringing the bell and banging on the door. How he smashed the glass and stumbled across the dark room to turn off the alarm, knocking over the pedestal ashtray. His actions when he first saw the body. Why he picked up the ashtray and how he was standing over the body, realising that it must have been the murder weapon when the Police arrived.

"And that's about all I can tell you, Inspector."

"As a regular visitor to the Singhabahu's house, didn't you have a key? Why smash the glass?" Harrigan asked.

"I, well yes, I do have a key. It is on my car keys. I don't know why I didn't think of it. I remember I'd left my keys in my car and, my goodness, the keys are still in the car, I hope someone doesn't steal it!"

"Your car is safe, Heathwich Police are bringing it over here. Please, continue telling us about the broken door glass."

"As I was saying, I'd left my keys in the ignition and I...I just didn't think to get them. I panicked I guess. All I wanted to do was to get inside as quickly as possible. Nothing else mattered. For heavens sake, Inspector, you talk as if you suspect *me* of killing Aysha."

"If you didn't kill Mrs Singhabahu, who do you think did?"

"I don't know, Inspector. How could I know?"

"Did she have any enemies?" Bill Buckle asked.

"No! Aysha could not have enemies."

"A jealous lover, perhaps?" Harrigan baited.

Ramachandran sprang to his feet. "No! Aysha was not like that!" He thumped the table as his voice reverberated around the sparsely furnished room.

"Please, sit down, Mr Ramachandran," Harrigan said quietly.

"Yes, of course. I'm sorry, Inspector."

"That's the second time today you've lost your temper over Mrs Singhabahu. I know this is a very trying time for you, Ram, but I must admit, I think there's a little more to it than that."

"More?"

"Yes. I think jealousy is the primary reason for your outbursts of temper." Harrigan remained deliberately calm.

"Jealousy, Inspector?" Ramachandran laughed as he also returned to a level of quiet control. "Aysha was a married woman. What right would I have to be jealous?"

"You and Aysha were lovers, Ram, and she is, was a beautiful woman."

"Yes, I cannot deny she was a beautiful woman." Ramachandran had regained his composure.

"Did you love her?"

"Aysha was my partner's wife. I had no claim to love."

"But it was alright to have an affair?"

"There is a big difference between trying to come between two people and satisfying the physical desire of one of them. Manjit and Aysha were never in love; it was an arranged marriage. I simply filled a need."

"Did you know that in many situations like yours, it's the *lover* who is the most jealous?"

"What has that to do with me, Inspector?"

"You *really* don't know what I'm trying to say to you?"

"No. Please tell me."

"I think you were insanely jealous of Aysha's other affair," Harrigan said bluntly.

"*Other* affair! What the devil are you talking about?" The tone of ignorance did not quite work.

"Her affair with Mahmood." Harrigan took a long shot.

Ramachandran raised his voice and slammed an open hand on the table. "That's preposterous! I will not hear such things of Aysha."

Harrigan was no longer the quiet and calm questioner. He was now the inquisitor. "Aysha was having an affair with Mahmood, and don't try and tell me you didn't know!" Harrigan sprang to his feet and leaned with both fists firmly on the desk top. He started down at the angry man opposite. "You were eaten up with jealousy Ramachandran, not only because you thought you were being betrayed, but also because there was nothing you could do about it."

"No!" he screamed.

"I know Aysha telephoned you early this morning, but not to beg you to come over. She rang to gloat that Mahmood was going to take her away. She was to become his mistress."

Bill Buckle had no idea how Harrigan knew about the affair between Mahmood and Aysha. What he didn't know, of course, was that Harrigan didn't know! He was just trying his luck.

"No! No, that's not true!"

Harrigan walked around the table. He leaned close to Ramachandran's frightened face. "You killed Manjit so you could have her for yourself, and—"

"No! No! I had nothing to do with Manjit's death."

"And when Aysha rang and told you she was going to leave and live with Mahmood, you lost control. In a fit of jealous rage, you raced over there, and when Aysha was too frightened to let you in, you smashed your way in, picked up the ashtray and killed her! That's why you didn't use your key. That's why you smashed the door glass. Now isn't that the way it happened? Isn't that the truth?" Harrigan's threatening voice boomed across the room.

Ramachandran went quiet. He sat back in his chair, bowed his head, his hands clasped in his lap.

"I think it's time I had my lawyer," he said quietly. "I'm not saying another word."

Harrigan moved back to his side of the table and reached for the tape recorder button. "Interrogation ended at 1.00 p.m. Let's go, Sergeant."

The two policemen left the room.

"Constable, arrange for Mr Ramachandran to call his lawyer. Offer him a cup of tea or whatever he wants, within reason, of course. But make sure there is always somebody with him."

"Yes, Sir."

"Sergeant Buckle and I will be in my office. Call me when his Brief gets here."

"Certainly, Sir."

"Come on Sergeant, let's put the Billy on."

Bill Buckle nodded and they walked to the kitchen. They talked small talk as they shared the duties of tea making. Harrigan filled the kettle and got the lemon juice and sugar, Bill Buckle the mugs, tea, and milk. The biscuits were soft.

Before joining Harrigan in his office, Bill Buckle excused himself, walked to the front desk, and spoke briefly to Sergeant Davis.

Harrigan and Buckle spent the next twenty-five minutes talking about the case to date and planning the sergeant's investigation into Wei Lee the next morning.

"I can't impress upon you enough to be bloody careful, I don't want you ending up like Aysha Singhabahu."

"You needn't be concerned, Sir, I've been around a long time."

"Just take extra care, that's all."

The telephone rang. It was an internal call. Harrigan looked through the glass toward the front desk as he lifted the receiver.

"Harrigan."

"Sergeant Harris, Sir. Mr Ramachandran's lawyer is here. He is with Ramachandran now."

"Thank you, Sergeant."

"Let's go, Sergeant."

As they entered the corridor leading to the interrogation rooms, Harrigan noted the improved illumination. He looked towards Bill Buckle.

"Sergeant Davis must have had the tubes replaced, Sir, he's very efficient." Bill Buckle said.

"Sergeant Davis, eh? I don't suppose you had anything to do with it?" He nodded to the constable standing outside the door of interrogation room one.

"Any problems, Constable?"

"None, Sir."

They entered the room.

A very distinguished man with silver-grey hair, smooth light-olive-coloured skin, wearing a dark blue tailored pin striped suit and tie stood and faced Harrigan.

"Abraham Steinbeck. I am Mr Ramachandran's legal representative."

Harrigan shook the outstretched hand displaying three enormous gold rings.

"I'm Inspector Harrigan; this is Sergeant Buckle. Mr Ramachandran is indeed fortunate to have such eminent representation."

Harrigan knew of Steinbeck. He was one of London's senior criminal lawyers with a reputation of ruthlessness and winning at any cost.

"My client tells me you have already interviewed him and accused him of some very serious crimes, Inspector. I trust you advised Mr Ramachandran that he was entitled to legal representation before you took such aggressive action?"

"I not only advised him, I recommended he get legal representation. It was Mr Ramachandran's choice not to be represented. I can play you the tape."

"I don't need to hear it at this time. Mr Ramachandran has filled me in. I'll get a transcript later."

"Alright, then, let's get this over with." Harrigan started the tape and again introduced the parties in attendance, this time including the legal man.

"Mr Ramachandran, can you tell me of your whereabouts on the evening of Monday the twelfth and early morning of Tuesday the thirteenth?"

"I was with Aysha." It was obvious that Ramachandran was back to his confident self.

"From what time?"

"I went to her house at around eight p.m. I stayed all night."

"Can anyone verify that?"

"Only Aysha."

"And she's dead."

"Yes, Inspector, unfortunately she is."

"Anyone else see you that night? Did you stop for petrol? Buy flowers? Anything?"

"No, Inspector."

"What about the neighbours?"

"You'll have to ask them."

"Are you telling me that you were nowhere near the Goldberg building?"

"How could I be? I was at Aysha's."

"Did you kill Manjit?"

Ramachandran restrained his legal representative. "No, Inspector, I did not."

"Did you know Mr Wei Yu Lee?"

"Was he the other man found in the ruins?"

"That's correct."

"No. I have never heard of him."

Harrigan produced a photograph of Wei Lee. "You have never seen this man?"

Ramachandran picked up the photograph and studied it closely. "Well I'm not one hundred percent sure, Inspector. Orientals all tend to look alike to me, but he has a strong resemblance to one of our clients. Mr Lee Fong."

"What was your relationship with Mr Fong?"

"He was an importer-exporter. We conducted his shipping business, Inspector. That's what we do, we're a shipping company." He looked to Steinbeck who just smiled.

"Do you have any idea why his passport identifies him as Wei Yu Lee?"

"I have no idea, Inspector. You'd have to ask him. But then he is no longer with us either, is he?"

Harrigan knew he was getting nowhere. He changed his attack to the murder of Aysha Singhabahu. Ramachandran stuck firmly to his story.

"Come now, Inspector." Steinbeck finally interrupted. "We are just going around in circles. My client has denied your accusations and the time has come for you to either charge my client or release him."

Harrigan didn't argue. He knew Steinbeck was right. He probably had enough evidence to hold Ramachandran on the Aysha murder. He could establish motive and opportunity. He could definitely establish Ramachandran was there and that his fingerprints were the only ones on the murder weapon. But there was one part of Ramachandran's story that left Harrigan uneasy.

Harrigan noted the time and turned off the tape recorder. He stood.

"Thank you for helping us with our inquiries, Mr Ramachandran. You are free to go. Your car is parked outside, and the desk sergeant has the keys. But please, do not leave London, and I will require you to surrender your passport."

"Really, Inspector!" began Steinbeck. "You have no right—"

"It's alright, Abraham," Ramachandran said, "I didn't kill those people, and I'm not planning to go anywhere. My passport is at my office. If one of your men would like to accompany me?"

"Thank you, Mr Ramachandran."

* * *

Bill Buckle occupied his usual chair in Harrigan's office. Harrigan stood at the liquor cabinet, his back to the sergeant.

"Whisky, Sergeant?" Harrigan spoke into the cabinet.

"Just a small one, Sir."

Harrigan carried two substantial Ballantines to his desk and, having placed one in front of himself, passed the other across to Bill Buckle. Looking at the quantity of liquid in the glass, Bill Buckle was glad he had only asked for a small one.

"I know you're wondering why I didn't charge him with Aysha's murder, and to be honest with you, I am not overly certain myself."

"Then why didn't you, Sir?"

"The timing of the alarm, Sergeant. There's just something that doesn't quite fit. If you remember, Ramachandran said he rang the bell, knocked on the door, smashed the glass, opened the door, and the alarm went off. He said he stumbled across the room in the dark and turned off the alarm. He then switched the lights on and saw Aysha lying on the floor."

"That's correct, that's his story," Bill Buckle agreed.

"The witness' story agrees with that. The witness also says that the police only took two minutes to get there."

"Maybe it took longer," Bill Buckle suggested

"Maybe it did, but not much longer. Senior Constable Blake said they were in the next street. So, if Ramachandran is lying and he did kill her, when did he do it? Before he turned off the alarm...in the dark?"

"I see your point." Bill Buckle thought for a minute. "It must have been after he turned off the alarm."

"Then where was Aysha? Would she have just stood waiting in the dark for this jealous lover to turn off the alarm, turn on the lights, pick up the ashtray, and bludgeon her to death? Highly unlikely I'd say."

"Are you saying that Ramachandran didn't kill her?"

"No. I'm saying we have to be absolutely sure we can prove it. I've just given you the scene as Steinbeck would portray it in court. What could have happened, was that after Aysha had telephoned Ramachandran to brag that she was to be Mahmood's mistress—"

"How do you know she was going to be his mistress?" Bill Buckle challenged.

"The suitcase. On her previous visits she had taken an overnight bag. This time, she took a suitcase. I'm guessing she was moving out for good. And don't forget, Fadhel came around to pick her up that morning."

"With respect, Sir, that doesn't prove anything."

"No, not in itself. But remember the items that were packed in the suitcase. All her personal trinkets. Two of her favourite photographs and *all* her jewellery. More importantly, she had packed only the basic clothing needs." He took a long thoughtful draught of whisky. "This, Sergeant, suggests she was moving away from her old life, or at least thought she was going to move away from the old life. Going to start over. And when a woman like Aysha starts anew, what is she going to want?"

"A new wardrobe of clothes."

"And shoes, Sergeant, don't forget the shoes."

It was the Sergeant's turn to take a thoughtful drink, as he listened as Harrigan continued to hypothesize.

"On the other hand, what *could* have happened was that Aysha realised how stupid it had been to ring Ramachandran and became frightened. When he arrived, she left the lights off and tried to hold the door shut, hoping the noise would attract attention and someone would come to help her. Neighbours... maybe even Mahmood's man. Of course, Ramachandran was much too strong, forced open the door, grabbed Aysha, and dragged her to the alarm pad and turned off the alarm. He turned on the lights, grabbed the ashtray and killed her. He was standing over her body when the police arrived."

Bill Buckle pictured the events as described and agreed it was possible. "You said she *thought* she was going to move away from the old life. You think Mahmood might have had other ideas?"

"Aysha was a very dangerous woman, Sergeant. She had been married to the murdered Manjit. She had been sleeping with Manjit's partner. It would be difficult to believe that she didn't know a lot about the more...intimate details of the Sidhu Trading operation."

"Pillow talk?"

"That's right. I have no proof, yet, but I suspect Sidhu Trading is not as squeaky clean as the image it likes to portray. As a

Shipping company, Sidhu Trading is in the perfect position for certain illicit operations."

"Importation of drugs?"

"Could be."

"You think Wei Yu Lee could be connected with some drug operation?"

"It's on the cards. But Wei Lee aside, let's just say I'm right and Sidhu Trading is mixed up in the drug trade. If either Manjit or Ramachandran had spilled the beans in a moment of heated passion, Aysha could have been a very dangerous woman to some people."

"Including Mahmood?"

"Especially Mahmood. And remember, Aysha had also been having a bit of the other with Mahmood as well."

"He's not the type to let something slip.'"

"No, but Aysha was an ambitious woman. She wanted to impress Mahmood. Maybe she hinted at what she knew."

"If she knew anything."

"Granted, but let's assume she did know something and she told Mahmood. If Mahmood's reaction to Margaret Willis' comments in the taxi is anything to go by, Aysha wouldn't have needed to know much to put her in danger."

Harrigan lay back and stared at the old sergeant as he again took a long, soothing swallow of the golden liquid.

Bill Buckle placed his glass heavily on the table. A small drop of whisky bounced out onto the table. "Let me get this right, Inspector. Are you suggesting that Mahmood may have set this whole thing up? Get rid of Aysha and blame Ramachandran?"

"It wouldn't have been difficult for Mahmood to persuade Aysha to pack a few personal items. To leave everything behind and start afresh. We must remember she *wanted* to believe it."

"Mahmood's man could have forced Aysha to make the telephone call," Bill Buckle suggested.

"Maybe, but I am more inclined to think she probably did it willingly. She was a spiteful woman."

"And knowing Ramachandran would rush over, Mahmood's man killed Aysha, and cleaned off the fingerprints." Bill Buckle was beginning to share Harrigan's enthusiasm.

"Or wore gloves," Harrigan said.

"Yes, or wore gloves, and then left the ashtray somewhere, where it would be in the way."

"Ramachandran picking up the ashtray may just have been a bonus, but either way, he would have been at the scene. The police patrolled the area constantly and would hear the alarm and come quickly. It wouldn't take much to build a case."

The two men finished their drinks and sat staring thoughtfully at the desk. The loud ticking of the clock was the only sound.

"So, Inspector, who do you think killed Aysha Singhabahu, Ramachandran or Mahmood's man?"

"I wish it were that simple, Sergeant. We mustn't forget the people in the drug trade itself. They're not known for their kindness and compassion. If Manjit had become greedy and double-crossed some illicit drug organisation, maybe it was they who killed both Manjit and Aysha. "

"So which one was it, Sir?" Bill Buckle asked, continuing to push Harrigan for an opinion.

Harrigan reached across the table and with the index finger of his right hand, wiped the spilled drop of whisky from the table.

"I have no idea, Sergeant." he replied honestly as he sucked his finger.

CHAPTER EIGHT

Monday morning at Stonegate was a hive of activity. Bill Buckle hadn't stayed for another drink yesterday afternoon, choosing instead to *"pop down to the Hound's for a couple of pints."* Harrigan hadn't been all that concerned with being left alone; if the truth were known, it was what he'd needed. With more twists and turns than a coast road in Scotland, this case was proving to be most difficult. Of course, his stirred emotions towards Margaret Willis, plus his concern for her safety, added to his mother being in hospital, and hadn't had any positive effect on his concentration. He needed some time alone to put his thoughts in order. Not that he was one for being overly absorbed with getting things into too much order, much like his father, really. *Little ducks in a row mentality* was his father's expression. His father had always been respectful of authority, but as a child, Harrigan would often hear his parents talking in the kitchen. *"Damn bureaucrats,"* he would hear his father say, *"spend too much time getting all their little ducks in row, instead of concentrating on the main game!"* To which his mother would reply, *"would you like another cup of tea, Dear?"*

Bill Harrigan preferred a well-thought-out, overall or general strategy, which gave direction with flexibility. With the comfort of two very large Ballantines and the ticking of the old clock, Harrigan had spent two hours of quiet contemplation. He was satisfied with the evidence they had gathered so far, and he was sure he was close to finding out what had happened. But there were still a few gaps preventing it all from fitting together. Not to his satisfaction, anyway. There was still more evidence to be gathered, and that's what needed to be done, now. Knowing some of the answers was a long step from proving what happened beyond all reasonable doubt. That was always the hard part. He'd left the office the previous evening feeling much more content with the world.

The buzz of Monday morning chatter filled Harrigan's office. Bill Buckle sat in "his" chair opposite the desk. Patricia Hedrich sat in the other chair against the wall. She didn't like to intrude into the conversation. She saw her position as listening quietly and noting the tasks that would need to be done behind the scenes. Those seemingly unimportant tasks that held the fabric of the whole thing together. Colin McIver leaned against the cocktail cabinet with Malcolm Watts walking uncomfortably around the room.

"For heavens sake, Constable, find somewhere to settle!" Harrigan said impatiently.

"I'm sorry, Sir."

It wasn't so much the situation that made Malcolm Watts uneasy, he just wasn't used to the idea of coming to work without his uniform. He had been wearing that uniform for a long time.

He wore his uniform with pride, drawing confidence from its respect and tradition. He felt almost naked wearing street clothes.

"Don't worry, Malcolm," McIver whispered confidentially, "you'll get used to it." The DSC's understanding tone eased some of his anxiety.

"Thank you, Senior."

Silence fell over the room as Harrigan positioned his now empty tea mug to one side of the desk and sat back noisily in his chair.

"Good morning again, people. Sorry there are not enough chairs, but we'll get this over as quickly as possible. You are all familiar with the facts of the case, and I am not going to waste everyone's time going over them again in finite detail. If anyone has any questions, see me later. Broadly, we have three bodies. All three deaths occurred in distinctly different ways. The mutilated and charred body of Manjit Singhabahu, the suffocated body of Wei Lee, and Aysha Singhabahu struck on the head and killed early yesterday morning. We have a selection of suspects, all with opportunity and a variety of motives. We also have one of the world's richest and most powerful men in the equation, and that, of course, means we have the bloody Home Office breathing down our necks, watching our every move." He paused as he leaned forward and rested his arms on the desk. "And we all know how I feel about the Home Office sticking its nose in, don't we?"

There was a sound of general uncomfortable shuffling.

"The other thing we all know is that results are the only way to keep them at bay. So, Bill, I want you and Senior Watts to go to Chinatown."

"London, Sir?"

"London, Birmingham, Manchester. I don't particularly care, Sergeant. I want you to take a photograph of Wei Yu Lee and see if you can find out some more about him."

"Yes, Sir."

He had already talked to Bill Buckle about this, but for the benefit of the others in the room, Harrigan continued. "I think there is a good chance that Wei Lee had a connection to the illicit drug trade." His attention returned to Bill Buckle and Malcolm Watts. "I want you to be careful. No heroics. Keep your eyes out and watch your backs. We don't know what toes Wei Lee may have trodden on so take every precaution, is that clear?"

"Yes, Sir," the two voices replied in unison.

His attention transferred to Colin McIver.

"I'm afraid your job is nowhere near as exciting, Senior. I want you to investigate the financial affairs of Ramachandran and Manjit Singh. Look at Aysha Singhabahu as well."

"What am I looking for?"

"I'll be able to tell you that, once you've found it. I also want you to do some more investigation on Lee. I want to know how long he has been a citizen of America. What he does there. Get your friend in the Embassy to help you."

Anticipating the question he knew they all wanted to ask but did not believe it their place to ask, Harrigan leaned back and placed his hands behind his head.

"In case you were wondering, I'm going to reopen the Lapsley-Midwinter disappearance case."

"Lapsley-Midwinter? Wasn't he the Supreme Court judge who disappeared in the paedophile case that involved Lord... Lord..." McIver struggled to recall the name.

"Banbury. That's right, Senior Constable, you know your business."

"Thank you, Sir. But may I ask why you think that that case has something to do with this case?"

"I'm not sure that it does. It's the Mahmood connection I'm interested in. Remember, Mrs Willis was threatened because of the connection she made with Mahmood and the paedophile case," Harrigan reminded everyone.

"But how does that help *this* case?" McIver was determined to understand all there was to know about this case.

"Mahmood is a very cunning man, Senior. He is an expert in gaining the upper hand. I figure that if we can investigate him on two fronts, it may distract him enough to put the odds a little in our favour."

He sat forward. "Anything else?"

He was met with silence.

"Alright then, let's get to work."

As the room emptied, Harrigan sat quietly and checked his in-tray. With nothing of any importance to take him away from the current investigation, he reached for the telephone. It was nine-thirty in the morning, so there should be someone at Scotland Yard who could arrange for him to have access to the Lapsley-Midwinter file. He had only dialled three numbers, when a brief knock on his door announced his superintendent. Harrigan replaced the hand piece and stood.

"Good morning, Sir."

"Good morning, Inspector." Wilkinson walked across the room and dropped two fairly substantial files on the desk. "The file on the Lapsley-Midwinter case. I picked it up from the Yard this morning. Take good care of it."

"Thank you, Sir." Harrigan was somewhat taken aback by the Superintendent's cooperation in the matter. Without saying another word, the senior policeman simply nodded the way bosses do and walked to the door. As he reached the door, he called over his shoulder. "I don't like paedophiles, any more than you do, Inspector." It was Harrigan's turn to smile.

He settled into his chair and removed the huge rubber band from one of the manila folders. He flicked through the file scanning the typed documents. Thousands of words typed on hundreds of reports, many he recognised as his own. He paused as memories of working at the Yard filled his mind.

* * *

As Bill Buckle left Harrigan's office, Patricia Hedrich called him over and handed him a photograph of Wei Yu Lee.

"That was the best one in the file, Bill."

"Thanks Patricia."

With the photograph nestled in the inside pocket of his tweed jacket, Bill Buckle and Senior Constable Malcolm Watts rode together on the tube train. If there was one thing that Bill Buckle hated more than driving in London, it was trying to find somewhere suitable to park. As he didn't possess his inspector's cavalier attitude toward parking, he found it more convenient to use the train. It was probably quicker in the long run anyway.

They left the Underground at Leicester Square and took the Little Newport St. exit.

Chinatown in London was like the many similar Chinatowns across the world. All welcomed visitors through a large Green and Red pagoda, usually decorated with dragons and flanked by two fairly ugly lions. Generally, the streets had an appearance of being narrower than one would expect and, of course, they were always crowded. Thousands of visitors from all parts of the world were drawn to these areas by the flavour of mystique and hypnotic aroma so abundant in any Chinatown. But despite this mixture of race and skin colour, people of Chinese appearance always dominated.

Bill Buckle had rarely visited Chinatown. It wasn't that he deliberately stayed away, he just never found a reason to go.

Being a well-trained and instinctive policeman, he stood at the head of the street trying to gain a small insight into the character of the area. This was very important in police work. When entering into unfamiliar surroundings, a policeman should always try to absorb some degree of *feel* for the area. In areas where the British culture had been clouded with cultures of other lands, the *feel* wasn't always easy to find.

The first thing that struck him as his eyes searched the streets and buildings, was the wide variety of what he would describe as *social difference* that seemed to co-exist here. The elegantly dressed young Chinese businesswoman in her tailored suit, looking striking against the man garbed in tee shirt and baggy trousers, unloading plastic crates from a dented and rusty delivery van; the young men smartly dressed, albeit in casual clothes; the supermarket owner standing at the doorway, arms folded, watching suspiciously up and down the street; his wife working behind the counter of his shop and an old man with stooped shoulders filing the shelves.

The shops and restaurants had mostly exotic names while the advertising, although bright, was generally boring. In the old sergeant's opinion, the suggested mystery implied in the name the East August Moon Restaurant seemed to lose some of its mystique when it was written in red tubular neon letters.

Looking at the almost overpowering quantity of gaudy advertising up and down both sides of the street, he came to the conclusion that the latest S Class Mercedes, radiant in contrasting black and parked outside the Jin Wan Sang Martial Arts academy, just had to be the property of the man who owned the neon light factory.

"Well we might as well get started," he commented unnecessarily.

They entered a small Chinese delicatessen. The old lady's head was barely visible between the rich brown carcasses of what looked to be cooked rabbits and ducks that hung from hooks above the counter. The counter itself was over-loaded with a variety of cellophane packets of ingredients foreign to the Bill Buckle's palate. He picked up two bags and read the labels. Dried mushrooms and dried shark cartilage, interesting.

"You want to buy?" It was a demand more than a question.

"No, no thank you." With some element of embarrassment, he replaced the two packets.

"Then what you want?"

"My name is Sergeant Buckle, and this is Senior Constable Watts. We're from the Stonegate Police." The old lady stared closely at the ID across the counter. She looked up warily.

"What you want?" There was more than a hint of impatience in her repeated demand.

He bowed his head below what was one of the biggest fowls he had ever seen.

"I wondered if you recognise this man."

Again she stared closely, this time at the photograph of Wei Yu Lee. Considering it was taken after his death, he looked fairly peaceful. He could have simply been asleep.

"He dead?" She asked.

"Do you recognise him?"

She turned away sharply and called loudly to someone Buckle assumed to be in the back room.

"You wait," she ordered, as she disappeared behind a pile of greenery labelled *Ting Yen Dried Seaweed*.

Bill Buckle looked at his companion who by now wore a look of quiet amusement. "What are you bloody smiling at?"

"How'd you like to be married to her?" Watts replied.

It was Bill Buckle's turn to smile.

"What you want?" The two policemen turned toward the male voice that had uttered the now familiar question.

"Good morning, Sir." Bill Buckle said to the old stoop-shouldered man. The man was dressed in what most people from other cultures would picture a hard working Chinese person to wear: slippers with no socks, baggy trousers that always appear just a little too short, and a loose fitting tee shirt upper garment. Introductions having been completed, the old man looked at the photograph.

"Never see."

"Are you certain you don't know this man?"

"Never see!" The old man shoved the photograph roughly into Bill Buckle's hand. "Now you go!"

"Well that went well," Malcolm Watts commented, as they stood on the footpath outside.

"I think we may well be used to it by the time we've finished here today."

"You won't get any argument from me about that."

And their prediction wasn't far from the truth. While the reception they received may have varied, the level of cooperation didn't waver.

From supermarkets stocked with seaweed cookies and tinned Leechee Nuts, to the watchmaker with hundreds of hand-made clocks ticking loudly on the walls, every clock with a tassel of either red or gold, dangling from each ornate crevice, the answer was the same. The fast food BBQ shop with its roasted ducks hanging by their necks, darkened restaurants lit only by a soft glow reflecting off pastel wall murals. Shops selling frozen Shark cartilage, powdered shark cartilage, shark cartilage capsules, Ginseng soup and Jasmine tea. It was the first time that either man had visited a twenty-four-hour karaoke nightclub. Malcolm Watts considered asking his Sergeant how you could have a twenty-four-hour *night*club, but thought better of it.

The jewellery shops, souvenir shops, and currency exchange were all very polite but still there was no recognition of the man in the photograph that, by now, was looking a little the worse for wear.

"Don't say we didn't leave the best to last," Buckle said, as he looked up at the old painted sign above the narrow doorway.

"Jing Wan Sang Martial Art Academy," he read aloud.

The dusty windows of the three-story building were either half-open or broken. What was left of the security speaker alongside the open doorway hung by one red electrical wire. A once proud brass plaque remained screwed to the wall, embarrassed by its pitted and stained face. He looked through to the old wooden stairs at the end of the darkened hall. A tenant board hung awkwardly on the smoke-stained walls. The sizes of the once white plastic letters pushed into the black notice board, varied as they had been replaced over time. Many letters that had been taken or had fallen off had not been replaced.

The sound of martial arts combatants going through their paces and the smell of scented cigarettes filled the hall.

"So this is an Academy," Bill Buckle said, failing miserably to hide the sarcasm.

"It must be, Sergeant, it says so on the sign out the front."

It took just under half an hour to visit Charlie Chan's Poolroom, the Adult Book shop, a small and untidy business advertising Novelties and, of course, the Martial Arts Academy. The fifth tenant was more interesting. Gabriel Ye owned and operated the Eastern Import and Export Company. His answers to Bill Buckle's simple questions were sufficiently vague to encourage the police Sergeant to continue his line of questioning.

"Alright, Mr Ye, let's go back to the beginning. Why don't you tell me and the constable here, exactly what it is you actually import and export."

"I've already told you, Sergeant, we don't export very much. England not very good at making things for export."

"You don't have to rub it in, Mr Ye, we already know that."

"Sorry to upset, Sergeant, but I only tell truth," he continued before Bill Buckle had time to react. "But we import all types of things. Clothes, souvenirs, tin food, that sort of stuff. Most of it goes to stallholders at markets. All over the country," he said proudly. "You wait. I get you some Bills of Lading, I can show you." He began to rise.

"That won't be necessary, Mr Ye, not at this time." He motioned for him to retake his seat.

"Have you heard of Sidhu Trading?"

"Of course." He looked away.

"Do you do business with them?"

"Sometimes. You must do business with organisation that size," he continued to talk to the wall beside his desk. The cockiness in his voice had been replaced with a quiet mumble.

"*Must* do business?" Bill Buckle pressed harder.

"Please, Sergeant, what you are looking for?" He leaned forward, resting on the old wooden desk. "Why you here anyway?"

"I told you, routine inquiries. Now what did you mean when you said *must* do business?"

"Sergeant, I have nothing to tell you. You been here too long, please go. People around here will know who you are and, and they will think I've been talking."

"Talking about what?"

"It no matter. We are a close community, Sergeant. We take care of our own business. We don't need others interfering in our affairs, it is as simple as that. Please Sergeant, if you have something to ask me, please you ask, then you go. If not ask, will you and your colleague please leave?"

Gabriel Ye's command of the English language varied enormously.

"Do you know this man?" Bill Buckle threw the photograph onto the desk.

The reaction from the man sitting across from Bill Buckle, although fleeting, was enough to tell the old sergeant that he'd recognised the man in the photograph. Now it was a matter of seeing if he would admit to it. Gabriel Ye slowly picked up the photograph.

"He…he looks dead."

"He is," Malcolm Watts said.

The photograph dropped back to the table.

"Well, who is he?" Bill Buckle urged.

"Who is he?" Repeated Ye.

"Yes, don't tell me you don't know who it is, you obviously recognised him."

"No, Sergeant!" he replied a little too quickly. "No! I've never seen him before!"

"That's not what your expression said when you first looked at the photograph."

"That was because he looked dead. I have never seen a dead man before. I am a simple businessman. I know nothing about people like that."

"People like what?" Buckle was desperate to get to what this man was hiding.

"Like that dead man. The man who's been killed."

"I didn't say he'd been *killed,* did I Constable?"

"No, Sergeant." Malcolm Watts felt pleased he'd been brought into the conversation.

"He may have died of a heart attack, in his sleep."

"Why would you be asking questions if he died in his sleep?"

Bill Buckle could not think of a logical answer to Ye's question. He returned to the Sidhu Trading issue.

"Mr Ye, I will give you one more chance to answer my question as to why you feel you *must* deal with the Sidhu Trading and Shipping company before we all go down to Stonegate Police Station and continue our little talk down there."

"Look, Sergeant." Ye appeared to be gaining in confidence "All I meant was that Sidhu Trading is one of the largest shipping companies around. For someone in my business, you can't avoid dealing with the largest companies from time to time. That's all I meant."

"May I use your 'phone?"

"Certainly."

Bill Buckle rang Stonegate Police and asked for Inspector Harrigan.

"Harrigan."

"Inspector, Sergeant Buckle."

"Yes, Bill, what's the matter?"

Bill Buckle sat looking directly at Gabriel Ye as he relayed the general gist of their conversation to his superior. "Do you want me to bring him in for further questioning?"

"I think that would be a damn good idea, Sergeant."

"Very well, Sir."

The man on the other side of the desk got to his feet in protest. Before he had a chance to either say something or move to one side, the huge hand of Malcolm Watts clamped on his shoulder and pushed him roughly back to his chair.

"Everything alright there, Sergeant?"

"Yes, Sir, Constable Watts has it in hand."

"Good. See you back at Stonegate."

* * *

While Bill Buckle and Grahame Watts were in Chinatown, Harrigan read through the files. By the time he had finished, the disgust he had felt in his stomach at the time of the investigation had returned. Men in high places and in positions of trust performing lurid acts on children, mostly underage boys. Stuff-shirted old men sitting in judgment over others while spending their leisure time putting their podgy fingers down little boys' trousers, and worse.

It was in fact the boys, who had eventually approached a television programme and accused some of the most respected people in the community of offering huge rewards for sexual favours.

It made Harrigan physically ill. And why was it that these young men felt they could only go to a damn television programme to get their case brought before the public? What great testimony to modern society that was.

Unfortunately, like many of these cases in the past, and probably many more in the future, it was never really brought to a satisfactory conclusion. Despite all the accusations and hours of humiliating testimony, most of the evidence was branded, by another group of stuff-shirted old men, as *unreliable* and, of course, the old favourite, *not admissible*.

Doubts about the integrity of the boys' stories were also fuelled by the fact that those championing their cause were seen by the masses as do-gooder social workers who were easily conned by a soft story. Although this populous view annoyed Harrigan, he had no option but to reluctantly admit to himself that, in many cases, history had proven the view of the sceptical public correct. Unfortunately, social workers were often conned. It was always a difficult task, trying to separate fact from fantasy.

In fairness, this case did suffer major disruption just a few weeks into the trial. The trial centred mainly on two accused men, Lord Banbury, a wealthy businessman with four children, three of whom were in the legal profession and one a medical doctor, and Archibald Lapsley-Midwinter, a High Court Judge. Unable to face the shame, Lord Banbury drove to the Appin Forrest, put a revolver in his mouth, and blew his brains out, all over the interior of his Bentley.

Lapsley-Midwinter simply disappeared.

Unfortunately, although utterly predictable, once the frenzied headlines of the death of Lord Banbury and the disappearance of Lapsley-Midwinter had subsided, the main media thrust of the case lost its momentum.

The inclusion of a Lord of the Realm and a High Court Judge in such a case was extremely newsworthy. Newspapers and news broadcasts quite happily filled their reports with the intrigue and shocking revelation that stirred the minds and imagination of the audience, an audience who weighed its guilt of wanting to know, against the thrill of seeking out each and every detail.

But to maintain the general public's enthusiasm over a single issue was a difficult task. Evidence continued to be presented against others of high profile, including a senior clergyman and two businessmen and, while the crimes were still as vile, the passion had gone, replaced with legal jargon and points of law. While remaining sympathetic to the boys' experiences, the general public became bored, and the media, seeing no immediate opportunity for that all-important by-line or increase in sales, also lost interest.

Much of the final evidence was eventually ruled as not admissible, unreliable, and inconclusive. The victims were paid small, yet not unsubstantial, amounts of compensation, and the file was allowed to slip into quiet oblivion.

Harrigan recalled that, despite a definite lack of support from those above him, he continued for months, trying to gain a small lead on the whereabouts of Lapsley-Midwinter. It was very difficult to disappear. Even people in a witness protection plan, created by the most powerful law enforcement agencies in the world, are often tracked down and killed. There was always a trail. There was always some small clue to follow. The transfer of money was often a good place to start. Lapsley-Midwinter had cashed in everything he could in a short period of time and had amassed an amount estimated to be in the region of seven and a half million pounds; there could easily have been more. That sort of money cannot be transferred without leaving a trail, and Harrigan had doubted Lapsley-Midwinter would try to carry such an amount around with him, especially when going through Customs.

Of course, the money could be split and transferred in smaller amounts to different countries, but a man on the run can't travel regularly from country to country; the risk is too great. He needed to find another identity and settle. Despite enlisting the help of law enforcement agencies across the world, Harrigan could not find one trace of that money.

No stone had been left unturned. Family connections were traced, airlines, shipping companies, and Immigration Department records were also scrutinised. With time and patience any traveller could be tracked. It might be an unusually complicated travel itinerary or a traveller who fails to complete an itinerary can be a beginning. Any clue that would allow a chase to begin would do. Once the first steps of a trail of a man fleeing from justice could be established, the rest of it became relatively easy. You just needed that start. In the Lapsley-Midwinter case, however, that start never came. He had just simply disappeared.

Harrigan often considered the possibility that maybe he had been smuggled out by one of the many people-smuggling rackets that operated throughout the world. But how many of these rackets originated in the England? And, anyway, would he dare join a group of illegals carrying a suitcase with seven and a half million pounds in it? Not likely. Being a rich man on the run was bad enough, but being a poor man? Harrigan didn't think that Lapsley-Midwinter would take such a risk. There had to be another answer.

Harrigan went to the filing cabinet and took out the file Muhammad Singh had given him at Sidhu Trading's Bichirst office. He sat thoughtfully reading the movements of contain ers and recording the container identification numbers delivered to each regular warehouse. It soon became obvious that, apart from the Goldberg building and a warehouse closer to Tilbury Docks, there was no real pattern. Containers just moved around the world, as the demand took them, but the Goldberg building and, more recently, an address in East Grinstead only received three particular containers. A trip back to Bichirst seemed the next logical step.

He asked Patricia Hedrich to try and contact Colin McIver.

"Tell him I want him back here pronto."

"Yes, Sir."

Harrigan spent the next twenty minutes on the telephone.

"I missed you last night, Bill."

"I explained when I telephoned last night. I had to do some washing and pop around and see Mum."

"I know, but I still missed you. How is your Mother?"

"Fine. A few more days and she'll be home."

"That's good to hear." Margaret paused for a few moments. "Bill, are you sure all this police protection business is necessary? I feel like I'm in a cage."

"Just hang in there a few more days. Do it for me, if you don't want to do it for yourself. Don't say a word, but I think I may have a lead on the Lapsley-Midwinter disappearance, and so, for now, I'll feel better with the police there at the moment."

"What sort of lead?"

Harrigan told Margaret what he had read in the files. "And I think I now know how Lapsley-Midwinter got out of the country," he concluded, finding difficulty in containing the excitement in his voice. "I'm just waiting for McIver, and then I'm off to test my theory."

"Do be careful, Bill, I worry about you, too."

"I know and I will." His voice softened. "See you tonight."

"I'll be waiting."

Harrigan had enough time to walk to the men's room, wash his hands, readjust his clothing, and return to his office before Colin McIver entered.

"You want to see me, Inspector?"

"Yes, Colin. Leave your coat on, we're off out."

"Right, Sir," he replied, as he followed Harrigan out the door.

"We'll be about two hours, Trish. I'll be on the mobile."

"Very good, Sir." Patricia called after them.

As they walked across the car park, Harrigan pushed the little black button attached to his key ring and watched as the indicator lights flashed once and the door lock knobs rose into view.

"May I ask where we're going, Sir?" McIver asked, looking across the roof of the Mazda.

"Bichirst." Harrigan disappeared from view as he climbed into the driver's position. McIver settled into the passenger seat. "I want to have another talk to Muhammad Singh, about containers."

"Containers, Sir?"

"Yes, Colin, containers. You know, those big rectangular things you see on ships and backs of lorries."

"I know what they are, Sir, what I don't know is why." McIver became angry. He hadn't yet developed the patience or understanding of the older Bill Buckle. He had to learn that someone like Bill Harrigan didn't like to be forced on any issue. He would tell you when he was ready.

"More importantly how did you go this morning?" Harrigan asked, ignoring McIver's mood swing.

"Only alright," he replied a little sulkily.

"What happened?"

"My friend at the Embassy made some initial inquiries while I was there."

"And...?"

"Wei Lee appears to be a bone fide resident of the United States. There doesn't appear to be any, what can I say..." He paused, searching for the right words. "It all seems honest and above board, Inspector." He could not hide his disappointment.

"Don't be disheartened, Colin. You're new to this type of investigation. You get used to the highs and lows. And don't worry, you are doing very well."

"Thank you, Sir." His spirits lifted immediately.

"You just have to learn to be patient. Trust me. If Wei Lee's documents are the real thing, I'll drop my pants in…" He looked toward Colin McIver. McIver had a surprised look on his face, eyebrows raised. "Well, let's just say I'd be surprised and leave it at that."

He screeched to a halt in a bus stop in Bichirst. McIver watched as Harrigan placed a notice in the window that had a photocopy of the Metropolitan Police Service coat of arms, and the words "Stonegate Police, Official Business" printed in large letters.

The seven employees at the Bichirst office were still at their desks. The piles of paperwork had not diminished from the last time he was there.

An East Asian woman wearing traditional dress and displaying a red spot of colour in the centre of her forehead rose from the front desk and walked gracefully to the counter.

"May I help you, Gentlemen?"

Harrigan did the introduction and offered his ID.

"May I speak with Mr Singh, please?"

"I'm very sorry, Inspector, Mr Singh is on annual leave. He won't be back for another two weeks."

"Annual leave? Mr Singh didn't mention he was going on annual leave last time I spoke with him. Do you know if this was a sudden decision?"

"I do not know, Sir. Mr Singh is the manager; I do not question him."

"So, are you in charge?"

"I am the acting manager, Sir, yes."

"Do you know if Mr Singh was going away for his annual leave?"

"Going away?"

"Travelling, maybe abroad."

"Oh no, Sir." She half laughed the answer. "I wouldn't dream of being so intrusive."

"Very well, Miss, I didn't get your name?"

"Alam. Mrs Alam."

"Very well, Mrs Alam, I'm after two pieces of information. Firstly, I would like Mr Singh's home address, and secondly, I want to know if a container has been shipped from the Sidhu Trading's East Grinstead warehouse in the last couple of days."

"Just give me a few moments, Sir." The ever-so obliging Mrs Alam glided away from the counter.

Harrigan stood resting against the counter. McIver walked to the front window.

"There's a traffic warden looking rather unfavourably at your car, Sir."

"Go down and flash your badge. Tell him I'll cut his balls out if he puts a ticket on it."

"I can't, Sir."

"You can't? You can't go down and flash your badge!"

"Yes, Sir, I'll go down immediately and flash my badge." As his head and shoulders disappeared down the stairwell, he called over his shoulder. "But tell him you'll cut his balls out...it's a woman."

Harrigan smiled. He liked Colin McIver. He had spirit.

"Here you are, Sir." She pushed a hand-written note across the paper. "This is Mr Singh's home address; it's not far. Just around the corner, really."

Harrigan picked up the note and read it.

Unit 43 / 127 Harold Wilson Close West Grinstead.

"It's a small Council Housing unit, Sir. Mr Singh lives alone."

"Has he ever been married?"

"I don't think so, Sir. He's a solitary man." She unfolded a large computer printout. "These are the container movements for the last three weeks; there were only two from East Grinstead. Do you know how to read this, Sir?"

"Yes, thanks. Mr Singh gave me quite a bundle last time I was here."

"I know, I printed them for you."

"Well, thank you again, Mrs Alam. You have been most helpful. Tell me, will you be here until Mr Singh returns? You're not planning to take annual leave as well?"

"Oh no, Sir." She laughed.

"Well, I might see you again. Goodbye for now, Mrs Alam."

"Goodbye, Inspector Harrigan."

Colin McIver was obviously having difficulty with the Traffic Warden. Harrigan should have gone over immediately, but McIver's flamboyant mannerisms were just too fascinating to be interrupted. If only Bill Buckle were here.

"Having trouble, Senior?" Harrigan asked, when he eventually joined the two combatants.

"Sir, the Traffic Warden is proving to be very stubborn. She just won't listen to what I'm telling her."

"Oh, I'm listening alright, but you're not saying what I want to hear. You young upstarts with your fancy badges. You think you can come over here and park anywhere you please! Well, not in my area you don't!"

"That's what I told him, Warden! You can't park here, I said to him. I'm a police inspector, and even *I* wouldn't do a thing like that!" He leaned closer to the old lady in the distinctive black and yellow uniform and whispered furtively. "Young people today, no respect, that's what my dear old mum says."

"I'm glad you're with him, Inspector. You might be able to teach him a thing or two."

"I'm trying, Warden. I'm trying."

Harrigan put his hand on a stunned McIver's shoulder. "Now you get into the passenger's seat young man, it's obvious I'll have to take the wheel!" He shut the door firmly. "Thank you, Warden; it's people like you that make my job of training these young whelps and setting the standards a whole lot easier."

"It's my pleasure, Inspector." The old warden folded her book, and with a newly found spring in her step, marched down the busy street towards a Ford Escort, parked with its front wheel on the unbroken red line..

"See what a mess you got me in to?" Harrigan accused.

"Me? Might I remind you, Sir, that it was you who parked the car in the bus stop, not me!"

"Details. Details." He waived a dismissive hand and pulled into the traffic. "Come on, let's take a quick look at West Grinstead."

The Council Housing units at West Grinstead were typical of the blocks of units built by councils at the time, with multi-storied concrete buildings, each block of units with its own particular colour, painted on stair railings, doors, and window trim.

Harrigan parked the Mazda in a parking area with spaces for eight cars. He stopped close to a Morris Marina, the only car in the area. The Marina had no wheels and was sitting forlornly on concrete blocks. Every panel had some degree of damage, and all windows had been smashed.

"The old marina's seen better days," McIver remarked, looking back over his shoulder, as they walked towards the bright yellow stairway.

"Morris Marinas didn't have better days, Colin."

They stopped at the bottom of the stairway and waited for a young mother and her son to come down the stairs. Harrigan guessed the boy to be around four years of age.

"'ello, Mister." He smiled as he reached the step, second from the bottom.

"Hello young man." Harrigan returned the broad smile.

The creaking sound of the mother's red plastic minicoat sounded, as she hit the boy across the top of the head. "Shurrup," she scolded, "'ow many times I got t' tell ya not t' talk to th' filff."

Sensing McIver was about to say something to the young woman, Harrigan took a firm grip on his arm and propelled him up the stairway. "You first, Senior Constable."

McIver led the way. "What was the Unit Number?" he asked angrily.

"Forty three."

"Did you see how hard that bloody woman cracked the little fellow over the head? We should have said something!"

"And if we had said something, he would have copped twice as much around the corner."

"How did she know we were the police anyway?" McIver continued, brooding still evident in his voice. "We're not in uniform and, with all due respect, Sir, the Mazda in no way resembles an official vehicle."

"They can smell us. Now get over it. We've got work to do."

Unit forty-three was on the fourth floor, two doors to the right of the stairs. A Holland blind was pulled down behind the only window. McIver knocked on the freshly painted yellow door.

"You'll not be gettin' any answer to that door," the old lady said, standing in the now open doorway behind Harrigan.

Harrigan was surprised he hadn't heard the door open.

"Oh? He not there?"

"No he is not. He's gone on 'oliday."

"Mr Singh tell you this himself?"

"Aye. Strange it was, too, I thought, him telling me that. He never speaks you see. Keeps to 'imself."

Harrigan noted that the old lady only seemed to drop her "h's" on the last word of a sentence.

"Did he say where he was going for his holiday?"

"Oh no. But he did say he would be away about two weeks. Maybe a little longer."

"Did he take much luggage?"

"An overnight bag and a suitcase. That was all."

"And you have no idea where he was going?"

"No, no idea." She looked left and right and moved closer, lowering her voice. "He was coloured you know. Who knows where coloured people go for their 'olidays."

Having secretly divulged this piece of vital information, the old lady began to retreat hurriedly back into her home.

"Thank you, Ma'am." Harrigan said to the closing door.

"That's alright officer. Always glad to co-operate with the police." The door closed firmly.

Harrigan looked at his watch. Twenty minutes past one.

"Let's make one more stop before we head back to the station."

Harrigan led the way down the stairs. McIver fought the urge to ask where they were going and remained silent. He was slowly learning that the inspector would tell him where they were going in his own time.

It was about four minutes into the journey before Harrigan volunteered the information.

"I want to have a look at the Sidhu Trading warehouse in East Grinstead; it's not far from here."

Harrigan turned into the High Road at East Grinstead. "I think if we go up this road for about a mile and turn left just through the town, we'll almost be there."

"Would you like me to look in the A to Z, Sir?"

"No, don't bother, I know where it is."

McIver sat quietly and watched as Harrigan stubbornly turned from one street to another, every now and then saying reassuring things like, "Ok, now I'm right," or "It's not far now." McIver was beginning to experience that feeling of satisfaction that comes when the boss makes a complete ass of him or herself and has to admit he or she is wrong or at least have to look at the A to Z. The feeling was short lived.

"There it is, just ahead of us," Harrigan declared proudly. "See, I told you I knew where it was."

With disappointment flooding through him once again, "Yes, Sir," was the only answer McIver was able to muster.

Like the other old wooden warehouse buildings in the block, the front of the building they were about to visit was, to say the least, dirty and uninteresting.

"It's the back entrance I want to have a look at," Harrigan said, as he took the next right-hand turn and then turned right again. They travelled slowly, along the rear lane. As many delivery drivers know, it is often difficult to find the building from the back lane. Very few buildings have a name or an address displayed at the rear and, many times, it's only through clues, such as the rubbish in the yard indicating the type of business operated, that the right address can be found.

The rear of the building Harrigan was looking for was easy. It was almost identical to the Goldberg building. He drove in and stopped next to the container platform.

"This is identical to the Goldberg building," McIver said unnecessarily, as they walked towards the rear door.

Several loud knocks on the rear door soon established that there was no one in the building.

"Well, what do we do now?"

"I didn't come to look inside the building, Sergeant. I want to look at the container platform. More accurately, I want you to look."

"Me, Sir?"

"Yes. Open the end door and tell me what you see."

McIver crouched down, opened the wooden door and looked into the black void.

"It's difficult to see, Sir. It's pretty dark inside. But it looks as though it's empty."

"Ramachandran told me they use the same space at the Goldberg building to store cartons, and they use the trapdoor above your head to take things in and out. It's not a bad idea, except for one thing."

"What's that, Sir?"

"Feel above your head, Sergeant, and open the trapdoor."

Just like Bill Buckle had done at the Goldberg building, Colin McIver unbolted the trapdoor and lowered it downwards. Light immediately shafted in through the opening.

"Now can you see what is inside, Sergeant?"

"No, Sir."

"Why not, Sergeant?"

"Because the door swings away from me and it blocks my view."

"Exactly, Sergeant, just like it does at the Goldberg building. The door is hinged on the edge closest to the centre of the platform and swings inwards, which means that when the door is open, it blocks the storage space from the hole through which Mr Ramachandran said they pass the stored cartons through.

"Then Ramachandran wasn't being truthful?"

"They may very well use the space for storage, but they don't use the trapdoor for that reason."

"What do they use it for, then?"

"That, Detective Senior Constable, is the one-million-dollar question."

Harrigan was first back to the car.

CHAPTER NINE

It was almost two thirty when Harrigan and McIver returned to Stonegate. Patricia Hedrich told Harrigan there were no messages; she'd taken care of all the queries, and offered to make a cup of tea. The two men took up her offer.

Once in Harrigan's office, McIver brought a chair over to the desk and sat opposite the inspector. He was sure that Harrigan had more than a hint to the answer to the *one million-dollar question* he had referred to at East Grinstead. He waited somewhat impatiently for Harrigan to elaborate. Harrigan, on the other hand, sat relaxed, drinking slowly from his mug of black tea with a dash of lemon juice. He returned the mug to its place on the coaster and reached for the manila folders on his left.

"O.K. Let's get into it."

"At last!" thought McIver.

"These folders are the relevant reports on the Lapsley-Midwinter case. I call it the Lapsley-Midwinter case because he is the only one I am currently interested in."

He flicked aimlessly through the thick wad of papers "I won't go through all the detail…"

"I know the gist of the case, Sir."

"Good. So suffice to say that, shortly after Lord Banbury blew his brains out, Lapsley-Midwinter disappeared."

Harrigan began, in relatively close detail, to go through the work he had put in trying to get a lead on Lapsley-Midwinter after his disappearance. It was almost as if he was cross-examining himself. "But try as I might—," the ringing of the telephone interrupted him. He snatched at the receiver.

"Harrigan." He growled, annoyed at being interrupted.

It was impossible for McIver not to listen to Harrigan's comments into the telephone.

"It's OK, Bill, what's the matter?"

There was a long pause, as he listened silently to Bull Buckle's report. "I think that would be a damn good idea, Sergeant," Harrigan eventually replied. About to hang up, something in Bill Buckle's tone stopped him, and, as a frown of questioning crossed Harrigan's face, he continued. "Everything alright there, Sergeant?" Another short pause.

"Good. Get back here ASAP!"

He had almost hung the telephone up when he heard a shout coming through the telephone. Even McIver heard it. He returned the hand piece to his ear.

"Yes, Sergeant?" He looked across to a now attentive McIver.

"What do you mean, you're waiting for a car? What's wrong with the car you went down in?" He was silent, as he listened to Bill Buckle respond to his question. "You went by bloody train!" he exploded. "You went by train?" he repeated incredulously. He sat in silence, as he tried desperately to regain some equilibrium. "Well, get here as soon as you can!" He hung up.

"I'd be lying if I said I wasn't curious," McIver ventured cautiously.

"It seems that Sergeant Buckle and Malcolm Watts have found a Mr Gabriel Ye who is reluctant to tell what he knows about our Mr Lee. They're bringing him in for questioning."

"What was that about a train?"

"They didn't take a car to Chinatown; they went by fucking train!"

Deciding that discretion was the better part of valour, McIver said no more about that subject. Besides, he wanted to get back to the disappearance of Lapsley-Midwinter. His curiosity was going to have to wait. Harrigan closed the file.

"Let's have a bite to eat. We can continue this after we've spoken to Mr Ye."

"Very well, Sir." McIver was getting much better at hiding his disappointment, so he stood and began to leave the room. "I have some sandwiches in my desk."

Harrigan had given up eating at his desk about four years ago. He'd read an article in a magazine while waiting to have his haircut that said having your lunch at your desk heightened your level of stress. The stress increased your risk of heart attack or stroke, or something equally diabolical, which he could not now remember. Since then, he'd always made sure he went out somewhere. Even if was just to sit in the small park around the corner and have a sandwich. He took his coat from the coat rack and told Patricia he'd be back in half an hour.

"And, if Sergeant Buckle gets here before I'm back, have him set everyone up in my office. Including DSC McIver."

He thanked Sergeant Harris for arranging transport for Bill Buckle and left the building. He hadn't had a decent meal for the last couple of days and was feeling decidedly hungry. He crossed the road and walked one block to a little Indian restaurant with the unimaginative name of *The Indian Curry House.*

The proprietor of the restaurant approached him, as he stood inside the entrance. Despite the name, this was by no means just another curry house; this was *the* curry house, where the *beautiful people* come to dine. Harrigan had never seen himself as one of the beautiful people; he just liked a good curry. It was also one of the few restaurants that didn't close between the traditional hours of lunch and dinner.

"Inspector Harrigan, welcome to my humble eatery." Nhanda Rajagopola's polished tone reflected his Oxford University education and years as a high ranking and respected officer in the Indian Army.

"Thank you, Nhanda, I don't get to come here often enough." It was difficult not to imitate the polite bow of acknowledgement.

"Your table still awaits you."

Harrigan was ushered graciously to his favourite table. He ordered Lamb Curry and a jug of iced water.

* * *

Margaret Willis was not a woman who took kindly to being caged, especially in her own home. She realised Bill was only thinking of her and she liked that; it showed he cared. But she had to get out, just for a little while. She stood on the front porch and spoke to Valerie Brideshead, the constable on duty at the front door.

"But you are not supposed to leave the house, Mrs Willis. I will get into trouble." Constable Brideshead pleaded her reply to Margaret's announcement she had telephoned the hairdressers and had an appointment in thirty minutes.

"I'm going to the hairdressers for goodness sake! What can go wrong?" She allowed time for the constable to consider the implied innocence of the question. "You can come, too," she added brightly.

"It would be my duty, Mrs Willis, but I don't know. I'd better check with the inspector."

"Oh come on, Constable!" Margaret turned away impatiently and spoke to the wall of the house. "Look, to be honest with you," she turned back to the policewoman, "I don't want the inspector to know. He's coming around later and I would like to, well, you know, have my hair done and look nice. You're a woman! Surely you understand."

"I could still get into trouble."

"No one will know."

"The inspector will, when he sees you. He'll notice you've had your hair done." Valerie Brideshead pointed out, before adding, "won't he?"

He'd damn well better Margaret thought. "Constable, stop worrying, I'll take the blame if anything happens." She turned and closed the door behind her. "Besides, I have already decided, and I don't want to be late for my appointment. So if you want to come, come on." Margaret waved the keys of her late husband's Jaguar, still parked at the far end of the driveway. It was rarely used these days. "I'll even leave the BMW where it is, to make it look like I am still at home."

Margaret Willis sympathised with the constable's dilemma and didn't want any unpleasantness. After all, she was only doing her job. But, damn it, she wasn't under arrest and could go anywhere she damn well wanted to.

"Alright, but just give me a minute to tell Jack."

Constable Brideshead hurried to the rear of the house. She told her counterpart what had happened and explained that she would go with Mrs Willis.

"You'll just have to try and watch the front and the back until we return," she called, as she turned and hurried away before he could offer any objection.

She slid into the passenger seat. "I feel like a naughty school-girl," she said to Margaret, now waiting patiently in the driver's seat.

Margaret looked at her and smiled, as she pushed the key into the ignition and held it between her thumb and forefinger. She looked across at the young constable and decided against using the obvious, *where would we get a naughty schoolgirl at this time of day,* line and, without giving it another thought, prepared to turn the key.

"Wait!" Constable Jack Downing shouted, as he came running towards the car. Margaret pressed a black button nestled in the walnut trim and the driver's window glided open. He rested both hands on the sill of the door and leaned down to speak.

"Where shall I say you've gone if someone asks?"

"Just say I've gone to the bloody hairdressers!" Feeling guilty at the impatient tone in her voice, Margaret nodded kindly and added softly, "Angelica's, on the High Road. Now stand back, we're about to blast off!"

Margaret Willis tightened her grip as she began to turn the ignition key.

There was something almost awe inspiring in the roar of the exhaust of a well tuned V12 motor as it strangled its way down matching exhaust pipes.

Thirty-four seconds after the engine had burst into life they had disappeared from view, and an anxious Constable Downing returned to the duty of watching the now empty house.

* * *

Harrigan returned to an office full of people. Extra chairs had been brought in, and Bill Buckle, Colin McIver, and Constable Malcolm Watts were all deep in conversation. A sad faced man of Chinese appearance sat in a chair positioned at the desk, directly opposite Bill Harrigan's empty chair.

"Good afternoon, Gentlemen…don't get up."

There was a chorus of greetings from the three policemen.

"And who do we have here?" He looked directly at Ye.

"Mr Gabriel Ye, Inspector. He runs an importing and export-ing business in Chinatown."

"Oh, Yes, I remember, you told me over the telephone. He has a problem with certain parts of his memory if I recall?" Harrigan's cold eyes stared fixedly at the man slumped in the chair opposite.

"That's correct, Sir. I showed him this photograph and, although he obviously recognises the man, he can't remember anything about him."

Bill Buckle placed the photograph into Harrigan's right hand. Harrigan's eyes remained still as he passed the photograph to Gabriel Ye.

"You know this man?"

Gabriel Ye didn't look at the photograph; he simply placed it on the desk in front of him. "I have seen him."

"Where have you seen him?"

"In Chinatown."

"Do you know his name?"

"No."

"Do you know who he works for?"

"No!" A hint of fear flashed across his face.

"Does he work for Sidhu Trading?"

"Look, Inspector. Just by bringing me to this police station, you have put my life at risk. Even if I knew something, I could not tell you. I would be killed. Please, just let me go, I know nothing."

"Mr Ye," Harrigan said quietly and spoke slowly, "you talk as if your life means something to me. Let me make it perfectly clear to you right now, it doesn't. The only thing I care about right now is to find out what you know about this man. And the one thing you should understand is that the only way you are going to get out of here is to tell me. Do you understand?"

"I understand you can't hold me here. I want a lawyer!"

Harrigan prodded the photograph with his finger. "Mr Ye, this man is dead. I am certain you are right when you said that, by bringing you here, we might have put your life at risk. I am also certain that the people you are frightened of killed this man and will not hesitate to kill you, too, even if they only *think* you told us something."

"Please, Inspector, I know nothing. I can tell you nothing. Please, let me go." The terror in his voice chilled the pleading tones.

"I want you to listen to me very carefully, Mr Ye, and I mean *very* carefully. Do you understand what I mean when I say very carefully?"

"I…I think so."

"Good. You may think that if you refuse to tell me what you know, you will be safe, that you will not be harmed by those you are trying to protect."

"I am not trying to protect anyone, Inspector. I am simply looking out for myself, keeping myself out of trouble."

"So how much trouble do you think you would be in if I let it be known on the streets that you told me what I wanted to know? That you named names."

"You wouldn't! That's against the law! You are the Police!" Ye stood violently. His body shook, and his mouth twisted as he shouted the words.

Harrigan sat motionless and stared into the frightened man's face. Bill Buckle held a restraining hand on McIver's arm, a warning not to interfere. "I was at Scotland Yard for enough years to know what goes on in your area, Mr Ye." Harrigan hissed. "I know the names and have no doubt in your mind that I *will* name them. And I will spread the word that you gave them to me. What would your life be worth then, Mr Ye?"

Several tense moments passed. The sound of Harrigan's fin ger knocking on the wooden desktop as he prodded the photograph once more filled the room. "Now stop wasting my time and tell me all you know about Mr Wei Lee."

Gabriel Ye sank resignedly into his chair. "His name is not Wei Lee."

"Would you like a cup of tea?"

"Yes, please, Inspector."

For the first time since Harrigan had sat down, he moved his eyes from the face of Gabriel Ye. As if on cue, Patricia Hedrich entered and took Mr Ye's order.

English breakfast, no milk or sugar.

"His name is Xiao Chen. He is, was, an enforcer with the largest illegal drug syndicate in London." His voice quickened as he added, "you must believe me when I tell you I know nothing of the operation of the syndicate."

Harrigan did believe him. "Go on with your story."

The Chinese businessman's story was short and to the point. It was a story not unfamiliar to Harrigan.

Gabriel Ye had been an honest businessman, importing mainly food for the local Chinese supermarkets and articles for sale in souvenir shops and the markets across the country. One day, he was approached by the drug syndicate and offered a simple business deal. He was to allow drugs to be hidden in his imported goods or he or his family would be killed. Gabriel Ye had no family. They had drowned when a ferry in his homeland China, carrying two hundred and thirty passengers, sunk in a wild storm, so the threat was aimed directly at him. Gabriel Ye was not a brave man, and so he'd done the bidding of the syndicate whenever he was told. Drugs would be hidden in his goods and brought into the country. He knew that eventually he would most probably be caught. But like so many others in his position, he knew very little about the actual Syndicate, had no idea of the identity of syndicate bosses or any knowledge of the operation. He would pose no threat to the overall organisation, so he would be destined to serve a prison sentence and then live out the rest of his life a poor and unwanted man. The only person he ever had contact with was Xiao Chen and his two rather large and violent companions.

Gabriel Ye took a sip of his tea.

"Do you have any idea why Xiao Chen could be on the run?" Harrigan asked.

Ye smiled for the first time. "Greed has no conscience or reasoning, Inspector. Xiao Chen was a trusted employee of the syndicate. He had access to many millions of dollars of syndicate money. You should realise that the syndicate does not only deal in drugs. There is prostitution, gambling, and the latest money-spinner is the smuggling of people." All traces of broken English had disappeared from Ye's conversation.

"And Chen decided to take his cut on the side?"

"That's what I have heard. Many large sums of money have been spoken about, Inspector, but I think the figure is around twenty-five million pounds."

Malcolm Watts let out an involuntary whistle. Harrigan glared at him for breaking his silence.

"You must understand that that is not a large sum of money in those circles," Ye continued, "but the syndicate frowns severely on anyone who tries to rob them. Especially trusted employees." He finished his tea.

"Thank you, Mr Ye, I know how hard that must have been for you." Harrigan said, with genuine understanding in his voice.

"Is that all you want to know, Inspector?" An inference of surprise lingered in his voice.

"That's it, Mr Ye. If you had told that to Sergeant Buckle in the first place, you could have saved us all a lot of inconvenience and risk to yourself, of course."

"I don't need to be reminded."

"Sorry, but if it is any consolation, you have my word this conversation will go no further than this office."

Ye nodded appreciation.

"Do you want me to arrange for a ride back to your office?" Harrigan offered.

"No thank you, Inspector, getting a ride here was bad enough. If you take me back, they will definitely think I've cooperated."

"I understand." Harrigan stood as Gabriel Ye prepared to leave. "Thank you, Mr Ye."

Gabriel Ye stopped at the door and looked back at Harrigan.

"As a matter of interest, Inspector, would you *really* have spread those rumours if I hadn't talked?"

"Do you remember a few years ago, a small-time pusher named Kim Yu?"

"Yes, Inspector, I remember Yu. His main target was the local schoolyard." Ye winced before continuing. "He was killed by the syndicate for giving information to Scotland Yard. I'll never forget it, his throat was cut, and his tongue had been removed, as a warning to others. His body was found in the lane way near my office."

"Well, for your information, Yu didn't tell us a damn thing. He didn't say a word."

The blood drained from Ye's face as he left the room.

Harrigan looked at the three pairs of unblinking eyes staring at him. "What?"

"That Kim Ye business," McIver began accusingly.

"Kim Yu." Harrigan corrected.

"Alright, Kim Yu business," McIver continued. "Was there any truth in what you said?"

"Ye told us what we wanted, didn't he?" Harrigan said impatiently, as he opened the container records given to him by Mrs Alam.

"Yes, but that man, Kim Yu. He was killed! We're the police for God's sake!" McIver persisted.

Harrigan looked up sharply at the indignant McIver.

"Sir." McIver added.

Harrigan dropped his eyes to the file, McIver looked around the room for support. His questioning expression was met only by stony-faced glares.

"Let's get on with the business at hand, shall we?"

The three policemen repositioned their chairs to be better able to see the papers on the desk. Harrigan looked at Bill Buckle and Constable Watts.

"To bring you two up to date, earlier today, Senior McIver and I went to the Sidhu trading office at Bichirst. I wanted to talk further to Mr Singh about container movements from the Goldberg building and the East Grinstead Warehouse. We were taken a little by surprise when told that Mr Singh had taken annual leave two days previously."

Harrigan briefly picked up the container records.

"But, anyway," he continued, "a Mrs Alam, the lady currently in charge at Bichirst, was very cooperative and, after asking her for a record of container movements from East Grinstead for the last month, she gave me these."

He paused as he allowed the records to fall back to the desk.

"We then went to Singh's home address and a neighbour confirmed that he had left with a small amount of luggage and would be away for around two weeks. She also made the comment that he was generally uncommunicative and she thought it was unusual for him to tell her that."

"You say that like it was important, Sir, is it?" Malcolm Watts asked.

"On its own, probably not, but as part of the whole picture, yes, I think it is. Having struck out at Singh's address, McIver and I then went to the rear yard of the East Grinstead warehouse. Do you want to continue, Colin?"

McIver was still feeling, not so much embarrassed, but more the odd man out over the Kim Yu affair. He began tentatively. "Well, we discovered there, er, was no one. At the warehouse that is. The inspector said it wasn't important because we were only there to look at the container platform."

"Was it like the one at the Goldberg building?" Bill Buckle asked.

Bill Buckle's question put McIver at ease. "Exactly like the Goldberg building."

"Tell them what you could see when you opened the trap door." Harrigan instructed.

"Nothing, Sir," he answered, "I could see nothing."

"Then it really is exactly like the Goldberg building," Bill Buckle repeated.

"Ok. Thank you gentlemen." Harrigan took control of the conversation once again. "When I saw the way in which the trapdoor opened at the Goldberg building, it was obvious that it was not possible to be underneath the platform, and receive cartons through the trapdoor, the way Ramachandran had told us, because the trapdoor got in the way. The Goldberg Platform simply made me suspicious, but the second platform at East Grinstead confirmed my suspicions."

He sat quietly, sensing the growth of anticipation. An inspector he'd had in his early police years in Sydney had once told him, *Timing keeps an audience attentive. Remember, without timing, a comedian isn't funny.* It was just one of those things that stuck in Harrigan's mind. Like 1066 and the Battle of Hastings.

"I believe that the only plausible reason for those trapdoors is to put something into, or take something out of a container that is sitting on top."

Comments came from across the room.

"But that's impossible!" Watts said, being the first to react.

"The floors in those containers are rock solid!" McIver added.

Bill Buckle said nothing.

"Why is it impossible? If we can have a trap door in the platform, why not one in the container?" Harrigan reasoned.

"Because," Watts replied hurriedly, a tone of triumph creeping into his voice, "not all containers would have matching trapdoors, Inspector. You wouldn't know which container was arriving."

"Ah ha!" Harrigan had counted on someone jumping in with that question. "That's where you're wrong, Constable." Harrigan turned the records around so that the three men could see them.

"Do you see that container number?" He stood up behind his desk, so he was better able to point to the container that had left East Grinstead the previous day. "ISL 2647?

Everyone nodded silently.

He walked to the filing cabinet and retrieved the shipping records given to him by Muhammad Singh on his earlier visit to Bichirst. He closed the filing cabinet drawer, returned to the table, and opened the files.

"Constable, have a look at those records and see if you can find Container ISL 2647." Harrigan sat back contentedly, as the constable searched eagerly. Bill Buckle and McIver were also reasonably confident they knew what Malcolm Watt's answer would be.

"There." He ran his finger down the columns. "And there... and there...but that's amazing, Sir!" He looked up at the inspector.

"That's right, Constable. But not so amazing for a company that owns the containers, the warehouses, the ships, and the trading company. And you can take my word for it that there are three other containers that continue to reappear at either the Goldberg building or at East Grinstead. How is my trapdoor theory looking now?"

"If you are right, Sir, and I don't doubt that you are, what is it that they are loading or unloading, drugs?"

"People, Sergeant." Harrigan was also pleased that question had been asked.

"People, Inspector?" Bill Buckle asked.

"Yes, Bill, people, refugees. But not your average refugee. You need too many of your average refugees to make a lot of money. And the more people you move, the higher the risk of being caught. No, we are talking of the rich and desperate refugee."

"That sounds like a good title for an afternoon soapy, Sir." Watts blurted out.

Three heads turned simultaneously toward the constable.

"Sorry," he said.

Harrigan smiled momentarily.

"Do you really think there are enough of these rich and desperate people, as you call them, to make it worthwhile?" Bill Buckle reasoned, as he brought the conversation back into line.

"That's what I wondered at first. But just think about it. I think we would all be very surprised to know how many anonymous villains there are who want to disappear. Con men wanting to disappear, taking their swindled millions to a place where they can live the life of luxury with no questions asked. Embezzlers, underworld figures, who have turned state's evidence and don't trust the witness protection program. People who take from the mob, the list goes on. And let's face it, I can only see three containers and they have a pretty slow turn around. If they are moving these ne'er do wells from country to country, as I suspect, we're probably only talking around eighteen, maybe twenty a year. And what would it be worth to someone who desperately needed to disappear? And disappear without a trace! One, two million pounds....maybe more? A tidy tax-free sideline."

"Are you suggesting that Xiao Chen might have been one of your rich and desperates?"

"Yes, I am, Colin, that's exactly what I'm suggesting. It's my guess he was supposed to be in that container when it left, but for some reason, he found himself in the warehouse at the time of Manjit's murder and the subsequent fire."

"He hid under the bathtub and suffocated to death. So his death really could have been an accident. Wrong place at the wrong time?"

"You were there at the scene, Colin. It could very well have happened that way." Harrigan did not elaborate any further. He left that for Bill Buckle.

"So where's the rest of the twenty five million pounds Ye said was missing?" Before allowing anyone else to offer any suggestions, Bill Buckle continued to answer his own question, not even stopping for a breath. "In the container is my bet." He paused thoughtfully. "And who was it that was so damn anxious to get that container reloaded and out of there?" This time Bill Buckle allowed someone else to answer.

"Ramachandran," McIver obliged. "But *I* reloaded the container, and it was completely full of cartons."

"Are you sure, Colin? Tell me, how many cartons did you reload?"

"I have it here in my note book, Sir. If you bear with me, I'll let you know exactly."

While McIver flicked through the pages of his pocket notebook, Bill Buckle continued, "Is this why you reopened the Lapsley-Midwinter case, Inspector? Do you think this is how he managed to, to just, disappear?"

"Yes, Bill, and that's why I have protection on Mrs Willis. That threatening telephone call to Margaret was always about the Lapsley-Midwinter disappearance, not the fire at the Goldberg building. Mahmood was afraid that the investigation into the fire and murders would lead to us uncovering the smuggling racket."

"If there is a smuggling racket," Bill Buckle commented

"There's smuggling racket alright, Bill; you couldn't put enough money on it."

"And Mrs Willis' comments to you that night in the taxi could help link Mahmood with the racket?"

"Maybe not link him, Bill, but at least steer us in his direction. Now maybe you see why I was so insistent. Margaret is in real danger"

The telephone rang. Harrigan picked it up impatiently.

"I'm sorry to bother you, Inspector, but I thought you'd want to take this call. It's Mrs Willis."

"Thank you Trish. Hello? Margaret? "

"Oh, Bill, I'm glad you're there. My car…It's been…It's…"

"Margaret what's happened?"

"My car…there was a bomb…I—"

"Are you alright?"

"Yes, just shaken…please come."

"I'm on my way. Now don't move until I—"

"I'm not at home, Bill. I'm at Angelica's, a hairdresser's in the High Street."

"You're where? Oh never mind that now, just wait. Don't go anywhere." He slammed down the telephone.

"I've found the number of cartons—"

"Not now, Sergeant." Harrigan said impatiently as he stood quickly, slamming his chair backwards against the wall. "Someone has just blown Mrs Willis' car to pieces. Come on, Bill," he said to Sergeant Buckle, as he grabbed his coat. "And, Colin, you and the constable catch up on your reports; we'll be back as soon as we can."

He looked at the clock as he hurried to the door. "On second thoughts, it's half passed four, you may as well go home and we'll see you tomorrow…oh and Colin, let the super know, will you?"

"Consider it done, Sir."

Despite the flashing blue light, the glaringly obvious non-police car image of the ZX Mazda made emergency driving across London at four thirty in the afternoon extremely difficult. While

Bill Buckle might have described Harrigan's driving as being almost combatant in nature, Harrigan's confidence in his own driving ability was infectious, and the old sergeant in the passenger's seat felt almost relaxed—*almost*, because he did get a little anxious when Harrigan moved his concentration from the road and dialled a telephone number on the mobile.

"Patricia Hedrich, Stonegate Police." Her voice resounded from the hidden speaker.

"Trish, Bill Harrigan."

"Are you there yet, Inspector?"

"Not quite. Listen, will you contact the East Binstead Police and tell them there should be a man by the name of Fadhel staying at The Badgers. Tell them I want him brought to Stonegate ASAP."

"Just *Fadhel*, Sir?"

"I did hear his family name at Aysha Manjit's house. Sahneed, Sahjeed...no Saheed. I'm fairly certain it's Saheed. But there can only be one Fadhel there, surely."

"Leave it to me, Sir."

"Thanks, Trish." The telephone went dead.

The fire engines and police cars around the area made identification of Angelica's in the High Street a simple matter.

Harrigan brought the Mazda to a screeching halt.

"Have a look around, Bill. I'll find Mrs Willis."

There being no need for further conversation at this time, the two men went their separate ways.

Harrigan showed his ID at the front door of Angelica's.

"The chief inspector is inside, Sir. He is expecting you."

The salon was swarming with police, staff, and three terrified customers with hairstyles in various stages of completion. Harrigan looked through the rear window at the wrecked vehicle.

"Inspector Harrigan?"

Bill Harrigan looked toward the owner of the booming voice. He was a rather short man of corpulent build and a receding hairline, which was well compensated by a huge walrus-style moustache. He was well dressed, complete with waistcoat and watch chain.

"Howell. C I Howell. I've been expecting you," he announced.

The two men shook hands in the traditional manner.

"Yes, the policeman at the door told me you were expecting me, Sir." Harrigan hesitated, somewhat thrown off guard by this extraordinary man's *Battle of Britain* personality. "If it is not an impertinent question, Chief Inspector, how did you know I was on my way?"

"Telephone call from the Skipper," Howell's voice boomed again. "I assume he must have received a 'call from your chap. Some theory that this may be linked to a case you are already working on."

"That's right." Harrigan even struggled to come up with that simple reply. He could almost hear Vera Lynn singing in the background.

"Protocol, old man. Best to let the man already on the job take over. Cooperation across the ranks, that sort of thing."

"That's very understanding and much appreciated, Chief Inspector, but I really don't want to take over. I'd just like to be involved from the sidelines. I'm sure your investigation will be thorough and efficient, and I'm more than happy to wait for your results." Harrigan had enough on his plate without taking on another full-scale investigation. "It is your turf after all," he added.

"Jolly good, Inspector, jolly good show."

"I would like to speak to Mrs Willis, though, and inspect the vehicle before it's moved. I'll then leave the rest up to you. If that's alright."

"That's topping."

Topping? Harrigan could not believe this man had just said *topping.*

The C.I. raised a short chubby arm, covered by a dark blue pinned striped suit sleeve and, with a well manicured hand, beckoned at a young uniformed constable standing awkwardly between two oversized hairdryers.

"What ho, Constable!" he called. "What ho!"

What ho!?

The young policeman hurried across the room. "Yes, Sir?"

"The inspector wants to speak with the lady who owns the damaged vehicle. I want you to show the inspector the way, and arrange for a spot of tea if the inspector requires."

The young constable snapped to attention. "This way, Inspector."

"Thank you, Chief Inspector Howell." The full title seemed justly appropriate.

Harrigan followed the eager young constable.

Margaret was sitting in what was obviously the tearoom. Constable Valerie Brideshead sat next to Margaret at the Formica kitchen table so common in most staff tearooms.

"Inspector, I'm terribly sorry," Valerie Brideshead began apologetically. "I asked Mrs Willis not to leave the house, but she wanted to look nice and she—"

"That's alright, Constable. Mrs Willis is not under arrest; she's a free woman. You did the right thing." He cupped her hand in his. "Now go and have another cup of tea and stop worrying."

"Thank you, Sir."

Margaret stood slowly. Although still strong in appearance, she was visibly shaken. She wanted to throw her arms around her man and sob into his chest, but the situation did not allow such behaviour. She stood discreetly in front of him.

"I'm very glad you're here, Inspector, thank you for coming."

Harrigan reached out and drew her to him. Valerie Brideshead returned the teaspoon to the drawer, took the young constable by the arm, and ushered him into the narrow hallway. She closed the door behind them.

"Police business." Valerie told the young constable quietly.

"What happened?" Harrigan almost whispered.

Margaret slowly pushed away and took her seat at the table. "I'm sorry, Bill, I'm acting like a bloody schoolgirl." She wiped her eyes. "I'm all right now. It was the shock I guess."

Bill sat next to her. "I do really need to know what happened, when you're ready."

"There's very little to tell, really, when you think about it. I wanted to get out of the house, and please, don't blame Valerie."

"Valerie?"

"The young female constable. Like she said, she tried desperately hard to have me stay at home, but I wouldn't take no for an answer." She placed her hand on Harrigan's knee. "I wouldn't listen to you, either, I'm sorry. It's plainly obvious now, you *were* right."

"That's not important now. What is important is that you weren't hurt, and I've already cleared it up with the constable. Now tell me what happened here."

"I had finished having my hair done—"

"It looks very nice too."

"Flatterer." Harrigan liked it when she smiled. "And I was standing near the register with my Visa when the telephone rang. To my surprise it was for me. I thought at first it might have been you."

"Me?"

"Yes. I thought you must have called around to the house and discovered where I was."

Harrigan simply nodded.

"But it wasn't you. It was a man. I didn't recognise his voice. He said something like '*you were told to keep your mouth closed. You were told to say nothing, especially to that boyfriend inspector of yours. You obviously thought we were joking. We don't joke. Next time, you won't be so lucky.*' And then he hung up. I must have looked surprised because Laura, the receptionist, asked me if I was alright. I said yes, and signed the receipt. As I turned towards the back door and began walking to the rear car park, I was wondering what the caller had meant when he said '*next time you won't be so lucky.*' I soon found out the answer to my question, because it was then my car just exploded. I could see it through the rear window."

"There was no one in the car park?"

"No, thankfully. Valerie was in the salon with me. She never let me out of her sight. And mine was the only car in the parking area."

"Do you remember anything else?"

"No, I'm sorry Bill. That's all there is to it."

He sat thoughtfully for a few moments before taking her hand and holding it gently. "Are you feeling a little better now?"

"Yes, thank you Bill, I'm fine. It was just the thought that in another few minutes, I might have been in the car. I could have been killed!"

"I don't think it was their intention to kill you. Not this time."

"*This time?*" She sat up straight and pulled her hand from his. "And what makes you think that whoever it was who blew up my motorcar wasn't trying to kill me *this time,* as you so quaintly put it."

He remained calm. "Well, granted I've only had a glimpse at your car, and from a distance at that, but it looks like it was the fire after the explosion that's caused most of the damage, not the explosion itself. Of course the explosion did some damage, but it could have been as lot worse. If whoever set the bombs in your car *really* wanted to kill the occupant or occupants of the vehicle, a much larger amount of explosive would have been used. Just think about it, even the rear window of the salon wasn't broken."

Margaret subconsciously glanced at the window. She sat silent.

"If you're feeling better, I'll send the constable in and go and test my theory with the chief inspector."

"You mean Biggles?"

"Biggles?" Harrigan repeated, before nostalgia overtook him."Ah yes, Biggles. James Bigglesworth. Pilot and adventurer of the 1930s who, for thirty years, was the hero of every boy in England and Australia. Who can forget *Biggles Flies Again*; *Biggles in the Jungle*; *Biggles — Secret Agent*. Those were the days." Harrigan returned from his memories. "You're right, Margaret, our DCI is a bit that way, isn't he? I must say that when he leaves, if he doesn't wear a white scarf and drive a British racing green open top Morgan I will be most disappointed."

He kissed her lightly on the lips. "I'll get the constable."

Although only preliminary investigation had been undertaken at this stage, there seemed common acknowledgment of Harrigan's theory. While the explosion had caused damage to both the engine bay and the boot area, which would indicate there had actually been two explosions, not one, it was the fire that had done the most damage. This would also indicate that if anyone had been inside the vehicle, they would have had time to get out. It was definitely looking more and more like a warning and not an attempt on Margaret's life.

In answer to Harrigan's question, Sergeant Gates of the bomb squad confirmed that there had in fact been two explosive devices. One fitted under the boot lid, the other in the engine bay. The devices had been placed in such a way as to ensure that the force of the explosion had gone away from the vehicle, not into the cabin.

"Would the explosives take long to put in the right position?"

"It would take some time, Sir. Both devices needed to be fixed, secured if you like, and both the bonnet and boot lid needed to be opened."

"So it would have been reasonably difficult to position the devices without being seen?"

"Very difficult, Sir." Gates replied.

Harrigan looked around carelessly. "Not done here in the car park?"

"Not likely, Sir; it'd be too risky. You can be seen from inside the salon and you'd have no way of knowing when someone else might drive into the car park. No, I'd say the explosives were already fitted when Mrs. Willis drove in here."

"Set off by some form of radio controlled mechanism?" Harrigan asked the obvious question.

"Without a doubt. We'll know more, once we take the car back for a full investigation."

"Thanks, Sergeant. Let me know the result." He gave the Sergeant his card.

"Certainly, Sir."

Bill Buckle had little to add to what Harrigan already knew, and at Harrigan's suggestion they went back to the tearoom. Margaret had just finished boiling the water.

"I was about to find you and ask if you wanted a cup of tea."

"You shouldn't be doing that, Margaret." Harrigan scolded.

"That's what I told her, Sir," the constable interrupted. "I did offer, but Mrs Willis wouldn't let me."

"It's alright, Valerie," Margaret assured her. She turned to Harrigan. "For heaven's sake, Inspector, the crisis is over! Please stop fussing, sit down, and drink your tea. You too, Sergeant. I made one for you, as well."

There was no more said until all four were sitting at the table.

"You might be right about *this* part of the crisis being over," Harrigan was the first to speak. "But let's not lose sight of the fact that the threat still remains. There are just too many questions to be answered to allow us to let down our guard now. Not the least of which is, when were the explosives put into the vehicle?" Harrigan took a sip of the tea. As there was no lemon juice, Margaret had put two sugars in it. "Constable."

"Yes, Sir?"

"You've been on protection detail at Mrs Willis' house. Would there have been any opportunity for someone to lift the bonnet and the boot lid of the vehicle and fit the explosives inside? Before you answer," he added quickly, "the explosives actually needed to be secured to something, not just laid inside, so it would have taken some time."

The Constable thought for a few moments before responding. "Even if they hadn't needed to be secured, Sir, I very much doubt it. There may have been short periods of time when the vehicle wasn't being watched, and even considering it was parked away from the front door—"

The constable stopped in mid sentence as Harrigan slapped his forehead. "Of course! You weren't driving your BMW!"

"No. I left it behind to give the impression that I was still at home. The Jag needed the run, anyway." Margaret offered.

"But I *still* doubt anyone would've had time, Sir, no matter which car it was." The constable persisted. "Whoever did it not only had to take the time to place the explosives, they would have to get up to the car, unlock it, do whatever it was they had to do, and then get away. Now that might not be impossible, but it would be highly improbable."

"As far as the BMW is concerned, yes, Constable, I would have to agree it is highly improbable, but the Jaguar?" Harrigan needed more convincing.

"Well I haven't been there all the time, Sir, but whoever had been on duty would have known the routine. I doubt anyone could've got to the Jaguar undetected, either."

"Maybe you're right," Harrigan said unconvincingly.

Margaret watched as Harrigan put another half teaspoon of sugar into his cup and stirred slowly.

"So, OK. If we are to assume that Constable Brideshead is correct, and I can see no real reason not to, that means the explosives were put in place *before* the police operation started."

"Before? Are you sure?" Margaret asked.

"No, Margaret, I'm not sure, but it's the best we've got," The slight uncertainty of the improbable made Harrigan edgy.

"Sorry I asked."

Bill Buckle brought the conversation back in perspective. "As the explosives were detonated by remote control, it could have been the plan to blow the Jaguar up in the driveway of the house."

"That's what I'm thinking, Sergeant. And while we obviously can't be certain, because they used the Jaguar, a vehicle Mrs Willis rarely drives; it probably supports the theory that the explosion was only a warning. It might well be that, when they saw

Mrs Willis drive away in it, they panicked. It might even have forced their hand."

"Blow it up in the car park before I could drive it home again?" Margaret asked.

"And if that is what happened, it definitely was only a warning," Bill Buckle concluded. "There is *one* certainty in all this, Inspector."

"And what would that be, Sergeant?"

"Whoever's behind it is no fool. He, or she, must have anticipated that the first telephone warning could very easily result in some form of police protection, and something like this explosion would need to be prepared ahead of time."

"I couldn't agree more, Sergeant." Harrigan finished his tea and looked at Margaret. "Alright, let's get you home and then Sergeant Buckle and I will go back to Stonegate." Then, turning to Valerie Brideshead, Harrigan continued. "It's probably a bit late now Constable, but we should've sent word to your partner at Mrs Willis' house."

"I called the station immediately after the explosion, Sir, and asked for extra patrols around the area of the house, just in case this was a diversion. I also requested one of the patrols to pass on a message."

"Good work, Constable. I'll make sure I put that in my report." Harrigan was a firm believer in giving the young constables the recognition they deserved.

"Thank you, Sir," she said, unable to hide a smile of satisfaction.

Technically speaking, the Mazda had seating capacity for four people. In a practical sense, however, the two people occupying the rear seats would hotly debate that claim, and with sighs of relief echoing throughout the vehicle, Harrigan stopped the crowded Mazda in the driveway of Margaret's home and walked her to the front door.

"Will I see you later?" she asked.

"As soon as I finish at Stonegate."

"Will you stay over?"

"If you want me to, but I'd better sleep in the front room. I don't want too much talk going around the station."

It hurt Margaret that their true feelings for each other were forced to be almost clandestine. She understood why, but it still hurt.

"I'll see you when you return. I'll prepare some dinner."

"You've had a trying day—" he began to object.

"For heavens sake, Bill, do you want some damn dinner? I've got some lovely loin chops," she tempted.

"Will they be *well done?*"

"Well done, just as you like them." *God only knows why,* she thought.

"How can I resist? I'll give you a ring before I leave Stonegate."

He stopped at the edge of the porch and turned back towards her. "I did tell you your hair looks nice, didn't I?"

"Yes you did, but I don't mind you telling me again."

She exchanged a knowing glance with Valerie Brideshead, smiled and subconsciously patted her hair as she watched the red coupe drive away.

Bill Buckle broke the silence. "They must be watching the house, Inspector. How else would they have known she'd gone to the hairdressers?"

"I'm glad you kept that question to yourself until we were alone, Bill. I was hoping no one would bring that up in front of Mrs Willis at the salon. But, yes, you're right. And they must have even been watching her in the salon. They knew exactly when to call and when to activate the explosives." The graphic truth behind Harrigan's statement wasn't lost on the old sergeant.

"Not a pleasant thought." Bill Buckle sat thoughtfully before continuing. "With that house standing alone the way it does, and the two blocks of units not too far away, it will be almost impossible to find whoever it is doing the watching."

"They could be anywhere, Bill. No, I think we have to forget the middleman and go right to the top."

Bill Buckle looked questioningly at Harrigan. Harrigan stared directly ahead.

"Muhammad Asif Mahmood," he announced.

"Mahmood!?" Bill Buckle's eyes shot up, as he looked unbelievingly at Harrigan.

"Who else?" There was no hint of a question in Harrigan's remark.

Bill Buckle had a high regard for his inspector. He knew Harrigan to be extremely capable and a man who could get things done. His total disdain for bureaucratic red tape and political protocol allowed Harrigan to achieve results no other man could hope to attain. But Mahmood! Mahmood was in a different league! The old sergeant began to worry that Harrigan was allowing his personal feelings for Margaret Willis to cloud his judgment. Harrigan wouldn't be the first man in history to fall into that trap.

As if reading Bill Buckle's mind, Harrigan looked understandingly at his companion. "Don't worry, Sergeant, I know what I'm doing."

They were almost at Stonegate when the mobile telephone rang. Harrigan pressed the little green button. "Harrigan."

"Inspector Harrigan, this is Sergeant Mudford, Upper Binstead," his voice boomed.

"Good afternoon, Sergeant. And there is no need to shout, the mobile telephone is a very efficient instrument."

"Sorry, Sir, I haven't had too much to do with those sorts of things."

"That's alright, Sergeant." Harrigan purposefully spoke softer than normal, trying to lead the way for the country sergeant. "Have you picked up Fadhel?"

"I'm afraid not, Sir. Mr Saheed is not in attendance at the Badgers at this time," he replied, his voice now several decibels lower.

"Has he left permanently, Sergeant?"

"I don't think so, Sir. Just out for the night I'd say."

"Let's hope you're right. Ok. Just keep an eye on the place and bring him in when he gets back. I'll be at Stonegate at around eight in the morning. It would be nice to have him there when I get in."

"Very good, Sir."

"Thank you, Sergeant."

"A pleasure to help the boys from the Metropolitan, Sir." his voiced boomed once more.

Harrigan quickly ended the call.

"Buggar it," he said quietly, under his breath. He drove into the Police Vehicles Only car park and, as most people had left for the day, he stopped the Mazda close to the door of the station.

"I'll see you in the morning, Bill, bright and early."

"You knocking off now, Sir?"

"No, not yet. There are a couple of things I want to do before I leave."

"Well, don't work back too long; tomorrow's another day."

"Thanks, Sergeant, see you tomorrow."

"Good night, Sir."

Harrigan sat in the Mazda for about five minutes. He knew he should begin writing a preliminary report on this case, but it had been a fairly long day and, well, there was always tomorrow. Like many of his age, Harrigan had studied Latin at school. He'd always thought it to be a waste of time during his studies and nothing had happened in his life after school to change his opinion. He had forgotten most of what he'd learned, but a few words still stuck. He could still hear Mr Sinclair telling the class, *"the word 'procrastination' is from the Latin word 'Cras', meaning tomorrow. So Pro plus Cras means to put off until tomorrow."* He was also fond of saying *"Procrastination is not only the thief of time; it is also the thief of ambition."*

"But then, when did I ever listen to anything Mr Sinclair said?" Harrigan asked himself as he started the Mazda and selected reverse gear.

It was just after six when he opened the front door of his home. The house was cold and had that empty feeling. There was nothing of any importance in the mail, so he had a shower, put on a fresh change of clothes, and threw some toiletry items into his green tartan shaving bag. The bag had seen better days. The zipper was broken, but when it was wrapped in a towel, it was ok, nothing fell out. He looked in the refrigerator, emptied the milk into the sink, and with a cursory glance around the house, left again by the front door.

He telephoned Margaret, as he drove to the hospital. "I'll just pop in and see how Mum is and then I'll be over."

"I'll put dinner on in about an hour."

"That'll be fine, 'bye." He sat contentedly as he drove slowly toward the hospital. His thoughts only of Margaret.

* * *

"The nurse told me you would be coming home soon, Mum," he said cheerily, as he sat on the hard hospital chair beside his mother's bed and repeated the message he'd received twenty-four hours earlier.

His mother looked very frail. Ignoring his cheery remark, she placed her hand on his. "Are you alright, son? Is your friend taking care of you?"

"Margaret? Well, yes." He paused, taken a little by surprise at his mother's question. "In fact," he continued cheerily, "I'm off to have dinner with her this evening." He didn't mention he'd be staying overnight.

"I had my reservations about her, William, but then, you already knew that, didn't you?"

"I had a suspicion." He smiled.

"Well, for what it may be worth, she seems to be a sensitive lady, and you have my blessing." She gave a gurgling cough.

"Are you ok, Mum?" he asked, glancing around quickly, looking for a nurse.

"I'm fine. Off you go, now, and have a nice evening." She pulled the sheet up to her chin and put both hands under the bed coverings.

"What are you having for dinner?" she asked, as an afterthought.

"Lamb chops."

A gentle smile creased her drawn face as she lay back into the pillow. "Your favourite."

Harrigan watched her eyes close as she passed into fitful sleep.

The nurse at reception assured Harrigan that his mother was being well taken care of and that it was always difficult with a person of her age. He left Margaret's telephone number with the hospital and, despite their assurances, he felt very ill at ease as he drove to Sprigham Wells.

* * *

"Am I late or is everyone early?" Harrigan asked Patricia Hedrich as he stopped briefly by her desk.

"We're all early, Inspector." She put the lid on her lipstick and checked the accuracy of the application one last time before dropping the compact mirror and the lipstick tube into her bag. The clasp on her handbag gave out a loud sound, as she snapped it closed. "And not only are all the boys in, you also have a Mr Saheed waiting in number two interrogation room."

"Well, it looks like a perfect start to the day."

"How is Mrs Willis, Sir?" Patricia Hedrich asked the question out of genuine concern, but recognising a look that fell somewhere between suspicion and guilt cross his face, she added hurriedly, "I thought you might have heard?" She needn't have bothered. He knew what she meant.

"She's fine, thanks, Trish." He leaned forward and spoke quietly. "Ask everyone to come into my office in five minutes? I'm just going to make a cup of tea."

"I'll get it for you, Inspector."

"No, it's ok, I'll get it. But thanks, anyway." Harrigan stopped in the kitchen and switched on the jug. While the water was boiling, he walked down to interrogation room two. He knocked on the door and turned the handle. A young police constable stood up.

"Good Morning, Sir."

"Good morning, Constable. Hello Mr Saheed."

"What's all this about, Inspector? Why have I been brought here?"

"Just routine. I see you have a cup of tea."

"Your officers have been most polite, but I do wish you would tell me why I am here."

"Like I said, it's just routine. I'll be back in half an hour or so. Constable, see that Mr Saheed is given everything he needs."

"Yes, Sir."

Harrigan ignored Fadhel Saheed's protestations and returned to the kitchen. He pressed the button on the jug to make sure the water was completely boiled, prepared a mug of his favourite English Breakfast tea and went into his office.

He was returning the large brown key to the top draw of his desk as Sergeant Buckle, Colin McIver, and Senior Constable Watts entered the office. Morning pleasantries were exchanged and they settled in the same chairs they had used previously.

"We're told Mrs Willis is none the worse for her ordeal," Bill Buckle offered casually.

"Mrs Willis is a very resilient woman, Sergeant, and speaking of Mrs Willis' experience, that brings us back to where we left off yesterday afternoon." Harrigan looked at McIver. "If I remember, we were talking about the internal measurements of the container?"

McIver opened his notebook and continued from where he'd left off the day before.

"That's right, Sir. I checked my notebook and there were," he paused once more while he found the correct page, "fourteen rows of cartons and nine cartons to a row."

"How wide was the inside of the container, Sergeant?"

"I...I don't know, Sir."

"Well, let's guess. The width of a lorry tray that carries a Container is around, what, eight feet?"

There was a general nod of agreement.

"The walls of a container are fairly thick so let's assume the inside width is somewhere around seven to seven feet six inches. It was also probably about as high as it was wide, maybe a little less." He looked at McIver. "If I remember correctly, each row was three cartons across and three cartons high?" He ignored the fact that McIver had already said there had been nine cartons per row.

"That's correct. I made a note of that in my notebook," McIver re confirmed.

"And, if I also remember correctly, each carton was as deep as it was wide so, taking all that and making a few assumptions, each carton measures somewhere around two feet by four inches in each direction which gives us," Harrigan paused as he took a small calculator from his drawer and made some calculations. "Gives us," he repeated, "a carton of just over twelve cubic feet." His fingers continued over the face of the calculator. "If we multiply that figure by nine cartons by fourteen rows we get," another pause, "one thousand, five hundred, and thirty-three cubic feet. Markings on the back of the container clearly stated that it had a capacity of two thousand, three hundred, and ninety cubic feet."

"That means there is eight hundred and fifty-seven cubic feet unaccounted for."

"That's absolutely correct, Sergeant Buckle." He secretly admired the old sergeant's capacity for mental arithmetic. "Even though our calculations are a bit rough, there is still a lot of space not filled with cartons." His thick fingers once again began to torture the little calculator. "And if we look at it another way, we know the container is forty feet long, because Sergeant McIver assured me of that the first day. But, if we multiply the carton depth by the number of rows, we come up around eight to ten feet short."

"So there is an area of about seven feet by eight feet at the *end* of the container, used to smuggle people?"

"Why not?" Harrigan looked at Malcolm Watts. "As we said yesterday, the money's good and, let's face it, the chances of getting caught are fairly remote. Customs don't check every container, far from it. And sniffer dogs are usually looking for drugs."

"But why didn't it seem obvious when the container was empty?"

"I thought about that too, but Mrs Willis gave me the answer. I felt right from the start that there was something not quite right about that container, so I went for a drive to Tilbury Docks, just to have a look around. As Mrs Willis had not been given official police protection at that time, I took her with me. We saw some containers in the yards that had been stored with their doors open. Why the doors were open, I couldn't tell you; maybe they were smelly or something, but who cares? Mrs Willis remarked that they looked bigger on the inside than on the outside. When I asked her what she meant, she said it was like an empty room, it looked bigger than it really was until you put the furniture in it."

"Well, I saw the container empty and it certainly didn't look bigger to me."

"Exactly. It didn't look *bigger*, that was because in fact it was smaller. However, it did look about the right size, am I correct?"

"Yes. So in fact, it did actually look bigger than it was. But that means the back wall was false. I must say, Sir, I looked inside that container very carefully, and the back wall didn't look false to me. It looked absolutely genuine."

"That's right, Colin, that's because it was a genuine back wall. You can't have a removable false wall on the inside of the container. It would be easily detected. And besides, the person couldn't get out if the container was full. Each operation would involve a lot of people if you did it that way, and we all know that the more people who know, the bigger the risk. Similarly, the outside wall and the top of the container also must be genuine."

"Then how do they get the people in and out?" Watts asked.

"That's the clever part about this operation. This is what sets it apart from the rest. They use the bottom of the container. Through the floor," Harrigan said.

Wouldn't the discrepancy in the cubic feet used against the cubic feet available show up on the documents?" Colin McIver asked.

"That's what I wondered, Senior. I've been told, however, that it's only when a container has more that one consignee, would detailed information like carton size and space used, be recorded on the Bill of Lading. But because Sidhu Trading are paying for a full container, Customs are not really interested in how much space is used, just what goods are inside. It wouldn't be questioned."

"Was there a car parking space between the container platform and the building at East Grinstead?" Bill Buckle asked Colin McIver.

"Yes, I think there was, Sergeant," McIver replied, looking at Harrigan for confirmation. Harrigan gave a slight nod.

"The same as the Goldberg building," Bill Buckle continued. "Bloody simple, really. They leave a car or small van or whatever parked in that space. Once the container is loaded onto the platform, the trap door underneath is opened and, when everyone has gone home, the person inside simply undoes the trapdoor in the floor of the container, unloads his possessions—"

"Or her possessions," Colin McIver just couldn't help himself.

Bill Buckle paused, looked briefly at McIver, then towards Harrigan with a, *well I did tell you,* expression on his face and then continued in a strained voice, "and then disappears. Only one person at either end of the journey need know. That's almost perfect."

"That's right. And on top of that," Harrigan continued, "if the person travelling has his *or her* own set of false identity documents, the true identity of the person need never to be known to anyone, or at most, only known to the person who supplied the documents. No one else needs to meet the person face to face. As you said, Bill, almost perfect. All we need to do now is tie it all together and then we can go home."

Harrigan looked at Bill Buckle, then at the other two policemen.

"Alright then, who wants to have a go?"

"Have a go, Sir?" Malcolm Watts still had a lot to learn about Harrigan's willingness to involve those around him. A trait rarely demonstrated by those of higher rank.

"That's right, Senior, have a go. Give it a shot. Tie it all together." He looked at Bill Buckle. "Bill, why don't you start?"

Bill Buckle shifted in his seat. "I was afraid you were going to say that. OK," he began after a few moments thought.

"I'll get the white board," Colin McIver rushed to the door.

"Bugger the whiteboard, Sergeant, let's just toss it around first." Harrigan was in no mood for that nonsense.

McIver slouched back to his chair.

"OK..." Bill Buckle repeated, "first of all, the people smuggling. I think we all agree that the people-smuggling racket is a reality and that someone or maybe more than one person at Sidhu Trading is behind it. We know that a racket like that depends on secrecy, which means the least people involved the better. This leads to the next question, how many would you need? My guess is two at this end and one involved in a minor way at the other. Why do I say three? Let's look at the operation. You need someone in charge. This person would also be the initial contact. He," he paused and looked at Colin McIver, "or she, would also arrange the false papers and a vehicle at the other end. This is the only person who could know the personal details, or some of the personal details of the person fleeing the country. The second person involved must take care of the containers. The routing, the paperwork, and the loading and unloading of the containers."

"Do you want to put some names to these people?" Harrigan prompted.

"Obviously, I have no idea of the identity of any third person overseas, but the mastermind here, I would say…" he thought briefly before declaring, "Ramachandran."

The others in the room nodded in cautious agreement, as Bill Buckle continued. "Muhammad Singh must be lead contender for the second role."

"Colin?" Harrigan said, as he looked at McIver.

"I don't think there is any doubt that Muhammad Singh is the container man, and I agree that Ramachandran is probably the main man. He seems too much an integral part of the organisation not to know of the operation. But why couldn't Manjit Singhabahu also be involved? He travelled the world. He was in a perfect position to be the third person. He could easily organise, for want of a better description, the *other end* operation."

"Because if Manjit Singhabahu *was* the other end operation man, *why* murder him? It would certainly disrupt Ramachandran's lucrative business." Harrigan explained.

"Are you saying that Manjit was *not* the person looking after the other end of the operation and that Ramachandran murdered Manjit for some other reason, Inspector?" Colin Watts asked.

"No. All I'm saying is that if Manjit was the other end operations man, Ramachandran would not have killed him."

"Well, if Ramachandran didn't kill him, who else had a motive?" Malcolm Watts was desperately trying to come to grips with the format of the meeting.

"A dissatisfied client." It was Colin McIver's turn.

Harrigan was disappointed at McIver's offering. "Xiao Chen was the latest client, Senior, and he was packed and ready to go. I don't think it likely he murdered Manjit, hacked off his hands and feet, went away and disposed of the body parts, came back, set fire to the building, and then threw himself under the bath. I would rate that as extremely doubtful."

"And any other client who didn't like the accommodation is on the other side of the world and hardly likely to come back to complain," Bill Buckle added.

There was to a long silence. Colin McIver felt an obligation to re-ignite the discussion. "Alright, Inspector, let's assume it wasn't some dissatisfied client, and forget about Manjit either being or not being involved. Do you have any suggestions as to why he was killed or who killed him?"

"I think it a little early yet to say who killed him, but three things do stick in my mind. Firstly, the way in which the new secretary at the head office of Sidhu Trading had Manjit's itinerary on hand. Why would Ramachandran telephone the secretary and make such a big deal about it. And then there was the car at Gatwick Airport. Obviously, the person who killed Manjit wanted us to believe he had caught a plane according to the itinerary. This means the person involved knew Manjit's movements. And lastly, would Manjit agree to meet someone at three in the morning in that desolate warehouse, unless he trusted that person?"

"Again you point to Ramachandran."

Harrigan ignored the comment. "We don't know a great deal about Manjit Singhabahu, but his reputation seems to indicate he was a kind and honest man. Maybe it was his honesty that had been the motive. Maybe he found out about the smuggling, that his trips, which he thought were for the improvement of living standards for the underprivileged, were actually only a front for the racket, and he threatened to expose Ramachandran."

"That could be closer to it," Bill Buckle said.

"What about jealousy, Sir?" Watts asked.

"Jealousy, Malcolm? Ramachandran killed Manjit because he wanted Aysha for his own?"

"Something like that, Sir."

"A possibility. Jealousy is definitely one of the more common motives of murder," Harrigan acknowledged. "But would a greedy man jeopardise several million pounds per year for the love of another man's wife? Especially as he was getting what he wanted from her, anyway?"

"Maybe she had given him an ultimatum. Get rid of Manjit or no more nooky," Bill Buckle suggested.

"Now that, Sergeant, is a lot more probable. A lot more probable indeed."

"It may also be a contributing factor in the motive for Aysha's murder," Colin McIver continued enthusiastically.

"Oh?" Harrigan asked.

"Yes, Sir! Ramachandran killed Manjit to appease his lover, but instead of Aysha falling into his arms, she told him she was going to leave him for Mahmood. He snapped, raced over there and, in a fit of jealous rage, he killed her too." He leaned back triumphantly in his chair.

"You sound like a police prosecutor, Senior Constable."

"You must admit it sounds plausible," McIver said confidently.

"Yes," Harrigan warmed to the connection with Mahmood. "It certainly does. In fact, it's so plausible I want you and Senior Constable Watts to mount twenty-four-hour surveillance on our Mr Ramachandran."

The room remained silent as Harrigan stood slowly and walked to the window behind his desk. They watched his back as he continued.

"I don't want him out of your sight, and if he shows any indication he is going to leave the country, arrest him."

"On what charge, Inspector?" McIver asked.

"Do I look like I really care, Colin? I just don't want him getting away, especially not now."

"Very well, Sir." McIver sat quietly, not sure whether to ask his next question. He asked it anyway. "Sir, if I might ask, Mr Ramachandran has shown no indication that he has any intention of running up to date. Why should he start now?"

Harrigan turned and sat on the window ledge.

"Because I am about to try and talk the superintendent into approving Sergeant Buckle and myself having a little chat with Mr Mahmood. I am still convinced that Mahmood is somehow connected to all this, and if I am not mistaken, Ramachandran is already under surveillance from Mahmood's men."

"And you don't want any reaction Mr Mahmood may have to your visit to unnerve Ramachandran?"

"You've got it." Harrigan returned to stand behind the desk. "If you must pick him up, Colin, try and use the people-smuggling racket. It's all pretty thin, but we have more chance of getting him to admit to a charge of illegal traffic in persons, than to a charge of murder."

"And what happens if the superintendent refuses your request, Inspector?" McIver asked.

"Oh, I'm sure I'll find another way," Harrigan replied off-handedly.

Colin McIver stood sharply and gently patted his hair into place.

"I don't want Ramachandran getting away, Colin," Harrigan said firmly.

"Don't worry, Sir, it'll be done properly. Come on, Constable, let's find Mr Ramachandran."

Bill Buckle watched as McIver left the room with a flurry of almost dramatic hand movements.

Harrigan looked at the still motionless constable. "Off you go, Constable, and don't be concerned, Detective Senior Constable McIver is a very capable policeman."

"Yes, Sir." He looked at Bill Harrigan, raised his eyebrows, and left reluctantly.

Harrigan stared at the old wall clock and drummed his fingers on the desk.

"Your Passport up to date, Bill?"

"I renewed it two years ago when Betty and me went to the Caribbean."

"Good." Harrigan stood and walked around the desk. "I have to pay a visit to the superintendent. Wish me luck."

"Good luck, Sir."

"Thank you, Sergeant."

* * *

"You want to *what?*" All eyes on the lower floor of the station rose to look through the glass section of the partition as Superintendent Wilkinson's voice exploded throughout the building. Harrigan's voice was inaudible beyond the enclosed office, but as they watched, they saw his hands rise in a gesture of overwhelming innocence.

"I just think it's the best way."

"I know I'm going to regret asking this, but please, explain to me why it's a good thing that you and Bill Buckle are taking a helicopter ride to some vague location off the coast of France, to speak to one of the most powerful men in the world about people smuggling, murder, and blowing up people's cars?" Wilkinson lay back with his hands linked behind his head. "Go on," he invited, "give it your best shot."

"Well, it was only *one* car and——"

"That's not a good start, Inspector."

"Sorry, Sir." Harrigan curbed his flippancy. He needed the superintendent on his side. "Sir, there is no doubt that Sidhu Trading is involved in a five-star people-smuggling racket for the rich and desperate. There have been two deaths directly linked to the Goldberg fire. One was definitely murder, the other might have been a case of the wrong place at the wrong time. We have a third murder linked to a Sidhu Trading director. Mrs Willis is under police protection because of her being able to associate Mahmood with Lapsley-Midwinter, albeit a brief and almost insignificant association."

"She overheard her now deceased husband make a comment on a telephone to an unknown person! Hardly an association, even an insignificant one, Inspector."

"Maybe so, Sir, but Mahmood himself almost told me as much during my visit with him at the Badgers. Nothing that would stand up in court, of course, but the threat was definitely there." Harrigan wasn't making progress. He needed more. "It *was* significant enough to have her threatened and her car blown up."

"Go on."

"I don't know how Mahmood is caught up in all of this. But caught up he is. Mahmood is the sort of person who stays ahead by knowing what is going on. His people are everywhere. He rules his empire by fear."

"Oh come on, Bill, you've been watching too much television." The superintendent leaned forward and placed his arms on the table.

"Believe me, Sir it has nothing to do with television. I've seen it first hand. An operation such as the people-smuggling racket, especially within Sidhu Trading, could not be carried out without Mahmood finding out about it. It's my guess he knew about it from the start."

"Even if I thought you were right, you'd never prove any of it, not without a confession."

"Exactly, and I am sure that Mahmood is not going to confess. Just as I am equally certain that Ramachandran, or whoever it is running the show, would not finger Mahmood. It would be more than his life was worth."

Harrigan uncrossed his legs and leaned towards Wilkinson. "But I am convinced that Mahmood knows a lot more about the whole business than we will ever be able to prove. And when I say the *whole* business, I'm including the murders and the harassment of Mrs Willis."

Wilkinson moved his hands to his lap and with a blank look on his face, sat silently, challenging his inspector to convince him to take the gamble.

"Sir, normal channels don't allow us to get close to people like Mahmood; the system doesn't permit it. People of his standing are beyond our level of justice. If I am to find out what Mahmood knows, or how he may be involved, I must push the envelope as far as possible."

"You don't have much time for our justice system, do you, Bill?"

"I believe in justice, Sir, probably more than most. There are races and tribes across the globe, and in these so-called modern times, even some communities within our own land, who continue to use a justice system that has served their community well for thousand's of years. And I must say, as barbaric as their penalties may sound to our namby-pamby society, justice is usually done."

"Namby-pamby?" Wilkinson repeated with some disbelief showing through. Harrigan ignored him.

"But the justice system of our society? It doesn't work, Sir. The system becomes more unjust the higher up the scale you go. Those at the bottom must pay the full price; those at the top pay nothing." Harrigan sat back and re-crossed his legs. "There is no mystery to it, of course. The simple explanation is that it was those at the top who created the system, and it remains that those at the top continue to run the system. Now I ask you, what fool creates and runs any system to their own disadvantage?"

The superintendent shrugged in resignation. "So, what has all this to do with your wanting to visit Mahmood in his lair?"

Harrigan was getting fidgety. He again leaned forward. "I don't expect to nail Mahmood on anything of any importance. Mahmood doesn't do his own dirty work; he gets other poor bastards to do that. Other poor bastards who are either so loyal or so scared they are willing to take the fall. If they don't, they are eliminated."

"You still haven't answered my question."

"I need to talk to Mahmood to make a deal."

"A deal?"

"Yes. I need answers. Mahmood has answers. I am never going to be able to bring Mahmood here for questioning; he wouldn't come, and the Home Office wouldn't let me, anyway. But if I arrange to meet him on his turf, well, water in this case, I may well be able to get Mahmood to throw me a sacrificial lamb or two in exchange for...for..." Harrigan paused, struggling for the right word.

"Immunity?" Wilkinson suggested.

"That's probably a little strong. Let's just say some peace and quiet."

"Margaret Willis part of the deal?"

"He leaves her alone. I leave him alone." "Why take Sergeant Buckle?"

"One policeman falling out of a helicopter or drowning overboard can probably be explained away, but two?"

Once again, Harrigan had put Wilkinson in a position where he must choose between his conscience and promotion. The superintendent only had a few more years to serve, and a promotion to Assistant Commissioner was a real possibility. He knew the Home Office would never approve the action suggested by Harrigan, but he also knew that Harrigan was right. The visit to Mahmood's Yacht was worth a try. But if anything went wrong, he could kiss any chance of promotion goodbye. He'd be lucky to keep his rank of superintendent.

"What about Interpol? It *is* an international matter." It was Wilkinson's last toss of the dice.

"Bringing in Interpol at this time would only serve to scare everyone off. The shutters would go down and, after a few well-placed telephone calls, the matter would be buried forever. Besides, it's a local matter."

"Smuggling people from one country to another is *not* a local matter."

"Sir, let me talk to Mahmood, and if that doesn't work, then we'll call Interpol."

"Another one of your deals?"

"If you want to put it that way, Sir."

Wilkinson waved his hand in dismissal.

"Ok. Go and have your chat with Mahmood, but remember yours isn't the only career you're playing with. Now get out."

"Thank you, Sir!" Harrigan hurried toward the door.

"Oh, and Inspector..." Wilkinson called after him.

"You're not going to tell me to be careful, are you, Sir?"

"Er, well...no," he paused, "Go on! Get out before I change my mind!"

CHAPTER TEN

Fadhel Saheed had been more than helpful. He'd telephoned his boss and given the telephone to Harrigan. Harrigan was heartened by the way that Mahmood had agreed to the meeting. There had been no hesitation, as he offered to make arrangements for all formalities to be in place by the time the trio reached the helicopter at the Little Woping Airport. He also insisted they stay overnight. Harrigan didn't say as much at the time, but he had little intention of accepting Mahmood's offer of hospitality.

Security at Little Woping was extreme to verging on the paranoid. Sniffer dogs inspected every vehicle, while Security guards discreetly passed very serious looking black metal detecting wands over every passenger. The search was thorough, polite, and efficient and took less than two minutes. The need for such security became more obvious as they approached the terminal. Harrigan had never seen so many corporate jets and helicopters in one place in his life. He made that comment to Fadhel.

"Little Woping is a fully functional international airport, Inspector. It is used mainly as a heliport, but the smaller corporate jet can use it at a pinch."

"I never knew it was here."

"Not many people do."

"How the hell do you keep something like this a secret?"

"Oh, it's not a secret. If you tried to keep it a secret, everyone would know about it."

Harrigan smiled at the wisdom of those words.

"No, Sir, it is not a secret, it's just not publicised."

"Surely the media prowls around the area, trying to find out who's coming and going?"

"Normally you would be right, Inspector, but while Little Woping is not a secret, it is well protected."

"But Security guards are not going to keep a journalist, bent on snooping out a story, away from the area."

Saheed gave a small laugh. "Ohhh, Inspector. The guards are only a small part of the security." He drove masterfully between the rows of helicopters of all sizes. "Little Woping has a much stronger line of defence against media people." He stopped and waited for a fuel truck to pass in front. "The world's major media moguls are partners in the Airport, so consequently, anyone employed within the major media are under threat of dismissal if a story about the place gets out."

"Everyone has a weak spot."

"Something like that, Sir."

"What about the people who live nearby?"

"You may not have noticed, but the countryside is sparsely occupied, by farmers mostly."

"It's a wonder the farmers don't complain about the noise upsetting their cows and chooks."

"*Chooks?* Excuse me, Sir, what are *chooks?*"

"Sorry, chickens. I spent my youth in Australia. It slips out every now and then."

"Australia," he repeated, and nodded with a, *that explains many things,* look on his face. He continued. "Under normal circumstances, I would agree that the farmers would be complaining about their cows and...*chooks*, but again, the land is mostly owned by those who support the airport itself. The farmers are allowed to stay at reduced rent and do whatever it is that farmers do, as long as they remain uncomplaining."

"Does the airport cost the taxpayer any money?"

Saheed manoeuvred the car into a large hanger and parked beside two British racing green Bentley's. "Oh no, Sir, well not directly. It's probably a tax write off, but the money all comes from the shareholders."

"Shareholders?"

"To use the airport you must be a shareholder. But like any other airport, you pay landing fees and for all other services." He unfastened his seatbelt. "Here come Customs, we'd better get ready to meet them."

Harrigan looked at the two uniformed officers approaching their vehicle. The smaller female officer was operating a battery-powered trolley, about the size of a hospital gurney.

Harrigan looked at Bill Buckle. There was just nothing to say.

"Good morning, Gentlemen, may I have your passports?" The male customs officer took the lead.

The three watched as he went through the familiar routine of checking the photograph and entering the details into a laptop computer, which was secured to one end of the trolley. The female officer was left to lift their bags and pass them under the portable x-ray machine at the other end. Harrigan and Bill Buckle stood in stunned silence.

"It seems everything is in order. Have a good journey, Gentlemen."

The whole episode took less than three minutes.

"It's time we left, Inspector. Sergeant." Saheed's comment bordered on being an order. Bill Buckle began to have bad feelings.

Fifteen minutes later, at ten minutes after one, the S-76 Sikorsky corporate helicopter lifted off the ground and sped along the six-mile length of the Woping Gorge.

Not being accustomed to the intercommunication system fitted to each helmet, Harrigan leaned forward and spoke loudly to Saheed.

"Where exactly is Mr Mahmood anchored?" he asked.

Despite having asked this question four or five times since the telephone conversation with Mahmood, Harrigan had not yet received a direct answer.

"Mr Mahmood is anchored just off the coast at St Jean de Monts."

Saheed looked towards the pilot. "It's about four hundred miles?" he asked.

The pilot replied with a simple nod.

"It will take about two and a half hours," Saheed concluded and looked directly ahead. As an afterthought he added, "Sit back, relax, and enjoy your flight, Gentlemen. You will never have a better view of France, and please, help yourself to the bar."

Once out of the Gorge, and at only one thousand feet above sea level, the pilot set the cruising speed at one hundred and fifty miles an hour, around thirty miles an hour below the maximum top speed.

There was little to no conversation. Bill Buckle and Harrigan occasionally nudged each other's arm to point to some interesting landmark.

With the exception of two mineral waters each, the bar remained untouched.

It was four-thirty-five when they flew over a large caravan and camping ground at St Jean de Monts. Their altitude and speed had been reduced to where they were now able to clearly identify people scurrying to and from the shower blocks, all in varying states of undress, with towels over their shoulders and carrying little canvas bags of toiletries.

Although the beach was almost empty, there were still a few swimmers left behind to enjoy the clear blue ocean water.

Bill Buckle had never been fond of helicopter travel; he preferred wings and engines on either side. Flying over water in a helicopter lifted his fear to a completely different level. With white knuckles straining in the huge fists tightly clenched to the arms of his seat, Bill Buckle stared directly at the back of the pilot's seat. He was convinced his soon to be watery death was simply an inevitability. The spell Bill Buckle had cast over himself was broken as Harrigan nudged him and pointed to the white vessel anchored ahead. As they approached, the magnificence of the vessel slowly became all too obvious.

"Flippin' heck, will you look at that boat?" Bill Buckle's fear of death suddenly vanished as his involuntary observation spewed forth, failing miserably to capture the true essence of the sight before them.

"Magnificent, isn't she?" Fadhel Saheed spoke with affection in his voice.

"That belongs to Mahmood?"

"To one of his companies, yes."

"How big is it?" Harrigan was not easily impressed, but the sheer elegance of this vessel, as it gently kissed the embracing water of the low swell, was enough to entice even the hardest of men.

"The *Dei Lucrii* is four hundred and fifteen feet long and seventy-two feet wide. She is powered by six diesel motors with up to nine thousand horse power. She has five floors or decks if you prefer. There are five bedrooms, all with ensuite, a master bedroom, two dining areas, plus a formal dining room. There is also a fully operational commercial centre, including satellite links to all Mr Mahmood's business operations, two secretaries, each with an office, Mr Mahmood's office, and a luxury Board room. Crew facilities are on the bottom deck, of course."

"Of course. How many crew are there?" Harrigan didn't really care, but he *was* interested in knowing the strength of the force he and Bill Buckle might be facing in a short while.

"There is a crew of thirty-five, plus security."

"How many security?"

"We had better prepare to land," he replied, security obviously not being a subject open for discussion. "Please sit back and make sure your seatbelts are securely fastened. Mr Mahmood would not want any harm to come to his guests."

Bill Buckle squeezed his eyes firmly shut as the pilot skilfully manoeuvred the helicopter onto the helipad positioned at the rear of the vessel.

Saheed ushered Harrigan and Bill Buckle from beneath the still rotating blades and down a small flight of steep steps leading onto the main deck.

"This way," he directed.

They walked quickly along the non-slip finish of the shining wooden boards. Brass fittings glimmered in the late afternoon sun.

Saheed stopped at a large wooden door and opened it outwards.

"Mind the step, Inspector, and please, wait for me at the bottom of the stairs."

Harrigan carefully negotiated the narrow stairway. He was grateful for the more than ample light that came from brass lanterns of the shape traditionally associated with sea going vessels. He waited at the next level for his companion and his guide.

Saheed passed him hurriedly and moved swiftly towards two doors of black glass. He slid his security card through a slot in the small grey box on the wall beside the doors. Three pairs of eyes were drawn to the little red light and waited apprehensively for the little green light to appear. They didn't wait long. A voice sounded from a hidden speaker.

"Please wait," it asked politely.

It took about fifteen seconds before a panel, about the size of a man's hand, appeared in the wall below the grey box. There was a glass cover and the panel was lit brightly in red. The notice on the panel said, *Do Not Touch – Electricity,* and there was a sign with that bolt of lightning symbol, used to indicate electricity.

As the glass cover rose, the light turned green. The sign changed to *Proceed*.

Saheed took a pace forward and placed his right hand on the panel. Almost immediately, Harrigan and Bill Buckle heard the two massive glass doors begin to slide open. Again, Saheed went ahead of them.

"Please stay behind me." This time, it was a definite order.

They followed him into a small vestibule. He stopped in front of five yellowish beams of light that barred his way. The doors behind them slid quietly closed. Not until they had closed completely and the sound of the locks refastening had ceased, did the beams of light disappear. The trio were now faced with a single black glass door. They stood patiently.

It was at least a full sixty seconds before the door slid open and Saheed led the two policemen into one of the most luxurious rooms either men had ever seen, or were likely to see again.

Wooden furnishings, upholstered with the finest leather and etched with pure gold leaf, filled the room with the smell of obscene wealth. While the rear wall behind them was square, the wall directly opposite, and one quarter of both side walls were of a semi-circular shape.

The top section of both the side walls and the opposite wall gave a panoramic view through shining glass. Harrigan suspected the windows had been manufactured of the same inch and a half thick, one-way glass, used for the doors through which they had just walked.

Muhammad Mahmood stood in silhouette against the far wall, but there was ample light to see a small tumbler of golden liquid held in a hand adorned with three overly sized gold rings.

"Welcome, Inspector, Sergeant, to my," he paused, "I won't say *humble* abode, for I fear that may indicate a little, shall we say, vulgar ostentatiousness?"

If he means he's a showy little bastard and he wanted to make a point, he's right, thought Harrigan.

"Maybe a little," Harrigan replied courteously as he walked slowly around the room. I must congratulate you on your good taste and obvious success," he added.

Harrigan wasn't given to envy and was always willing to acknowledge others' successes. He did not necessarily agree with some methods used to gain such success, but success in any form should at least be respected.

"Thank you, Inspector." Mahmood cautiously accepted Harrigan's praise. He shifted his gaze slightly and looked over the police inspector's shoulder. "And what about you, Sergeant, I am sure you would like to familiarise yourself with the rest of the yacht? Fadhel!" Mahmood called.

"Yes, Mr Mahmood."

"Please show the sergeant to his overnight quarters, and show him around the *Dei Lucrii*."

"Yes, Sir! Please follow me, Sergeant."

Bill Buckle looked at Harrigan who offered an agreeable nod. "It's alright, Sergeant," he replied, and looking directly Mahmood, added, "I'm sure I'll be able to contact you if I need you."

Mahmood moved his shoulders in an, *of course he can,* manner.

Bill Buckle turned resignedly towards Saheed. "Come on, Fadhel," Bill Buckle invited, "show me over this tub. She's a bit different to what I used to sail on in the Navy."

Saheed bowed politely. "Yes, Sir."

The two men left.

"Drink, Inspector?" Mahmood asked, as he walked slowly towards a well-stocked liquor cabinet. The only place Harrigan had seen a larger stock of liquor was the liquor aisle in his local Salusbury's store.

"A small scotch, thanks."

Mahmood selected a square bottle. "Ballantines I believe?"

"Thank you." Harrigan was impressed; this man certainly did his homework.

But Harrigan was not there to be impressed. *If a man takes the trouble to learn and remember what brand of whisky you prefer, it's for sure your preferred tipple isn't all he knows about you,* he quietly warned himself.

"This is certainly a magnificent view, Mr Mahmood, how do you ever get any work done?"

"Discipline, Inspector, but yes you are right." He stood beside the policeman and handed him his Ballantines. "It is indeed a magnificent view."

Two more different men you wouldn't find; yet to find two more similar men would be an equally difficult task.

"But you did not come here to admire the view, Inspector, so please, select a chair and let's begin our…is it an interrogation, Inspector?"

"Oh, it's not an interrogation, Mr Mahmood." He selected a chair beside an enormous bookcase and allowed the soft leather to envelop him. He began to wonder at the wisdom of interviewing such a powerful man on his own territory. "Let's just say it's an exchange of truths. A *confidential* exchange of truths."

"That sounds like it could be very interesting," Mahmood said cautiously.

"It's more than a *could be,* Mr Mahmood. I'm counting on it."

They toasted each other and each took a meaningful sip of the liquor of their choice.

"Truths about what, Inspector?"

Harrigan knew his reply would be a make-or-break response, and it was no time to pussyfoot around. "Mainly your involvement in the subsurface movement of people around the world," he said, as bluntly as possible.

The casual manner in which he delivered his answer, in no way indicated Harrigan's pounding heart. He knew there was not another person on this Earth who would dare speak to a man of Mahmood's position in that manner. He also knew that Mahmood's answer would determine the future of this conversation.

Mahmood did not flinch.

"What an interesting statement." He showed no emotional reaction. Tension-filled seconds crept by as each man tried to hold the edge. Harrigan knew that in Mahmood's game plan, it was now his turn to speak. He remained silent.

Harrigan stared motionless as Mahmood took another sip from the not overly large but elegant tumbler. *A small, almost unsure type of sip,* Harrigan thought.

"Please, go on, Inspector." Mahmood was forced onto the back-foot.

Harrigan smiled inwardly and placed his Ballantines on the small table to his left. He crossed his legs and placed his hands on the ample arms of the chair.

"Without going into all the boring details, I know about the *not-quite five-star* accommodation compartments in some of your shipping containers."

He took his notebook from inside his jacket and read aloud three container numbers. He looked at Mahmood who, with a slight hunch of his shoulders, shook his head indicating the numbers meant nothing to him.

"Not that actual container numbers would mean much to you," he continued, somewhat negating Mahmood's nonchalant response, "but they do mean a lot to me. Those numbers enable me to follow those containers around the world. I do have the records in my office."

"Fascinating." Mahmood's feigned indifference heartened Harrigan. Mahmood wasn't reading the situation correctly. Feigned indifference to such allegations was wrong. *Outrage* would have been an innocent man's reaction. Harrigan replaced his hands and arms openly along each armrest. "I even know for whom that accommodation is, or should I say *has*, been used. The name Lapsley-Midwinter immediately springs to mind."

Harrigan needed to give Mahmood time to think. He tipped a few drams of the soft liquid into his mouth and allowed it to caress his inner palate, before it trickled slowly into his throat. His actions were delayed, almost laborious.

"Lapsley-Midwinter?" It was the best reply Mahmood could eventually come up with. He knew it wasn't good enough, and Harrigan knew he knew it wasn't good enough. It was akin to saying *pass* in a game of cards.

Harrigan slammed his glass down dramatically and stood impatiently.

"Oh come on, Muhammad!" Harrigan figured it was time to drop the Mr Mahmood malarkey. "I thought we agreed we would be truthful, that's the whole purpose of this visit!!"

He walked to the semi-circular window and spoke to the coast of France. "If you're going to stick with the story that you don't know who Lapsley-Midwinter is, you're either a liar or you think me stupid."

It was Mahmood's turn to stand. "How dare you call me a liar!" he shouted.

Harrigan turned slowly and walked to within six inches of Muhammad Mahmood. "Because you," Mahmood felt the hot breath on his face as Harrigan whispered, each word laced with menace, "have threatened Mrs Willis and had her car blown up, because you think, she can connect you with Lapsley-Midwinter."

Mahmood made to argue and then stopped. He took a step back and picked up his empty glass. "Another drink, Inspector?"

Harrigan retrieved his glass and drained the last few drops. "I'd love one, Mr Mahmood."

They eventually returned to their seats.

"What is it you *really* want to know?" Mahmood's manner was relaxed and conciliatory. The tension had left the room.

"I want to know what you know. I have three bodies. Two have been murdered, one may have been accidental." Harrigan gave Mahmood the highlights of the case. Manjit's body, the dead Chinese, and the murder of Aysha. The illegal movement of undesirables around the world. The escape of people such as Lapsley-Midwinter. The harassment of Margaret Willis was also high on the agenda.

"Do you have any strong suspects?"

"Generally, the evidence points to Ramachandran."

"Evidence that points to the murders or the traffic of people?"

"Both. He had motive and opportunity in the murder of Aysha, which he strongly denies of course."

"Of course."

"As far as the Manjit murder. There was too much effort put into trying to convince us that Manjit had gone away on business. The car at the airport, the secretary having his itinerary at her fingertips. And I believe that Manjit's murder is somehow tied in with the illegal trafficking. Whoever I can tie in with the trafficking, I can tie in with the murder of Manjit."

"You mean me?" Mahmood asked.

"I mean you," Harrigan replied.

Mahmood respected Harrigan's directness and honesty. It had been many years since he had met a man who was not intimidated by his position and power.

"Ramachandran had the opportunity and very few others would need to be involved," Mahmood mused.

"That's right. He had access to, and was responsible for, the movement of the containers. Of course, Muhammad Singh must also have been involved with actually arranging the movement of the containers, but they could have managed it together."

"Just the two of them?"

"At the UK end, yes. The success of such an operation depends on the least number of people knowing about it."

"Then haven't you just presented the case for my defence? Is that not a reason why I should *not* have known about it?"

"Normally yes. But there are two things that trouble me. Firstly, your overreaction to a brief comment made by Margaret Willis. Why was there such a violent reaction? The information was virtually useless in any court of law. It was at best hearsay. Mrs Willis overheard one side of a telephone conversation, which mentioned both you and Lapsley-Midwinter. What would that prove? It probably would not even be allowed in evidence."

Mahmood said nothing.

"I'll tell you why the reaction. It wasn't that the evidence was of value; it was that a statement, no matter how valueless it may eventually be, that linked you with the disappearance of a paedophile, would affect your reputation. And, Mr Mahmood," Harrigan gestured boldly at the opulence of the room, "despite all your wealth, I believe your *reputation* is your prized possession. I realised your obsession for acceptance in elite circles, the night I saw you at Ali's with people who would normally be seen as foreign to your world. An Archbishop? A High Court Judge? Come now, Muhammad, are they really your kind of people? I think not! Not socially anyway. I'm sorry to have to tell you, but your desire to belong in this reputable and elite world, appears not only to be your driving passion but also your Achilles' heel."

Harrigan felt he might have gone too far and that the conversation would be terminated. He was surprised at Mahmood's calm reply and candour.

"Yes Inspector Harrigan, I fear you could be right." He paused. "But you said there were two things?"

"I have been amazed and I must admit to a little admiration, at your far reaching control. There is very little that would escape your watchful eye. I imagine you have eyes and ears in every part of the globe."

"Everywhere there is a need."

"Exactly. I also know that anyone who does not play the game to your rules is dealt with, shall we say, very severely?"

"You could say that." Mahmood soaked the praise from this man.

"And that is my point. Ramachandran would not dare double-cross you. He wouldn't dare run such a lucrative operation without your knowledge. Money, no matter how much money, is worthless to a dead man."

It angered Mahmood that he had again allowed Harrigan to take the upper hand. Mahmood struggled within himself. If it were not for that damn sergeant, Harrigan might have had an accident. It was easy to fall overboard and drown, even for a policeman, especially when he'd had too much to drink. But *two* policemen? No, there had to be another way. Harrigan had obviously prepared well for this encounter. He would allow this man, whom he had obviously, grossly underestimated, to continue to play his game towards its conclusion. There might be a way out along the way.

"If we assume for a moment that you are right, and please don't take that to be an admission, you have no evidence. Not against me."

"I don't need evidence. I have Ramachandran. I have enough evidence to convict *him* for crimes that will lock him away for the rest of his natural life." Harrigan lay back in the chair and again spread his arms along the well-padded armrests. "But as for you, I do not need to take your freedom away. I will deprive you of the very thing you hold in the highest. On the route to Ramachandran's convictions, I will take away your respectability."

Harrigan watched closely as his last words sparked instant hatred inside Mahmood. His countenance took on a demonic glow. Harrigan waited a further twenty seconds, timing was everything.

"Of course," he continued, "none of all that unpleasant business need occur. In fact, I have no real desire to pursue that course of action."

Mahmood's mood softened as the not too subtle hint of a possible deal surfaced into Harrigan's words. Mahmood liked men who were willing to make a deal.

"As I explained at the beginning, I just want to know what you know. I want to be told everything you know about this affair, not just what you think I *ought* to be told." Harrigan took a sip from the tumbler. "The difference between now and the start of our conversation is that you are now fully aware of the consequences, even if I only *suspect* you are holding something back."

Like Harrigan, Mahmood admired a man good at his craft. He continued to relax. "I don't know what it is you are after, Inspector, but go ahead, ask your questions. I'll do my best to be as truthful as possible."

"Thank you." Harrigan replaced the tumbler on the side table and opened his notebook. "I suspect that until recently, Manjit Singhabahu had no knowledge that his beloved charity works were simply a cover for the more lucrative Sidhu Trading migrant service. Am I right?"

"Yes." Mahmood told Harrigan of Manjit's visit. He also explained that he had asked Manjit not to say anything to Ramachandran.

"Why did you do that?"

"I was concerned that Ramachandran might do something foolish. I explained that to Manjit."

When Harrigan was a boy, growing up in outback Australia, his mother used to tell him that if he told a lie, he would get a big black mark on his tongue. He would give anything at this moment to have a look at Mahmood's tongue. There was simply no point to Mahmood's answer. His answer indicated that it was his intention to protect Manjit and punish Ramachandran. Why would he do that? There was nothing in that for him. *No*, Harrigan thought, *he more than likely called Ramachandran and told him to get rid of Manjit.* But Harrigan was satisfied so far. At least he'd been right about Manjit finding out about being used.

"How would you describe Manjit's attitude when he came to visit you. Was he angry?"

"I wouldn't say angry." Mahmood paused while he considered his answer. "Manjit was an honest man, Inspector, and like most honest people who devote their lives to doing good, they refuse to see the other side of people. The real and ugly side of people. They pretend that everything in the garden is rosy. A weed in a garden is simply a misunderstood flower."

Harrigan allowed himself a slight smile as Mahmood again paused meaningfully before continuing.

"I mean, take the affair between Ramachandran and Aysha. Don't tell me Manjit didn't know that it was going on! He had to know! But, in the true nature of the righteous, if you don't admit it's happening, then it isn't."

Mahmood was talking a little too much. He obviously wanted the affair between Aysha and Ramachandran brought into the conversation. It was beginning to look like Mahmood was trying to finger Ramachandran in a left-handed kind of way.

"What did you think of one of your directors having an affair with his fellow director's wife? Not a great image for Sidhu Trading if something like that got out," Harrigan probed.

"Maybe I am also touched with the nature of the righteous," Mahmood offered, but even he was forced to give a little smile at the ridiculousness of the statement.

"You still haven't answered my question about Manjit's mood. Give it to me in one word."

"One word?" He looked to the ceiling. "Disappointed."

"Did he swallow your line about being worried that Ramachandran might do something foolish, and to keep it to himself?"

Mahmood was momentarily thrown off guard. He thought Harrigan had believed him. "Er…er, I, I think so," he replied brokenly.

Harrigan gave a quiet, doubtful "mmm" and made notes in his small book. "Did you mention this conversation to Ramachandran?"

Mahmood knew this was a most important question. No matter what answer he gave, it would lead to his knowledge of the trafficking business and eventually connect him to the murder. Not that what he said could be used against him. It was his word against Harrigan's, and he knew Harrigan was not carrying a tape recorder or bug of any kind. The three men had been x-rayed and scanned for any electronic devices while they stood in the vestibule. On the other hand, he was not going to admit too much.

"Let's just say Ramachandran knew that I was aware of his, his extra curricula activities. Maybe I was foolish to allow it, but I have never been one to stifle the entrepreneurial spirit. I was concerned that if Manjit went to the authorities and reported Ramachandran's, migrant service I think you called it, it would reflect badly on the business and, in turn, on me. So, yes, Inspector, I called Ramachandran to my home on Constopolu and told him that Manjit had found out about his activities and he was to fix the problem immediately. '*I do not want Manjit going to the Authorities,*' I told him. At no time did I mean to suggest that Manjit's life should be taken. Goodness me, just a satisfactory compromise, that was all I was looking for."

"Are you suggesting that Ramachandran killed Manjit?"

"Of course not!" The look of annoyance that had been planted carefully on his face to coincide with the emphatic denial was allowed to fade slowly into a look of understanding. "But I see how you *could* think that, Inspector." His voice trailed off. Then suddenly, "But no! It's impossible! Unthinkable! Ramachandran wouldn't do such a thing!"

The defence of his director was admirable. Utter baloney, but admirable.

"Did Ramachandran report back to you after he had reached a compromise?"

"Yes. He told me the problem had been fixed."

"When was this?"

"The day after the fire at the Goldberg building."

The answer was too readily available.

"And Ramachandran telephoned from Aysha Singhabahu's home to tell you this?"

"I believe so."

"Did he tell you he had killed him?" He put the question as bluntly as possible.

"Come now, Inspector, do you really expect me to answer *yes* to such a question? Even if it *were* true, which it isn't. Ram told me he had reached a compromise, that's all."

"And you weren't curious as to what the compromise was?"

"I have learned through the years that curiosity can be an adversary. I am a true Leo, Inspector, but I am well able to control the feline curiosity."

Mahmood watched closely over the rim of the glass, as Harrigan made several notes in his book. Unlike the detective stories in the movies, he was unable to tell what the policeman was writing by watching the movement of the top of the pen.

Harrigan returned the pen and notebook to the inside pocket of his jacket.

"I only have four more questions, Mr Mahmood, before we get on to the final matter. I must have honest answers. Yes or No will be fine."

The finality of his demand left no opportunity for an answer. Mahmood sat quietly, almost obediently.

"Did you contact Aysha Singhabahu and tell her she was to come and live with you."

"Yes."

"Did you think at the time she would contact Ramachandran and tell him she was going to be your mistress?"

"Yes."

"Did Aysha know of the trafficking racket?"

"Yes."

"Did you send Saheed to kill her?"

"No."

It was as if he'd been waiting for the question. But Harrigan believed him.

"You said there was a final matter?" Mahmood asked.

"I want you to call your dogs off Mrs Willis."

The two men sat holding the other's stare. The seconds ticked by. Harrigan felt the sting in his eyes, as they cried for him to allow the eyelids to close and coat them with soothing moisture. His eyes went in and out of focus. His face remained stony cold.

Mahmood stood and walked to the window.

"*Your* Achilles' heel, Inspector?"

Harrigan let the question pass. He decided he should allow Mahmood a little dignity in what both men knew was defeat.

"Let us just say, that as the conversation Mrs Willis overheard is now a matter of record in my files, there is nothing to be gained from her harassment, or indeed, harm. And I should also add that any police investigation that was the result of any harassment, or worse still of any harm that might befall Mrs Willis, will be far more damaging to you than any piece of hearsay conversation will ever be."

Mahmood turned, but failed to look directly at Harrigan.

"Do I detect a threat, Inspector?"

"Not at all, Mr Mahmood, just good advice."

Mahmood walked to the telephone on the desk and pressed a speed dial number. He then pressed a second button. Harrigan heard the telephone ringing on the loud speaker. It rang three times.

"Yes, Mr Mahmood?" A heavily accented voice said.

"Mrs Willis no longer needs to be under our observation, Mahindah, remove all surveillance immediately."

"Yes, Mr Mahmood." The telephone went dead.

"Is that all, Inspector?"

Harrigan was suspicious. "Aren't you concerned that your telephone may by tapped?"

"That line is fitted with a scrambler, Inspector. For commercial reasons you understand."

"For commercial reasons," Harrigan repeated. "I should have realised."

Harrigan stood. "Thank you for your candour, Mr Mahmood, and like I said at the start, this conversation didn't take place."

"I hope it helps with your investigation, Inspector."

"Oh it helps alright. In fact, I know all the answers now; I just have to prove them."

"I could use a man like you, Inspector. If you are ever looking for a job?"

"Thank you, Mr Mahmood, I'll keep that in mind."

"I am surprised that a person of your ability remains at the rank of inspector."

Harrigan smiled. "Let's just say that higher ranking officers don't always see my methods as politically sound."

Mahmood pressed another button on the telephone.

"Yes, Mr Mahmood?"

"Where are you and the Sergeant, Fadhel?"

"In the main lounge area, Mr Mahmood."

"The inspector will join you shortly." Mahmood clicked off the telephone.

"The helicopter will arrive at eight thirty tomorrow morning, Inspector." As if anticipating Harrigan's request to be returned to London immediately, Mahmood continued. "Arrangements, flight plans, and the like have already been made. Until that time, please relax and enjoy the hospitality on board."

He ushered Harrigan toward a wall mural of three rather large, full-bodied and very naked Greek maidens sitting around a well. As the two men approached, two ladies were separated from the third as a panel in the wall slid open.

A huge man, wearing grey trousers and a starched white casual shirt stood, arms folded, in the carpeted alleyway.

"Joseph will take you to your companion. Good bye, Inspector."

"Good-bye and thank you again, Mr Mahmood."

CHAPTER ELEVEN

The helicopter lifted off at exactly eight-thirty the next morning. The two visitors had to admit their night on the *Dei Lucrii* had been most enjoyable. It must be said, however, that with both men having a more pedestrian taste to that which Mahmood's personal chef was accustomed to catering for, their evening meal, while delicious, was a little too *gourmet*.

Harrigan had needed to contact Colin McIver, away from ear-shot of the crew. McIver was on duty watching Ramachandran, so he had one of the Station's mobile telephones with him. Harrigan had tried earlier, but his mobile telephone didn't work from his cabin, and up until mealtime, he'd been unable to get out on deck without one of Mahmood's men being there to *"show him the way."* At the evening dining table, he made sure he was first to order. A medium to rare pepper sauce steak for the main course.

"While you gentlemen order I must just go up on deck for a minute. I won't be long. Don't anyone get up, I know the way."

Bill Harrigan had then excused himself, and made his way to the main outside deck. He prayed his mobile telephone had a signal. Luck was with him. He dialled the number and waited.

"McIver," came the reply.

"Colin, it's Bill Harrigan. Sergeant Buckle and I won't be into the station until around midday tomorrow. You still watching Ramachandran?"

"Yes, Sir."

"Good. I want you and Malcolm to pick him up immediately."

"The Senior is just down the road, getting some refreshments, do you want me to pick Ramachandran up on my own or wait for Watts to return?"

"Well, there should be two of you there now; that's why I sent *both* of you." The rebuke wasn't lost on McIver. "But as you're the only one there, if you think you can handle it on your own, do it now. You're the one there; you'll have to make the call. I just don't want any unnecessary delays, do you understand?"

"Right Sir. What's the charge?"

"No charge. Take him in for questioning. Use the Aysha murder; it's the best bet. And, Colin, once you have Ramachandran in custody, don't leave him with any policeman you don't know. I don't give a damn about rank or what the story is, I want either you or Malcolm Watts with him at all times. He must not be left alone with anyone else. Do you understand?"

"Yes, Sir!"

"Good. Now hop to it, and hope you are not too late. See you tomorrow." He rang off.

Harrigan had no idea if his telephone call could have been intercepted. He wouldn't have been surprised, but he couldn't chance to delay the call any longer; he had to get Ramachandran into protective custody.

It was doubtful that Ramachandran would involve Mahmood, no matter what he may or may not, eventually be charged with. To involve Mahmood would mean almost certain death. However, Harrigan had not dismissed the possibility that Mahmood might need more assurance than that. It was always the loose ends that got you. A frightened Ramachandran was one thing; a dead Ramachandran was much safer. It would certainly allow Mahmood to rest more easily, not to mention an easy target to take all the blame. Harrigan could almost see the report now.

Victim: Khalil Ramachandran.

Cause of Death: Murdered by a "dissatisfied client."

Mahmood would deny all knowledge of the illegal traffic in persons and, although expressing disappointment in Ramachandran's dishonesty and completely unexplainable acts of homicide, would also show dismay at his director's murder.

Ramachandran would be named as being responsible for the deaths of Manjit and Aysha Singhabahu, and the death, albeit unintentional, of Xiao Chen. He would also be blamed for the entire people-trafficking operation, and his murder put down to retribution from some unidentified villain-on-the-run. The case would never be completely finalised and, in the modern-day equivalent of some old dusty drawer marked cold case murders, it would simply fall into the bowels of history.

Having made the telephone call, Harrigan returned to the meal table.

Despite the offer of fulfilment of any need, and *any* was underlined, Harrigan and Bill Buckle spent the rest of the evening in the private film theatre drinking Bass beer and watching Lethal Weapon One and Two.

* * *

McIver knew that the stakeout on Ramachandran's home could be a long and tiring affair. He and Malcolm Watts hadn't stopped for refreshments on the way, and McIver now realised that had been a mistake. "We should've stopped for some food and drink, Malcolm. I'm hungry already."

"There's a fish and chip shop just down the road. It won't take me long to pop down and get something," Watts offered.

McIver glanced into the rear view mirror and saw the reflection of the fish and chip shop in the distance. It was a fair distance down the road, but still in sight. He decided to chance it.

"Good idea, Malcolm! What'll we have?"

They spent a few minutes making a list of not only fish and chips for now, but soft drinks and nibbles in case the night dragged on. McIver watched Malcolm Watts disappear into the distance behind them for a few moments before returning his attention to Ramachandran's house.

Ramachandran lived in a modern estate of townhouses. A kind of up-market terrace house row, designed to give the occupant a feeling of separation and a little more garden than would be normally expected with a townhouse. Kings Hill was one of those new suburbs that, although being built in the heart of an older suburb, had been given its own identity to attract those who wished to move up a rung of the class ladder. Kings Hill actually shared the same postal area code as Lower Hackney. Having said all that, McIver did have to admit that, while Lower Hackney and Kings Hill shared postal codes, in the matter of character, they were miles apart. Lower Hackney was a typical working class area. Old style terraces lined the footpaths of narrow streets. With the exception of the weekly outing to Bingo, the corner shop with the occasional stall out front, and the local pub were the main areas of social gathering. But the people of Lower Hackney had something the newcomers to Kings Hill would never have. They looked out for each other, especially the "littl'uns." They stuck together like one large family. They had their squabbles, like any family, but they kept themselves to themselves. Those of Kings Hill didn't know the names of their neighbours. The only time they spoke was if the neighbour's Porsche was parked too close to *their* boundary. They shopped in "a more acceptable area" and drank only "the best" wine, even at home.

Each to his own, thought McIver, as he settled more comfortably into the driver's seat. It was then that Harrigan had rung.

McIver pressed the end-call button. There had been a great deal of urgency in Harrigan's voice, and he was in two minds about whether to get Malcolm Watts or ring Stonegate. It would obviously be quicker to get Constable Watts from the shop down the road than it would be waiting for back up from Stonegate, but that would mean leaving his post.

He looked down the road then back to Ramachandran's home. The front door of 23 Elizabeth Grove could be seen, albeit in the distance, from the shop. He decided to get Malcolm Watts.

The 1.8 litre motor of the Metro burst forth in asthenic energy, as McIver hurriedly did a U-turn and drove down the hill, watching the house in the rear-vision mirror all the time.

He thought of Harrigan as he parked illegally on the corner and, with a final glance at Elizabeth Grove, dashed inside to find Watts.

Neither of the two occupants of the black Mercedes paid any attention to the happenings at *"Reg's Fine Fish Emporium"* as it drove past.

It took McIver a long and agonising three minutes to locate Malcolm Watts. He'd been in the Men's room.

"Come on, hurry," he said urgently grabbing the arm of the larger man. "The Inspector said we have to take Ramachandran in. It sounded urgent."

"But what about the order? It's already paid for," Watts complained.

"Now!" Came the one-word reply.

As he followed McIver towards the door, Senior Watts looked wistfully at the plump battered fish pieces, chips, and scallops frying in the deep fryer.

Once outside, McIver looked immediately towards King's Hill. "Bloody hell, come on!!" He yelled as he saw the headlights of the Mercedes reflecting off the garage doors of number 23.

The flashing blue light on the dash spun faster than the front drive wheels, and the motor screamed in pain as the little Metro gave its master all it had. The two policemen could see figures struggling in the driveway. It was too dark and too far away to determine exactly what was happening, but it was for sure that someone was trying to force another person into the car.

As the struggling figures heard the sound of the approaching police vehicle, the two officers saw the silhouette of someone being thrown to the ground. The dark car reversed recklessly from the driveway, and McIver saw what looked like a flash from a gun. The door of the car slammed closed and the now blacked out vehicle sped past them.

"Let them go. Just pray that nothing serious has happened to Ramachandran," McIver said. "For our sake, as well as Ramachandran's." McIver knew he had really cocked things up this time, no matter what condition Ramachandran might be in.

But their prayers were not answered. Ramachandran lay in a pool of blood. McIver called an ambulance while Watts knelt helplessly beside the wounded man.

McIver tried to call Harrigan. There was no answer from Harrigan's telephone, so he left a message.

* * *

Harrigan's mobile telephone had no signal in his cabin, and he hadn't had any other opportunity to use his mobile telephone in private. Mahmood might have been cooperative and, at times, even pleasant, but Harrigan still didn't trust him. *As Mahmood doesn't trust me,* he thought.

Saheed accompanied them in the helicopter and it wasn't until they had landed at Little Woping that Harrigan walked to an open space away from the hanger where the car was garaged and switched on his telephone. The battery indicator showed he had half the battery left, but there was a full signal. He read *message received*, and dialled the number. A pleasant voice told him he had two new messages.

He waited.

"Inspector, this is Colin McIver. Mr Ramachandran has been shot and is in intensive care at Our Lady of Mercy Hospital at Bushgate. I will stay with him, until I receive instructions from you." There was a pause before the message continued. "The assailants arrived in a large black Mercedes, while I was getting Constable Watts. I had the house under surveillance, but, but I was too far away to stop the shooting. I'm sorry, Sir."

Harrigan clenched his jaw. Anger flowed through him. He knew there had been a chance that Mahmood would try and get rid of Ramachandran, but there had been something inside him that had hoped he would be wrong. Something that enticed him to believe that Mahmood had enough respect for him to act, well, *honourably* was probably not the word, but at least act in the *spirit* of their conversation. He wondered now, if could trust Mahmood when it came to Margaret.

The next Message announced itself. He listened.

"Mr Harrigan, this is Sister O'Leary from St Luke's hospital. We need to speak to you urgently." The sister gave the telephone number. Harrigan fumbled for his notepad and replayed the message. He wrote down the number, cleared the telephone, and rang St Luke's. Sister O'Leary was not on duty and he spoke to the new ward sister, Sister Jones. He introduced himself and explained he had only just received Sister O'Leary's message.

"How is my mother, Sister? Is there something wrong?"

"I think you should come over straight away, Mr Harrigan."

"What's happened? Is my mother alright?" His tone was urgent, almost impatient.

"We cannot discuss your mother's condition over the telephone, Mr Harrigan," she replied firmly in that tone of authority that all Ward Sisters must obviously go to special training for. "I can only urge you to come to St Luke's immediately. Ask for me." She terminated the conversation.

Harrigan hurried to the car. He sat heavily in the front passenger's seat and turned to Saheed.

"Saheed, I want you to detour via St Luke's hospital at North Finchenham. If you have to check with Mahmood, do it on the way."

"Mr Mahmood instructed me to take you where you want to go and then wait at The Badger's, in case you need me." He waved to the Security guard as he drove through the front gates. "It'll be quicker if you direct me."

"Fine, fine. Just get onto the M25, I'll show you from there."

"How is your mum?" Bill Buckle asked with concern.

"To be honest with you, I don't know. There was a message on the mobile. I spoke to the day sister and she told me to come over immediately. She sounded very serious, but then Ward Sister's always do. It's probably some medical procedure needs my approval." There was silence as the car left Little Woping and sped towards London. "It'll be some bloody red tape," he added, trying to sound as convincing as possible.

It was twelve-thirty-five when Harrigan told Saheed and Bill Buckle to wait in the car and he would only be a few minutes. The two men watched as he hurried up the old stone steps, taking two at a time, the corners of his coat flapping open.

The time dragged by. Apart from a few questions and answers about the *Dei Lucrii*, Bill Buckle and Saheed had little conversation. It was after all a difficult situation, because Saheed was a potential suspect in a murder case and Bill Buckle one of the investigating police.

Bill Buckle looked at his watch. Harrigan had been gone over thirty minutes. "There must be a lot of papers to sign," he said aimlessly.

"Here he comes now." It was Saheed who first noticed him.

Harrigan walked slowly down the steps, his coat now firmly buttoned. His head moved in a constant jerky kind of motion, looking up, and then down, then up then to the side and down again. He opened the door and slowly eased himself into the front seat.

"How is she, Inspector?" Bill Buckle asked quietly.

"She's dead, Bill." The words choked in his throat.

That kind of heavy silence that hurts your eardrums filled the interior of the car. Bill Buckle looked down into his lap. Saheed's gaze remained fixed towards the windscreen.

"She asked for me last night," Harrigan continued softly. "They couldn't raise me because the mobile was turned off." He paused as he silently went through a short period of self-recrimination. As he continued, a sad smile hinted at the corners of his mouth. "She told them her son was a policeman, and if they couldn't contact me, she would understand. They were her last words."

He fell silent.

Bill Buckle leaned forward and placed a hand on his shoulder. "I'm sorry, Sir. If there is anything Betty and I can do..." His voice trailed off.

Harrigan half looked over his shoulder. "Thank you, Sergeant."

This felt like a formal occasion, and not to use Bill Buckle's formal rank seemed inappropriate. Besides, his mother always did frown at his familiarity with the lower ranks.

He acknowledged Saheed's condolences. "I want to call at Mrs Willis' house on the way, Saheed. I'll direct you. Just turn left at the gates."

He'd telephoned Margaret from inside the hospital.

"I'm sorry, Bill," she'd said then added, "You know I'm here if you need me."

"Thanks, Margaret. I'll call 'round on the way to Stonegate."

"I'll keep a look out."

Saheed's lack of experience driving through the traffic of Greater London made the journey slower than Harrigan was used to, not that there was any great hurry.

The journey was taken in silence, only broken by his own words, *"left at the next roundabout"* or *"right at the next set of lights."*

He appreciated the silence. It gave him time to gather his thoughts. Although always well meaning, those almost inane words of platitude that people feel obligated to offer at a time like this were usually more irritating than comforting.

Margaret had been watching at the front window, and as the car came to a stop, she was standing at the open doorway. She stood aside as Harrigan walked past her and stopped in the hallway. He turned to her as the door closed and they stood in each other's arms.

"Can you stay long?" she asked eventually.

"Just a few minutes. I still have a lot to do at the station."

"Come into the front room. Have you time for a cup of tea?"

"No thanks. I'll have something stronger a little later." He sat on the settee. "I was half expecting it you know; she'd lost a lot of her fight lately."

"She was just ready to go, Bill. They say we all know when it's our time."

"Yep, that's what they say."

Margaret sat beside him. "I suspected it was something serious when the hospital rang here last night, looking for you. When I told them you weren't here, they said they had your mobile number and they would try that. I asked if I could do anything." A tone of annoyance crept into her voice, "but as I wasn't family, they said there was nothing I could do, nor could they tell me anything."

"Hospitals have their rules; it's not their fault."

"I wasn't suggesting it was; it's just so bloody annoying sometimes."

He put his arm around her shoulder, as she moved closer to him and laid her head on the side of his chest. "I tried to ring you a few times," she said.

"You should have left a message."

"The people at the hospital said they were going to leave a message, so I thought you didn't need me bothering you."

"You don't bother me," he said, as he squeezed her shoulder and kissed her lightly on the top of her head. "If the truth was known, her zest for life began to slide after Dad died. She never got over him."

Margaret sat silent. She knew he was leading to something.

"I'm going to take her ashes to Australia," he announced. "I want to bury them in Dad's grave, if that's allowable. I'll make some enquiries later."

"I'll do that for you."

"You don't have to."

"I want to, Bill. This is important to you and so it is important to me, too."

"Thanks." The sadness in his tone raged in opposition to his faint smile. While Margaret understood and shared his grief, she was not about to allow him to become absorbed by it. She felt compelled to try and steer his mind to other things.

"How'd the trip go? Did you accomplish what you set out to do?"

This bold change of direction, albeit led with a softness only a woman in love could deliver, created some uncertainty in his mind.

"Well I thought so, but now with the Ramachandran thing."

"What Ramachandran thing?"

Harrigan suddenly realised that Margaret had no way of knowing that Ramachandran had been shot. It was the kick-start he'd needed. Harrigan told her the whole story. When he got to the part that involved her, she sat up sharply. It was strange really, because she suddenly felt gratitude toward Mahmood. The fact that it was Mahmood that ordered the threats and the destruction of her car in the first place seemed to get lost somewhere.

"You obviously believe that Mahmood is behind the shooting?"

"Who else?"

"Will he keep the deal and leave me alone?"

"I think so," Harrigan replied quickly, hiding the uneasy doubt that had crept in since Ramachandran's murder.

"Well, come on, hop up. I must get to Stonegate," Harrigan said. They both stood and walked towards the front door. "Let's go out tonight, somewhere simple."

"What about your local? You know, the one with the dog. Do they serve meals?"

"They certainly do. The best Steak and Kidney pie in town!"

She kissed him lightly on the cheek. "Well, off with you. I'll need time to get ready." She had to prepare herself in more ways than one. She hated Steak and Kidney pie.

At Three o'clock, Harrigan directed Saheed into the Stonegate police station car park. "Just park over there."

Bill Buckle put his overnight bag in the boot of his car. Harrigan had left his bag in Margaret's hallway.

The three men walked into the station. Bill Buckle led the way to Harrigan's office, Saheed in the middle and Harrigan at rear. Harrigan wanted to give the impression that they were bringing Saheed in for questioning, just in case Wilkinson saw them. If the superintendent thought they had a suspect, it was a sure bet that he wouldn't expect an immediate report on his visit to Mahmood.

Patricia took the tea order.

"Can we have a few biscuits too, Trish? We've had nothing since breakfast."

Harrigan lifted the telephone receiver and dialled. The telephone rang three times.

"Detective Senior Constable McIver."

"Senior, Inspector Harrigan. What's happening? How is Ramachandran?"

"Well, Sir, Mr Ramachandran remains in a coma. He was shot twice. Once in the chest, once in the stomach. I only saw one gun flash, but he has definitely been shot twice. It's the stomach wound that's caused the damage; the bullet in the chest missed all the vital organs."

"What are his chances?"

"Not good I'm afraid, less than fifty-fifty."

"Are you taking all precautions? I don't want someone finishing the job at the hospital."

"Constable Watts is at the door of the ward, and I'm with Ramachandran. I have issued orders that no unidentified person is to enter the ward, and no one is allowed to give medication or make any adjustments to the life support apparatus unless the Ward Sister is present."

"What about any change of shift of hospital staff?"

"Constable Watts and I each have a roster sheet, and the current Ward Sister will bring her relief and introduce her to us."

"Good. Now what else can you tell me about the incident? What actually happened? What about the car?"

"Not much more than I have already told you, Sir. It was a large model Mercedes. The latest shape. But not much else."

"What about the registration Number?"

"It was blacked out, Sir. So were the windows. We had no chance of seeing the occupants."

"What about the bullets?"

"The doctor has removed a standard thirty-eight slug from his chest. The stomach wound is too difficult at the moment."

"Keep me informed." Harrigan's tone was decidedly icy.

"Yes, Sir."

"You and Watts had any sleep?"

"None, Sir."

"I'll get some relief to you as soon as possible. Until then, you'll have to keep going."

"Very good, Sir."

Harrigan replaced the handset.

"Ramachandran has less than a fifty-fifty chance," Harrigan said to no one in particular, as he passed the telephone to Saheed.

"Get your boss on the telephone. I have a few things to say to that man." The tone in Harrigan's voice left Saheed no choice.

Saheed dialled the number and waited.

"Rowena? It's Fadhel Saheed. Put me through to Mr Mahmood." He paused irritably. "I have my reasons, just put me through!" Harrigan guessed that this Rowena had asked Saheed why he hadn't dialled Mahmood's direct number. Harrigan could've told her. Saheed obviously didn't want Mahmood's private number recorded anywhere it might be traced.

"Mr Mahmood, Inspector Harrigan wishes to speak with you." He handed Harrigan the telephone.

"Mahmood! Harrigan! What the hell's going on? I thought we had a deal!!"

"Come, come, my dear Inspector, calm down. I must assume you are talking of the shooting of Ramachandran?"

"Yes I am. And tell me, how do you know about that?"

"I've told you before, Inspector, I make it my business to know what is happening." He paused. "Inspector, surely you don't think *I* had anything to do with Ramachandran's injuries?"

"As unbelievable as that may sound to you Mahmood, yes I do."

"Why would I do that?"

"With Manjit and Ramachandran both dead, you can claim your innocence and shock to find out that they had been in cahoots together and that you are appalled at their deception!"

"As tempting as that may sound to you, Inspector, I gave you my word. Not directly of course, but you were entitled to believe that nothing would happen to Ramachandran, not from my end, anyway. And it hasn't."

Harrigan wanted to believe him but not for any reason to do with the murders. If he could believe Mahmood about this, he could believe his promise to leave Margaret alone.

"I am a very busy man, Inspector. Have Saheed contact me if I can be of any further help." The line went silent.

Harrigan picked up a shortbread biscuit and thoughtfully dunked it in his tea. Shortbread crumbs spread slowly across the top of the black liquid.

"If we assume Mahmood is telling the truth and he did have nothing to do with the shooting, who else would want Ramachandran dead?" As he dunked the biscuit the second time, the end fell off and sunk to the bottom of the cup. He picked up the teaspoon and carefully tried to retrieve it without it breaking up and filling the cup with soggy dough. He was only partially successful.

"With what we know, there is really only one other possibility," he said eventually.

"Xiao Chen's connections?"

"That's right, Bill, and it is their style. Big black Mercedes, gunning their victim in the driveway of his house. Serves as a warning to everyone else."

The telephone rang.

"Inspector. I want to see you. Come into my office immediately." It was Wilkinson.

"Bill, get as many people as you can trying to identify UK owners of the latest model black Mercedes; try the top of the range first. Check Channel crossings too; it may gives us a lead."

"What about me, Inspector?"

"I think we are finished with you at the moment, Saheed. Thanks for driving us around. Will you be at the Badgers?"

"Yes, Sir."

The telephone rang again. Harrigan picked it up quickly. "I'm on my way, Sir."

It took Harrigan almost twenty minutes to fully brief his superintendent.

"And that's about where we're at, Sir," Harrigan concluded.

"And do you think Mahmood had anything to do with the shooting of this Rama…what's-his-name fellow?"

"Like I said, at first I was damn positive. But after speaking to Mahmood on the telephone, I, I think I might have been wrong."

"He has a bloody good motive. It would tie up a lot of loose ends."

"I can't argue with you there, Sir. The prime suspect for three deaths, the trafficking racket, and the fire at the Goldberg building, shot in a gangland style operation by a person or persons unknown. It *would* be very convenient." The previous doubts about Mahmood's involvement began to re-emerge. Wilkinson allowed Harrigan time to wander uncertainly through his indecision. "I have no doubt that Mahmood is quite capable of ordering the shooting,—"

The telephone rang. Wilkinson grabbed the handset. "I said I did not want to be disturbed!"

He was silent as he listened to the other voice. He handed the handset to Harrigan.

"It's for you! It sounds important."

"Harrigan, here." It was Harrigan's turn to sit silently and listen.

"Thanks, Colin." Wilkinson heard him reply to the caller. "Just tidy up there, and make sure the bullet in the stomach gets to forensic as soon as possible. Then you and Watts better get some rest. I'll see you tomorrow." He gave the handset back to Wilkinson. "Thank you, Sir. That was DSC McIver at the hospital. Ramachandran didn't make it."

"So now it's officially murder. Damn, what am I going to tell the commissioner? He'll want to make some statement to the press. Not that you'd care about that," he added.

"It's not that I don't care, Sir, it's just that talking to the press is simply not that important right now. For fuck's sake, doesn't the commissioner realise the press isn't after facts or the truth, just a story? Any bloody story!"

"I still have to tell the commissioner something," Wilkinson insisted.

"Well, if you must, tell him something, stick to the story that Ramachandran committed all the crimes and was murdered in a revenge killing by overseas drug barons," Harrigan suggested resignedly.

"But is that the truth?"

"Some of it probably is…but honestly, Sir, who cares?"

"The commissioner cares! We mustn't tell him something that will eventually make him look a fool!"

As Harrigan began to open his mouth, Wilkinson continued hurriedly. "Don't say it, Inspector. The commissioner is our superior."

"Officer, Sir." Harrigan completed, "superior *officer*."

Wilkinson stifled a smile. He stood and placed his hands, thumbs forward, on either side of his waist. "Very well, Inspector," he said, his voice straining, as he arched his back. "Let's assume that's what we tell the commissioner." He sat down and rested his arms on the desk. "Where do we go from there?"

"Well, Sir, There are a few smaller things that need tidying up. Xiao Chen's history, the owner of the Mercedes, that type of thing. Sergeant Buckle and McIver and, of course, Malcolm Watts are more than able to follow that up."

"And you?" the superintendent asked tentatively.

"I want to make a few arrangements and fly to Houston to meet the container that left the Goldberg building just after the fire."

"Do you really have to go in person? Can't our counterparts in force over there look after that?"

"I think there is upwards of twenty-five million pound in bank notes and gold in that container, sir, put there by Xiao Chen, and I would like to be there when it's opened." He thought he should add a sweetener. "That'll probably be all the evidence we'll need to wrap this whole thing up." Harrigan stood and added, "It will also give the commissioner something to tell the press."

"Very well, I'll leave it up to you." Wilkinson picked up a biro from his desk. The conversation was over.

"There is *one* more thing, Sir."

Wilkinson looked up, still holding the biro above the typed report on the desk.

"When this is all over, I'd like to take four weeks leave."

Wilkinson looked at the report and absently made some corrections. "Four weeks leave?" he asked incredulously. "My God, man, you could go to Australia in that time." Harrigan interrupted before he had time to add, *"It's out of the question."*

"Yes, Sir. That's what I intend to do. My mother died in hospital last night, and I want to take her ashes to be buried in my father's grave."

Wilkinson stopped writing and slowly laid the biro on top of the report.

"Inspector," he said, as he looked up slowly, his voice echoing that mournful tone adopted by most people when told of news such as this, "I am so terribly sorry. Take whatever time you need."

"Thank you, Sir." Harrigan replied respectfully. "Four weeks will be plenty. I may need a few hours in between to make arrangements."

Wilkinson waved his hand dismissively. "Of course. Of course. Take whatever time you need."

"Thank you again, Sir." Harrigan left the office.

As he walked thoughtfully to his own office, he noticed Bill Buckle and several other officers busily checking vehicle records, faxed from the Motor Registry Regulatory Authorities. He sat in his chair, and with his elbows placed on each arm of the chair, he intertwined his fingers and rested his chin on two outstretched thumbs.

He raised his eyes, as he heard a slight knock, and Patricia Hedrich poked her head around the door.

"Feel like company, Sir?"

"Come in, Trish. Close the door and have a small drink with me."

He poured two generous portions of Ballantines. Trish preferred it with ice.

She raised her glass. "To mum's," she toasted.

He raised his glass to share the toast, but before taking a sip, he slowly moved his tumbler to hers and the glasses clinked.

"And good friends," he said with a smile.

Patricia Hedrich's eyes moistened, and she hastily took a sip of the golden brown liquid.

It was a little before twenty minutes after six, when Bill and Margaret left her address and headed for the Kings Arms. They sat closely in Bill's Mazda.

"I notice my Bodyguards are still on duty," Margaret remarked, as they drove out the driveway and waved to the police officer standing at the front of the house. "You said you think Mahmood will honour his word, do you have doubts about that?"

"No, not really," he stated unconvincingly. "Maybe I'm just overcautious where you are concerned."

She squeezed his thigh gently,

"Have you contacted your insurance company yet? Are they going to pay for the Jag?"

"Yes, there doesn't seem to be any problem. They said that once they receive a report from Chief Inspector Biggles, the claim can be processed."

"Would you like me to arrange the report?"

"No, it's all been done. In fact, I find Biggles quite charming, in his way."

"I don't know if I shouldn't be getting jealous about now," he said good humouredly.

They drove the rest of the way in silence. It wasn't that they had nothing to say; they each had plenty to say, just nothing that would fit comfortably into such a short journey.

The Kings Arms was busy but not over crowded. As Harrigan walked to the bar, Sarah, the publican's wife, placed Joe Feigan's half-pint of Bitter on the drip tray and came towards Harrigan.

"I'm sorry to hear about your mum, Bill. If there's anything me or Roy can do, you only have to yell out."

"Thanks, Sarah, but just a pint of Bass and a large gin and tonic will do nicely at the moment."

Sarah nodded to Margaret who stood facing the wall, looking at photographs of Sarah's husband, taken during his days in the RAF.

"She'll do you with a bit of nicely, too," Sarah said with a twinkle in her eye. "Now off you go and sit down, and I'll get Roy to bring your drinks over…on the 'ouse." She gave him a saucy wink.

Table service for drinks was not a usual custom at the Kings Arms.

As he took two large menus, each bound with red leather and finished off with a gold cord and tassel, Harrigan mouthed a polite *"thank you."*

"Where do you want to sit?" he whispered over Margaret's shoulder.

She tilted her head back slightly. "You choose."

He took her gently by the waist and guided her to a corner table. The Kings Arms was the typical English pub. Highly-polished wooden dining tables were fixed to the wall, with bench seats either side. A partition divided each table, and an imitation gaslight above the centre of the table twinkled through an Elizabethan-style glass lampshade.

The table in the corner, however, was free standing with four high-back leather chairs in attendance.

Margaret settled into the padded leather seat and looked around politely.

"This is very nice, Bill."

"It does me," he answered simply.

"Here we are, Bill," a voice sounded from behind. "A pint of bass for the gentleman and a large G & T for the lady."

Harrigan looked up at his host. "Roy, may I introduce Margaret Willis. Margaret, Roy." He leaned forward and whispered loudly, *"don't take any notice of him, he only owns the place."*

"Very pleased to meet you, Ms Willis."

"Please, call me Margaret," she invited, as she offered her hand.

"Margaret," Roy repeated, as he accepted her hand in a firm, yet polite, manner. "It is a pleasure to have your company. I can't say the same for your companion, I'm sorry to say."

"Thanks, Roy, you can go now."

They all laughed in accordance with the protocol expected of such repartee.

"Sorry to hear about your mum, Bill. If there is anything Sarah and me can do…"

"Thanks, Roy. I appreciate it."

They were alone at last. They picked up their menus and held them high towards the dim light. Margaret reached across the table and removed the menu's tassel from the heady froth at the top of Bill's tankard. He looked around the edge of his now half-closed menu. "Thanks, I always do that. You'd think I'd learn by now."

Having eventually selected their preferences and noticing that the bar was now fairly busy, Harrigan went to the bar and ordered their meal. Both would have the shrimp cocktail for an entrée. For the main course, he would have the Steak and Kidney Pie and Margaret, having summoned the courage to tell him she just couldn't bring herself to eat kidney, would have the Chicken Kiev. He also ordered one serving of garlic bread and one mixed herb.

He returned to the table.

"I told Wilkinson I wanted four weeks leave when this Mahmood, Ramachandran thing is over."

"What did he say?"

"I think he was about to laugh in my face until I told him about Mum, and wanting to take her ashes back to Australia. He told me to take all the time I wanted."

"I spoke to a local funeral director this afternoon, while I was getting ready."

"What did he say?"

"He didn't think it would be much of a bother taking your mother's ashes back to Australia. I have to ring him tomorrow with all the details. He'll chase it up and make the arrangements if that's all right with you."

"That's more than alright."

Another round of drinks later and having finished their entrée, Harrigan sat with both elbows on the table, closely inspecting a piece of garlic bread from the second order of the same.

"Will you come to Australia with me?" he asked, as nonchalantly as he could.

Margaret had been dreading the moment when he would ask her to go with him. It wasn't that she didn't want to go, far from it, but she was afraid of the consequences. She was in love with this man, even though they had only *really* known each other for a matter of days. And there lay the problem. Their relationship hadn't yet been given time to be nurtured into maturity. Would such a trip so soon be fatal for their future together? Was she willing to take that chance? On the other hand, what would be his reaction if she refused? Although not a mother's boy by any stretch of the imagination, he had been very close to her. To be invited to share the moment when his mother and father were re-united for the final time, could only be taken as a gesture of love and must be handled with the care and understanding equal to the issue of the invitation itself.

"Margaret?" His voice interrupted her thoughts. "If you don't want to come with me, I'll understand."

He'd done it again. It was as though he could almost read her thoughts and had chosen to offer her the way out. She knew he was being truthful, if she refused, he *would* understand, and that made up her mind. "Of course I'll come with you, Bill."

He laid an upturned hand across the table, and as her hand fell into his, he squeezed it gently.

"Come on now, none of that in 'ere." Sarah said gruffly, as she brought two well-filled dinner plates.

For the rest of the evening, Margaret and Bill tuned out the rest of the world and simply enjoyed one another.

* * *

Thursday and Friday were filled with the dull and boring routine police work, rarely seen by the general public. Seventy-four likely Mercedes owners had been identified, and to speed up the investigation, three investigation teams had been formed to track down each vehicle. Each team consisted of a police driver, a constable and either Bill Buckle, McIver, or Watts.

The car driver in Bill Buckle's team, waited for directions. Sergeant Buckle sat in the passenger side of the police vehicle and carefully scrutinising his team's list. One address suddenly caught his eye. Mr Lee Ho Tung, fifteen to seventeen Little Wardour Lane. London Chinatown. WC2. City of Westminster.

"Let's go to Chinatown. Little Wardour Lane. Do you know where it is, Constable?"

"I know Chinatown, Sergeant, but not Little Wardour Lane. There's a Wardour Street."

"Head for there. I'll look it up in the A to Z."

Bill Buckle inwardly chastised himself. *I must be getting old,* he thought, as the mental picture of the S class Mercedes parked outside the Martial Arts Academy flooded back into his memory.

Despite his efforts, Bill Buckle could not find a Little Wardour Lane in the A to Z. He slammed the book shut.

"They have either missed it or it's not there. Let's have a look anyway."

After thirty minutes driving around Chinatown looking for the address and being assured by several locals and two taxi drivers that they had never heard of it, it was the consensus of the vehicle's occupants that the address did not exist.

"Where to now, Sergeant?"

He looked at the list. He was about to give the next address, when he suddenly gave the paper to the driver and opened the door. "Just wait here for a minute. There's someone I want to talk to before we leave."

He crossed the narrow street and entered the Jen San Sang Martial Arts Academy building. It was as dark and dingy as he remembered it. He went directly to the office of the Eastern Import and Export Company. The door was locked. He knocked firmly and waited.

He knocked again.

"Mr Ye!" he called loudly. "Are you in there? This is Police Sergeant Buckle. Open the door!"

"He hasn't been there for a couple of days."

Bill Buckle turned and looked at the man with the greased hair and bright red silk shirt standing in the doorway of the Adult Bookshop. "Unlike him really," he continued. "He spent most of his time there. Day and night." The sound of a telephone ringing inside the bookshop prompted the man to withdraw from the doorway.

Bill Buckle again knocked on the door and tried the doorknob, this time with a little more urgency. It was to no avail.

"Is there a building caretaker I can contact?" he called into the recently vacated doorway. He assumed it was the man with the red shirt who laughed.

He moved back to the locked door and raised his left leg. It only took one solid kick to splinter the old door jam. Gabriel Ye sat behind his tired wooden desk, the cord of the telephone handset disappeared over the far edge of the table. Ye must have dropped the handset when the bullet hit him in the centre of the forehead.

Bill Buckle pulled the door closed as best he could and hurried back to the police vehicle. He told the driver to wait with the car and not to let anyone in or out of the building. "You, come with me." He ordered the young constable in the back seat. Bill Buckle and the young constable hurried back to Gabriel Ye's office.

"Wait here at the door, Constable. Make sure no-one who shouldn't come in, comes in, right?"

"Yes, Sergeant."

Bill Buckle went to book store across the hallway and used the telephone. Twenty minutes later, the office of the late Gabriel Ye was swarming with police officers, forensic investigators, and the medical examiner's office.

Harrigan swore down the telephone at the news of Ye's murder. As slender as it may have been, Gabriel Ye had been their only link to the Drug Syndicate.

"I'm not too far away. I'll come right over." He arrived fifteen minutes later.

"To be honest with you, Inspector," Bill Buckle answered Harrigan's first question, "when I studied the list of addresses a little more closely, I remembered seeing an S class Mercedes outside this building when Watts and I came here the other day."

"By train," Harrigan commented.

The old Sergeant ignored the jibe. "Well," he continued, "when we came here today and couldn't find the address, I thought Ye might be able to give us a lead, so I came up here, and you know the rest."

"It looks like someone else thought he might be able to give us a lead too. Come on, we can't do much here." He stopped suddenly in the doorway. "Bill, tell the medical examiner that if the bullet that killed Ye is a thirty-eight calibre, I want it sent to forensic urgently and compared with the bullet found in Ramachandran."

"Yes, Sir. Speaking of bullets, what about the bullet in Ramachandran's stomach? Any news yet?"

"All we know is that it was a high calibre hollow point. Exploded inside him. The poor bastard never stood a chance. Probably fired at close range, so it most likely came from inside the car."

"That explains why McIver didn't see the flash."

"I'd say so." Harrigan moved from the doorway. "I'll be in the Bookshop," he called over his shoulder.

Bill Buckle spoke to the medical examiner and followed his inspector. As he entered the bookshop, he saw the man with the red shirt sitting on a wooden chair, beads of sweat oozing from beneath the slick back hair. Harrigan leaned on both arms of the chair, his face barely inches away from the man's trembling face.

"And unless you want to be involved in a murder charge, you had better cut out this *I know nothing* crap and tell me what I want to hear!"

"Alright! Alright! Yes I have seen a big black Mercedes parked outside! Several times! Three men sometimes came to visit Ye.

One smaller man and two much bigger. I never asked who they were."

Harrigan took the picture of Xiao Chen from his inside pocket and held it in front of his face.

"Was this one of them?"

The red shirt began to stain as sweat soaked the shiny material.

"Is it?" Harrigan shouted.

"Yes!"The man slumped into the chair. "Yes, the smaller man."

Harrigan stood and returned the picture to his pocket.

"Get this man's particulars, Sergeant, and I want him kept available," Harrigan ordered Bill Buckle as he strode towards him. "I'll see you back at the station," he whispered with a wink as he passed closely.

Back at Stonegate, Harrigan spoke to a Sergeant Henry Washington (call me Hank) Bradford Junior the Third, of the Houston Police Department. He told the Texas police officer of his intention to attend the unloading of a container at the Port of Houston.

"Only too willing to *co*operate," he declared with an accent that distinctly separated *co* and *operate*. "Can you *in*form me of a few more of the *de*tails?"

While not fully declaring the twenty-five million pounds he suspected was in the container, he did say he was looking for a large amount of cash. Hank suggested this kind of thing would come under the jurisdiction of the FBI and he would guarantee to make all the necessary arrangements.

Harrigan thanked him and said he didn't care who was there.

"Do you know when you'll be arriving? I'll meet you at the airport."

Harrigan said he would inform him of all the flight details once he had booked.

"What about the ship you're looking for?"

"I'd like to keep that under my hat for a little longer, Hank, no offence."

"Hell no. No *offence*. I understand these things."

They said their good-byes, and Harrigan told him he would be in touch.

While Harrigan had no reason to doubt Sergeant Henry Washington Bradford Junior the Third's honesty and good judgement, he held a high respect for Mahmood's influence around the world, and he didn't want the container experiencing some mishap, like being lost at sea. The close detail must remain highly confidential and only on a *need to know* basis.

* * *

The cremation was on Saturday. It was a rainy day and felt cooler than normal for this time of year. It was a small ceremony. A few neighbours, Bill and Betty Buckle, Roy and Sarah, Margaret came of course, and an Auntie Lou, whom he didn't remember from the times before they emigrated. She wasn't a real Auntie, just a family friend, really, but most families had at least one family friend cum Auntie or Uncle. Auntie Lou had read his mother's name in the Death Notices and made the trip from the other side of London.

The minister attached to the crematorium presented a standard, yet warm, eulogy sermon, only glancing at the pages of the small book during the passages that required the name of the deceased to be uttered.

Ten minutes after the start of the sermon, the soft organ music began playing in the background, as the rumble of rollers announced the casket had begun its final journey.

Harrigan sat silently watching as it disappeared behind closing velvet curtains. He tried to think of everything that he should have said to his mother while she was alive, but didn't. He offered silent apologies for all the things he did say but shouldn't have. He tried to remember all the good times, the things his mother had done for him over the years. There was so much to think of and so little time. As the velvet curtains embraced the rear of the casket, the shape of the casket showed clearly. But as the droned rumble of the casters carried the casket farther away, the outline slowly faded, and the curtains returned to hanging in the straight position. The rumbling ceased and the music faded away.

Bill Harrigan felt Margaret's hand take his arm. "Are you alright, Bill?"

He nodded, keeping his head bowed. He stood and allowed Margaret to urge him toward the door. The sad faces of the mourners only served to stir his emotions. He clenched his teeth in a desperate effort to maintain the dryness in his eyes.

Outside, the rain had stopped and patches of clear sky greeted the sombre group. They stood on the front steps of the chapel each taking their turn to offer their condolences before agreeing to meet at the Kings Arms.

They moved away from the chapel, clearing the way for the mourners who were already gathering for the next ceremony.

* * *

Bill Harrigan stayed at Margaret's house for the next few days. There was no reason not to, really. It seemed a waste to leave his house in Finchenham just lie empty, but then, the other half of the mansion Margaret lived in, the section that her late husband had used during their separation, had laid empty a lot longer.

They spoke about this on Sunday as they rode the charter vessel up the Thames to Windsor. It was a sunny morning, and Harrigan just wanted to get away for a few hours.

The Sunday papers appeared with pictures of the commissioner telling the world that *his men* had solved the recent spate of murders. Ramachandran had been responsible for the deaths of Manjit and Aysha Singhabahu. He was also indirectly responsible for the death of Xiao Chen, a prominent figure in the world if illicit drugs, who had stolen over twenty-million English pounds of drug profits from the organisation. Ramachandran had also been supplying illegal International passage to the rich, undesirable element. While the details of how this was done remained *confidential at this time*, journalists went into great detail speculating about persons who may or may not have used Ramachandran's services. Ramachandran had been brutally slain by members of the illicit drug trade for his part in trying to spirit Xiao Chen away and, while his force did their best to maintain law and order, illicit drugs were an international problem. Mr Mahmood, owner of Sidhu Trading was shocked and horrified to be told that one of his most trusted employees had been so deceptive and dishonest.

"What are you smiling at?" Margaret asked, as he folded the paper.

"They love the good news."

"Who?"

"The chiefs, the managing directors, politicians, police commissioners, the lot of them. Give them a bit of good news, and they are all over you like a rash, but hint at something gone wrong, something difficult, a time when leadership is vital and you won't see them for dust."

"You're a cynic."

"I live in the real world. And speaking of the real world, this is it!" He stood behind her and put his arms around her slim waist. They stood at the rail and watched the trees, the parks, and the neat houses pass by as they glided along the Thames towards Windsor.

"We'll have to think seriously about where we'll live," Margaret remarked casually. "That house of mine is too big, and all that space next door is simply a waste. Maybe we should sell it and move into your house. That is a more sensible size."

They spoke as if they were married or at least had set the date.

"I'd like a fresh start. Sell the lot and start anew. Something that is ours, not something that once was yours or mine," Harrigan said.

And so the conversation went.

They had a midday meal at the *Numero Uno* Italian restaurant in Church Street, not far from the castle. It was their intention to take an afternoon tour of Windsor Castle. Unfortunately, too much pasta, at least one order of garlic bread over the limit, and two of the most delicious bottles of Chianti Harrigan had ever tasted, put paid to any chance the tour might have had.

It was after seven in the evening when they returned home, tired but relaxed.

"I was so grateful for the police protection, but I must admit, I am equally pleased to see them gone," Margaret commented, as she put the key in the front door lock.

CHAPTER TWELVE

Forty minutes after the published take-off time, British Airways flight BA2025 left Heathrow airport bound for Houston. Bill Harrigan sat in an aisle seat halfway along the economy section. A combination of the steep angle of take-off and the thrust required to lift the large aircraft into the sky, forced his body into his seat. The large movie screen and overhead locker doors shuddered violently as the pilot banked into the low clouds.

Harrigan enjoyed flying. Apart from his love of actual travel, it gave him the opportunity to indulge another of his favourite pastimes, the study of people. People were always the most interesting during times of emotion, or when in unnatural surroundings; and flying was definitely not a basic human instinct.

Understandably, airline passengers usually feel most vulnerable during take-off and landing and cope with the mixed feelings of excitement or fear in various ways. Harrigan broadly categorised airline passengers into three main groups. The nervous passenger, the first time passenger, and the regular passenger.

Nervous passengers get seats in the centre row. They close their eyes and grip anything within reach very tightly. With their current situation firmly shut out of their lives, nervous passengers are then able to think of Hawaiian beaches and beautiful sunsets. They deny their conscious minds any thought of actually sitting in a long metal tube-like vehicle, hurtling down the runway at three hundred miles per hour.

First-time passengers are nowhere near as complicated. First-time passengers are so excited at being on a flight they have been saving for, for over three years, they simply don't have time to think about being nervous. They clamour for window seats, marvelling at the unforgettable view that accompanies every take-off and landing. They take large quantities of pictures with their brand new, duty-free pocket cameras, the automatic flash reflecting off the window, lighting up the cabin with every masterpiece. They will learn with disappointment that the x3 zoom lens on their Cannon will not produce the results they imagined at the time of taking the photographs.

Most interesting of all groups are the regular passengers—not *all* regular passengers, of course. The well-seasoned traveller learns to cope quietly with the boredom of long-haul flights. The regular passenger is the one who has flown at least once before and feels duty bound to ensure that everyone crammed into the economy section is fully aware of that fact. These passengers quickly develop a well-choreographed and rehearsed routine, specifically designed for that purpose. The first clue comes around the time the majority of passengers initially take their seats and are coming to grips with their allocated space. Regular passengers will stand in the aisle, take-off their coats and nonchalantly toss them in the overhead locker. They casually push everything in the locker back a fraction before closing the lid, because they *know* how difficult it can be to close these lids. They are the last passengers to put on their seatbelts and always the first to undo them. They leave their tables down until that almost indefinable moment immediately before the flight attendant tells them to lock it in the take-off position. The regular passenger usually has some form of *terribly important document,* which is placed on the lap for serious and in-depth study. After take-off, they undo their seatbelts the instant the little *ding* from the warning chime announces that the seat-belt sign light has gone out. When doing this, it is important not to look at the sign. Regular passengers *know* what the little *ding* means.

During the flight and despite the *terribly important document*, their bodies jolt upright as they listen ever so intently to any mes-sage that mentions Frequent Flyer passengers.

The final display of the regular passengers' routine is to never watch the flight attendant during the safety lesson. Non-watching must be done with an air of *"I don't need to watch this because I've seen it before. You on the other hand should all watch because it is terribly important."* This expertise is only gained through experience.

There is another more difficult presentation, given only by the very experienced regular passenger. Immediately following the little *ding* and the removal of the seatbelt without reading the sign, the true exponent of the art will stand and immediately walk directly to the toilet and open the damn thing without as much as a fumble.

Harrigan looked at his watch, and mindful of the person behind him, tilted the back of his seat slightly, laid his head back and closed his eyes. As he drifted into a restless sleep, he won-dered just how valuable that little whistle on the life jacket would actually be, once the plane had plummeted thirty thousand feet and crashed into the ocean at eight hundred miles an hour. The added problem of simultaneously blowing into the little whistle and the manual inflation thing as you bobbed up and down in forty foot waves, was pushed quickly to the back of his mind.

* * *

Nine hours and twenty three minutes after take-off, the wheels of the aircraft thumped onto the tarmac at Houston International Airport; the time was ten minutes past four in the afternoon, Houston time. During the last hour of the flight, Harrigan had thought of his interview with Sir Charles Reece that had been held in Wilkinson's office yesterday afternoon. Harrigan was ready for the usual lecture about diplomacy and the obligatory, "*Don't forget you are representing the Met, and when you represent the Met you represent me.*" But to Harrigan's surprise, the lecture didn't come.

"Inspector Harrigan," Sir Charles had begun. "It is my duty to inform you that you have been promoted to the rank of Chief Inspector…effective immediately." He held out his hand. "Congratulations."

The two men shook hands respectfully.

Harrigan looked at Wilkinson who shrugged in a, *it's news to me, too,* kind of way.

"That'll be all, Chief Inspector," Sir Charles had said, as Harrigan was dismissed.

Harrigan had stood to attention, said an official, "Yes, Sir. Thank you, Sir," and left the office. It was obvious the commissioner had serious reservations about the promotion, or worse still, had not been consulted on the matter. Whatever the reason, he'd left no doubt as to his feelings about Harrigan's sudden and unexpected rise through the ranks.

Harrigan was also surprised that he had been offered the promotion. Not that he wasn't qualified, he was. It was just that he had never done anything to endear himself to those of higher rank, more to the contrary if the truth was known. There had also been no warning that a position was coming up. Wilkinson had told him later that afternoon, he would remain at Stonegate and he was pleased that the station had been upgraded to a level that warranted a Detective Chief Inspector.

Margaret couldn't care less where the promotion had come from and beamed at the news. She'd also demanded they go to Ali's that evening to celebrate.

Harrigan thought of his mother and how proud she would have been.

The pilot taxied to the terminal and a few moments before the seatbelt sign was extinguished, the regular passengers were retrieving their belongings from the overhead lockers. Urged on by the passengers in the inner seats of Harrigan's row, Harrigan stood, removed his bag from the locker and joined the urgency of the moment by standing shoulder to shoulder in the crush of other passengers, waiting for the doors to open.

He had no luggage in the Hold and once through immigration control, he walked directly to the green exit. The watchful eyes of the Customs officials studied the faces of those walking innocently toward the outside world. Although Harrigan genuinely had nothing to declare, and despite every effort to look innocent, he knew his effort probably made him look as guilty as sin.

At the end of the narrow ally leading into the arrival hall, waiting friends and relatives reluctantly left just enough room to squeeze through. Harrigan saw an enormous man holding a sign that read *Inspector Harrigan*.

"Hank?" Harrigan asked, as he walked to him.

The giant offered Harrigan a broad smile and held out a hand bigger than a cow's face. "Howdy, Inspector. Welcome to Houston."

"Thank you, Sergeant, it's good to be here."

The Texas policeman took Harrigan's overnight bag. "You sure travel light, Inspector. Follow me," he said as he turned. "I have a vehicle waiting out front."

The large white police vehicle with black wheels was not difficult to identify. A wide, light-blue strip interrupted with the word *Police* covering the front and rear doors, ran the length of the vehicle. In smaller lettering, positioned above and to the left of the large *Police sign*, was the word *Houston*. A Houston Police badge positioned across the blue strip on the front mudguard looked a little like an afterthought and tended to take away from the power of the otherwise simple, but affective, design.

They put Harrigan's bag in the boot and, as they moved to each side of the car, the two men collided.

Harrigan then realised his mistake.

"Sorry, Sergeant," he apologised. "I forgot it was left-hand drive."

They disentangled themselves and Harrigan headed for the right-side passenger's door. "Where you staying, Inspector?" Hank asked, as they entered the vehicle.

"The Hotel Spatial. It's apparently only ten minutes from here."

"Yeah. It's on the Sam Houston Parkway. Do you want to check-in on the way?"

Harrigan looked at his watch; he had set it to Houston time during the flight. It was just a little after four-thirty and check-in time began at three.

"Why not? I won't have to worry then."

Harrigan watched with admiration as the huge man expertly manoeuvred the large vehicle out of the airport precinct and towards the Hotel Spatial. Their conversation consisted of the usual small talk that follows questions, such as, *"How was the weather when you left? How was the flight?"* And of course the essential, *"What was the food like on the plane?"*

"Just around the next corner, Inspector, and we're there."

"Why don't you drop the *Inspector* business and call me Bill?" Harrigan offered.

"If my *su*periors heard me *add*ress you that way, they would cut my balls out. If you don't mind, I'll stick with *Inspector*."

"I can understand that." Harrigan smiled.

"But please, Inspector, call me Hank."

"You won't lose your balls if I do?"

"No, Inspector. It doesn't work the same way coming down the line. With all respect, Sir," he added quickly.

"Don't worry, Hank, it's the same the world over."

It took over half an hour before Harrigan returned to the car.

"Everything ok, Inspector?"

"Fine. It looks extremely comfortable as a matter of fact."

"Ok, then, let's visit the FBI."

Hank briefed Harrigan on his talks with the FBI. They had shown a great deal of interest and were looking forward to meeting with the inspector.

They sped down Route 45, turned right onto Route 610 and shortly after, exited just before E.T.C. Jester Boulevard. The Houston Field Office headquarters of the FBI was in E.T.C. Jester Boulevard, and it was only a few minutes before the two policemen signed the visitor's book in exchange for large visitor's passes for prominent display at all times whilst in the building. They rode the lift up several floors and barely thirty seconds after announcing themselves at the reception area, a door opened, and a woman of Amazonian proportions strode confidently towards them. This woman of astounding beauty and absolute proportion made Wonder Woman look like a pussycat.

Sergeant Henry Washington Bradford Junior, the Third, obviously knew what to expect and showed no reaction at the appearance of the FBI operative.

"Ms Benecke, may I introduce Inspector Harrigan, of London's Metropolitan Police."

This coloured enchantress matched Harrigan's stare as her outstretched hand approached him like some deadly missile.

"I am very pleased to meet you, Chief Inspector, welcome to Houston."

Harrigan displayed no recognition of his surprise that the FBI was already aware of his most recent promotion. He was, however, impressed, and in his own disrespectful way figured that the FBI must have an intelligence system almost equal to Mahmood's.

Harrigan took her hand in his and returned the firm handshake. He liked a woman with a firm handshake and, as an added bonus, she hadn't given him a "high five."

"Thank you, Ms Benecke; it's good to be here."

"Please follow me." She turned sharply on her heel and returned to the doorway from which she had appeared.

Except for the offer of coffee or tea, there had been no further small talk. Angelina Benecke was a very direct and astute person. There was no requirement for lengthy explanations, and you were able to get straight to the point. As they would say in Australia, there was no need to *beat around the bush*.

In response to Ms Benecke's request, Harrigan gave a crisp rundown of events since the fire at the Goldberg building. He also gave them the name of the container ship.

"The FBI is very interested in this method of moving selected illegals. Using shipping containers for illegal immigrants is not new, but this niche-market thing is something we have never considered. It is so brilliantly simple."

"The good ideas usually are the simplest."

"Y'know, we have many hundreds of missing." She became silent, as she searched for the right words. "How shall we describe them, rich and infamous persons? When someone disappears without a trace, and I mean without a trace, you tend to figure that they have come to an untimely death, that they are somewhere at the bottom of the ocean, or in a road bridge, but this way..." she paused again, "they can be completely anonymous, take their wealth with them, and start a new life where no one will find them, not even the FBI."

The last observation spoiled it a little for Harrigan.

Angelina Benecke came back to the moment. "Alright, how can we help?"

Harrigan explained they believed that there was up to twenty-five million pounds in gold and cash in the container and they wanted to get it back.. He needed to know the exact day, time, and location the *El Hal Monarch* would be berthing. "And I don't think we should intercept the container at the docks. I am interested in seeing where it ends up," he concluded.

"Won't the delivery dockets tell us that?" the FBI agent challenged.

"The delivery docket will only tell us what is on the delivery docket, Ms Benecke. It doesn't guarantee that's where the container will end its journey."

Angelina Benecke quite rightly suspected that Harrigan wasn't quite telling the whole story. She let it slide for the moment.

"True," she replied. "Please, go on, Chief Inspector."

"It goes without saying that we need to keep the container under observation at all times."

"Do you think that someone might intercept it?"

"It's possible. Twenty-five million pounds is a lot of money, and if someone else knows, or at least suspects, it's in there? I think it's worth the effort. It's also possible, that instead of intercepting it, they be waiting at the drop-off point."

"Agreed."

"The final thing of course is we mustn't be seen. We don't want to frighten anyone off."

"I'll have our person at the terminal put a bug on it. We'll be able to follow it at a distance." She looked at her visitor's worried expression. "Don't look so worried; we won't lose it. We're very good at this."

She smiled and turned to the keyboard of the computer on her desk, and Harrigan watched as long and nimble fingers worked quickly over the letters. Every now and then, she'd hit the *enter* key with a little too much force.

"Alright, now let's see." She studied the screen silently, occasionally looking down at the keyboard and striking a few more times.

"The *El Hal Monarch* is on time," she announced as she clicked the mouse button. "It will dock at Berth four at the POH Container Terminal tomorrow morning at eleven-fifteen."

She pushed her keyboard away.

"We'll keep an eye on it for you, Chief Inspector, and contact you at the Spatial if there are any changes." She looked at the sergeant. "Will you pick the chief inspector up in the morning, Sergeant?"

"Yes Ma'am."

"Good. We'll meet you tomorrow at Morgan's Point around eleven. It's no use being any earlier." She remained behind her desk, as she stood erect. "As it is, we'll be in for a long day."

They said their good-byes and very shortly the big white Ford left the underground car park of the FBI building.

"I'm sorry, *Chief* Inspector...I didn't know you had received a promotion."

"Forget it, Hank. It's only a new thing."

"Well let me be one of the first to congratulation you, Sir," he said. "I'd say that calls for a celebratory drink, or two."

"Maybe the odd one," Harrigan agreed.

* * *

Considering the time he eventually got to bed and the amount of food and alcohol consumed the night before, Harrigan felt surprisingly fit the next morning. Hank had arranged to pick him up at nine-forty-five and, having completed sixteen laps in the indoor swimming pool, showered and dressed and fully satisfied himself at the hotel's first class breakfast facility, at twenty minutes to ten, Harrigan waited in the foyer. As he sat in a leather chair and with legs crossed, holding the *Houston Chronicle* in front of his face, he unwittingly re-created a scene so common in every B-grade mystery movie.

He heard a voice he assumed to be the concierge. "Excuse me, Chief Inspector, Sergeant Bradford has arrived."

Harrigan looked up. He was right. It was the concierge. "Thank you, Claude."

The big white Ford with *Police* emblazoned on either side had been replaced with another big Ford, this time a tan coloured earlier model. It carried a few body scars and was obviously not supposed to look like a police vehicle. Harrigan didn't have the heart to tell Hank the truth.

"Good morning, Chief Inspector, how do you feel this morning?"

"As well as can be expected. What about yourself?"

"I've had better mornings."

The journey to Morgan's Point took just under an hour. They didn't hurry, and Hank pointed out some of the highlights of Houston. Hank was a very proud Texan. They passed through Pasadena, Deer Park, and La Porte and, once onto East Barbours Cut Boulevard, Hank slowed the vehicle.

"Not far now; we should see Benecke's car soon." He slowed even further. "There it is, just ahead." He stopped behind the dark coloured vehicle. Angelina got out of the driver's seat. Her two male companions walked behind her and, as she approached the newly arrived policemen, the two FBI agents stopped a discreet distance from the trio, legs astride and arms folded.

"Good morning, Gentlemen, the *El Hal Monarch* is berthing now. I have informed the Operations Director that we may need to visit the terminal this morning."

Harrigan's immediate concern showed on his face.

"No need for concern, Chief Inspector. They don't know why we're coming. A visit from us is not an uncommon occurrence. It won't raise any suspicions."

"Thank you for your diplomacy, Ms Benecke."

"We are not amateurs, Chief Inspector." She made no attempt to disguise her displeasure at Harrigan's innocent remark. "Please follow us." She returned to the driver's seat and, without a second glance, drove toward the main terminal gates.

"I have to admit, Hank, I never know whether to call her Agent Benecke or Ms Benecke."

"She prefers Ms Benecke."

"I thought she might."

The two vehicles were waved through the main gates and, after driving through a maze of containers, cranes, and lorries, stopped at the operations room. The operations room was a building similar to those air traffic controllers' towers used at all major airports.

Jimmy Kleczkowski, the Operations Manager, was extremely cooperative. He gave Hank and Bill Harrigan a brief tour of the operations room. He offered the assistance of any of his staff and not once, did he ask why they were there, or what ship they were interested in. He had been doing this job a long time and any novelty or excitement that might have been associated with illegal activities on the wharves had long been extinguished. Bill Harrigan thanked him for the tour and access to any records required and left him to return to his work.

"Nice chap," Harrigan commented to the lady operative.

Angelina Benecke ignored the comment and held a clipboard in a position for Harrigan to read. The first four pages on the clipboard had been folded over the top of the board and held in position by her fingers at the back.

She pointed with a long, well-shaped finger on her right hand.

"Here, this is your container, Chief Inspector. It looks like it will be one of the first off."

She handed Harrigan the clipboard.

"It'll be taken to one of the transit sheds and picked up from there. All we have to do now is wait."

It was six hours before Benecke's mobile telephone rang for the last time before they moved.

"Benecke. Yes…good…yes, I've got that." She ended the call.

"We're on our way." She called a thank you to Jimmy Kleczkowski and once back at the vehicles, she briefed Harrigan.

"The container is being loaded onto a truck from Gerry's Transport. It is a self-loading container rig and is painted blue with a yellow stripe. It has one of those plastic bug deflectors on the front with *Gerry's Pride* painted on it. It should be easy to spot."

"Did your man get the bug on it, just in case we lose it?"

She smiled. "All done."

She quickly wrote down an address. "Here, give this to the sergeant; it's where the container is supposed to be delivered. We'll follow you. It's your show now."

"Thank you. And, Ms Benecke…" He stopped.

"Yes, Chief Inspector?"

He was about to comment on her nice smile but thought better of it. She would probably think it to be some sexist remark, not an innocent compliment. Pity really.

"Nothing, it doesn't matter."

Gerry's Pride rumbled through the front gates of the terminal a short time later. Hank displayed a high degree of competence in staying far enough back so as not to be noticed, but never losing sight of the container. He assumed the FBI were a similar distance to the rear.

The convoy rolled back through Pasadena, on to Mission Bend, and eventually into an area known as Emmaville Industrial Estate. The estate was one of the older industrial estate designs, and the ambience of the area seemed to fit with the clandestine nature of their operation. Harrigan could no longer see the FBI vehicle, but he knew it would be there somewhere and immediately re-focussed his mind on the job at hand.

They watched as *Gerry's Pride* pulled into the rear of a warehouse building. Despite nightfall almost being on them, and being a considerable distance from the yard, Harrigan was still able to distinguish the familiar raised platform. He watched as the driver, who he assumed to be Gerry, lowered the hydraulic rams to stabilise the vehicle as he unloaded the container.

"I can't see any other vehicles here, Chief Inspector. It looks like your theory that someone might be waiting for it is not going to materialise."

"See if we can get closer, Hank." Harrigan said, ignoring Hank's observations.

Hank started the vehicle and drove towards the warehouse. As a blacked out vehicle would attract attention, he switched on the headlights and drove along the street like he should have been there. As they approached, he saw a driveway opposite and drove in. He reverse parked into the parking bay labelled Managing Director, switched off the lights and looked at Harrigan.

"OK?"

"Perfect."

The parking bay was underneath the office block and partially obscured by shrubbery growing along the fence line of the property. With the aid of the spotlights on Gerry's Pride, Harrigan watched through the shrubbery, as Gerry unloaded the container.

Once completed, the rams on the vehicle were withdrawn and locked into position. Gerry returned to the driver's cabin, and with a swooshing sound, released the airbrakes. As Gerry changed through the many gears of the now empty truck, the sounds of the rise and fall of the loud exhaust slowly faded, until the last of the echo disappeared and left the area in silence.

The two men sat quietly. Their ears throbbed, as they strained to hear some tell-tale noise. Their eyes stared into the darkness of the poorly-lit area. Hank searched in the distance for any sign of an approaching vehicle.

Nothing. Nothing moved. There was no sound.

After what seemed like an eternity, Harrigan quietly opened the door.

"Let's take a look," he whispered.

Harrigan led as the two men walked silently across the road. He stopped at the far end of the container, the end where he believed there to be the trap door. He looked at the vehicle parked behind the platform. *Well, the getaway vehicle is in place,* he thought to himself.

"Well there's no one here to meet——."

"Ssshh!" Harrigan put his fingers to his lips indicating for Hank to remain silent.

"Why are we still whispering?" An impatient Hank asked, "there's no-one here! Let's open it up!"

"I'm not so sure, Hank, I'm not so sure."

Right on cue, a sound came from inside the container. Harrigan again raised his finger to his lips and walked around the end of the container. He folded his arms, leaned against the vehicle, and stared at the wooden door in the end of the platform. One minute later the lock on the door was released, and a short man of Middle Eastern appearance wearing a built up shoe came out of the darkness.

"Well I'll be damned!" Hank said.

"I trust you had a pleasant voyage, Mr Singhabahu?"

"Wha…? Who are y…?" Is all Manjit Singhabahu could manage before collapsing to the ground.

A voice sounded from the darkness.

"So that's what you were keeping from me, Chief Inspector."

"Well, if I'd been wrong, I'd've looked a right idiot, wouldn't I, Ms Benecke?"

CHAPTER THIRTEEN

With the threat to Margaret Willis now over, Margaret and Bill Harrigan had chosen to spend a relaxing night at Ali's. They sat in their favoured area, looking out at the lights of London.

"I would've given anything to have seen the look on your commissioner's face when he heard that you had arrested Manjit Singhabahu." Margaret smiled, as she sipped on her second gin and tonic.

"It wouldn't have been a pretty sight. I think we are all probably better off for not being there." Harrigan fondled the cigarette lighter in his pocket. He'd not yet noticed that she hadn't had a cigarette for the past week. In fact, not since that night at Bognor Regis.

"When did you first suspect that the body was not that of Manjit, and in fact, he might even be the murderer?"

"That's the exact question Bill Buckle asked me in my office, the afternoon I arrived back from Houston." Harrigan said as he settled back in the high backed leather chair, drank from his tumbler of Ballantines and ice, and looked out at the Thames. *Ali must spend a fortune on window cleaning*, he thought.

He allowed his mind to recall the events of that afternoon.

Everyone at Stonegate had been eagerly awaiting his return from Houston, everyone except Patricia. Well, that is to say that she was the only one not to show it. She had simply asked him if he'd like a cup of tea and called him an evil little bastard. Only Patricia could get away with something like that.

Bill Buckle had sat in his chair opposite the desk and against the wall, McIver, in the second chair opposite the desk, and Malcolm Watts, the chair against the far wall next to the filing cabinet. Superintendent Wilkinson had popped out for a few minutes to buy a birthday present for his granddaughter's second birthday.

"That's difficult to answer, Bill," had been his reply. "I must admit that, right at the beginning, I thought Ramachandran was the guilty party."

"Why'd you suspect Ramachandran, Chief inspector?" Watts had asked.

"It was the way he offered to help identify the body under the bathtub." He'd held them in suspense as he thanked Patricia for his tea and watched as she walked across the office. She'd refused Malcolm Watts' offer of the chair and, so she could keep one eye on her reception desk, had leaned against the wall near the doorway.

"You see," he'd continued answering Malcolm Watts' question, "I had told Ramachandran we found two bodies and that one was unidentifiable. I didn't tell him *which* one. But when we went into the ruined building, he offered to help identify the one *under the bathtub*. Now, how could he possibly have known that the *other* body was the one that could not be identified unless he'd seen it before?"

"Or been the killer himself?"

"That's right, Sergeant, or killed the person and mutilated the body himself."

Margaret brought Harrigan back to the present. "But wouldn't the fact that you thought Ramachandran could have been the killer strengthen the theory that Manjit, his fellow director, was the victim?"

"Yes, and it did, at the start."

"So, when did you start to doubt it?" she asked, fascinated with the intrigue,

"I suppose after the first few days. The evidence was too convenient. There had been too much evidence that pointed to Ramachandran being the murderer. Well, maybe not *evidence*," he corrected himself, "*suggestion* would be a better way to put it. I was trying to explain the difference this afternoon when the Superintendent came in." Harrigan returned to the events in his office earlier that afternoon.

"The Commissioner is not pleased, Bill." Superintendent Wilkinson had announced, as he joined Bill Buckle, Colin McIver, Malcolm Watts, and Patricia in Bill Harrigan's office. He'd nodded to the others in the room and sat in the chair opposite Harrigan's desk, just vacated by Bill Buckle. Colin McIver had stood from the other chair opposite the desk and gestured for the old sergeant to take the seat. McIver moved to the far wall, motioned to Malcolm Watts to stay seated and stood beside Patricia Hedrich.

"With respect, Sir, I did advise against any announcement to the media." Harrigan had tried to explain.

"But you didn't tell us about Manjit Singhabahu being in the container! You allowed us to believe he was the victim, not the murderer." Wilkinson had obviously had a bollicking from higher up the chain.

"And he may well have been the victim. I only had a *suspicion* that he was still alive." Harrigan then thought for a moment. "Well maybe a little more than a suspicion but—"

"Modesty doesn't become you, Chief Inspector. But please… go on."

"As I was saying, Sir, although it looked on the surface that Ramachandran was the murderer and Manjit the victim, there were just too many obvious clues, many filled with inconsistencies."

They'd waited patiently as he tried to prioritise the evidence.

"For example, the body had been burned, the mouth area destroyed, and the hands severed. All measures taken to disguise the identity of the body. But the feet had also been severed. Why do that?"

"Because Manjit had a club foot and would be detected," Colin McIver had said.

"That's right, Colin, but the removal of the feet also suggests that the victim had an identifiable foot complaint. And in complete contrast to the mouth and hands mutilation, because Manjit had a clubfoot, the removal of the feet only served to identify the body. And what about the UCFAC buckle? An object so identifiable should have been removed. It just didn't make sense."

"So Manjit wanted us to think that the killer tried to remove the identity of the victim but, at the same time, lead us to the identity of who he wanted us to think it was." Bill Buckle secretly admired the cunningness of the plan.

"That's it exactly."

"Who was the victim?" Patricia asked.

"Zahid Manjoo, a homeless drifter who used to help out with some of the charity organisations Manjit dealt with in Scotland.

He was the right build, had no family, so no one would miss him, which made him the perfect choice."

"Poor Bugger." A tone of sympathy was blatantly absent from the Superintendent's words. "What set Manjit off in the first place?" He'd then asked.

"There was a mix up in one of Manjit's flights from Cairo and, instead of arriving at Gatwick, he'd landed at Heathrow. He called into the Hawgate office unexpectedly and discovered Ramachandran talking to Chen. Although Ramachandran made up some cover story, Manjit had overheard some snippets of conversation as he'd entered the office, and didn't believe Ramachandran's story. He began to investigate and soon discovered that Ramachandran was using his charity work as a cover for his illegal operations."

"So he got mad," Bill Buckle said unnecessarily.

"You could say that, Bill. In fact, he went to talk to Mahmood and told him what he'd found out. When I interviewed Manjit in Houston, he told me that Mahmood was furious and told him not to say anything so he would have time to carry out a complete investigation, and nail Ramachandran *good and properly,* I think the expression was."

"But Manjit couldn't wait," Colin McIver prompted.

"There's more to it than that, Colin. He hadn't been totally convinced of Mahmood's truthfulness. Manjit had been a loyal employee and done good work. He was a good man. But there's often a fine line between being a good person or an evil person. Both traits have a strong emotional base, and when emotion loses its control, well, Manjit is the typical case. He simply crossed over the line. He'd brooded about Ramachandran's betrayal of his charity, not to mention the affair with Aysha, which he'd known about for quite some considerable time. His mood changed to one of uncontrollable anger and, blinded by hate, he set out on a rampage of murderous revenge."

"Did he kill Aysha too?" Margaret could no longer sit quiet, listening to Bill relay the conversations of the afternoon.

"I'll come to that."

The waiter at Ali's brought two fresh drinks. Margaret resettled in her chair and longed to reach for the cigarette case she still carried in her handbag. She resisted the temptation.

"Manjit's plan was carefully thought out. He would kill a substitute for himself and place it in the warehouse. He would lure Ramachandran to the warehouse and kill him. He would do this on the night before the container Chen was to travel in, was picked up for transporting to the docks. He then intended to kill Chen and escape in the container and dump Chen's body in the middle of the Atlantic Ocean. Once he reached Houston, he would take the car left for Chen, and Chen's twenty-five million pounds and disappear into the sunset. By the time the two bodies were found, he would be long gone."

"How would he dump the body at sea if he was inside the container?" Malcolm Watts had asked the obvious question.

"I said this was five-star accommodation. The ship was built in such a way that the last eight feet of the container, which was always placed on the bottom outside row of containers in the bulkhead area, hung over the bulkhead. The end of the container was on a purpose-built stand. This meant that, when all the other containers are stacked around it, the occupant inside the container could undo the trapdoor and move around in a sort of cave-like area. They had to be careful not to fall overboard, but it saved on batteries, gave them plenty of fresh air, and allowed them to empty waste over the side, like the chemical toilet for example."

"And the odd body," Margaret contributed.

"And the odd body," he agreed. "But unfortunately, as the Superintendent said to me this afternoon…"

"Things obviously didn't go as planned."

"No, Sir." Harrigan had agreed. "Manjit had found his substitute victim, done the business, and placed the mutilated body in position in the warehouse. He'd contacted the new secretary in Sidhu Trading's Hawgate office earlier that afternoon, said he was Ramachandran, and told her that he, that's Manjit, wouldn't be in the office for a few days. This wasn't unusual. He had also placed his car at Gatwick—"

"In an obvious place so we would find it quickly, and left enough clues that would lead us to think, that someone had left the car at the airport for the sole purpose of making it *look like* Manjit had left the country, but obviously hadn't. An obvious red herring, again for the purpose of establishing Manjit as the victim in the warehouse." Bill Buckle had completed the sentence.

"Correct, Sergeant. He had little trouble getting Ramachandran to meet him. He had told him he knew about Ramachandran's illegal activities and wanted to discuss them where they wouldn't be disturbed. The early hours of Tuesday Morning at the warehouse seemed a good place."

What Harrigan *didn't* tell his audience, was that he suspected Ramachandran was under instructions from Mahmood to get rid of Manjit and that when Manjit had suggested the meeting, he'd seen it as the perfect opportunity to carry out the deed.

"When Manjit returned to the warehouse, things started to go wrong. After he'd placed the body in the warehouse, he realised that Chen wasn't in the container. Against instructions from Ramachandran and despite the risks, Chen had been out exchanging gold for cash, and he was resting in the warehouse before getting into the container. As Chen was trying to explain to Manjit what he was doing in the warehouse and Manjit was trying to coach him back into the container so he could use the silenced .38 pistol in his pocket, Ramachandran arrived outside. Manjit told Chen that Ramachandran would be furious if he found him out of the container and may cancel the deal. He told him to hide under the bathtub until Ramachandran had gone and then he would help him back into the container."

Harrigan had finished the mug of cold tea. For the first time, Patricia didn't make any move to replenish it.

"Manjit took the pistol from his pocket, and with his heart pumping heavily, waited inside the back door. He'd watched Ramachandran creep into the warehouse and call out his name. He didn't answer. As Ramachandran stood in an area lit by the streetlights, he took aim. But before he had time to squeeze the trigger, Ramachandran found the body and bent down to study it. Manjit was forced to wait for another opportunity. It never came. As he watched and waited for the chance to come, Ramachandran recovered from his shock, and having decided to burn the body and the building, Manjit watched as Ramachandran began to pour the strong smelling liquid around the building. When he realised what Ramachandran was going to do, he began to panic. He didn't want to get caught in a fire. He became frightened for his life and, when Ramachandran went to the front of the building, he escaped out the rear door and climbed into the container. He sat quietly in the container, thinking of what had happened and what might happen. If he was lucky, Ramachandran would do everything in his power to get the container shipped on time. He wouldn't want the authorities snooping around the container. But what about Chen? That was simple. If Chen got out of the fire and came into the container, he would revert to his original plan. If Chen was trapped and died in the fire, the police would probably think he was a vagrant hiding in the warehouse, or even better was responsible for the other body. The body of Manjit Singhabahu. The belt buckle he left would establish it was Manjit Singhabahu. He'd begun to feel easier, it was going to work out anyway. Providing the walls of the building didn't collapse on the container, he might still get away with it. What Manjit didn't know was that Chen still had some of the gold with him. Of course, the other risk would be at Houston. Ramachandran might decide to be there. If Chen did die in the fire, Ramachandran would think the container was empty, and the temptation to collect the money he knew would be in there would have probably been too much. Manjit told me he had smiled about then, when he realised he still had the pistol in his pocket. If Ramachandran was waiting at the other end, Manjit would finally tie up all the loose ends."

"Are you saying that Manjit was inside the container all the time? Even when I unloaded and reloaded it?" McIver had asked.

"Yes."

"If Manjit was inside the container, then it must have been Ramachandran who killed Aysha?" Malcolm Watts asked the almost rhetorical question.

"No."

"Then who did?" Superintendent Wilkinson could not sup press his curiosity.

"Muhammad Singh."

Margaret knew little of Muhammad Singh, so Bill Harrigan was forced to leave the related story of the afternoon and explain to Margaret how Muhammad Singh fitted into the picture, including where he worked and what his responsibilities in the shipping company were.

"So you see," he concluded, "he was in the perfect position to manipulate the movements of the containers."

"But why would he kill Aysha?" Margaret could not piece it together.

"Singh was an orphaned beggar on the streets of Pakistan when Manjit first found him. There was something about the lad that intrigued Manjit, and on his return to England, Manjit persuaded Ramachandran to use his influence and sponsor the lad. It was not long after that Singh was in England with a job at Sidhu Trading. As the years passed, Singh showed potential and, eventually, Ramachandran started to have a substantial influence over him. With promises of future riches, Singh became part of Ramachandran's trafficking operation. He would arrange the false documents, the right containers on the rights ships, the car at the other end, all the boring ground work. But unfortunately for Singh, the riches never came."

"Did he know of Mahmood's knowledge of the operation?" she asked.

"I don't think so. Anyway, he was becoming very dissatisfied with what Ramachandran was paying him. He still drove the company van and lived in a council flat. He wanted more, but what could he do about it? He couldn't go to the authorities; he was part of the operation, so he was stuck with it. That is until Manjit started his investigation into Ramachandran and found out how unhappy Singh was. Manjit was apprehensive about bringing Singh into his confidence, but he needed a new identity, and Singh knew how to arrange it. He offered Singh half a million American dollars to arrange the papers. Singh argued that if he took the half a million dollars, how could he spend it? If he bought a new car or a house, Ramachandran would want to know where he got the money. No. If he was to arrange a new identity, he would need two million dollars so he could disappear himself."

"Did Manjit agree?"

"Yes...and no. He agreed to pay the two million, but on one condition."

"That he kill Aysha!?" Margaret asked unbelievingly.

"Yes. The deal was, half a million up front, and Singh arrange a new identity for Manjit. He would then kill Aysha and meet Manjit in Texas for the balance of the money."

It was at this point of the story earlier in the afternoon that Bill Buckle had made the questioned observation that Singh was in the container that left East Grinstead. Harrigan had agreed.

"Singh would give Manjit the papers," Harrigan continued to Margaret, "and proof that Aysha was dead, and Manjit would give him the rest of the money."

"Where is Singh Now?"

Harrigan looked at his watch. "I would say that, if everything has gone to plan, FBI agent Benecke is just about fitting the cuffs on him at this very moment."

"What about Ramachandran? Was it Chen's associates who, who shot him?" she stumbled.

"I think so. Bill Buckle found the car in Chinatown. There was a spent shell in the front that matches, well could match— forensic isn't one hundred percent sure—the fragments in Ramachandran's stomach. I would say that his death was a warning to anyone else thinking of helping someone steal from the cartel."

He took a sip from the crystal tumbler. "Bill's still working on it, but I don't hold out much hope." He paused as he looked towards the opening lift doors. "Well, well, well, look who's coming in."

Three well-dressed businessmen passed the area Harrigan and Margaret occupied. The fourth man stopped and addressed Harrigan.

"Congratulations on your success."

"Thank you, Mr Mahmood."

"No loose ends?" Mahmood asked.

"Not on my side," Harrigan replied.

"Is that supposed to mean something?" Mahmood's eyes narrowed slightly.

Harrigan moved closer to Mahmood and lowered his voice. "We had a deal, and as far as I am concerned, we have both honoured it. I would, however, suggest to you that there may be one loose end. On your side of the ledger."

"Oh?"

"Lapsley–Midwinter." Harrigan looked over Mahmood's shoulder at the three men seated as Mahmood's guests. "I would say that for a person as rich and famous as Lapsley-Midwinter was, to be able to simply vanish, would take the assistance of someone, who," he paused as he returned his gaze to Mahmood, "is also rich, and of course, very powerful."

Mahmood stood silent.

"Now that I am reasonably sure I know how Lapsley-Midwinter managed to disappear, he will be much easier to trace. Once I return from my visit to Australia, I will probably re-open the case and go looking for him. I doubt Lapsley-Midwinter will take the rap all by himself...if you get my meaning."

Mahmood looked deeply into Harrigan's unblinking eyes. "I think I must agree." The two men stood apart. "Thank you, I believe it is now, *Chief* Inspector?" he added all too knowingly.

"Yes, that's correct." Harrigan's voice trailed off as he began to realise where the push for his promotion had come from.

"Oh, and that job offer is still open."

"Thank you, Sir, I'll remember that."

Mahmood straightened to his full height and, with a slight click of his heels, he nodded politely towards Margaret and strode towards his waiting guests.

As Harrigan raised his glass, the distant lights of a cruise ship sailing slowly along the Thames worked their passage through the golden liquid.

"To us," he toasted.

* * *

It was seven weeks later. Harrigan sat on the top floor balcony of a suite in the Golden Sands Hotel, located north of Cairns on the coast of eastern Australia.

Margaret wore a brief bikini as she sat in front of a wooden easel, painting enthusiastically on a canvas they had purchased two days before. Margaret had bought a book from a second-hand book stall at the local weekend markets, that explained how simple it was to paint in watercolour. Harrigan had to admit she appeared to have a natural talent for it.

He turned the page of the *Queensland Tribune* newspaper and read the headline of the article at the top of page five. *Explosion Rocks Caribbean Island* it announced. He read on: *A violent explosion which completely destroyed a luxury cruiser, killing the wealthy recluse owner who had moved to the island over three years ago, rocked the peaceful community yesterday. While the man's identity has been a closely guarded secret speculation has it that...*"Harrigan closed the paper and raised his face to the sun.

His closed eyelids hid the unmistakable mischievous glint of satisfaction.